# Rory Clements

Rory Clements lives in a seventeenth-century farmhouse in Norfolk and is married to the artist Naomi Clements-Wright. As well as writing, he enjoys village life and a game of tennis with friends. There are five books in the *John Shakespeare* series of Elizabethan mysteries, all published by John Murray.

## Praise for the John Shakespeare novels

'Enjoyable, bloody and brutish' *Guardian*

'Sixteenth-century London comes alive in all its tawdriness' *Daily Mail*

'A world spiced with delicious characters . . . The novel wears its historical learning lightly, and Clements seasons it with romance and humour' *Mail on Sunday*

'Beautifully done . . . alive and tremendously engrossing' *Daily Telegraph* *****

'A cracking plot full of twists right up to the last minute. I look forward to the next' *Sunday Express*

'Colourful . . . exciting . . . vivid' *Sunday Telegraph*

'Sharp and challenging, this book is missed at one's peril' *Oxford Times*

'Clements can be seen as doing for Elizabeth's reign what C. J. Sansom does for Henry VIII's . . . What's impressive in the latest is how much of Tudor society it crams in, from the court and Derby's estate to outlaws and the soldiers in its concluding scene' *Sunday Times*

'Marvellous . . . intelligencer John Shakespeare . . . administers what can only be described as ruff justice' *Daily Telegraph*

'Engrossing . . . we can expect to see more of the brothers Shakespeare. They will be welcome' *Washington Post*

'A historical thriller to send a shiver down your spine. Atmospheric . . . it demonstrates energy, élan, a fine ear for dialogue and a grasp for the intrigues of Elizabeth I's court. Clements also demonstrates the compelling eye for detail and character that Bernard Cornwell so memorably brought to Rifleman Sharpe . . . I could not tear myself away, it is that good' *Daily Mail*

'Real quality . . . faster moving than C. J. Sansom . . . very, very well done' *Front Row, BBC Radio 4*

'This is a first-class mystery steeped in authentic sixteenth-century intrigue; the evocation of the stench and squalor of Tudor London is sans pareil' *Good Book Guide*

'Step into the world of Elizabethan intelligencer John Shakespeare and you put your very life in peril, whether it be by the blade, the rope or the rack . . . High adventure has never been more exciting' *Northern Echo*

*Also by Rory Clements*

Martyr
Revenger
Prince
The Heretics

# Traitor

## RORY CLEMENTS

HODDER

First published in Great Britain in 2012 by John Murray (Publishers)
An Hachette UK Company

Hodder paperback edition 2014

4

Maps drawn by Rosie Collins

A CIP catalogue record for this title is available from the British Library

ISBN 978-1-84854-432-1
Ebook ISBN 978-1-84854-431-4

Typeset in Adobe Garamond by Servis Filmsetting Ltd, Stockport, Cheshire

Printed and bound by Clays Ltd, St Ives plc

Hodder & Stoughton policy is to use papers that are natural, renewable and recyclable products
and made from wood grown in sustainable forests. The logging and manufacturing processes are
expected to conform to the environmental regulations of the country of origin.

Hodder & Stoughton Ltd
338 Euston Road
London NW1 3BH

www.hodder.co.uk

*To the memory of my mother,*
*the heart of our far-flung family*

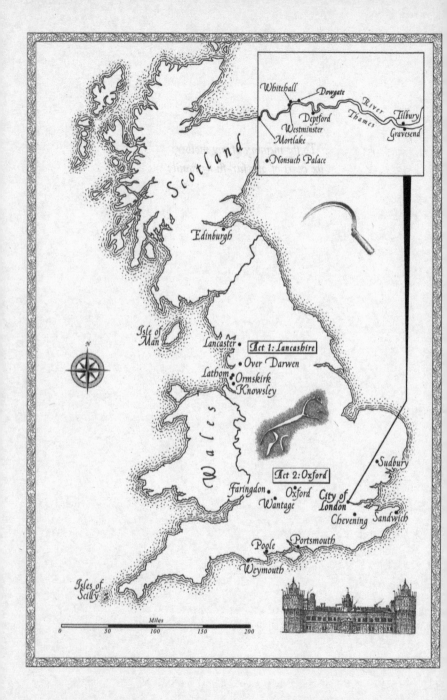

Whitehall
Dowgate
River Thames
Deptford
Westminster
Tilbury
Mortlake
Gravesend

• Nonsuch Palace

Scotland

Edinburgh

Isle of
Man

Lancaster
**Act 1: Lancashire**
• Over Darwen
Lathom • Ormskirk
Knowsley

Wales

**Act 2: Oxford**
Faringdon •
Oxford
City of
London
Wantage
Chevening Sandwich

Sudbury

Poole • Portsmouth
Weymouth

Isles of
Scilly

N

Miles
0    50    100    150    200

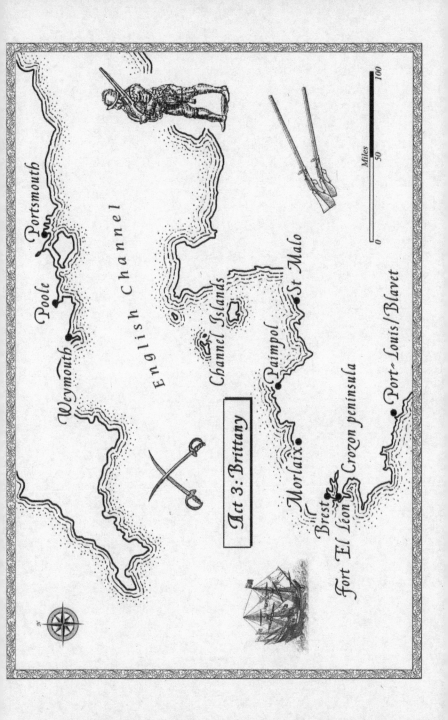

Act 3: Brittany

Portsmouth
Poole
Weymouth
English Channel
Channel Islands
St Malo
Paimpol
Morlaix
Brest
Fort El Léon
Crozon peninsula
Port-Louis/Blavet

Miles
0    50    100

# Act 1
## To Lancashire

# Chapter 1

WILLIAM IVORY TOSSED his cards across the table and picked up the coins. Three shillings, a sixpence, two farthings. He was aware of the resentful glares of the other players, but did not acknowledge them. He had all their money now; there was no point in staying. Without a word of farewell, he thrust the coins into his jerkin pocket, already bulging from the rest of his winnings, and strode to the doorway. It had been a long night and the tavern was heavy with the stench of smoke and ale.

At the doorway, he stopped, surprised by the glare of the dawn sun. He took a deep breath of the fresh air. As his eyes adjusted to the light, he looked about him. He resisted the temptation to pat the side of his dun-coloured jerkin where the perspective glass was secreted, tied hard against his ribs with leather straps. The street was busy, but his keen eyes told him no one was watching him.

The alehouse stood in a narrow alley close to Portsmouth docks. It was wedged between a broad-fronted ship-chandler's shop with sail lofts on one side and, on the other, a noisy whorehouse where mariners paid for stale flesh with the spoils of their long months at sea. Ivory walked to his own house, in the next street. He lived alone, close to the bustle and noise of the dockyard. It gave him the anonymity he needed and the gaming houses he craved. He took out a heavy iron key to open the door, then changed his mind. He would eat before sleeping.

It was a cool morning, braced by a breeze blowing in from the Channel. He should have seen the watcher. At sea, he could spot a Spanish ship on the horizon hours before other men, yet here on land his senses failed him. He did not detect the presence of a predator ten paces away, nor did he see the pistol he held in the capacious folds of his cloak.

Ivory drew on a long, ornately carved pipe, filled with rich tobacco. He had acquired the pipe from natives on the coast of *La Florida* back in '86, in a trade for a common English knife. He exhaled a thin ribbon of smoke, which was instantly gone on the wind. With a last look about him, he stepped back out into the street and headed down towards the quayside to buy herring and bread. A man in his mid-thirties, he wore long whiskers and combed his straggling grey-black hair forward across his brow. He looked what he was: a man of the sea. With his lean chest, his weather-lined hands and salt-engrained cheeks, there was little to pick him out from all the others in this seafaring town. His gait was rolling like all the rest of them: bodies that could never quite forget the pitch and heave of the ocean swell. Only the precise sparkle of his luminous, cornflower-blue eyes set him apart.

All around him there was noise – traders calling wares, seamen singing shanties as they hauled at cables, gulls cawing as they swooped for manavilins of fish, whores and gossips screaming oaths at each other, idlers laughing. Who could hear a heartbeat or a footfall above such a din?

The man with the wheel-lock pistol shuffled forward with the crowd, protected by it. He was unremarkable and stocky, totally enveloped in a cloak that billowed about him like a top-gallant sail and cowled his face. His weapon was loaded and primed, ready to kill. Not quite yet, though, not here, not now. Not with all these people about. His present name was Janus Trayne, though that was not his real one. He had had many names in his forty years.

He followed his quarry down to the quay where men from a laden smack were hauling their catch ashore. He watched Ivory bargain for a pair of fish, all the while puffing at his strange pipe, then followed him to the baker where he bought a two-pound loaf and some butter.

Janus Trayne was not from these parts. He was in the pay of Spain, though not a native of that nation. His mission was to prise something from William Ivory, some instrument that he kept about his person at all times. Trayne did not understand what it was, nor did he care. All that mattered to him was that his masters would pay handsomely for it – two hundred ducats of gold.

He held back twenty yards from Ivory. His chance would come soon enough.

From the baker's, Ivory walked on a little further, to the cook-house that stood in the front bank of houses, close to the harbour. The low sun was blanked out by the towering fore-castle of an armed merchantman, moored for refitting before its next voyage. At the cookhouse window, he handed over his two fish to a large, sweaty goodwife for scaling, gutting and frying. She tried to engage him in conversation, but he ignored her and walked down to the water's edge to smoke his pipe and wait.

Less than ten minutes later, the drab called to him and he collected his food on a wide trencher, paying her a penny. He settled down in a quiet spot at the waterside to eat. First he laid his smouldering pipe beside him, then, with a sharp blade, he cut into the tender flesh of the herring and released the succulent juices and savoury smells. He ate slowly, chewing at hunks of bread and butter between bites of fish, taking his time, enjoying the food and the perfect day.

The events of the next minute happened at bewildering speed.

There was the hard touch of a hand on his left shoulder, then the cold muzzle of a pistol at his right temple. Ivory dropped the trencher from his lap and tried to scramble back from the assailant.

'Give me the instrument.' The voice was low, growling. 'You know exactly what I want, Ivory.'

So they had come for him at last. But it was not him they wanted, it was the glass.

'I do not have it,' he said, wrapping his arms around his chest as he leant away from the pistol. 'Not here—'

'Then I will cut it from you.'

And suddenly there was the shadow of another man, bearing down on them like a clawed demon. The demon's talon-like right hand pulled the assailant's pistol down while the left arm came past his neck, across his chest. Trayne might have been strong, but the demon was quicker. Clenching a blade, he thrust upwards into Trayne's wrist. The man gasped with shock and pain as the sharp steel sliced up through tendons and flesh, into the very bone of his right arm. His gasp turned to a deep howl. The wadding and ball rolled harmlessly from the muzzle of his pistol. His finger pulled the trigger, igniting powder with a flash and a loud report. Fire spat out and smoke billowed, but there was no shot. The gun fell from his weakened grasp.

Ivory watched in fascinated horror. Within the space of a few seconds a man had held a pistol to his head and now that very man was squatting there with a knife protruding through his wrist, a knife thrust into him by a second assailant.

The wounded man leapt to his feet with surprising agility. Gritting his teeth, he wrenched the knife from his wrist. Blood gushed forth, splattering across the harbour wall. He hesitated a moment, instinctively shielding his face, then he ran, followed by a trail of blood drops.

Ivory watched him go, mouth agape in astonishment. Then he looked at the man who had saved him. It was a face he had not seen in many years, not since they had sailed the world together. A face he had had no interest in seeing again.

'Boltfoot Cooper! What in the name of God are you doing here?'

'Saving your life, Mr Ivory. Saving your worthless, poxy life.'

## Chapter 2

'IN DAYLIGHT? ON the quayside where anyone might have seen what he was doing? Christ's tears, Mr Shakespeare, your man Cooper has surpassed himself this time.'

'It was necessary, Sir Robert. The man was about to blow a hole in Ivory's head.'

'Gunfire, blood all over the quayside ... If this reached Her Majesty's ears, she would be most unhappy. She will not have men knifed in her towns and seaports in full view of passers-by.'

'It was *necessary*, Sir Robert,' Shakespeare repeated, slightly too sharply. 'In defence of the realm ...' His voice trailed off, wondering whether he overstepped the mark in talking to Elizabeth's first minister in such tones. 'Forgive me for speaking plain.'

Sir Robert Cecil laughed, a dry little laugh. He was small in stature, not much over five feet tall, with a hunch of the shoulder that he tried to disguise by pulling back his head. He had a tidy spade of a beard and dark, inquiring eyes. John Shakespeare, six feet tall, with flowing hair, towered over him as they walked across the beautiful inner courtyard of Nonsuch Palace. Water gushed from a marble fountain. The walls seemed to close in with their profusion of intricate plaster reliefs of figures both noble and godly. Across the court and dominating all was the statue of the Queen's father, Great Henry, his menacing, magnificent figure seeming to hold the very gods of Olympus in thrall.

As if on cue, the Queen herself emerged into the sunlight from the state rooms on the far side of the courtyard. She wore a French gown of white pearl, flourished with gold and silver, embroidered with tiny harts and stags. In her hand she carried a fan of white feathers with a handle of ornate gold. She shone in the sun's glare, an aureole among the courtiers who thronged around her.

The Queen stopped a moment to breathe in the fresh spring air. Her courtiers stopped, too, responsive to her every movement. Chief among them was her favourite, the Earl of Essex, markedly taller than his companions. His eyes flitted from his sovereign to the bosom of a young lady-in-waiting two steps behind. On Elizabeth's other side stood the bluff, handsome figure of Sir Thomas Heneage, her greatest friend and Chancellor of the Duchy of Lancaster. He was whispering some tittle-tattle in her ear and she smiled.

Also there was Sir Edward Coke. As the Queen stepped forward again, Coke moved too, a spring in his step, puffed up from his appointment that very morning as Attorney-General. Cecil's father, Lord Burghley, hobbled behind, the pain of his gout evident in his expression. Southampton clasped Essex's arm with one hand and with the other ran his silky fingers through his own long hair. Behind them Shakespeare spotted the squat, white-haired figure of the torturer Richard Topcliffe, and shuddered. No courtier's elegant attire could disguise that feral, stale-sweat brutality.

Bile rose in Shakespeare's gullet at the sight of the white-haired Queen's servant. Their paths had crossed too many times and the loathing between them ran deep. Topcliffe had done his utmost to persecute Shakespeare and his family, believing them tainted by Catholicism. Shakespeare, in turn, had seen the inside of the private torture chamber Topcliffe maintained in his Westminster home. It was there that he had brought the natural father of Shakespeare's adopted children to the point of death with his foul instruments of rope and iron. Shakespeare could smell the stench of pain and blood that hung there even now, and knew the torturer would not rest until he had destroyed him and all he held dear. As the royal party drew near, Topcliffe caught his eye and smirked. Shakespeare's expression did not change, did not reveal his revulsion, nor his contempt.

He and Cecil both bowed low and went down on one knee at the Queen's approach. She looked at them and for the briefest of moments her eye caught John Shakespeare's. At this proximity he could not but notice what he had not seen from a distance – how marked her face had become by time, how tarnished her glow. Her golden hair was dry, her skin coated white, like a badly rendered façade. She did not acknowledge him, simply looked away and walked on with her courtiers and the ladies in her train. Topcliffe turned as he swept past and threw Shakespeare a half-smile that denoted nothing more than loathing and disdain.

Cecil rose and touched his hand to Shakespeare's elbow to signify that he, too, should rise. The statesman's gaze followed the departing group.

'My lord of Essex has been swearing eternal love and devotion to his virgin queen,' Cecil said in a low voice in Shakespeare's ear. 'Yet before the hour is out, he will have *that* wanton's skirts about her waist with never a thought for Her Royal Majesty.' He nodded towards the woman whose breasts Essex had been contemplating. The corners of Cecil's mouth turned down in distaste. 'Come, John, let us walk in the gardens, away from ears.'

Shakespeare was surprised by the note of bitterness in Cecil's words. His enmity for Essex was well known, but it was unlike him to reveal so much of his inner feelings.

They ambled through the gatehouses. Chaffinches and sparrows sang with the promise of spring. Fruit trees burgeoned with blossom buds. From the outside, the fantastical turrets of Nonsuch Palace dazzled beneath blue slate and red-brick chimneys. Cecil patted the spaniel at his heels and then glanced up at a large lanner falcon that swooped and ranged above them and around them, hunting for food. He shook his neat head in admiration and acknowledged the falconer, who bowed to him. Cecil pointed out the bird to Shakespeare.

'That is my lanner, John. Is she not comely?' He paused and looked around. There was no one within earshot. 'So tell me, now that we are in a quiet place, what do we know about the attacker?'

'Nothing, except that he wore a large cloak, which concealed a German wheel-lock pistol, which we have. He ran like a hare. Boltfoot, with his club-foot, had no hope of giving chase. Anyway, he was more concerned to stay with Ivory.'

'Did they follow the blood trail?

'As far as it went, into the next street. After that, nothing.'

'Would they recognise the man again?'

'Unlikely – he closed his cloak about his face. This was no common felon, but a mercenary, a hired man.'

'From Spain?'

'We have no way of knowing.'

'But not a common footpad after Mr Eye's gold?'

Shakespeare grimaced. 'No. Mr Ivory confirmed that he demanded the perspective glass. However, there is still a chance of identifying the assassin. Here . . .' He withdrew the would-be killer's pistol and handed it to Cecil. 'It is a fine-wrought piece.'

Cecil handed it back. 'Give it to my man, Clarkson. He will pass it on to Frank Mills to deal with. I have other requirements of you. This incident in Portsmouth has worried me greatly. Where are Mr Eye and the perspective glass now?'

'I have them both safe, Sir Robert.'

'And you do not think they should be parted? The glass kept safe in the Tower, perhaps?'

Shakespeare shrugged his shoulders. 'That is for you to decide.'

'But I would appreciate your opinion, John.'

'Well, the glass is our priority, but Mr Ivory is also of great value to us. It seems rational to keep them together.'

Cecil smiled briefly. 'My thoughts exactly. Keep the Eye and the implement secure. Tell no one where they are except Clarkson. And beware of men in cloaks with scarred wrists. I fear we will need Mr Eye again very soon.'

Shakespeare bowed solemnly. There were times when Cecil required obedience, not debate, and this was one of them. Many men loathed him, calling him Robin Crookback or Robertus Diabolus – mocking names, spoken with a tinge of fear – but there were few who did not respect him. Shakespeare went further. He liked to think he understood Cecil. He worked for him because he believed they shared some human creed and aims – peace and justice, the security of the realm, a prosperous commonwealth, the hoped-for triumph of good over evil. And if that sometimes meant being harder and more devious than the enemy, well, so be it.

'I must tell you, John,' Cecil continued, 'that this perspective glass has assumed great significance. I do believe the very fate of the realm might rest on our strange instrument. We have culverins, we have ships-of-war, we have courage, yet this glass is our greatest weapon of all – for we alone have it. As the sparrowhawk's eye provides its killing vantage, so it is for us.'

Shakespeare considered what he knew of the perspective glass. It was made of stiffened pig-hide and it concealed curved pieces of glass, like those used in spectacles to remedy feeble sight. These glass discs were precisely ground, highly polished and so conformed that, when a man looked in one end of the tube, the impossible happened – distant objects drew near.

As chief officer in Cecil's intelligence network, he was one of a mere half-dozen men privileged to have used it. It had been at Greenwich for a demonstration in front of the Queen. When Shakespeare looked through it, he had clearly seen the markings of a deer a mile away and the freckles of a maiden hanging out her mother's washing. Astonished, he had gazed through it for a full minute and then handed it back to Cecil suddenly, as though the glass contained some magic that might burn his hand or eye.

That had been a year ago. The next Shakespeare had heard of it was last month. Cecil had ordered him to assign Boltfoot Cooper to protect the glass's keeper, William Ivory. Word had reached England from a spy in the court of King Philip that Spain had become aware of the glass's existence – and wanted it.

'We will keep Ivory and the glass safe.'

'Good. Your man Boltfoot did well. But I must now tell you why I am so concerned that we will need the glass again very soon.' He signalled to a liveried servant, who had been dogging their steps at a discreet distance. The man approached and bowed. 'Give Mr Shakespeare the paper.'

The servant proffered a document. Shakespeare took it and instantly recognised his associate Frank Mills's hand. It was a decoded intercept. He read it quickly and began to go cold. His eyes met Cecil's.

Boltfoot lost Ivory in the busy street of Shoreditch. One moment, they were riding at a slow walk, a little way apart, the next he was gone into the throng of people, livestock and wagons.

'A plague of God,' Boltfoot rasped beneath his breath. He was furious with himself. Progress had been slow. It had taken them over three days to get home to Dowgate from Portsmouth. And now, just an hour out on the way to join Jane and the family in the safety of Suffolk, he had let his guard drop. Standing up in his stirrups, he tried to look above the heads of the mob.

Boltfoot's hand went to the hilt of his cutlass. He wished very much to do some injury to Ivory. Well, he would just have to find him; even among this teeming mass of humanity and animals, there was only a limited number of places he could be. He kicked on into the crowd.

Shakespeare read the message again. It was from a French intel-ligencer in Brittany to his masters at the royal court of Henri IV, and it revealed that the Spanish army of Don Juan del Águila was building a fort on the southern headlands that dominated the entrance to Brest Harbour.

'The fort is almost complete, John, and will be powerfully equipped with long-range cannon and at least four companies of men. The Spanish will control the entrance to Brest Harbour – and will hold the port in thrall. If Brest is taken, with its deep-water harbour, they will be able to assemble a far more deadly armada against us than was attempted in '88. And they will have liberty to pick their time, when the wind and weather are in their favour. Hawkins tells me the great danger is that the harbour is to windward of Plymouth, so their ships could use the prevailing winds to make a sudden attack. I do not know how we could withstand such a force. Our coffers are empty, our fleet is in disarray, our land is overrun with vermin-ous bands of rogues and vagabonds. These are straitened times. *Dangerous* times.'

'What can be done?'

'What indeed? Sir Roger Williams has been sent secretly to survey the fort to see whether it can be taken. But the omens are not good. The forces we have in Brittany are woefully lacking after four years of skirmishing. General Sir John Norreys is down to his last thousand men, of which half are non-effective through sickness or wounds. They are holed up in the fishing port of Paimpol. Only now does Her Majesty see the importance of this forgotten war. She is summoning Norreys home to confer.'

'What will you recommend, Sir Robert?'

'That he must be reinforced. With seasoned men, new recruits, a siege train and a fleet. I have already sent out an order to the lords lieutenant to recruit men throughout southern England. And we will move a number of battle-hardened troops from the Low Countries. But it may all be too little, for we will be up against a well-equipped Spanish army and a constant patrol of galleons. Brittany is in turmoil, with French troops on both sides. Marshal Aumont's army supports the English, but Mercoeur's Catholic League militias are with the Spanish. In such circumstances of disarray, we need every advantage we can muster.'

'The perspective glass.'

'As Erasmus told us, in the country of the blind the one-eyed man is king. So in the world of dull-eyed pigeons, the hawk's-eye kills.'

Shakespeare bowed. Ivory would be protected until he was needed. It would not be easy. He was prickly and churlish and would not take kindly to being nursemaided by Cooper. Reports suggested he lived a solitary life, communing with his fellow man only when he wanted a game of cards or a whore to satisfy his carnal desires. No one would ever have noted him except for his one great talent: his eyesight. Vision so precise that his crewmates called him simply Eye, or Mr Eye. Even before the perspective glass, Drake had used his skills to good effect on the great circumnavigation of the globe. The glass had given him almost godlike powers to observe the land and sea.

One thing puzzled Shakespeare.

'Sir Robert, could we not make more perspective glasses now that we have the secret? Surely the mechanism can be copied? There could be one on every ship-of-war and in every coastal fortress.'

Cecil shook his head impatiently. 'No. It is out of the question. The Queen won't have it, nor will the Privy Council and neither will I. Protecting *one* glass is hard enough. How would we keep safe a dozen or more? How long would it be before one of them fell into Spanish hands – and then where would our advantage be?' He stopped in the shade of a new-leafed horse-chestnut tree. 'You realise, of course, John, that the incident in Portsmouth was but the beginning. There will be other attempts.'

'Indeed.'

'But protecting Mr Eye is not sufficient. There are two other men who must also be safeguarded – the men who constructed the perspective glass. If the Spanish cannot get to the glass itself, they may seek to abduct one or both of the men who made it and learn their secrets.'

'Dee and Digges . . .' Shakespeare muttered.

The two most learned sciencers in England were Dr John Dee, alchemist, spiritual seeker, stargazer and ingenious deviser of machines, and Thomas Digges, mathematician, military theorist, architect of forts and professor of navigation. Digges had been Dee's student. Some men said he had now surpassed his master in the sciences.

Dee and Digges, both remarkable but very different. In 1580, fourteen years ago, Lord Burghley – Cecil's father and Lord Treasurer of England – had commissioned the two men to devise a perspective glass. They had assured Burghley that, with the best glass crafters and with time, the device was possible. There were difficulties, however, mainly in calculating the exact conformation of the glasses and in grinding and polishing them with the required precision. Dee had given up the struggle, leaving the country for Prague. Only after his return, and with the onset of open warfare with Spain, did he and Digges begin to overcome their difficulties. The invasion attempt by the Armada accelerated their efforts, which at last came good.

'Do we know where they are, Sir Robert?'

'Thomas Digges is at his country home, in Kent. He is writing a new volume on warfare science, but he ails. Frank Mills is organising his protection. Two men watch him day and night and Frank will follow them there.'

'And Dee?'

Cecil looked pained. 'Ah, yes, Dee. He is more difficult, and that is your task. Since his return from Bohemia, he has been impoverished. He continually solicits my father and Her Majesty for grants or church livings. It is utterly tedious. He wants the chancellorship of St Paul's or the mastership of St Cross, but he will have neither. His dabbling in the dark arts makes him most unsuitable for such positions and, anyway, he is an irritant. In truth we wish him away. My father has hinted to him that he might have the wardenship of the collegiate church in Manchester. Dee has now gone there to spy out the land, so to speak.'

'That is almost as remote as Prague,' Shakespeare said wryly.

Cecil laughed. 'I believe he views the prospect with some reluctance, but it is a good living with extensive lands, and he has few options. It would remove his infernal begging and complaining.'

The lanner at last landed on the arm of the young states-man's falconer with a fluttering of wings and took the shred of meat.

'Come, John, for we must talk on this further and Sir Thomas Heneage must be included. As he is Chancellor of the Duchy of Lancaster, the palatinate of Lancashire is his domain – and there are local sensitivities in the county. I have asked him to detach himself from Her Majesty's presence and wait on us in my apartments.'

Ivory's grey gelding stood patiently in one of the smaller, quieter streets, to the north of Hog Lane. The animal was teth-ered to a post. Boltfoot slid from the saddle and looked around. There was only one house it could be, the one with the youth sitting outside, idly drinking a gage of ale.

'How much for a woman?'

The youth eyed him up and down with scornful boredom. 'For a maggot like you? Sixpence. Tuppence for me, the rest for the wench. Take your pick?'

Boltfoot handed him two coins and went into the dingy hovel. Three girls sat on the floor in the sawdust. The room stank of sweat and scent. Without thinking, the whores bared their breasts to him. He ignored them and examined his sur-roundings. There were two interior doors, one closed.

Boltfoot pushed open the closed door. In front of him, less than a yard from his face, was Ivory's white arse. His hose and stocks were down about his calves and ankles and he was at his business with a plump young woman who was moaning by rote. Boltfoot laughed. 'You've got five minutes, Ivory, then I'm dragging you out.' He closed the door again. He had his man.

# Chapter 3

'WHILE DR DEE is in Lancashire, he is staying at Lathom House with the Earl of Derby. You are to go there and bring Dee away, John. Bring him down south to the home of Thomas Digges in Kent. Once there, you will hand him into the protective care of Frank Mills. That way Dee and Digges will both be in safe keeping.'

Shakespeare acknowledged Cecil's instructions with a nod, then his gaze drifted sideways and his eyes locked with Heneage's. The older courtier's eyes seemed permanently amused and friendly. He was a well-built handsome man in his early sixties, the sort of fellow you liked the instant you met him, the sort you might confide in at short acquaintance. He sat, apparently relaxed, but he was listening intently.

'But you will tread carefully, John,' Cecil went on. 'While I have little time for Dee, for he is a nuisance, the Queen retains affection for him and relies on his auguries.'

'I understand, Sir Robert.'

Cecil seemed to hesitate. Shakespeare noted it. There was clearly more to this than just the removal of the sciencer and conjuror John Dee from Lancashire to Kent. Shakespeare said nothing. Cecil was not a man to be prodded for information.

'Bear one other thing in mind, John: Dee's circumstances are so dire that one must consider the possibility – however unpleasant – that he could be tempted to sell his knowledge of the perspective glass. Such a secret could fetch him much gold.'

Dr Dee had a curious reputation. There had been scandalous talk about him over the years. Some said he was a Simon Magus – a demonic magician with godlike aspirations; others merely called him a conjuror, which was defamatory enough. But never had Shakespeare heard a suggestion that the man might be a party to treason. Still, he had encountered stranger things in his years of working in the world of secrets.

Shakespeare turned again to Heneage, but he still said nothing, merely observing the proceedings with amused detachment.

'What do we know of Dee's character?' Cecil said. 'Is he treacherous? We have no reason to think so. But we do know that he is easily intimidated. I have seen his terror of my father. His hand shakes like barleycorn in the breeze when he is in the old man's presence.'

Afraid of old Burghley? That was reasonable enough, given the power he wielded. Only a fool would be duped by his kindly face and white beard.

'We know, too, that Dee has no guile. That might seem an admirable attribute in a Christian gentleman, but in Dee's case it simply means he can be deceived. For a man who claims to understand the heavens, he is mighty gullible here on earth. I fear a man would not have to be the most skilful cozener in England to lure a secret from him. Why, a pretended scryer could find out all he wished by informing him that the angels insist he reveal the secret of the perspective glass.' Cecil laughed again, drily. 'My father always had doubts about Dr Dee, John, and I share them.'

Shakespeare did not laugh, but he smiled at Cecil's cruel jest about the scryer and the angels, for he understood its scandalous provenance. During Dr Dee's years in Prague, he had been persuaded by an 'angel' to exchange wives for a night with his scryer Edward Kelley. It was said that the comely young Jane Dee wept uncontrollably as her husband despatched her to Kelley's quarters to be ravished – while Dee received Kelley's rather less alluring wife, Joanna, in return.

Yes, Cecil was right, Dee was gullible. There could be little argument about that.

'Consider, too, the company he keeps,' Cecil continued. 'Kelley apart, Dee made some unsavoury friends during his time in Prague. The city is a hotbed of treason and Catholic intrigue. And we know, too, of the Earl of Derby's unfortunate connection with that city and its English traitors.'

Shakespeare stiffened. From the straightforward task of protecting Dee, Cecil was lurching into high politics. The Earl of Derby, with whom the doctor was now staying at Lathom House in Lancashire, was one of the premier claimants to succeed to the throne of England. This was not merely *high* politics, but *dangerous* politics: the earl's religious sympathies had come under much scrutiny these past months.

Cecil nodded in the direction of Heneage. 'Sir Thomas, if you would . . .'

Heneage smiled warmly. 'Thank you, Sir Robert.' His eyes met Shakespeare's again. 'I have long admired your work on behalf of England, Mr Shakespeare.'

Shakespeare bowed. 'Thank you, Sir Thomas.'

'No, no, England must thank you. Sadly, there are those in our country who are not so loyal to our sovereign lady. My own county, Lancashire, I am afraid, has a great portion of such traitors and those who harbour them. Every week, new intelligence reaches my office of Jesuits and seminary priests walking our northern towns openly and without hindrance. It shames me, sir, as Chancellor of the Duchy, that such a state of affairs continues.'

It was ever thus, Shakespeare knew. Mr Secretary Walsingham – four years dead now – had been driven half insane by reports of Catholic defiance in Lancashire. He had continually ordered purges with heavy fines to be paid for recusancy – non-attendance in the parish church. The priest-hunter Richard Topcliffe kept maps of the county marked with names and homes of prominent Catholics, each one underlined and circled with the frenzied scrapings of his quill.

'In truth, Mr Shakespeare, there are many in my county so disaffected that they would rather sever their fingers than sign the Bond of Association.'

Shakespeare's jaw tightened. He shared the loyalty of those who had signed the Bond, but could also understand anyone's reluctance to put their name to the paper. It had been formulated ten years ago, in 1584, by Walsingham and Burghley in the dark days following the Throckmorton plot against the Queen. All those who signed it made a pledge to do away with anyone who harmed or conspired to do harm to the Queen. It was dressed as an act of pure patriotism, but to Shakespeare it was a licence to kill, legitimised murder.

'But that,' Heneage continued with a wave of his elegant hand, 'is by the by. I mention it merely so that you will know the dangers of the territory you are about to enter.'

'Thank you, Sir Thomas. I have a good understanding of the situation in Lancashire. I, too, have seen the reports from the county.'

'Good. Then I am sure all will be well and you will remove Dr Dee safely. But before you do so, there is someone I wish you to make contact with there. Her name is Lady Eliska Nováková, and she is the daughter of a very dear friend of mine, sadly deceased. I have a letter for her, full of fond remembrances. I would be grateful if you would put it in her fair hand.'

‡ 22 ‡

Heneage took a sealed paper from his gold and wine-red doublet and held it out. Shakespeare took it.

'Of course, Sir Thomas. Where shall I find the lady?'

'That is easy. Like Dr Dee, she is a guest of the Earl and Countess of Derby at Lathom House. He has few enough visitors these days, I believe.'

Janus Trayne clutched the reins with his left hand. His right arm was held in a blood-stained sling fashioned from old rag. The horse he rode was slow and stubborn. Worst of all was the pain, the deep throbbing pain from his wrist where the knife had penetrated. Every so often he stopped and put his left hand to the injury, feeling for heat, wondering whether it was about to turn bad.

He could not stop thinking about how nearly he had had the instrument within his grasp at Portsmouth. He had been so close to success, only to have it snatched away. But who was the assailant? Who thrust the dagger blade so deep into his flesh and bone? Somewhere, in the distant crannies of his remembering, there was a name attached to that stumpy body and grim, weathered face. Had he seen him before? If so, then in God's name where?

The road to the north-west was long and hard, yet he had to ride on, for although his empty pouch would not make him welcome, he was expected. He realised well enough that there would be more work to be done. This was not over yet. The chance of earning two hundred golden ducats was not to be passed up. Spain would have what it so desired, and he would have his gold.

As Heneage strode from the offices, Cecil stayed Shakespeare with his hand.

'Not you, John. We have a little more business.'

'Sir Robert.'

Cecil closed the door and walked towards the table, where he had a goblet of French wine. He took a sip, then sat down close to the window. Shakespeare remained standing.

'Well, John, your thoughts . . .'

'This is about a great deal more than the safety of Dr Dee.'

'Yes, the Lady Eliska.' Cecil's tight mouth creased into a grimace. 'Let us say that she is of great interest to me. Her father was a fervent Protestant, who died at the hands of the Inquisition. He worked closely with Sir Thomas for many years, trying to advance the Protestant cause in the German lands and the Dutch estates. Now she seems to wish to further his work against Rome. Heneage is certain she can be of great help to England, and we may well have a use for her. But I wish *your* opinion. Observe her, John, and report back to me. Is she to be trusted?'

'From her name, I would suspect she is from the East.'

'She is Bohemian, from Prague.'

Prague. That city again. The place where Dee had gone in his strange peregrinations, the place whence so much trouble had come down upon the head of Lord Derby. Shakespeare's raised eyebrow posed the question to Cecil.

'How could she possibly help England?'

Cecil looked ill at ease. He shifted the hunch of his shoulder. 'As yet, I am not certain. But Sir Thomas is convinced. Though he is to marry Mary Wriothesley this summer, I sometimes wonder whether there might be some place in his heart for his young Bohemian friend. Love can cloud any man's judgment.'

Shakespeare said nothing. Walsingham had once believed that love had clouded *his* judgment, when Shakespeare fell for Catherine Marvell, the Catholic governess who became his wife and mother to his child.

Cecil continued, 'For all I know, the lady Eliska might be all that Sir Thomas claims and more. But I would like to hear your impressions. You will have little enough time with her, for you must remove Dee at speed. All I ask is that you find out what you can.'

'And my lord of Derby?'

Cecil hesitated again, then stood and looked out the window. At last he turned back.

'Yes, it is true. I wish to know the state of things there. Do what you would do wherever you find yourself: keep a watchful eye. I fear, like a stag at bay, he lies isolated in his northern fastness. Since the events of last September, I know he feels endangered and cut adrift. He fights with his brother and is in conflict with the Duchy of Lancaster. As for those who would have made him king, the Jesuits, I believe he has received a death threat from them. Many of the more militant Catholics feel betrayed by him and desire revenge.'

'That does not surprise me.'

Shakespeare knew enough of the perilous situation Derby had faced seven months earlier in the early autumn of '93. A man named Richard Hesketh had approached the earl with a treasonable letter from the Catholic exiles in Prague, entreating him to be their anointed chief in England, their king-in-waiting. Derby had turned Hesketh over to the authorities, and the wretched man had been butchered on the scaffold for treason. But had the earl simply sacrificed Hesketh to save his own skin? Was he, as many still suspected, a crypto-Catholic with designs on the crown of England?

Cecil lifted the flask from the table and poured wine for them both. His mood seemed to lighten.

'Come, John, tell me a little of your family. How do they fare? I was glad to help your boy Andrew go up to Oxford. These have been hard months for you all since—'

Shakespeare's hand went up. 'I am sorry, Sir Robert, I

cannot talk about it. Forgive me.' The death of Catherine was as raw today as ever. Sometimes he feared the pain would never ease.

'I understand,' Cecil said softly. 'But sup with me, John. Take a little wine and sustenance. You have a long ride ahead.'

# *Chapter 4*

T HE ROAD NORTH-WEST took Shakespeare through Oxford. He considered stopping to visit his adopted son, Andrew Woode. He could spend a few hours with him and bring him news of their family from London. He worried for Andrew constantly, for the boy's Catholic passions seemed to run deep, and England was a dangerous place for anyone with such a powerful attachment to the sacraments of Rome.

Shakespeare shook the reins. He would lose the rest of the day if he stopped now – a day that he could not afford. Reluctantly, he rode on, resolving instead to stop the night here on his return journey with Dr Dee.

For the next forty hours, save a five-hour sleep at an inn, he drove northwards relentlessly, urging on post-horse after post-horse, exchanging them for fresh animals as soon as they flagged.

Two hundred miles later, John Shakespeare was deep into Lancashire. It had been a rough slog, leaving him saddle-sore, angry and exhausted. He had made good progress, but the thought that he had not taken the opportunity to visit Andrew nagged at him all the way. What worried him most – something he barely dared admit to himself – was that Andrew might leave the country.

Too many Catholic youths fled England for the seminaries

of Rheims and Rome and Valladolid; some of them sought freedom of worship, some trained to return to England as priests. Under the law of the land, it was treason for a Catholic priest to enter England secretly, and the punishment was death, martyrdom.

Andrew's college, St John's, was reckoned hard Protestant now, but nothing was ever that simple. There were still disturbances in the college, still Fellows whose hearts lay with the old ways. Shakespeare had a deep sense of foreboding.

As he rode on, he thought about the rest of his family. With Andrew gone, their large house in Dowgate, on the banks of the Thames in the city of London, seemed empty. It had been a school for the poor boys of London, dedicated to Andrew's mother, Margaret Woode, but it had been closed by two years of plague and showed little sign of reopening. It was a pleasantly appointed property in a fine setting, but Shakespeare found its echoing spaces unsettling and oppressive. He turned corners expecting to see Catherine, his wife, but she was not there.

These thoughts crowded in as he came down Parbold Hill from the sensuous folds of southern Lancashire towards the flatlands that led to the sea. He was within the last few miles of the market town of Ormskirk and of Lathom House.

From the hill, the land stretched out before him. Then he came once more into woods where the road narrowed and became more rutted.

Suddenly a gunshot rent the air. Shakespeare reined in the tough, flea-bitten post-horse. They were on a beaten track through a wood of oak and ash. Light played through the fresh spring leaves. He waited a moment, then walked the horse on, more cautiously. It was probably a huntsman with a fowling piece, but it paid to be wary along these outlaw-infested paths. Every lane of England seemed inhabited by criminal bands of vagabonds in these straitened times.

Turning a corner, he pulled his mount to a halt again. Revulsion welled up within him. There were three men at the side of the road, one of them with a hempen noose about his neck, his arms bound behind his back. The other two men were dressed in heavy cassock coats of the type worn by soldiers. They were powerful-looking and heavily armed. The smaller of the two had a smoking petronel pistol dangling from his hand and was picking up a dead rabbit. Neither man seemed concerned at the arrival of Shakespeare. They eyed him coldly, then continued about their business. One of them, the taller, a plough-horse of a man at six and a half feet with a muscled frame and a gaunt face that seemed to tell of battles fought and survived, held the loose end of the long hemp rope. Casually, he tossed it over a thick, ungiving branch of oak, perhaps ten feet off the ground. The other one slung his spent petronel pistol across his back, then tied the dead rabbit to the stirrup of his horse.

He looked up the road and saw Shakespeare, but ignored him and joined the bigger man. Together, they began pulling on the rope, hoisting the condemned man off the ground, his legs kicking frantically at the air. The executioners seemed unconcerned, bored even, as though this was their daily work.

'What is this?' Shakespeare demanded, urging his horse forward close to the hanging tree.

'Deserter. What's it to you?' the plough-horse man said.

The two hangmen nonchalantly knotted the loose end of the rope around a lower branch, to secure it. The man with the petronel wore the Queen's escutcheon on his tawny cassock and seemed to be in charge. There was a pitiless quality to his eyes. Half his face was badly disfigured, as though his cheek had been shot away. The remainder of his face had black spots, like parchment on which ink has been flicked. Shakespeare guessed it had been peppered with fragments of shot.

The rope creaked as the knot was pulled tight. Shakespeare moved his horse closer, drew his sword and slashed at the hempen cord, just above the condemned man's head. The steel blade, new-honed and as sharp as a scythe at harvest-time, sliced through the fibres with one strike.

The man fell helplessly to the hard, dusty earth, cracked his knees, crumpled and tipped face-forward with a juddering crunch to the nose and forehead. Shakespeare jumped from his horse and, pulling out his poniard, cut the noose away from the man's neck. He lay there, still, then sucked in a short, desperate measure of air. He gasped again, the breath rattling in his throat.

Four hands dragged Shakespeare away and flung him, sprawling, into a hedge. The leader, his pocked, callous face lacking any emotion – not even wrath – strode over and put his boot in the middle of Shakespeare's chest. He took a wheel-lock pistol from his belt and aimed it at the bridge of Shakespeare's nose, dead between the eyes.

'I could kill you here and now, you maggot's arse.'

Shakespeare grabbed at the booted foot and tried in vain to lift it and twist it so he could roll away and get up.

'You are wondering who I am. Well, my name's Pinkney. Does that mean anything to you?'

Pinkney removed his foot and Shakespeare rose to his feet, dusting himself down, then looked at the man. The name meant nothing.

'Provost Marshal Pinkney, under orders to press men for the wars in Brittany and hang deserters and outlaws. You have interfered with lawful business here. I should shoot you dead as I just shot that rabbit.' He nodded towards the wretched, skinny carcass hanging from the stirrup.

The half-hanged man was now on his knees, face down in the dirt with his hands still tight bound behind him, coughing and rasping as blood dripped from his mouth. He was struggling to say something.

'Rope him again, Cordwright,' Pinkney ordered his assistant. 'He hasn't done dancing his jig.'

'No, wait!' Shakespeare held up his hand. 'I am John Shakespeare, an officer of Sir Robert Cecil. I want to hear what the man has to say for himself.' He stepped forward and placed himself between the condemned man and the provost. Kneeling at the man's side, he cradled his battered head. 'Who are you?'

The man could not speak, but he looked like no common soldier or deserter. Shakespeare would have taken him for a clerk or scribe; the skin of his face and hands was soft and pallid.

'Who is this man, Mr Pinkney?' Shakespeare said, trying to lift the hanged man from the ground. 'Get me drink to wet his lips so that we may listen to him.'

'I say he is a deserter, so that is what he is. Martial law, Mr Shakespeare, martial law. These are hard times and I am authorised to work in the interests of England. Captain-General Norreys needs all the men he can get for the Royal Army, even vermin like this. And as this man won't go to the wars, though he has cost the Queen sixteen shillings for coat and conduct, and three shillings for a pikestaff, I say he is a deserter and will hang for it. Look at his good broadcloth venetians, his kersey nether-stocks and his new shoes! In faith, this is good English justice, Mr Shakespeare, and I will not be balked by you, Cecil or any man save Sir John Norreys himself.'

'Justice? This may be *military* law, but there is no martial law in place here. What trial has this man had?'

'Summary justice, as decreed by *martial* law. He is a master-less man, pressed for service. He took the coat and our food – and then he disappeared from camp. We found him hiding in this wood. He has no defence.'

Shakespeare snorted. 'You are collecting men a long way north for an expedition to Brittany. I have never heard of a levy so far from the ports of embarkation. Why, it is two weeks' march and more to Portsmouth or Poole.'

'Needs must, Mr Shakespeare. These are perilous times and I will take masterless men wherever I find them.'

'Well, I say he will not hang until he has been examined further.'

Provost Pinkney laughed. 'You have no jurisdiction here.' He turned to his man. 'Hang him, then relieve him of his boots and coat.'

Provost Pinkney stood in front of Shakespeare, one hand on the hilt of his sword, the other gripping the butt of his pistol, while his powerful foot soldier set about fashioning a new noose from the severed rope.

Shakespeare glared into Pinkney's grey, unblinking eyes and saw no hope of reprieve. Pinkney was a couple of inches shorter than him. The lower portion of his shot-ravaged face was covered in bristles. He had red, longbow lips and a chin that pushed forward aggressively from the canopy of his thick barley-harvest of hair.

The hangman wrenched the condemned man's head back and pulled it into the noose, dragging the rope choking-tight around his already damaged neck. Then he yanked the victim to his feet, roughly, by the bindings at his back. Guilty or innocent, the man was about to die and, at the point of a gun, there was nothing John Shakespeare, an officer of the most senior government officer in England, could do to stop it. This was martial law, summary justice, wolf law. No justice at all.

The thunder of an approaching wagon jolted the hangman to a halt in his grisly business. Shod hoofs on a hard, uneven road and the rattle of metal-rimmed wheels grew louder.

In a swirl of dust, a black carriage appeared from the woods.

It was a curious lightweight coach with a golden cupola atop each corner, driven hard by a coachman with a black cape and a long lash.

The soldiers and Shakespeare stood and stared at this apparition. The carriage, which was pulled by just one heavy black horse, was going fast and seemed about to sweep past them eastwards, in a clatter of wheels and hoofs. But the passenger inside banged at the coach's wooden casing, and the coachman reined in the horse in a fury of stamping and whinnying.

The horse was dripping with white-flecked sweat, its great barrel chest heaving with exertion. The coachman jumped down from his roost and opened the small door, bowing low to its occupant as he did so.

Without hesitating, Shakespeare brushed away the provost marshal's pistol and moved towards the carriage. The coachman tried to restrain him, but Shakespeare held his ground and peered in. A woman sat there, still, silent and veiled. So small and dark was she, seated in the corner, that at first he thought she was in widow's weeds. But as his eyes became accustomed to the gloomy interior, he saw that her clothes were, in truth, an exquisitely tailored black travelling costume and not at all in the English mode.

She seemed to be staring at Shakespeare as one might gaze at an alien creature imported from the southern seas. A tiny monkey with a long tail sat on her shoulder. It began chattering with little yellow teeth. Shakespeare bowed.

'My lady . . .' he began.

'Is there to be an execution here?' she said in a throaty, heavily accented voice. 'A hanging?'

Shakespeare could not quite place her accent, but it was unlikely there would be many foreign aristocrats in Lancashire. Was this the Bohemian woman whom Heneage had asked him to seek out?

'My name is John Shakespeare, my lady. I am an officer of Sir Robert Cecil.'

The word *Cecil* had an immediate impact.

'Cecil?' the woman said, pulling aside her black veil with delicate gloved fingers, to reveal a fair, unlined complexion. She was young, perhaps in her mid-twenties. Her expression revealed nothing except her interest. 'The son of Lord Burghley?'

'Indeed, my lady. May I inquire who you are?'

'You may, of course, Mr Shakespeare, but I may not wish to tell you.'

There was a sudden scuffling from behind Shakespeare.

'I've had enough of this,' the provost said. 'Get on with the hanging, Cordwright. If the lady wants to watch, that's her business. She can have a front-row seat.'

Pinkney's executioner threw the rope over the branch again and began to pull it taut.

'Stop!' Shakespeare bellowed.

The woman in the carriage leant forward and peered out. 'Pray, tell me, Mr Shakespeare, what is going on here?'

'I am trying to stop a murder, my lady,' Shakespeare growled. 'But I am outgunned.'

The woman laughed lightly. 'Well, I enjoy a hanging as much as the next lady, but if you say you are Cecil's man, then I believe I shall assist you in this matter.'

She nodded to her coachman who strode forward and, without ado, pulled the condemned man up by the scruff of his coat, removed the noose from his neck and, throwing him across his shoulder, carried him over to the carriage, where he laid him down on the ground, in full view of the passenger. The would-be hangmen looked on, astonished.

John Shakespeare took his water-flask from a hook on his saddle, his eyes all the while remaining on Provost Pinkney. Stepping forward, then kneeling, he held the clay flask to the lips of the half-hanged man. He sucked at the water thirstily, then coughed and spluttered.

'Who are you?' Shakespeare asked.

'Lamb ...' The voice was weak. 'Matthew Lamb. You cannot save me ...'

'Yes, I can.' He turned back to the woman in the coach. 'My lady, I entreat you, help me take this prisoner to Ormskirk. If there is evidence of wrongdoing, he will face a court of law.'

The woman smiled at Shakespeare, then said a few words to her coachman in her own language. He bowed.

Shakespeare held the flask once more to Lamb's lips. He drank, but coughed up blood. Shakespeare wiped his sleeve across the man's mouth. 'Take small sips,' he said.

'There is no time,' the man said, barely audible between hacking, painful coughs. 'You must save Strange, sir. I beg you, save Strange.'

'Strange? What are you saying, Mr Lamb?'

Lamb's eyes opened wide, for he saw what was coming. Provost Pinkney had stepped forward with his pistol and the muzzle was now aiming full at his body. Pinkney pulled the trigger.

# Chapter 5

T HE BALL FROM Pinkney's gun drove deep into Lamb's body. The crack of the shot jinked the carriage-horse sideways, shaking the coach from side to side.

The coachman leapt on Pinkney and put a wheel-lock of his own to the side of his head. Pinkney shrugged him off and looked dispassionately at his handiwork. He bowed in an exaggerated, scornful manner in the direction of the coach.

'My apologies for the disturbance, my lady. I trust your horse did not injure itself. If it needs attention, you may send the reckoning to Captain-General Norreys or to the Lord Lieutenant of Lancashire.'

Shakespeare stood up. His doublet, hands and face were spotted with the dead man's gore. 'You are a murderer, Pinkney.'

'A pustule on your prick, Shakespeare. If you have anything to say on this matter, I would refer you to the Lord Lieutenant, for I have no other master in this county.'

Shakespeare pulled back his fist, but the other soldier, Cordwright, restrained him.

'Please come here, Mr Shakespeare,' the woman called from the carriage.

Shakespeare lowered his fist. He shook off Cordwright's

restraining hands, turned and strode angrily to the lady in the carriage, wiping blood from his face on to his sleeve.

'I do not know what any of this is about,' she said, 'nor do I wish to. But I am exceedingly put out if, as you say, the poor man has been killed without benefit of judge or jury.'

'This cannot end here. I would ask you to help me lift the dead man's body so that I may remove it to a nearby town, where he can be properly identified and examined. The least he deserves is a coroner's inquest.'

'Then that is what we shall do. Solko.'

She nodded to the coachman. Solko picked up the body of Lamb and laid it across the back of Shakespeare's horse.

The two would-be hangmen looked back with indifference. With the coachman's assistance, Shakespeare mounted up in front of the corpse and bowed to the woman in the coach.

'Thank you, my lady. And may I ask you once again – who are you?'

She smiled. It was a smile of such beguiling innocence that a more credulous man than Shakespeare might have been entranced. 'My name is Eliska Nováková,' she said, then retreated into the depths of her carriage.

Before Shakespeare had a chance to say another word, the coachman closed the carriage door, mounted his perch and lashed the horse forward.

Ormskirk was a small market town. Shakespeare stopped at an inn in the central square. This was no market day. The dusty space was almost deserted, save for an old man sitting against the inn wall, whittling a stick to pass the time. Above him, a painted sign swung slowly in the breeze, creaking. It bore a picture of an eagle, clasping a swaddled child in its talons.

Ignoring the old man, Shakespeare walked into the taproom where he found the landlord, a broad-bellied, grim-visaged man of middle years, and told him he had a body outside, a victim of murder. He demanded he send for the coroner.

'He won't come unless you pay him a mark. He'll send his man to view and bury the body.'

'Tell him I am an officer of the Queen. And while you're about it, bring me the constable, too.'

'You could be an officer of Christ himself and the coroner still wouldn't come without his coin.' The landlord suddenly noticed Shakespeare's hand on the hilt of his sword. 'But I'll go and tell him what you say.'

'The body will be in here.'

'Not in my taproom, it won't. You'll bring me bad fortune, and I've enough of that already.'

'You'll have more if you don't make haste.'

As the landlord shuffled out, his head hung in gloom, Shakespeare went and hefted in the body, which was surprisingly thin and light, and laid it on a table. As he waited, he looked down at the dead man's face and recalled his last words.

*You must save Strange . . . I beg you, save Strange.*

What possible connection could there be between a deserter from Provost Pinkney's militia and the Earl of Derby? The Earl of Derby, who until the death of his father, the fourth earl, the previous September, had been known as Ferdinando, Lord Strange. Shakespeare paced the room in frustration. He had been delayed long enough. It was imperative that he got to Lathom House to put the matter to Derby himself . . . and to carry Dr Dee away to safety.

At last the constable arrived with the landlord.

'Where is the coroner?' Shakespeare demanded.

'Hunting duck. I left a message for him to come when he returns,' the landlord said, eyeing the body in his taproom with distaste. 'How long will that be there? Customers will be coming soon, thirsty yeomen. They won't want to share their ale with a corpse.'

'Is there somewhere else?'

'Out in the backyard, there's a workshop. Put him in there.'

'You two – you and the constable – carry the body.'

Reluctantly, the two men lifted Lamb's corpse from the table and carried it out through a postern door. Shakespeare followed them. It seemed to him that the constable was nervous. He was a big man, like most constables, with sweat on his brow and shifting eyes. So far he had said nothing, merely nodding in deference to Shakespeare.

'What is your name, constable?'

'Barrow, master. Constable Barrow.'

'Do you recognise this dead man?'

The constable averted his eyes and did not reply.

'What was his name?'

The constable said nothing.

'I shall have this information from you, constable, whether you like it or not. I am on Queen's business.'

The constable turned back and met Shakespeare's eye. 'Lamb. The man was Matthew Lamb, commonly known as Matt.'

'What was he?'

'A man of some private means. He was new to this area, came last year. Never wanted for a shilling or two, caused no trouble, so I had no dealings with him.'

'Did he have no trade nor master?'

'No.'

'Where did he stay?'

The constable looked at the landlord, as though unsure what to say next.

'Well, man?'

'He had no permanent lodgings, master. He came and went . . . stayed here and there.'

Shakespeare began to understand. 'Send a woman to prepare this body for the inquest and burial. I want her here quickly and she shall have threepence. In the meantime, leave me. I wish to examine him myself. Oh,' he turned to the landlord, 'and bring me a blackjack of your best bitter beer and some pie. Now go.'

Shakespeare removed the corpse's doublet first. It had a wide, ragged hole in the side where Pinkney's pistol had blasted its deadly ball. Beneath it, the dead man's torso was tightly wrapped in a stinking horsehair undergarment, which crawled with lice. Lamb had been mortifying his flesh. It was as Shakespeare had suspected from Constable Barrow's evasive responses: the dead man was a Roman Catholic priest, sent illegally from a seminary into England.

The door to the workshop opened wider and a thin, bright-eyed woman bustled in. 'Good day, master, good day,' she said cheerily.

'Good day, mistress.'

'Now, who have we here? Oh, Lord help us, it's Father Lamb.'

'You knew him?'

'Indeed, sir. He was well known in these parts.'

'What was he?'

'From the Society of Jesus. Brought his ministry to many people in this district. Has anyone said words over him?'

'Are *you* of the Roman faith?'

'What if I am, master? That is between me and God.'

'Indeed, mistress. All I wish is to get to the truth of this man and his untimely death.'

The woman moved closer to the woodworking bench on which Lamb's body lay. Shakespeare liked her face; he could see that she must have been comely before motherhood and the years took their toll, but she retained sweetness and mirth.

'Oh, poor man,' she said, touching the hairshirt. 'I had no idea he wore one of those. How could a man think for the constant pain and irritation in wearing such a thing?'

'Tell me, mistress, what is your name?'

'Goody Barrow, sir. I am the constable's wife, whom you have met. Did he not say words over Father Lamb? Such a craven man, but we must abide with what we have.'

'I believe there are many Papists hereabouts.'

'It would be difficult to find any other than a Papist, sir. We hold to the old way here, the *true* way.'

Shakespeare was surprised to find how openly the woman talked of her Romish allegiance. 'Do you not fear the consequences of recusancy?'

'What consequences, sir? There are not enough Protestants in these parts to apply southern law, though Derby tries his hand when he can, for appearances' sake.'

Shakespeare let the matter pass. 'Well, get on with your work, Goody Barrow. I want this body stripped.'

He drank beer and watched the goodwife go about her work. She was adept at removing the clothes with due reverence and cleaning the body with care.

While she worked, Shakespeare went over to the pile of clothes the goodwife had placed, neatly folded, on the floor and he picked up the dead man's doublet. He felt it carefully with the tips of his fingers, then sliced open the bottom seam with his poniard. Slipping his fingers up into the stuffing, he found a paper and withdrew it.

The goodwife looked over at him with curiosity and something else – fear, perhaps?

The paper was folded, stitched and had a wax seal. Shakespeare cut it open. It was a letter, written in a small, neat hand. It was addressed to 'His Eminence WCA'. A name sprang to mind instantly – William Cardinal Allen, foremost of the English

Catholics in exile and responsible for sending dozens of young men to martyrdom in their homeland. It was a poor way to disguise his name. Who but a cardinal was addressed as *His Eminence*? Shakespeare read on, for the remainder of the letter was not obviously encoded.

'*On arriving in Lancashire at the end of my long journey from Rome, I was heartened by the generosity of the reception from people great and low. All here hunger for the mass and are happy to receive me into their dwellings, so that I never have fear of discovery. My arrival has been the happiest possible, inspiring and cheering the flock in equal measure, for though there is less to fear here than in other parts of this benighted isle, yet they have felt dismayed and abandoned by the Church . . .*'

So the letter went on, detailing the joys and tribulations of the priest's mission in England. Shakespeare had seen many such intercepted letters from Jesuits and seminary priests to their controllers in Rome and Rheims. They were always careful not to divulge names, places or dates, and this was no exception. Their codes were subtle, so that there seemed to be no code. However, one phrase towards the end leapt out from the parchment.

'*As to the great enterprise, all is not well. We must pray, and hope, for better times ahead.*'

The great *enterprise*? King Philip of Spain had described his Armada invasion plans as the *Enterprise* of England.

Shakespeare's jaw stiffened. He read the words again, then stuffed the paper in his own doublet, bade Mistress Barrow good day and took horse for Lathom House.

# Chapter 6

THE HOUSE SOON came into view. It seemed to Shakespeare that it spilt across the landscape like a sleeping dragon. Its grey towers and turrets were the horns and its embattlements were the spikes and notches of the spine. The place was immense – on a scale with the magnificent Windsor Castle, and of similar appearance. No wonder men spoke of it as the Northern Court.

By now, Shakespeare was almost asleep in the saddle, but he reined in his mount and took a few moments to gaze on the scene. His eyes alighted on a small encampment of brightly hued tents that dotted the parkland outside the moat, not far from the main drawbridge and portcullis gate. Men milled about, cooked over open fires and smoked pipes. Outside a larger canvas pavilion, a group of half a dozen men were acting out a play of some sort. Shakespeare squinted into the evening sun. Among the players, he thought he spied the upright form and dark, swept-back hair of his brother.

As he steered the flea-bitten horse through the tents and heavy wagons he reflected: after all, why should Will *not* be here? He had often played with Lord Strange's Men, now, after Strange's accession to the earldom, known as Derby's Men. The earl had helped foster Will's career for many years.

Will held the playbook and seemed to be leading a rehearsal.

When he looked up and saw his brother, he put up a hand for the players to take a break and walked over to him, smiling.

'Have you come all this way to see us perform, John?'

Shakespeare laughed and slid from the horse. He embraced his brother, then stood back to look at him.

'I would, of course, go to the Moluccas to see you. But not in this instance. I have other concerns. You appear well, brother.'

'Well, it is always a pleasant part of England to spend a few days. The theatres in London and Southwark open and then close, then open again, then close. These plague years will do for us. In the meanwhile, my lord of Derby begged a light confection to cheer him, so I have brought a tale of faeries and spells and midsummer in the woods. I hope he will like it well.'

'When is it to be performed?'

'It was to have been this evening, here among these trees, but his lordship is indisposed with some sickness, so we must wait another day.'

'Well, I hope it will be my good fortune to see you play. But for now, I must go and pay my respects.'

The drawbridge was overgrown with weeds, as if it was never raised. Likewise, the portcullis was rusted solid up in its casing. As for Lathom House itself, it seemed out of its time, built for a more elegant age of warfare. Its crenellations, towers and castle keep spoke of knights and chivalry and boulders flung by trebuchet, not this modern era of gunshot and cannonfire. Turreted ramparts could not withstand a barrage of cannon-balls. Fortifications now were squat and brutish, with massive curtain walls, twenty or thirty feet thick, and solid bastions to cover against attack from every corner.

Shakespeare led his horse across the drawbridge and through the portcullis gate. A guard glanced peremptorily at his letters patent and signalled to a fellow guard to escort him in. Shakespeare handed the reins of the post-horse to a groom and followed the guard into the castle grounds. They walked briskly across a cobbled way to a grand doorway, which gave on to a long, handsome hall, to the left of the keep.

A liveried servant admitted Shakespeare to the hall, which was oak-panelled and high, emblazoned with coats of arms on the walls. The most obvious of these, the one that greeted him as he entered, was the eagle and child, like the inn sign at Ormskirk: this was the coat of arms of the Stanleys, the family name of the earls of Derby.

'I shall bring his lordship's steward to you straightway, Mr Shakespeare,' the servant said.

The household steward arrived quickly. A man of thirty or so, he had greying black hair and a clean-shaven face. He was attired all in black, like the lawyers Shakespeare once studied among at Gray's Inn, before Walsingham took him on as an intelligencer – work far more suited to him than the world of dusty books. The steward introduced himself as Cole and apologised to Shakespeare that the earl was indisposed.

'I understand you have letters patent from Sir Robert Cecil. My lord of Derby will certainly wish to see you when he is well, but I fear he is presently most grievously ill. In the meantime, I shall try to find her ladyship, Mr Shakespeare, for I know she will wish to receive you and welcome you. I shall have refreshment sent to you while you wait.'

'Thank you, Mr Cole.'

Wine and dainty dishes arrived. Shakespeare sat on a settle and picked at the food. Outside, through the window, he saw the sky darkening. Twilight. He had been on the move since before dawn and much had happened. Just as his eyelids were growing heavy, the Countess of Derby appeared, followed by three giggling girl children whose ages seemed to range from about twelve to six, all attired in fashionable taffeta, creamy white with silver threads.

Shakespeare stood up and bowed low. The Countess of Derby was dark-haired with spotless skin and a gracious smile. He had seen her at court before she was married, in the days when she went by her given name, Alice Spencer. He recalled her close friendship with the Queen and their shared interest in plays and poetry. She smiled at him, then looked at her daughters and clapped her hands.

'Off you go, young ladies,' she ordered, and they scuttled away. 'Now then, Mr Shakespeare, I am exceedingly pleased that you have come. Did you know that your talented brother is here?'

'I have seen him already, my lady.'

'He has promised me the role of the beautiful Titania in his new masque, if my husband allows me to play her. But I fear we shall have to wait some little while, for the earl is in poor health.'

'Is it a sickness of long standing?'

'It came on very suddenly, a vomiting sickness of most violent nature after he returned from the hunt yesterday. I would wonder whether it was something he ate, but no one else in the household is ill, and there are more than a hundred people here, including servants, family, players and guests, so it surely cannot be that. My lord believes himself bewitched, but that is the fever talking. The physicians are with him.'

*You must save Strange, sir. I beg you, save Strange.*

Shakespeare tensed once more at the recollection of the priest's final words. Save Strange from what?

The countess touched his arm. 'I am sure all will be well, Mr Shakespeare. My lord is always as fit as a hare and will withstand any small sickness. He will be up at the chase again in no time.'

'Do you think I might see him, my lady?'

She gave him a wan smile. 'You believe there is some mischief here, don't you, Mr Shakespeare?'

'I pray not. But, yes, it was the first thing that occurred to me.'

There was silence between them. 'I fear I know what you are thinking.'

He tried to keep his face neutral. 'I had, indeed, heard some suggestion that the earl was threatened.'

Silence again. And then she sighed. 'Yes. It is true. There was a letter . . .' The countess broke off, seeming to think better of it.

'A letter?' Shakespeare pressed her. 'What did the letter say, my lady?'

'It said . . . it said my husband would die in the most wretched manner if Richard Hesketh went to the gallows. It seems we are to be cursed by evil letters.'

Richard Hesketh had brought a letter, too. Hesketh, a name that tainted the Earl of Derby and would haunt him for as long as he lived. Shakespeare mentally rehearsed what he knew of him. Hesketh was a Lancashire cloth merchant whose large, extended family had for many years been close friends and retainers of the earl and his forefathers. By all accounts, Hesketh was a stout, yellow-haired fellow, who seemed to have led a largely blameless life. He was probably a Catholic, but that was hardly unusual in these parts. His life changed dramatically in the year 1589 when he became involved in a local dispute over cattle, in which a landowner named Thomas Hoghton died.

Forty men were arrested. Hesketh had been at the centre of the fight, but he had evaded capture and fled to Prague. There he fell in with other English exiles, including Jesuits and renegade members of the Stanley clan, the Earl of Derby's family. It was a city Shakespeare had never visited, but one he felt he knew well from the reports received by Walsingham and, more recently, Cecil. The place was thick with Protestant spies and riddled with Catholic plotters from Spain and the Vatican. Into this volatile mix, of course, were added the curious figures of the alchemist Dr Dee and his friend and scryer Edward Kelley, along with a few dozen more of the malign, misguided and beguiled. And now a new name had to be added to the cauldron of Prague intrigants: the mysterious and beautiful figure of Lady Eliska Nováková, friend to Heneage and now a guest of Derby. Who exactly was she and what she was doing here?

Before leaving Nonsuch, Shakespeare had pressed Cecil for more information, but none was forthcoming. 'I wish you to meet her without prejudice, John,' was all he would say.

The Earl of Derby must have gone cold as he read the letter Hesketh had brought from Prague, thought Shakespeare. As the earl was a direct descendant of Henry VII, and under the terms of Henry VIII's will was a prime claimant to the throne, the letter entreated him to become a figurehead for England's Catholics, and to snatch the crown for God and the Pope. *Become a figurehead for England's Catholics?* God's teeth, how could the earl not have recalled the grisly fate of the last Catholic figurehead – Mary Queen of Scots? That proud head had been lopped off at Fotheringhay Castle in a drenching of blood.

The earl did not seem the stuff of such martyrdom. He loved life too much. Poetry, plays, the hunt, gaming, his beautiful wife and daughters: that was where his devotion lay.

But as he read the Hesketh letter, he must have realised he was in an awful trap: if he even talked the contents over with the wretched Hesketh, he would be condemning himself in the eyes of the Queen and the Cecils. If he did not hand Hesketh over to the Privy Council as a traitor, then he, Derby, would be the traitor.

And if he did denounce Hesketh? Then he would make enemies of the whole Catholic world and of Hesketh's kin.

In the end, Derby had had no option: to have any chance of survival, he handed the letter over to the Queen and had Hesketh taken into custody. Under questioning by the relentless William Wade, clerk to the Privy Council, Hesketh maintained that he never knew the contents of this letter. He had collected it, sealed, from a contact near London and had then ridden for Lancashire. Eventually, however, he confessed his guilt to high treason and was executed by hanging, drawing and quartering at St Albans last November.

Derby had been left badly wounded by the affair. Many Catholics now believed him a betrayer for bearing witness against Hesketh and sending him to the scaffold, while many Protestants were still not convinced that he was not, himself, a Catholic with designs on the crown of England.

Now the earl was on his sickbed. Could any man believe this to be mere coincidence?

'This threatening letter, my lady . . . do you know who it was from?'

The Countess of Derby's proud head did not fall, nor did her shoulders slump. 'An enemy, of course.'

'May I see the letter?'

'It has been destroyed. We have no idea who sent it. One of Hesketh's family, perhaps, or an enemy at court. Any number of people. Sometimes I think we are hated by the whole world, Mr Shakespeare, and I do not understand why. We are Christians and have led Christian lives, cultivating the arts and literature and learning. Never has Ferdinando strayed into politics or joined a grouping to seek power.'

What was it Sir Thomas Heneage had said to him in Cecil's chambers at Nonsuch Palace? *Lord Derby has few enough visitors these days*. He did not press the issue, but asked the question he most wished answered.

'Does the name Lamb mean anything to you?'

The countess hesitated, as the constable had done.

Shakespeare waited for her.

At last she smiled, as if suddenly remembering. 'Why, yes, I have met Mr Lamb. He came here at Christmas, with some of the townspeople, to celebrate the birth of our Lord. Such occasions are not uncommon. My husband sees it as his duty to provide such entertainments for the local gentry and merchants.'

'You were not at court last Christmas?'

'Are you sent to spy on us, Mr Shakespeare? You seem to have a great interest in affairs that cannot possibly concern you.'

He shook his head. 'No, I am not here to spy on you. But, yes, this does concern me, as I shall explain.'

'Very well. My husband considered it unfitting to go to court at Christmas, following the recent stir. He was not sure how welcome we would be.'

Shakespeare understood. 'What do you recall of Lamb?'

'I did not mark him much, but I do recall I was introduced to him and thought him a pleasant man. He had an easy manner. Why, what makes you ask about him?'

'He is dead, my lady, shot as a deserter by a provost marshal named Pinkney, who claims to be responsible only to the Lord Lieutenant. His lordship your husband is, of course, Lord Lieutenant of this county.'

The countess was clearly shocked. Her fair skin blanched to a deathly pallor. 'Father Lamb is dead?'

Shakespeare nodded, noting the title. He had not mentioned that the dead man was a priest. 'He died with a plea on his lips – a plea that I should save his lordship, though he did not specify what I should save him from.'

Her hand went to her slender throat. 'Mr Shakespeare, if you are trying to frighten me yet more, I confess you are succeeding . . .'

'Would I be correct in thinking that you knew Father Lamb rather better than you have acknowledged?'

'What are you trying to say?'

'It has long been rumoured that my lord of Derby is of the old faith.'

Suddenly her manner changed. 'I ask again – are you sent here to spy on my lord of Derby? Shame on you, Mr Shakespeare!'

He shook his head. 'That is not why I am here. However, I am worried that I may have walked into something of great moment and I would be neglecting my duty if I ignored it.'

'Tittle-tattle. Assume nothing, Mr Shakespeare,' she said, almost spitting the words. 'Assumptions are dangerous, as neighbour Hesketh discovered at the cost of his head.'

'I apologise if I offended you, my lady. In fact, I am here to see Dr Dee, whom I gather is your guest, that is all, and to request your assistance in protecting him. It is feared he may be in some peril, which I shall explain to you.'

The countess's face softened again. 'Forgive me, Mr Shakespeare, I quite understand your concern on our behalf. But I would beg you to understand that these are trying times for our family. We are crossed at court and crossed in this county. My lord has enemies – powerful enemies – who would happily see his head on the block. Our complaints go un-answered. Even my husband's rightful request to be honoured as Chamberlain of Chester is ignored. He is snubbed. In his place, they choose the upstart Egerton, who was once our attendant. I do sometimes think he would take on our whole life if it were in his power.' She sighed heavily. 'And yet that is not the worst of it, Mr Shakespeare. For that you must look to Richard Hesketh's own brother, the attorney Thomas Hesketh, who speaks so ill of us that I doubt we have a friend left in the county. And you must know that this Thomas Hesketh is so close-coupled with Sir Thomas Heneage that a blade of grass would not pass between them.'

Shakespeare frowned. What was she intimating? Never had he heard a bad word said of Heneage. Everyone liked him. And yet there seemed to be some ill-will here. Perhaps Heneage had not been the earl's preferred choice to succeed Walsingham as Chancellor of the Duchy of Lancaster. He would delve no further. For the present.

He bowed. 'I am sorry these days have been so hard for you.'

She waved her hand. 'I had not meant to concern you with our worries. Please, Mr Shakespeare, tell me exactly what it is you require from me in the matter of Dr Dee. I shall do my best to provide every assistance.'

'I would ask for your two stoutest guardsmen. Dr Dee needs a permanent escort. I am charged by Sir Robert to bring him to Kent as soon as arrangements can be made and your guardsmen will need to come away with us for protection.'

'Is he not safe here? I would hate to think that a guest of ours was in some danger.'

'He has knowledge that our enemies would dearly love to obtain. No disrespect is meant to you or his lordship, but it is felt by Sir Robert that he could be more easily protected elsewhere.'

'Well, then consider it arranged. You shall have your guards, for you must know that we would do anything to help Sir Robert Cecil.'

*Was there an edge of disrespect as she spoke of Cecil? An edge of fear, perhaps?*

'Thank you, my lady,' he said. 'And the other matter? Might I be permitted to see your husband? I will not tax him if he finds my presence troubling.'

'I will talk with his physicians. In the meantime, I will have Cole take you to Dr Dee in his quarters. And please tell Sir

Robert how eager we were to cooperate and assist in every way possible. I greatly desire to retain his love and trust, as does my husband.'

Janus Trayne lay back on the narrow bed. Walter Weld looked down at him with scorn, then cracked the side of his head with a riding crop.

Trayne recoiled from the blow, but knew better than to cry out.

'Anyone could have seen you come here, you dog's pizzle.'

'No one saw me, Mr Weld, I promise you.'

Weld hit him again. 'I should kill you here and now, Trayne. What use are you to me? You were hired to bring me the perspective glass. Instead you bring me a worthless right arm, blood-stained apparel and a tale of woe. Worse, you jeopardise everything by coming here. How do you know you weren't followed?'

'Please, Mr Weld, I got clean away. And I will find it. I will bring the instrument to you. I pledge it. I can find where it has been taken.'

Weld twitched his crop but did not hit Trayne again. Instead he flicked the leather tip at his wounded arm. 'How bad is it?'

'Bad enough. I need a little time for it to mend. Two days, three perhaps.'

'You can hold a pistol with your *left* hand, can't you?'

'Yes, I could do that.'

'Good. Then we shall do our work here in Lancashire, for the prize we seek has fallen into our path.'

# Chapter 7

A<small>T THE AGE</small> of sixty-seven, John Dee was still a man of impressive bearing. His hand emerged from the wide, open sleeve of his richly embroidered artist's gown and clasped Shakespeare's right hand in a firm grip.

'Mr Shakespeare, I am pleased to meet you.'

'And I am glad to find you well, Dr Dee.'

The room was large with two leaded windows looking out across the battlements to the park and furnished with a table and stool, and a wooden crate of books. On the table Dr Dee had quills, ink, a crystal stone and a volume in which he had been writing when Cole brought in Shakespeare.

As Cole departed, Shakespeare began to explain his presence to Dr Dee and of Cecil's fears for his safety.

Dee looked puzzled. 'I cannot imagine anyone would wish me harm. I am but a poor sciencer. More than poor – impoverished.'

'And a deviser of engines.' Shakespeare lowered his voice. 'In particular, the perspective glass.'

Dee smiled. Above his long beard, his eyes shone and creased into the handsome face of his distant youth. 'Ah, my spying glass. So that is what this is about. Do they wish me to make another? I would require a great deal of money.'

'No, but Sir Robert is concerned that the one you have made

is in peril. You must know that it is in the keeping of a man known as the Eye. There has been an attempt on his life.'

Dee's smile vanished. 'By God's heavenly angels, what happened, sir?'

Shakespeare told him of the events in Portsmouth.

'This has made Sir Robert most anxious about your own safety. He fears that our enemies might try to abduct you or your collaborator Mr Digges and somehow attempt to coerce the secret from you.'

'Mr Shakespeare, you do me a disservice! I would never reveal the secrets of this realm to a foreign power.'

'I am pleased to hear that, Dr Dee. But you can surely understand why Sir Robert is concerned to look out for your welfare.'

'Yes, Mr Shakespeare, I suppose I do. But how do you propose to protect me? Surely, I am safe here at Lathom House?'

'I am to take you to the home of Mr Digges at Chevening in Kent. There you will be assigned to the keeping of my associate Francis Mills and his men. In the meantime, until we are there, you will have two men with you at all times. They will sleep outside your chamber and accompany you wherever you go. I will be billeted here, with you, inside this room.'

'So we are not leaving immediately?' Dee seemed relieved.

'Soon. But until we go, be circumspect, Dr Dee. Do not put yourself in danger. Consult me before you consider going anywhere.'

'Mr Shakespeare, I am a busy man. I must go to Manchester for a day or two, to the collegiate church of St Mary, and there are other matters—'

'Other matters?'

'Well, there is the honour I owe to my lord of Derby. I cannot leave while he ails, for that would seem most ill-mannered. But be straight with me, Mr Shakespeare. I may look old and befuddled to you, but there is more to this, is there not? There is something you keep from me.'

'No,' Shakespeare lied. 'I am being straight with you. There is nothing more than your safety.'

He could not tell this venerable man that Cecil doubted him, feared even that he might *sell* his secrets to Spain. Shakespeare changed the subject.

'But there is this new matter of my lord, the Earl of Derby. His illness worries me greatly in the light of the Hesketh affair.'

Dee sighed. 'It is most unfortunate. I can well understand why you might imagine some link between his illness and the unfortunate events of last year.'

'Can you explain it? Did you consort with Hesketh in Prague?'

'No. I had left Bohemia before he arrived. But, of course, I heard tell of his attempt to recruit his lordship for treason against the Queen.'

'So you knew nothing of him?'

'No, not at that time. I knew him before, of course. We were friends for a time in the early eighties.'

'You shared an interest in alchemy. Yes, I have read the reports.'

'Indeed. But we lost touch after that.'

'But you knew those in Prague with whom he would have dealt during his exile?'

'Some of them, yes. Mr Edward Kelley, for one. And the Jesuit, Father Stephenson, for another.'

'Stephenson?'

'Thomas Stephenson, a good man. He was at the College of the Clementinum, a Jesuit college in Prague. He was sent there by either Cardinal Allen or Father Persons, I believe.'

'Were they behind the letter that Hesketh brought back to England for Derby?'

Dee shrugged his shoulders. 'It would not surprise me, but I had also heard it testifed that Hesketh was given the letter in London. Is that not so?'

'That is what he said. He insisted he was approached by a boy and given the sealed paper at the White Lion in Islington. But you are a man of wit, Dr Dee. Explain to me why he was at the White Lion and why someone just happened to be there with a letter for him to deliver unless it had all been pre-arranged.'

Dr Dee thought for a moment, but just as he opened his mouth to make reply, he was stopped short by a scream from elsewhere in the house. It was a cry of piercing volume and intensity that seemed to well up from the depths of the earth and ring through the ancient halls of Lathom House, an unholy howl of terror and pain and despair.

*Chapter 8*

THE EARL OF Derby's chamber was shrouded in a sickly
gloom. The shutters were closed to keep out the evening
light and just one beeswax candle was lit. It guttered and
almost blew out as Shakespeare shut the door. The air was stale.

He had never encountered such a weird and spectral scene.
The earl sat on the edge of a great, carved-oak bed. He was
wearing a white linen nightgown, streaked with stains, and
was leaning over a silver basin, vomiting.

A physician held the basin for him, but averted his head,
cupping his hand over his nose and mouth to shield himself
from the foul stench of the earl's eruption. Two other physicians stood further away, by a table, clearly scared, their eyes
shining in the dim light. In a dark corner of the room sat an
ample-bosomed woman who rocked back and forth, chanting
words that meant nothing to Shakespeare.

She was stirring the contents of a small earthenware pot,
which she held clamped between her knees.

'My lord of Derby . . .'

The young earl, no more than thirty-five years of age, looked
up from his basin and wiped his sleeve across his mouth. His
face was heavy and drained, his eyes mere slits.

'Mr Shakespeare,' he said quietly, taking shallow breaths. 'I
had heard you were here. It is a long time since last we met.'

'Indeed, my lord. I have come to fetch away your guest, Dr Dee.' He looked at the earl's gaunt face. 'God's faith, I am sorry to find you in such straits.'

'I am bewitched, Mr Shakespeare. I fear the worst. There is nothing these three frauds can do for me with their physic.'

One of the two physicians who had held back stepped forward. 'Sir, I beg you to allow me to bleed you. There are ill humours that must be released.'

The earl tried to laugh, but immediately retched, then vomited again into the basin and beyond. Shakespeare was appalled; the earl was bringing up fleshy, rusty-blood matter that stank worse than a house of easement in high summer.

Shakespeare turned to the physician who had just spoken. 'How long has he been like this?'

'No more than a day and a half. It came on suddenly, when he was hunting at Knowsley. He stayed one night there, then demanded to be brought here.'

'Have any of you three any notion what is the cause of this sickness?'

They looked at one another uneasily.

'I am afraid we are divided in our opinions, sir. I believe it to be a natural inflammation of the gut and have treated him with three clysters of calomel, but he will have no more.'

The second physician wrung his hands together so that his knuckles cracked. 'See the colour of his skin. He has a jaundice,' he said. 'I fear his liver is decayed from a surfeit of activity, food and wine. Yet he will not allow me to bleed him to release the corruption within.'

'And you?' Shakespeare said to the third.

'Poison.' He mouthed the word, perhaps hoping the earl might not hear it.

Shakespeare nodded. His own thought, too.

'It could be one of many, though I have ruled out nux

vomica,' the physician continued. 'The red hue of his puke and the staining of the silver basin make me think cinnabar. I desire to apply bezoar stone or a powder of unicorn horn, for they are certain antidotes to all venoms. Yet my lord turns them away.'

Shakespeare said nothing. He walked across to the woman in the corner. She had her eyes closed while she chanted her curious words. In appeareance, she was a common goodwife, with a grey woollen kirtle and smock that had seen better days. Her hair was bound in a threadbare coif.

'Who are you?' Shakespeare demanded.

The woman opened her bright green eyes and looked up at him in silence.

'Well? Speak, woman.'

'I am one that would save my lord from the forces of darkness.'

'What is in there?' He pointed at the pot she stirred.

'Herbs, master. A broth of herbs. Feverfew to soothe him, spleenwort to purge him and as remedy for henbane, belladonna, ratsbane and other foul poisons.'

'You are a witch.'

'No, sir, I abhor the craft. I deal with naught but country lore, sir. I am a poor woman. My lord of Derby wishes me here, so I am here. He has been bewitched and the spell must be broken.'

'What reason do you have for saying such a thing?'

'A giant crossed his lordship's path twice in the day he fell ill.'

'A giant?'

'Nine feet tall or more. A stranger. No man in these parts has seen him before or since. That is not all. While my lord was out hunting, a hag asked him about his water. Now his water has stopped.'

Shakespeare glanced at the physicians. One of them nodded

in confirmation. 'It is true. We have tried means to provoke his piss, but to no avail. It causes his lordship great pain and distress.'

'Who was this crone he met? Does anyone know her?'

'A woman of the woods out by Knowsley,' one of the physicians said. 'Men say she has a lair of twigs and rags, and consorts with crows.'

'Today a wax figure was found at the crossroads a mile from here with a hair through its belly,' the woman in the corner continued. 'His lordship has been enchanted.'

Shakespeare turned away from her. This was the talk of village women who listened to tales. Ferdinando, Lord Strange, fifth Earl of Derby, had been poisoned. But with what and by whom was not clear.

He walked to the bed and bowed.

'If it please your lordship, I shall come and talk with you some more when you are better able to converse.'

Derby said nothing. He began gasping for air, his mouth hanging open and limp over the silver bowl.

Shakespeare bowed again, briskly. Without another word, he strode from the room and went in search of the earl's steward.

Boltfoot Cooper could not relax. He sat on a three-legged stool next to the fire, drawing on a pipe of tobacco. He closed his eyes momentarily as if to make the hubbub disappear, but it did not help. He had come to this house on the orders of his master, John Shakespeare, who had determined there could be no safer place in England to keep Ivory and the instrument, but he could not find peace here.

His five-year-old niece, whose name he could not recall, had just hit his twenty-month son John with a clay bottle and knocked him to the ground. Little John was now wailing. Two other nieces were squabbling over the last of the strawberry conserve. Jane, his wife, was talking with her mother and seemed oblivious to the noise. Boltfoot doubted he would be able to stand more of this without going mad.

They were in the cottage of Jane's parents in a village on the Essex side of the border with Suffolk. It was a timber-frame building with a thatched roof, kept in good condition by her father, an honest worker who took to market his master's live-stock and other produce, and who, though not wealthy, was allowed enough land to provide well enough for his large family. This cottage had been Jane's childhood home. As the oldest of twelve, all girls, she was accustomed to the din and chaos of the place. Not so Boltfoot; he had been brought up alone down in Devon, by his father.

The house was pleasant, with a large room taking up most of the ground floor. It served as kitchen, eating room and general living space, leading into a small pantry at the back. Above them, by way of stepladders and trapdoors, were three plain bedchambers, one of which had been set aside for the guests – Jane, baby John, Boltfoot and the two Shakespeare girls, six-year-old Mary and her adopted sister Grace Woode, who was eleven. The other members of the Cawston family still at home clustered in the other two sleeping rooms.

They were, thought Boltfoot with a grim sigh as he exhaled a cloud of smoke, as tight packed as wadding in a cannon barrel. He could put up with cramped spaces. He had spent more years than he cared to remember at sea under Drake, where men were packed a hundred or more in a space that would have felt crowded for a dozen. But the worst of it, here in this Essex household, was the presence of William Ivory, the Eye. Boltfoot had offered him a palliasse in his family's room, but Ivory would not have it. He preferred to sleep outside, under a makeshift shelter, beneath the stars. Boltfoot recalled that, even at sea, Ivory had done his utmost to sleep and eat alone; like a cat, he would creep off to some place, out on deck, perhaps in the lee of a gunwale or behind the whipstaff. The only time he wanted company was when the playing cards and coins came out.

In all the years Boltfoot had known him, they had scarce passed more than half a dozen words, and nothing had changed these past few days. Boltfoot was more than happy with Ivory's silence, but that did little to ease his concerns. Two things worried him: the first was that Ivory might simply slip away again; the second was that Mr Shakespeare was wrong in his estimation that this place was safe. Boltfoot did not feel secure here, and if he was not safe, then neither was his family.

Jane was standing in front of him with a beaker of ale. He took it with a grunt of thanks.

'The young ones will be abed soon, husband.'

He mumbled to let her know he was listening.

She lowered her voice. 'Did you note Judith?'

He nodded. Aye, he had noted Judith and didn't know what to make of her. She was one of the older girls, about seventeen, and once or twice he had caught sight of her slipping outside. She was gone again now.

'Got a swain, has she, Jane? She's pretty, like you. Or is it the fresh air she likes?'

'She likes talking with your Mr Ivory, Boltfoot.'

He frowned, then laughed. 'Talk with the Eye? She might as well chat away to a tree for all the converse she'll have out of him.'

'I wouldn't be so certain about that. Why don't you take a look? Mother saw her creep into that lean-to he's built himself in the yard with some ale for him.'

'What interest would a girl like that have in a grizzled old fool like Ivory?'

Jane looked at him strangely. 'You could be talking about yourself and me, Boltfoot Cooper. I dare say there's those that thought us an odd couple when first we courted, including Master Shakespeare.'

Boltfoot was about to say something sharp, but then thought better of it. He had been surprised himself when Jane took an interest in him. Surprised and delighted. But surely Ivory was a different matter? Sour-faced, silent as the grave, never a thought for anyone but himself, only happy in a tavern wagering money or when he was on his own at the top of a ship's rigging.

'Well, if that's the case, if the daft girl has gone soft on him, I don't like it. All I want is to keep the miserable gullion alive. Don't want him messing with your family, Jane. Tell her she's to go to him no more. I'll speak to him.'

Boltfoot stood up, shoved his pipe into his jerkin pocket and strode towards the yard door. He'd have it out with the man.

'Keep him happy, keep him safe, whatever it takes, Boltfoot,' Master Shakespeare had said.

Boltfoot hovered, then sat down again. Damn Ivory's hide, he could not go to him. Boltfoot picked up his caliver and started cleaning its ornate octagonal muzzle for the second time that day.

He was certain he would need it soon enough.

Cole was in his office, working on the household accounts with the Clerk of the Kitchen and the wine-butler.

'Twenty hogsheads of beer, seven pounds seven shillings and sixpence, three roundlets of sack, each of fifteen gallons, six pounds and a crown . . .' He looked up. 'Ah, Mr Shakespeare.'

'I would talk with you alone, Mr Cole.'

'Most certainly.' He turned to his under-stewards. 'Please leave us, Mr Amlet, Mr Dowty. Oh, and, Mr Dowty, talk to the butcher about the mutton. I swear it died of old age. He will lose our custom soon enough if he does not provide young and fresh-killed flesh. And the three firkins of butter – tell the dairyman that with so few guests we should be *selling* butter, not buying it.'

The two stewards bowed and retreated from the small room.

Cole rose from his chair. 'Can I order you refreshment, Mr Shakespeare?'

'No. I am worried about your master. He will die without better care.'

'He has the best physicians in all of Lancashire and Cheshire, sir.'

'I want to send to London by post. I need your fastest messenger. He is to go to a Mr Joshua Peace, the Searcher of the Dead at St Paul's and a man with greater knowledge of the body than any physician, and bring him back straightway. I care not what he is working on, he must leave it without delay and come here. There is no time to lose. Do you understand?'

'Of course. I shall send Robert Hearnshaw. He knows the road well and can ride by the most slender of moons. He has made London in thirty-five hours.'

'Tell him to better that time. And I will need your second-best rider to take a note to Sir Robert Cecil. Give me a quill and parchment. I must write letters.'

Shakespeare sat at the table and dipped the quill in ink as Cole went to the door and ordered a servant to summon the riders and have the horses saddled. Shakespeare wrote fast.

'*Joshua, there is a matter of utmost urgency. I believe my lord of Derby has been poisoned. There is foul sickness, rust-red, voiding of the bowels, much pain and inability to piss. Yet he is lucid. There is no other I can trust in this and none here who can help. Come immediately with the messenger. Your friend, John Shakespeare.*'

He folded and sealed the paper and turned to the next note to Cecil, which was more circumspect.

'*His lordship, the Earl of Derby, is sick and in mortal peril. I have sent to Mr Peace for assistance and will, meanwhile, do all in my power to secure the best physicians here present. Dr Dee is in good health and close-guarded. Your true servant, John Shakespeare.*'

He also scratched out a copy of the letter he had found in Father Lamb's doublet, added a discreet note explaining its provenance, and sealed it into his own letter.

Hearnshaw arrived, already booted and hurriedly pulling on his leather riding jerkin and a waxed cape. Shakespeare handed him the sealed letter for Peace and gave him instructions on how to find him, then handed him two small gold coins.

'Now go with the speed of a falcon, Mr Hearnshaw, and return as swift. Your lord's life may well depend on it. There will be more gold if I see you soon enough.'

The rider bowed and left, at a run, just as the other messenger appeared and took the second letter, addressed to Cecil.

Shakespeare breathed deeply. He realised he still had not slept. Outside the window, darkness had fallen. There were still matters to be settled.

'The countess promised me guards for Dr Dee.'

'They are already with him, awaiting your further instructions.'

'Would you trust them with your life?'

'I would, sir.'

'Good. Now tell me, Mr Cole, what has been happening here at Lathom House? Who is that woman in the earl's bedchamber?'

'She is Mistress Knott, a wise woman from the village. His lordship has consulted her before. He demanded her presence as soon as the sickness came on. I believe there is no harm in her.'

'Consulted her before, you say?'

'He has asked her for propitious days – for travelling, for his daughters' christenings, for the beginning of building works on his houses—'

'This is monstrous, Mr Cole. He dabbles in the occult!'

Cole looked stiff and uneasy. 'She insists she is no witch, Mr Shakespeare, but a Christian lady, battling the dark arts.'

'Well, she talks like a witch – tales of giants and wax dolls and crones in the forest. I want her out of that room.'

Cole sighed deeply. 'We all do, master, particularly the physicians, for they feel hampered and crossed in their efforts while she is there. Her ladyship, the countess, is most distressed by the woman's presence. But the earl will not listen. He is convinced he has been beguiled and considers her his only hope.'

'But you believe him poisoned.'

'I fear it is a grave possibility.'

Shakespeare saw the tension within the steward. Tension and something else – despair, perhaps. He was close to the edge. Shakespeare turned away. He had many questions to ask, but first he needed sleep.

Walter Weld had hoped it would not come to this. Trayne should have secured the perspective glass in Portsmouth; he had failed, but there was still the matter of Dr Dee. The earl had been conveniently biddable when Weld had suggested inviting the old alchemist to Lathom House. And so here he was, and he was vulnerable.

Weld paced his room close to the stables, alone. Trayne was in a house in a village three miles away. The widow who tended his wound had no idea who he was, only that he was a Catholic gentleman in need of assistance. She would ask no questions, and she would tell no one that he was there. And soon, pray God, he would be well.

In truth, Trayne's recovery could not come quickly enough. He could not abduct Dee alone. The holy fool Lamb was dead, so there was no help to be had there. Not that Lamb had ever been of much use: too interested in saving souls to care much for the hard business of insurrection. Lamb would never have countenanced an act such as the abduction of Dr Dee.

There was urgency now, for the earl was fading fast and the great house was in disarray. The moment might very soon be lost. There was more: he had heard from the grooms that a new guest had arrived, one John Shakespeare. It was a name he knew. Shakespeare was an intelligencer close to Cecil, right at the centre of power.

Weld smiled to himself as he pulled on his boots. It was time to take a look at this new arrival.

## *Chapter 9*

OXX AND GODWIT presented the most comforting tableau Shakespeare had seen all day. Heavily armed, strong and immovable, they stood outside Dee's door to ensure none could pass. They eyed Shakespeare with suspicion.

'I am John Shakespeare. I will sleep within.'

Oxx, the bigger of the two men, shook his close-shaven, thick-bearded head. His name suited him well, for his shoulders had the breadth and power of an ox-yoke. 'Not until we know for sure that you are who you say you are.'

At that moment, Cole appeared at the top of the staircase. 'All is well, Oxx, this is indeed Mr Shakespeare. He is to be admitted.'

'I am the *only* person to be admitted. At any time. Unless you have my permission, Mr Oxx,' Shakespeare said. 'Do you both understand? No one. No exceptions. Not even Mr Cole here.'

Oxx hesitated, looked at Godwit, then at their master, Cole.

'Do exactly as Mr Shakespeare orders, Oxx,' Cole said, though he sounded a little put out. 'He is here on Queen's business.'

'Thank you, Mr Cole. Should there be developments before dawn in the matter of his lordship's sickness, wake me.'

Below them, in the hall, Shakespeare saw two figures walk

towards the doors. A man and a woman. He recognised instantly the strange, beautiful woman from the coach. The man with her was slender and handsome, with light brown hair and elegant clothes. Her hand touched his arm. He turned and looked up. His eye caught Shakespeare's before he looked away and pushed his way through the door with the woman in his wake.

'What man was that, Mr Cole?'

'Walter Weld, sir. He is master of the horse to his lordship.'

'And the woman with him, what are they to each other?'

'Her name is Lady Eliska. To my knowledge there is no connection between them.'

'Is Mr Weld new here?'

'A few months – since last autumn time.'

'I would speak to him tomorrow. And I would speak to the lady. I wish to interview anyone newly arrived here.'

'Weld has apartments beside the stable block. You will find him there unless he is riding. Lady Eliska has rooms in the house. She is a stranger to this country and a guest of the earl and countess. Most of the retainers have been with the family for many years, though Mr Dowty in the kitchens is quite recent.'

Dr Dee was awake, his tall frame hunched at the table, studying by candlelight. He seemed to be looking at some chart or map. He smiled at Shakespeare diffidently.

'It seems you have me protected like the royal jewels. I know not whether to be honoured or afraid.'

Shakespeare nodded, but he was too fatigued for conversation. A fine mattress and bedding had been brought for him. He unfurled the mattress across the doorway, laid himself down and fell straight into a deep sleep.

*

Shakespeare awoke before dawn. From a few feet away, slumbering in the great four-poster bed, he heard the intermittent sleep-sounds of Dr Dee: a deep, pig-like grunt of a breath followed by a minute's silence, then another rasp. Each breath sounded like a death rattle.

Half dressing in breeches and shirt, he lifted the iron latch of the door, carefully so as not to wake Dee. Outside the room, a low-burnt candle cast light on the two guards. Oxx was asleep on the floor but stirred instantly at the opening of the door. Godwit was awake and his eyes were sharp. Good. That was how Shakespeare wanted it: one must always be alert while the other drowsed.

He nodded to the guards and walked down the dim stairway on soundless, bare feet. The first light of day etched the great hall of Lathom House in a grey tinge. From outside he heard the clatter of iron-rimmed wheels on cobblestones.

Pushing open the main entrance door, he was straightway confronted by a halberdier in a dazzling corslet of steel.

'Up early, master?'

'I am looking for the kitchens or bakehouse for meat and bread to break my fast.'

The halberdier held out his arm westwards, along the inside of the battlements. 'Past all these wains. Third door along, master. They're all in there working now. You'll have bread crusty and hot.'

'I arrived last evening. Where do guests normally eat, pray?'

'There's a second, smaller hall off the great hall. In ordinary times, all would meet there at eight o'clock, but this past day, with his lordship's illness, the ladies and gentlemen come and go at will.'

Shakespeare walked in the direction of the kitchens. The cobbled pathway was banked up with wagons and drays, their drivers waiting patiently to edge forward so that they might unload produce or collect empty barrels. Three men were shouldering kegs into a wide, double-doored entrance. He glanced in. It was a long, dark storehouse with a hundred or more casks of various sizes disappearing into the depths. Game hung from hooks. Further along, a second, smaller door opened on to a large scullery. Six drabs were at work polishing silver plate and copper pots.

Then came the kitchens, which were immense, the greatest Shakespeare had seen outside Windsor Castle. A central room was lit by three blazing fires in hearths that were each of sufficient size to roast a whole ox. This lime-slaked room gave out on to six more galleries. One, Shakespeare could see, was a store for flesh, another was a bakery, yet another the pastry house. Men and women, perhaps forty of them, came and went, sweating with the heat and energy of the place, working at stone benches and wooden blocks, carrying food and carcasses or tending the fires. None paid Shakespeare heed.

He stayed a man in a full-length apron, hoisting a basket of loaves on his shoulder.

'I wish to speak with Mr Dowty, the Clerk of the Kitchen,' he said.

'Are you delivering? He won't see you unless you have an appointment.'

'Just tell me where to find him. He *will* see me.'

The baker laughed. 'Well, you'll find him through there, shouting. Can't you hear him?'

Dowty was in the wet larder, using a three-pound pike to beat the head of a boy aged about ten.

'Call that scaling?' he berated the boy. 'You'll be drowned in the pond where the fish came from if you leave scales like that again.' Another smack on the head, then he spotted Shakespeare and his mood changed. 'Good morning, master.'

'Good day, Mr Dowty.'

Dowty pushed out his chest, then looked him up and down as if appraising a side of pig. His eyes came to rest on Shakespeare's bare feet.

'How may I help you, sir? Fresh manchet bread, some eggs, a pair of shoes? If you return to the hall, I'll have you served.'

'My name is John Shakespeare and I am on Queen's business. Mr Cole will have told you to expect me.' Shakespeare had noted the insolence in the man's tone and was having none of it.

'Indeed, but I have work to do. We have a large house and estate to feed with a company of players added on. And I am responsible for it.'

'There are questions I will have answered unless you wish to be taken into custody, held in shackles and arraigned before the Ormskirk justice.'

Dowty was a short man, but bulky and strong. He had little hair and his chins tumbled down over his collar. 'Ask your question, then, and be quick about it.'

'I shall take all the time I like, Mr Dowty. Firstly, what did the earl eat in the hours before he fell ill?'

Dowty slapped the pike into his hand. The boy he had been hitting shrank back nervously and took the opportunity to scuttle from the room.

'Do you think I poisoned him? Is that what you are suggesting? Well, if you must know, his food that day was none of our doing here at Lathom. He was at Knowsley. You'll have to go there.'

'And where were you while he was there?'

Dowty said nothing, merely glared at Shakespeare as though he would gut him and scale him like the fish.

'Who is his taster?'

'I am his taster.'

'You run his kitchens *and* taste his food?'

'Why should I not? If anyone wishes to poison my lord of Derby, they'll have to kill me first. And what cook would poison his master if, in doing so, he had to poison himself?'

'So who tasted his food when he hunted at Knowsley?'

'I did. I went with him.'

'Do I have to draw every piece of information out of you? Why are you not cooperating? Do you not wish your lord and master to recover?'

'Of course I want him to recover. But do you think I did not see this coming – the suspicion, the inquisition? I knew you'd be straight round here and I do not like it. Is there a more offensive slur than to come into a man's kitchen and accuse him of poisoning those he feeds? Oh, I'll answer your questions, but I also wish a plague of hornets on you—'

'How long has the earl used your services as a taster?'

'He never bothered until last September. The Hesketh matter changed everything around here. Since then he has not tasted so much as a mouthful of cheese without me trying it first.'

'So you were with him at the Knowsley chase. I ask again, what did he eat in the hours before his sickness?'

Dowty put the fish down on a slab, then held up his left thumb.

'One, he broke his fast with cold beef, cold pigeon pie, a half-pint of beer – small beer – Lancashire cheese, manchet bread, scrambled duck egg. Two . . .' He held up his index finger. 'He had a hearty stirrup cup of aqua celestis and two small saffron cakes. Three . . .' He thrust up the middle finger. 'We had a midday repast of roast venison and roast capon, with a beaker of songbird broth. And he had another hearty cup of brandy and a quart of beer. I love my master, Mr Shakespeare, but I would be lying to you if I denied he was a voluptuary. Enjoys his wine and food, the earl. And I sampled it all. If any of it was poisoned or bad, then I should be vomiting my guts up, too.'

'What, then, has caused this?'

'You're not from these parts or you wouldn't need to ask that. The Jesuits got him, that's what has happened. They're having their vengeance for the death of the traitor Hesketh. Beguiled him with their rites and magic.'

Shakespeare's brow creased. 'Are you suggesting Jesuit priests used witchcraft against him?' He snorted at the absurdity of the suggestion. 'They are more likely to *burn* witches than use their Satanic arts, Mr Dowty.'

Dowty sniffed. 'As I said, you're not from these parts. I'd inquire after one Lamb, if I were you, and then you can stop wasting my time and yours around these kitchens.'

'Tell me about Lamb.'

'He's a dirty Jesuit. Been sniffing around Lathom and Ormskirk for months, like a fox around a chicken coop. He's the one wants the earl dead – revenge for turning in their snivelling messenger boy Hesketh. They swore the earl would die in pain if Hesketh was taken to the scaffold, and now you see it happening. If it's not witchcraft, you tell me what it is. Because it's nothing he ate, I'll promise you that.'

Shakespeare did not mention that Lamb was dead.

'What of Mistress Knott?' he said.

'What of her?'

'Do you know her?'

'I know *of* her. His lordship has visited her on occasion. She lives in Lathom village. I reckon her harmless enough. Makes charts, I'm told. And if that makes her a witch, then so is Dr Dee, for does he not study the stars and make charts, too?'

'She mentioned strange things happening. A giant of a man, a crone, a wax effigy. Did you see any of those things?'

Dowty laughed. 'There was a large farmer, fair bit taller than you. Maybe even six and a half feet tall. Does that qualify as a giant? He had ideas about stopping the hunt riding over his new-sown field, which caused much merriment. But I know nothing of any crone, nor no wax effigy.'

Suddenly there was a clanging. A man in an apron was walking through the kitchens, swinging his bell like a night watchman.

'That means we have to get food on the tables, Mr Shakespeare. A hundred or more hungry souls to be fed this morning.'

Shakespeare met his eyes and tried to read them. Why was this man being so obstructive? Did he have something to hide?

'We will speak again in due course,' he said. 'I wish to know more about you, Mr Dowty.'

The dining hall was empty of guests. Half a dozen bluecoats stood at their stations, shoulders held stiffly back. Shakespeare sat down in the middle of the long oak table that took up most of the length of the hall, and proceeded to eat his fill of bread, eggs, bacon and cheese.

Feeling a good deal better, he did not linger but went back to his bedchamber to complete his morning wash and to dress himself properly. He was surprised and worried to discover that Oxx and Godwit were not at their posts outside the room.

Pushing open the door, he found, too, that Dr Dee was gone. On the table was a note, written in a fluid hand.

'*Mr Shakespeare, fear not. I have not been abducted, but have gone questing in woodland two miles north-west of Lathom House, accompanied by Mr Oxx, Mr Godwit and diggers. I will return before five of the clock.*'

It was signed Δ – the delta of the Greek alphabet, Dr Dee's signature. Shakespeare was alarmed. He knew of Dee's lifelong pursuit of buried treasure, but how was he to be protected –

even by men as sound as Oxx and Godwit appeared to be – in the middle of a country wood?

Cursing Dee for a fool, he washed, dressed and hurried out.

At the foot of the stairs, in the great hall, Shakespeare was astonished to see the Earl of Derby up from his sickbed and fully dressed. He was walking slowly, on the arm of his wife, the Countess Alice. She wore a simple day dress of cream and pearl. It was the earl's attire that caught the eye – a beautiful cerise doublet with sleeves slashed to reveal the family's eagle-and-child crest, intricately woven in thread of gold. Behind them walked three magnificent greyhounds.

Shakespeare bowed. 'My lord, I am delighted to see you up from your sickbed.'

He was not so delighted by the earl's appearance. His face was sallow, his dark, wavy hair now lank and slicked down. He had always had a squint, his eyes seeming to watch two places at once, but there was usually a keenness and life to them; now they lacked lustre and wit. His beard, once neat-trimmed, was like a dark-red hedge.

'I am weak as a new-born babe, Mr Shakespeare. I am wasted almost to nothing.'

'Your sickness, sir . . .'

'It eased in the night, thank the Lord. I have had no convulsions or vomiting for some hours and, what is more, I slept. Even better is that I have pissed. A whole river of piss, that carried away my pain. I think the curse is lifted.'

'The whole house has prayed, Mr Shakespeare,' the countess said. 'It is the power of prayer that has saved my lord.'

'What do your physicians say?'

'Those fools? They say I am cured. It is the first true thing they have said this week. Mistress Knott will not have it, however.'

The countess patted his arm. 'I do not know why you ever

listen to that mad woman, Ferdinando.' She smiled. 'Come, it is a fine morning. Come and sit in the sun and see if you can sip some cordial.'

Shakespeare bowed again. 'I would speak to you, if I may, when you are fully recovered, my lord.'

'As you will, Mr Shakespeare. I believe there is some alarm concerning the good Dr Dee?'

'Indeed.'

'Then we will speak anon. Allow me a few hours to get back my strength. I trust you will stay with us long enough to view your brother's new trifle? We have delayed too long and it shall be performed tonight.'

His wife shook her head, almost imperceptibly. 'I think we should leave it a day or two, Ferdinando – you will be too fatigued.'

The earl tried to laugh, but it caught in his throat. 'Do not listen to her, Mr Shakespeare,' he croaked. 'I believe my wife thinks me made of glass.' He patted one of the greyhounds and stroked its sleek head.

Shakespeare watched them walk away. It occurred to him that there were many who would happily break that glass. His instinct was to take Dee now and ride with him to Kent, but his reason told him he must stay a little longer. The last, dying warning of Father Lamb seemed to toll like a funeral knell for Derby.

# Chapter 10

T HE EARL'S YOUNGER brother, William Stanley, came out of Cole's office as Shakespeare was about to bang at the door to gain admittance. Shakespeare bowed to him, but he simply nodded curtly and hurried on.

As he walked away, William Stanley cut a commanding figure. Unlike his older brother, he was a man of bearing with gracious parts, tall and slender with short-cropped dark hair and a hot aspect that would serve well on the field of battle. Shakespeare wondered why he had not acknowledged him. They knew each other well enough. Stanley had travelled extensively in Italy, France and Spain during the mid-eighties and had brought much valuable information to Sir Francis Walsingham's attention. Well, Shakespeare would need to speak to him in due course. Cecil had suggested there was bad blood between the brothers.

Shakespeare watched him a moment, then turned away and entered Cole's office.

'I would like to resume our conversation, Mr Cole. And I will need the assistance of yet another of your men.'

If Cole was put out by being barged in on, he was too much the lawyer to show it. 'As you wish, Mr Shakespeare.'

'The earl has made something of a recovery, it seems.'

'The household is overjoyed. I do not mind telling you, sir, that we had feared for his very life.'

'And I see his brother is here.'

'He came from the Island of Man at Easter.'

'I had not known the brothers to be on speaking terms.'

'It is not my place to comment on such matters, Mr Shakespeare,' Cole said, a little stiffly. 'But I can tell you in honesty that I have detected no ill-will these past days.'

Shakespeare said nothing, but looked around. There were shelves of ledgers and correspondence; the whole workings of this complex and costly household were contained within this small room.

'What did Stanley want with you just now?'

'He asked me to arrange his baggage and retinue. He wishes to leave imminently. He is returning to Man.' Cole smiled, regaining his composure. 'Was there anything in particular that you wished to talk of, Mr Shakespeare?'

'Yes. In the first instance, I want one of your servants or riders to take me to where Dr Dee is engaged on his dig. While I am there, I would like you to draw up a list of all who work here and all your guests, both recently departed from the house and those still here. I would know who else is closeted in this great house – and why.'

'Naturally, I would require the earl's permission to disclose such information.'

'I am sure that the earl would do nothing to hamper the inquiries of an officer of Sir Robert Cecil.'

Cole inclined his head. 'Indeed, sir, I am sure he would not. I will make all haste with your requirements.'

'What guests are here apart from Dee and myself?'

'Well, there is Sir William, whom you have just seen. And Lady Eliska from the Bohemian lands, whom I have already mentioned. That is all. It is strangely quiet, sir.'

'Where is this lady?'

'She is out on some private business today. I believe she will return in the evening.'

'I would hear what you know of Mr Dowty.'

'Michael Dowty? He is our Clerk of the Kitchen.'

'He says he is the earl's taster.'

'That is true.'

'How long has he been at Lathom?'

'He arrived a little over a year ago.'

'That does not seem a great length of service for a man given a position of such trust.'

'He came with the most impeccable letters of reference, Mr Shakespeare – from the household of Sir Thomas Heneage, Chancellor of the Duchy of Lancaster. There can be none better, I think.'

Ah, Heneage again. It seemed he took his duties as Chancellor of the Duchy of Lancaster most seriously. Shakespeare smiled wryly to himself. If Sir Thomas Heneage trusted Dowty, why should any man not?

The muzzle of a petronel appeared from a thicket. It was thrust into the stomach of Shakespeare's escort and would have blown him away had the trigger been pulled. Oxx, who held the heavy pistol, emerged from the bush, his face uncompromising. He turned to Shakespeare, nodded in recognition and removed the weapon from the man's belly.

They had ridden out immediately after leaving Cole's office. Now Shakespeare nodded to Oxx.

'I presume we are close to Dr Dee's dig?'

The guard signalled with his head. 'A little further, beyond the spinney. There are three men with him. We searched them thoroughly, though we know them.'

Behind the clump of woodland, at the edge of a low-lying

meadow, Shakespeare found Dr Dee and his three assistants beside a mound of new-dug peat and a deep hole in the ground. There was no sign of Godwit. Shakespeare assumed he was as well concealed as Oxx had been; that, at least, was something.

Dr Dee was sitting on a three-legged stool, wearing his long gown and an exotic, embroidered gold and red cap with a gold-thread tassel. Two of his assistants, working men with their shirt-sleeves rolled to the tops of their weathered and muscled arms, were up to their chests in the hole. The third was standing a little further off, drinking from a beaker of ale and idly flicking a thin, catapult-shaped stick. He looked a different cut from the diggers, for he wore a buttercup silk doublet, its ties unfastened, and green hose.

Shakespeare took in the scene and dismounted. He dismissed his escort and turned to the man he was commissioned to protect.

'Dr Dee—' he began sharply.

'Mr Shakespeare. I trust you found my missive.'

'I did, and I was mighty displeased.'

'Oh, Mr Shakespeare, I am quite safe in the hands of Mr Oxx and Mr Godwit.'

'I have no reason to doubt them, but you must discuss your plans with me *before* you venture outside the house. Or even your chamber.'

Dee stood up from the stool. His long sleeves fell below his hands so that they were not visible unless he flicked back the cuffs.

'Mr Shakespeare, I have travelled to the farthest reaches of the world – through the Allemain lands to Bohemia and to Poland, along mountain tracks plagued by bandits and wolves. Do you think me less safe here in England's green bosom?'

Shakespeare was irritated. 'It is not so much *your* safety, Dr Dee, that concerns me as the safety of your knowledge. If an assassin's ball strikes you dead, then your secret remains secure. But all the while you live, I must protect the knowledge inside your head, whether you like it or not. Do not cross me in this, or I will restrict you further – and I will have the backing of Cecil and the Council.'

Dee, unperturbed, continued to press his case. 'But am I safer inside Lathom House than here in the open air? Is his lordship, the Earl of Derby, safer in the confines of his home?'

'You have said enough, Dr Dee. You know my feelings on this – and you will obey me. Who are these men with you?'

Dee smiled. 'My diggers are honest, hard-toiling peasants as you can surely tell from their callused hands and their skill with pick and shovel.' He swept his arm in the direction of the third man. 'My friend over there is Mr Ickman, my scryer.'

*Ickman.* Shakespeare felt a stab of alarm. The Ickman family had proved useful to Walsingham in the old days before the Armada fright, but Mr Secretary had never really trusted them. Was this man of that clan?

Shakespeare called over to him.

'Mr Ickman?'

The man approached and bowed with excessive display. 'Mr Shakespeare . . . Bartholomew Ickman at your service, sir.'

Shakespeare studied him more closely. Above the costly yellow doublet, he had a face of smooth, burnished skin, so unblemished that it might have been a maiden's, or an adder's. It was if he had never grown a beard, nor even shaved. His voice was soft and strangely ethereal.

'Do I know you, Mr Ickman?'

'I think not, but I certainly know of *you*, Mr Shakespeare, for I performed certain duties in the service of Mr Secretary, your chief man that was. You may know my uncle Richard, or brothers William and Ambrose.'

Shakespeare held his gaze steady. He certainly knew Richard Ickman, and a more villainous creature he had seldom met. He was a broad, rough bully of a man, who had made a great deal of money from his crooked dealings. He looked nothing like this sylph-like fellow.

'What are you doing here?'

'Assisting my good friend and patron, Dr Dee, as always.'

Shakespeare gave him a severe look. 'That is no answer. Why are you here at Lathom in Lancashire? And you, Dr Dee, why did you not mention his presence to me?'

'Bartholomew is my medium, my pathway to the great world of spirits beyond. Few have such a gift. I had once thought Mr Kelley – but that is another story. We are here, together, to find a hoard of Roman gold, of which we have sure information. This chart, on ancient parchment . . .'

Dee opened a wooden box that lay on the ground at his feet and produced the map that Shakespeare recognised as the one he had seen on the doctor's table the previous evening.

'. . . it is very fragile because of its great age, but it tells of a Roman governor of Deva Victrix – the city we now know as Chester. He had a country villa where Lathom House is now situated. The parchment implies that he buried the gold coin for safe keeping at a time of great unrest towards the end of the fourth century, intending to return for it one day. There is no reason to believe he ever had the opportunity to come back, so it should still be here.'

'And what is your role in this, Mr Ickman?'

Ickman held out the Y-shaped stick, one twig in each palm. 'This is my *virgula divina*, Mr Shakespeare. It may seem as naught but a stick to you, but to those with the power of divination, it is the guide to untold riches.' He turned his hands to lay open his soft palms. 'It is all in the sensitive touch of the hands. In this, I am merely the good doctor's tool in his quest for electric bodies. Are you sensitive, Mr Shakespeare? Would you care to hold my stick and see what you find?'

Shakespeare glared at him. 'Be careful, Mr Ickman. I am not a man to be toyed with.' He glanced again at Dee. 'You have not answered the second part of my question. Why did you not tell me of this man's presence here? How can I protect you if you keep secrets?'

'I had not thought it relevant. Mr Ickman is an old friend—'

'Is he roomed at Lathom House?'

'No.' Ickman spoke for himself. 'I have lodgings in Ormskirk.'

Shakespeare strode over to the new-dug hole and looked in at the diggers, thick with peaty earth and sweat. 'How much gold have you found thus far, Dr Dee?'

Ickman arrived at his shoulder. 'None as yet,' he said, twiddling his divining rod too close to Shakespeare's face. 'But given time, we will. I am certain we will.'

Shakespeare gripped the man's slender wrist.

'Be careful not to answer for others, Mr Ickman, lest I take you for someone other than you are. You may find I treat you with less gentleness than you believe you deserve.'

Shakespeare found his brother at the base of an oak tree, eyes closed as if asleep. Will was wearing a fantastical green costume with fringes of many colours and gossamer decorations, like a sprite. At his side lay a cheap crown of gilded tin.

'Will?'

'Brother . . .' Will opened his eyes.

'Did I wake you?'

'A daydream. This place is full of strange magic. I feed off such dreams.'

'Strange indeed. Stranger yet is the sickness, then sudden recovery, of my lord Strange, the Earl of Derby.'

'Yes. And now he is insisting we proceed with our performance this evening. Half of me fears he will die during the first act, yet the other half is greatly relieved. I do not wish to stay in these parts a moment longer than necessary for the discharge of my duties to the good earl.'

'You call him the *good* earl, Will? I confess I have always liked him well enough, but there are those who speak of him as having so haughty a stomach, and so great a will, that he believes himself fit for a crown. They say, too, that his arrogance will one day be his overthrow. When I saw him last night, I rather thought that day had come.'

'I will not listen to such talk. He has been a fine patron of players over the years. He gave me this life, you know. His troupe accepted me when no one knew my name. He is there for us still, even at this troubled time.'

Shakespeare prodded his brother with a foot and laughed. 'Never mind Derby's ambitions. You look as if *you* would be king.'

Will rose to his feet and bowed. 'Oberon, king of the faeries,' he announced with a flourish, then paused before sighing wearily. 'And my lady, the Countess Alice, will be my queen, proud Titania. What would the Master of the Revels say about a lady playing on stage?'

'Mr Tilney is not here, so fear not.'

'But usurping the role of a queen, a faerie queen? How would that news fare at court?'

'Not well, so say nothing.'

'Come, let us find cider, John. I have a thirst.'

Shakespeare followed his brother into a tent where a boy served them a powerful draught of apple cider from a flagon. They went outside once more and settled by a tree with a fine view of the magnificent old palace. It seemed a good time to talk.

'John, you are in a dark humour. You still grieve deeply.'

He shook his head. 'It is not just that. I have many worries. No, more than that – *fears*. Fears that I find hard to share.'

'This place would make anyone feverish.'

'I have as great a desire as you to be away from this place. I must take Dr Dee to Kent. But that is not my only concern. I also fear what lies behind this illness of the earl. And I worry about my boy, Andrew.'

'I will not ask why you must remove Dr Dee, and I can understand your concerns about Derby. As for Andrew, yes, I can see how he might give you sleepless nights. A lad of strong will.'

'He is thirteen, but he has the passions of a man. He has lost everyone he loved – his mother, his father and now Catherine, whom he loved as his own. He rages against their deaths and blames the English Church and this government for all that has happened. He sees me working for Cecil against the interests of Rome.'

'But now he is at Oxford. I am sure a change of place will help him. He will meet new people, immerse himself in a new world.'

If only that were the case. Shakespeare sighed.

'Am I not right, brother?' Will persisted.

'I pray it is so. But I worry that the opposite will happen. He would have no college but St John's. I had to engage the assistance of Cecil himself to persuade the Merchant Taylors to give him a place. I had to do something – Andrew was going as mad as a caged lion. We were all deep in mourning for Catherine, yet Andrew's dark presence left no room for light. Our house at Dowgate was a dungeon of despair.'

Will smiled. 'You have been through a great deal.'

'And so I arranged for him to go to St John's, even though I understood the perilous reason why it had to be that college. It was the *alma mater* of the Jesuit martyr Campion, you see. Andrew had heard tales of him from Catherine's lips and discovered some ill-founded inspiration there.'

'You think he wishes to emulate him and seek martyrdom?' Shakespeare nodded. It was exactly what he feared.

The brothers were silent for a while. There was nothing to be said. Both knew the dangers. As children they had seen the passion of the old faith in their own home. It was a passion that did not easily die nor succumb to threats. They drank their cider and refilled their cups. At last, Will touched John's shoulder.

'Walk with me a little way further, John. I would rather speak in low voices. Trouble dogs you, and I do not wish to be bitten.'

They strolled into the woodland. John, six years older and a little taller than his brother, was more soberly dressed in his felt cap, black and brown striped woollen doublet and black hose.

'Well?'

'They say he is bewitched, you know. All say it. The players, the ploughmen in the alehouses, the goodwives at their looms, the drovers with their cattle. All say the earl is bewitched.'

'He believes it himself. I think poison a more likely cause of his ills.'

'Indeed, but you should know what people say.'

'Thank you, Will. So who has bewitched him – and why?'

Will stopped. He looked about him, then his voice sank to a whisper. 'Some say the Pope, others say Dr Dee.'

'Dee!'

'They fear him. Children run screaming from his presence. The men call him conjuror and necromancer. He wanders about in a cloud, looking for gold, unaware of men's distaste for him and his ways. They do not trust him. Many would burn him as a witch.'

Shakespeare could not help laughing. Dee a witch! Had England not rid itself of such superstition along with relics and incense? Laughable as it was, however, that did not mean there was no threat.

'Thank you, Will. You have strengthened my resolve. I will remove Dr Dee from Lancashire as soon as I may.'

# *Chapter 11*

'I CANNOT STAY here, Jane,' Boltfoot said. 'I will go mad.'

'You know you must stay here, to protect Mr Ivory. Where else would you go?'

'I know not, but I must take him away. I do not like being indoors while he remains out. And I am concerned about Judith and her foolish attachment to him.'

'That is just a miserly excuse, Mr Cooper, and you know it. She is a pretty young woman and he is a man. It is the way of the world, no more.'

'It's not healthy, Jane, and I won't have it. The man's a dog. Never did I meet a seafaring man with such sly ways.'

They were in their cramped little chamber, in the early evening. Baby John slept in his crib. From below, the sounds of the family reverberated through the old walls. This feeling of Boltfoot's had been building all day.

Jane stroked her husband's face. 'I'll see what I can do, Boltfoot. There's a farmer in the next village who used to be friendly. Maybe he'll let you and Mr Ivory stay in his barn.'

Boltfoot rubbed his arm across his brow. It was hot in here and he was sweating. His throat and bones ached. He needed fresh air.

What he could not tell Jane was that he was eaten away by terror. He was not a man who felt fear for himself, but the safety of his wife, son and their other charges was another matter. And fear was gnawing at his heart like a deadly black canker. They weren't safe here. Ivory wasn't safe. The whole Cawston family was not safe. He had seen nothing suspicious, but this instinct of the gut had saved him on more than one occasion when faced with enemy shot or arrows in the Pacific isles. He had to go. Tonight preferably, tomorrow at the latest.

Walter Weld sat motionless astride his bay mare. He watched from the distance of a furlong as John Shakespeare strode across the outer courtyard towards the stable block. Weld's hand went to the pistol in his belt, but he did not draw it.

The presence of Shakespeare made things less simple. Two strong-armed men now guarded Dee. They would have to be blown away with pistol shot. It would be messy, and the abduction would be met by a hue and cry. Well, so be it. There were ways to get Dee away, get him to a place near by where he could be interrogated and his secrets drawn from him. The cause of Spain and God had friends enough in this county.

Weld took a last look at Cecil's man, then wheeled the mare's head and kicked on. This was no place to be today.

Unable to find Walter Weld, Shakespeare talked with men around the stables.

'Aye, he's the Gentleman of the Horse,' said the head groom, a man with a tongue as loose in his mouth as his belt was tight about his girth. 'Gone riding, most like.' His voice lowered. 'But I can tell you, master, that we have heard rumours bruited about. Folks say Mr Weld is a most devotional Catholic gentleman.'

'That does not seem to be a rarity in these parts.'

'No, but it is the manner of his devotions that has made men talk. Some say he is Christ's fellow, a boy-priest.'

Shakespeare understood the insinuation. 'Is there anyone in particular, any man, to whom he is close?'

The groom shook his head. 'I do not know, master.'

'Think carefully.'

'No, sir, no names come to mind.'

'What sort of man is Mr Weld?'

'Good with horses. Can pacify a nervy one. Gentle hands. A lean, well-formed man, always wears fine clothes. He is a fair master, but aloof. He likes the horses, but does not converse much with me or the lads.'

'And his family?'

'You'll have to ask him that. All I can tell you is that he's not from Lancashire. Comes from somewhere in the southern shires, I believe. I cannot tell you more, for I know no more. He has not been here longer than a six-month.'

'Take me to his chamber.'

The head groom eyed Shakespeare, but then shrugged his shoulders. 'As you wish, sir. Follow me.'

They went to Weld's room close by the stable block. It was protected by a heavy door, which was locked.

'Do you have the key, master groom?'

'No, sir.'

'Well, tell Mr Weld when he returns that John Shakespeare would speak with him on urgent business. He will find me in the great house.'

Young Andrew Woode had known much unhappiness. First the death of his mother, then of his father and, finally, the loss of Catherine Shakespeare, who had been like a second mother to him. It could not have occurred to him that life could get worse.

Hubert Penn was gazing at him in that unsettling way he had. At seventeen, he was four years older than Andrew and was in his second year at St John's. Andrew tried not to meet his eye, for he did not like what he saw there.

Fitzherbert, their tutor, came into the room.

'Have you scholars done your exercises? I did not see you in the quadrangle.'

'I have, Mr Fitzherbert, but Woode hasn't.'

'But I have run for a quarter of the clock, Mr Fitzherbert!'

'Are you calling Penn a liar?'

'No, sir, but he is mistaken.'

'You will run until the clock strikes nine, then you will continue with your studies by candlelight – and pray for an hour before bed.'

'Yes, master,' Andrew said.

He knew that if he argued, the alternative would be a great deal worse: a birch-rod flogging, half-rations for a week and the chores of every boy in the dormitory. He looked across at Hubert Penn, expecting to see him smirk. But his handsome face had the innocent cast of an angel.

'And you, Penn,' Fitzherbert said, 'shall have the privilege of sharing the comfort of my cot this night as reward for your honest dealing.'

A low stage had been erected close to the west wall of Lathom House among the grove of parkland trees. The evening was fine. Honoured guests from Ormskirk and the surrounding villages were arriving and quickly filling the audience enclosure.

They had been summoned in great haste, but none refused the invitation. All wanted to see the wondrous new play presented by the Earl of Derby's company. They wished, also, to pay their respects to the earl, their liege lord. But most of all, they were eager to see for themselves if the stories spoken abroad were true: that he had been bewitched and was now but a shadow of a man.

John Shakespeare leant idly against the trunk of an ash tree and watched. He held a silver goblet of Gascon wine, rich and unsweetened. Bluecoats flitted here and there with drinks and delicacies. He almost laughed as he saw a local dignitary hesitate before accepting a sweetmeat, as though fearful that it might be poisoned or cursed. Lathom House was gaining an unfortunate reputation.

Suddenly the world went dark. Instinctively, Shakespeare's own hands went up to throw off the two that were covering his eyes. As he did so, he saw they were small, feminine and neatly encased in soft cream gloves. He spun around. It was Lady Eliska. She smiled. The monkey on her shoulder bared its sharp little teeth at Shakespeare. It wore a collar around its neck studded with gemstones that looked very much like diamonds.

'Mr Shakespeare, I told you we should meet again. And here we are.'

He bowed. 'Madame. Lady Eliska.'

'We met in sad circumstances.' Her voice was husky and rich. 'It is pleasant to meet again in these more benign surroundings.'

'Indeed.' He fished into his doublet. 'And I bring you tidings from an old friend.'

He handed her the letter entrusted to him by Sir Thomas Heneage. She took it with a frown, then saw the distinctive red seal and smiled.

'Why, thank you, Mr Shakespeare. This is most welcome. I shall read it in due course, in the privacy of my chamber.'

'You will be pleased to know that he was in good health and spirits when I saw him most recently.'

As he spoke, Shakespeare could not help but be entranced by her appearance. She wore a slender-waisted gown of gold and black. The golden bodice descended dramatically to a sharp-pointed stomacher; the sleeves were black, cuffed with gold braid and a ring of intricate lace. At her neck was a small white ruff, delicate and unstarched, revealing her inviting and flawless skin. Her hair, uncapped now, was fair and Shakespeare fancied she might be Germanic, though her pronounced cheekbones suggested some Slav blood. She was exquisite.

She proffered her hand. He took it and kissed it. 'And I must thank you again for your assistance, my lady.'

Her hand lingered in his, then she stroked her pet. 'This is my little friend Doda. Or Lady Doda, perhaps.'

'I am told you are from Bohemia.'

'Has Sir Thomas been gossiping about me?'

'I assure you he said nothing indiscreet.'

She laughed. 'There is little enough to know. My father was a member of Rudolf II's court, a noble merchant of Prague and a patron of the arts. There – I have told you all you need to know. Now tell me, do you like my pretty little monkey, Doda? Is she not the sweetest thing?'

'No. I do not like your monkey,' he said evenly.

Lady Eliska took a delicacy from a passing tray and fed it to her pet. 'I like your honesty, Mr Shakespeare, though your queen might not. I believe she too has a monkey. In Prague, I could have had a man walled up and starved to death for saying an ill word about my little friend. Could your Elizabeth do that?'

Shakespeare changed the subject. 'Again, I owe you much gratitude for coming to my assistance on the road. It was a sorry affair.'

'You must tell me all about it later, after the masque.'

'Few grooms are as skilled with a pistol as your coachman.'

'Solko was my father's faithful servant, and now he is mine. That is why I know I can travel the world in safety.'

'What brings you to England?'

'The pleasure of meeting friends old and new. If you are

concerned, I will show you my letters of pass, issued by Lord Burghley himself.'

Yes, he thought, I would like to see them.

'Indeed, my lady, as an officer of Sir Robert Cecil, I consider it my duty.'

'After the masque, then. I will happily show you whatever you desire.' She kissed his cheek. Her lips were cool. 'Come to my chamber later. There are other matters I would discuss with you further.'

'Such as?'

'You will discover soon enough. I can assist you – and Sir Robert.'

'In which part of the house are you staying?'

'There is a stairwell from the smaller hall. I am sure a man of your ingenuity will find me.'

She smiled again and was about to go, but he stayed her with his hand.

'Mr Shakespeare?'

'I saw you in the hall, talking with Mr Weld, the earl's Gentleman of the Horse.'

'Indeed?'

'He is a man that interests me. What do you know of him?'

She laughed. 'That he looks after the horses, including mine.'

And she was gone.

Apart from a few stragglers, the guests had all arrived. The air was cool. Clouds were blowing in and Shakespeare gauged that the weather was about to turn. He looked again. Dr Dee was in the front row beside an empty settle adorned with cushions: clearly the place reserved for the earl. Oxx and Godwit stood behind Dee, their eyes alert. It would take determined men to get past them. The silent bolt of an assassin's crossbow could kill Dee easily, but that would not acquire his secret for Spain. Under the circumstances, he was as safe as could be.

The crowd murmured, then fell silent. The earl was coming from the main gate, carried on a chair by four servants. At his side walked Cole. The earl waved weakly, and the crowd stood and applauded. He was taken to the front row and helped into the settle, where he slumped back into the cushions. He nodded to his neighbour, Dee, but did not appear to say anything. Perhaps he did not have the energy for speech. On his other side, Shakespeare noticed, Eliska had appeared. She attentively touched the earl's sleeve and said a few words, to which he nodded. Her eyes then turned to Shakespeare and she tilted up her chin.

Will Shakespeare was in the centre of the stage, a few feet from the front row. He bowed low in honour of his patron. The earl motioned him over with a feeble wave of his fingers. Will approached the nobleman and went down on one knee in obeisance. Derby leant forward and took Will's forearms in his bony fingers, signalling him to rise. He clutched at him and mouthed some words. Will smiled and nodded, then backed away.

The play began. The scene was a Greek palace. The Duke of Theseus was discussing his wedding plans with his betrothed, Hippolyta. The action quickly moved to woods, into the land of faeries and dreams. John Shakespeare half watched it and half watched the crowd.

Cole appeared beside him.

'You know, Mr Shakespeare,' he said quietly, 'there was a time, not long ago, when an event such as this at Lathom House would have brought forth the greatest in the land – Southampton, Ralegh, Essex, Northumberland and scores more. Now no one wants to know my lord of Derby, except this rabble. And they are here only to see if he is alive or dead

– and for the pleasure of your brother's poetic verse. The Hesketh affair has left a miasma around his lordship. The great of the land shun him as though he trailed murrain in his wake.'

It was true. The faces of those here this evening might be well known in Lancashire, but none of the great men or women of the royal court was in evidence. Was this the circle of a man with a powerful claim to be king? The Earl of Derby's star had fallen to earth.

'Now that he appears better, do you still believe he was poisoned?'

Cole nodded. 'I do, Mr Shakespeare. I fear I do. I would suspect the Jesuits or some of the Heskeths, but there are others, too, who would wish him ill. I am greatly perturbed for the earl and countess. They feel abandoned, you know.'

Shakespeare was silent. He could see that Cole was stretched as tautly as a man on the rack. This affair was placing a huge burden on him as steward of the earl's household and estates. Apart from Oxx and Godwit, he was the one person in this house Shakespeare trusted.

'What do you know of the Lady Eliska?'

'She sent letters of introduction ahead and her name seemed to mean something to his lordship, but I confess I know little more than that.'

'How long has she been here?'

'She arrived two weeks since, Mr Shakespeare.'

The wind was whipping up from the west. Clouds scudded and threatened to hasten the gloom of the evening. But the play was well under way and the audience was appreciative. In the second act, there was a thunder of applause as Will appeared on stage as Oberon. He was closely followed by the Countess of Derby as Titania. The crowd gasped in admiration, then rose to their feet applauding. Alice, the countess, was attired in a peasant smock that had been decorated all over with leaves and flowers. At her back was a pair of wings made of thin osier bent to shape and stretched with fine gossamer linen; on her curled and tumbling hair, she wore a crown of pink petals and golden-yellow roses.

Shakespeare watched her, captivated. Edmund Tilney, the Master of the Revels and the man with the power to say Yes or No to any play or player, might not approve of a female on stage, but, Shakespeare decided, she had acquitted herself with grace and skill.

As the sky darkened, a series of pitch torches flared up and lit the action. The flames flattened and dashed in the squally wind, lending an eerie note to his brother's curious tale of love and magical spells in the forest.

The rain held off until the final scene of the fifth act.

'*If we shadows have offended,*' the mischievous Puck intoned as Titania and Oberon left the stage and the first drops of rain began to fall, '*think but this, and all is mended, that you have but slumbered here, while these visions did appear . . .*'

Suddenly the earl moaned, low and growling, and then howled in terror and pain. The same despairing scream Shakespeare had heard before, yet more hideous. All eyes were on the stage, expectant. Was this some final chapter in the tale? The audience sat forward, preparing to cheer or applaud, whichever was appropriate, for they knew the end was near.

Shakespeare ran forward to the settle where the earl now lay, crumpled, clutching his belly as though it were on fire. Titania was back on stage, a hand held to her mouth in horror. She ran down and joined Shakespeare beside her husband. The earl's physicians appeared, like carrion crows, rubbing their hands.

'Get him inside!' Shakespeare shouted at the nearest servants. 'Carry your master to his chamber.' As the four men who had brought him rushed forward with the chair, Shakespeare pushed it away. 'He cannot go on that. If there is no litter, carry him on the settle. Get more men.'

More men arrived. The heavy settle was hauled to their shoulders. Slumped across it, the earl was doubled up, convulsing, unable to talk or breathe properly. His mouth foamed with rust-red spittle. Every wasted sinew was in spasm, like the rictus of death.

Shakespeare ordered the men forward, towards the drawbridge, through the pattering rain and the gusting wind. Turning back for a moment he saw Dr Dee, deep in angry conversation with Lady Eliska. She seemed to be scolding him with sharp, threatening words, harrying him towards the shadows at the edge of the stage.

Shakespeare's blood chilled. Where in God's name were Oxx and Godwit?

## Chapter 12

Shakespeare stepped forward, his sword drawn, but then sighed with relief. He could see Oxx and Godwit there, just out of earshot in the gloom. Watching. Protecting. He looked again at Dee and Eliska. He heard her say something and laugh lightly.

'Enough of this, Dr Dee . . .'

And then she leant forward and kissed the ageing alchemist on the side of his face, while a soft gloved hand cupped the other cheek. Dee's face looked drawn, but then he seemed to smile and say something before stepping back from her. Shakespeare's frayed nerves relaxed a little.

Dee turned and caught sight of Shakespeare. He hesitated, then bowed, a mite too sharply.

'Mr Shakespeare, I hope you are not fearful for me in the presence of this beautiful lady. Do you think she has the face of a Spanish spy?'

Shakespeare looked from one to the other. 'If she was, then I fear she would be more than a match for you, Dr Dee.'

'We are old friends, from Prague,' Dee said cheerfully. 'Eliska Nováková was my muse, Mr Shakespeare. As bright a creature as any of the angels of the vasty deep with whom I communed.'

'I am pleased to hear it. I would not have wished you spirited away to Bohemia, caged like a lady's monkey.'

Eliska laughed while Dee gazed at her admiringly. 'I confess I sometimes wondered why I bothered to seek angels in the beyond, when my Eliska was here on earth.'

She touched his sleeve affectionately. 'Because you are a married man, Dr Dee.' She looked curiously at Shakespeare. 'Are *you* a married man?'

Shakespeare was about to say that yes, he was a married man and that his wife, Catherine, was the most beautiful woman God ever gave to the world. But then he recalled that he was a widower and Catherine's remains lay cold in the earth at the churchyard of St John in Walbrook. He shook his head, his jaw clamped tight.

'We have no time for this,' he said shortly. 'My lord of Derby is gravely ill. Do you know aught of medical matters, Dr Dee?'

'Nothing that will help the earl.' Dee looked up. The rain was beginning to fall properly. 'Come –' he offered his arm to Lady Eliska – 'let us go into the house. The evening's entertainment is over. It was a wondrous affair, though wasted on an audience of muddy provincials. Pearls before swine.'

Shakespeare did not move.

'You go,' he said. 'I will stay out here.' The air was healthier, though he did not say so. He signalled to Oxx and Godwit. 'Ensure the doctor is secured in his chamber.'

Walter Weld slunk back into the shadows and thrust his pistol back into his belt. Dee was too close-guarded. And yet there was hope. He had been to see Janus Trayne and was heartened by the improvement in his wounded wrist. More importantly, Trayne had dredged up some memory from the sink of his past. It was the memory of a name and a face, of a club-footed, limping man. The man with the knife at Portsmouth. A man named Cooper.

Weld allowed himself a smile; they would have the perspective glass yet.

'A fine play, brother.'

'You are generous. Do you think it would be considered ill mannered of me to leave for London? I have commitments. I would not have been here but for the love I owe my lord of Derby. My task is done.'

They were in Will's tent. Rain seeped in from all corners and from below. They drank deep from goblets of sack, which warmed their throats. It would be an uncomfortable night. Shakespeare could well understand why his brother would wish to be away from here without delay.

'I no longer like this place,' Will continued. 'It seems a very century since the Christmas of '91, when Strange's Men presented six plays before the Queen. Men no longer speak kindly of his lordship. I know not whether he is bewitched or poisoned, but in truth I am sure Lathom is cursed. There is nothing here for me.'

Shakespeare went to Dr Dee's chamber. Oxx and Godwit were outside, awake.

'Is he within?'

'Yes, master,' Oxx said. 'There has been no sound for half an hour. I believe he sleeps.'

'Do not let him go questing for treasure in the morning. He is to stay in the house.'

The guards nodded. Shakespeare left them and went down to the great hall. He guessed the time to be close to midnight. He had stayed with his brother too long and had drunk too much wine. They had talked of women and children and their family. It had been a warm interlude, but he would pay for it: he would feel the ache of the spirit in the morning.

Above him, leading off the gallery, he saw the entrance to the earl's apartments. All was quiet for the moment. Shakespeare imagined them there: the three physicians wringing their hands; the countess still in her faerie queen rags, soothing his brow. Perhaps Mistress Knott still in her corner, chanting and moaning and invoking spirits against the darkness that ate at the earl's body. Shakespeare's stomach clenched at the thought of the earl's agony. The Earl of Derby, the man who might have been king, was dying, he was sure of it. And there was nothing anyone could do.

He slipped through into the smaller hall. At the side, as Lady Eliska had described, was a wide stairwell. He climbed the stone steps and came to an oak door, half expecting to find the coachman Solko there, standing guard with his pistol, but no one was about. He knocked softly, then lifted the latch and walked in. She was waiting for him. Naked. The air was filled with the exotic scent of oil of spikenard.

He stared at her. She was lying on her bed, on a bank of pillows, reading a book by candlelight. Her body was exquisite. Well-formed breasts, smooth belly, a fair V of soft, golden hair. Slowly, she looked up from her book. Their eyes met.

'Put on a gown, madame,' Shakespeare said.

Outside, the rain tapped against the leaded window, which was far from watertight. Rivulets streamed in and ran down the inside of the wall, as they must have done for many years past, for they had carved brown, mouldy streaks.

Eliska put down her book and slid her legs from the bed to the floor. She stood up and faced him.

'Do you not like what you see, Mr Shakespeare?'

'I am a man. You are a beautiful woman. Now don a gown or wrap yourself in a blanket. I wish to see your passports from Burghley, and there are other matters to discuss.'

She shrugged her slender shoulders and picked up a loose

linen gown. Unhurriedly, she slipped her arms into the sleeves and fastened it at the front. The full curve of her breasts was still plain to see.

'Who sent you here, madame – and why?'

She frowned. 'I came to visit the earl. I am engaged on a grand tour. It is what I have been doing since my father died. The earl and countess were gracious enough to invite me to stay.'

'But why? Who are you? You said you could assist me. How? And why does Heneage write to you?' He found himself both stirred and angered by her.

She laughed. 'As I told you, I am the daughter of a noble merchant, who lived and traded in Prague, one young woman among many at court. With my beloved father dead, I travel the world with my coach, my Solko and my little monkey, finding entertainment where I may. I have more gold than I could ever need. I do not wish estates and castles in Bohemia; I want the whole world. As for Sir Thomas, he sends me his love and tells me to be kind to you.'

'And he speaks well of you, my lady.'

*But I will make up my own mind on that.*

Shakespeare stepped away from her and paced to the window so that his back was towards her.

'Do I disturb you, Mr Shakespeare?' she said.

Her voice was sweet and warm. It seemed to chase away the coldness of the rainswept night. The demon Succubus must have such a voice.

He had had enough and turned sharply. 'Do not take me for an imbecile. There is more to you than this. You speak English as though you have been here for many years, you say you are a friend of Dr Dee . . . You have links to Prague.'

All roads pointed to that exotic and distant city.

'And what do you suppose all that might signify?'

'Dee was in Prague, as was Richard Hesketh. Someone there sent him to England to discover whether my lord, the earl, would seize the throne of England for the Roman Church. Did you know Hesketh?'

She was thoughtful, as if attempting to recall a long-distant event.

'It is possible I met him,' she said at last. 'There were many English malcontents exiled in the city. I came across them from time to time. If I met him, he made no impression on me. No, I do not recall him.'

'You understand why I ask this, do you not? Has the news of what passed here reached you during your travels?'

'Yes, I have heard of the fate of Mr Hesketh. Hanged but cut down while he yet lived; his privies sliced from him with a butcher's filleting knife and held before his gaping eyes; his bowels plucked from his belly and tossed into the cauldron; his beating heart torn from his breast and thrown after his entrails; finally death – and then his body hacked in pieces and parboiled to be shown to the people as a warning. You English have a curious talent for punishment. The Spanish Inquisition with its burnings might learn from you.'

'You disapprove?'

She sighed. 'I neither approve nor disapprove. All who live must die. You will not find a swooning faintheart in this breast.'

He was silent a moment. Of what stuff was this woman made? He voiced his suspicions.

'Some might wonder whether you were not sent here by Roman Catholics in Prague to wreak vengeance on the Earl of Derby for causing Mr Hesketh's arrest and execution.'

She tied her gown tighter. 'Lord Burghley trusts me.'

She walked to a coffer at the side of the room and took out a pouch of fine kidskin. Opening it, she drew out papers and handed them to Shakespeare.

He read them slowly: they were passports for Eliska and her coachman; the hand and seal were undoubtedly those of Lord Burghley, the Lord Treasurer. Shakespeare handed the papers back to her and she replaced them in the pouch.

'Come with me, Mr Shakespeare. There is something I would show you, something I discovered by chance. Come – it's close by.'

Suddenly her monkey started chattering, high up, on the canopy of the four-poster bed. It leapt down and Shakespeare saw that it was tethered to the bedhead by a long chain attached to its jewelled collar. It lunged towards him, but the chain held it back. The monkey turned, squatted – and a jet of acrid piss shot across the floor.

Eliska ignored her pet, picked up the lighted candle and led Shakespeare to the door. The stairwell was lit by the flames of wall sconces. She looked about her, down and up, and saw that no one was there, then silently climbed the stairs. Shakespeare followed her.

On the floor above, a door opened into a library. Books were everywhere: on the floor, on a table, on shelves, stacked against the walls. Glancing at them, he noted that many were in Italian; more were in German and English and Latin. Eliska's candle threw shadows and light across the walls and ceilings.

'There is another door. Watch me.'

She let go his hand, approached a panelled wall at the side of the chimney breast, prised her fingers into an indentation and the panelling slid open.

She stepped through the little doorway. Once more, Shakespeare followed her.

The new room was slightly smaller than the library, perhaps eighteen feet by twelve. He saw instantly what it was: a chapel, with an ornate altar. A sculpted Madonna and child looked down from the wall above the altar. The altar itself was laid with a cloth of gold and silver threads, and furnished with a cross and the mass things – a chalice and paten, both wrought from fine gold. The faint whiff of incense hung in the still air and mingled with the candle smoke.

So it was certain. Cardinal William Allen and the Popish exiles in Prague and Rome had been right about where the Earl of Derby's true loyalties lay. He was no Protestant.

Eliska stepped further into the room and indicated something on the floor, to the left. A thin mattress lay there, furled up, with two blankets beside it. From a hook hung the cassock and surplice of a priest. A book lay on the floor. Shakespeare picked it up and looked at the pages. It was a beautiful Bible, in Latin, with illuminated lettering.

'I suspect that this is where our poor friend on the road dwelt, Mr Shakespeare.'

Shakespeare nodded grimly. Most likely. This was the hiding place of a seminary priest or Jesuit, and Father Lamb was the obvious candidate. This had been his home. He had been chaplain to this household, bringing the sacraments to the earl and others in this house who clung to the old faith. But that did not explain Eliska's part in it.

'And how, my lady, would you find a hidden room by chance in a house you do not know?'

'Soon after I arrived here I took a wrong way coming to my room and ended up in the library. Idly looking at the earl's collection of books, I discovered the door.'

'By chance you slid back the one false panel in a room full of panelling?'

'I thought it most unusual, too, Mr Shakespeare.'

He did not believe a word of it. He would watch her closely, whatever the feelings of Burghley and Heneage.

'Tell me what is *your* religion, madame?'

'Is it compulsory to have a faith in your country? In

Bohemia, people are free to worship – or not – as they please. Rudolf is an enlightened king.'

'Very well. I will not press you on that. But you bring this chapel to my attention, knowing that I am an officer of Sir Robert Cecil, and certainly knowing that the earl's faith is a matter of conjecture and great controversy in this country.'

'It was precisely because you are an officer of the Cecils that I showed you this room. I wish only to do right by your sovereign and the Cecils, as I am sure Sir Thomas has told you. I am a guest in your country and a friend.'

As she stood there in her light gown in this holy candlelit place, Shakespeare almost reached out his hand to draw her to him. It was so long since he had had a woman. Instead, he turned aside and prepared to leave.

'Say nothing of this chapel to anyone.'

'As you wish, Mr Shakespeare.'

# Chapter 13

S LEEP DID NOT come easily to Shakespeare that night. The mattress that had soothed him to sleep before now seemed too narrow. His shoulders hurt from the hardness of the boards beneath the thin palliasse and a draught seeping under the door blew against his exposed neck. In the early hours he woke amid fitful dreams and thought of Catherine. He felt a sudden rage at her for dying. He felt angry, too, at her stubborn clinging to the Church of Rome; she had been so like his own father in that. What, in truth, did any of it matter? For the man or woman communing alone with God, the difference between one Christian faith and the next was nothing but trappings.

He thought of the earl's secret chapel and of the letter he had found in Father Lamb's doublet. It did not take the devious nature of a Walsingham or a Cecil to wonder whether the 'great enterprise' Lamb mentioned referred to the Catholic attempts to persuade the Earl of Derby to lead a rebellion against the crown of England. The hapless Richard Hesketh had tried to persuade the earl once. Who was to say it had not been attempted again, by Lamb?

Andrew Woode woke at dawn to the sound of church bells. After all the running and the late prayers, he had slept deeply and without dreams. Groggily, he slid from beneath the blanket. Around him there was the bustle of the other scholars and their tutor rising from the beds. He reached for his black scholar's gown and recoiled. It was daubed red, as though washed in blood. He looked at his hand. That, too, was red. He tried to rub it off, but it was dry.

Paint. He had red paint all over his right hand. Confused, he looked up. All the other scholars and Mr Fitzherbert were staring at him.

In the morning Shakespeare spoke with Dee while the old doctor lay in bed.

'I do not want you digging for treasure today.'

Dee stiffened. 'I must, Mr Shakespeare.'

'I am not requesting this. I am ordering you not to go.'

'This is intolerable! I am in sore needs of funds, as I am sure you know. There is a possibility of a living to be had at the collegiate church in Manchester, but I would rather find other means to get wealth. I have no love for these cold northern climes.'

Shakespeare sighed. It would not do to antagonise the old man. Cecil had insisted he be persuaded rather than forced to cooperate.

'Show me the map. Where did you get it?'

Dee rose from his bed eagerly and fetched the fragile parchment from his table.

'It was in a chest, buried beneath the rubble of a ruined abbey. It was brought to me by a bookseller at St Paul's who knows of my interest and my success in deciphering such papers. I have great expertise in the quest for buried metal.' He went to a large box, opened the lid and took out a book. 'This is Agricola's *De Re Metallica*.' He held up the volume for Shakespeare to examine. 'It tells of earths and ores and how to discover them. In the past, I have discovered rare red soils that will produce gold, I am certain. With Ickman's powers of divination, we cannot fail in our present quest. This land is ripe with lost and forgotten treasure, ready for harvesting from the soil.'

Shakespeare was unable to hide his disdain.

'You are a coney, Dr Dee. The perfect gull for every trickster that ever lived. The booksellers of Paul's must wring their hands with glee at your approach. And why, in God's name, would you trust Bartholomew Ickman?'

If Dee was shocked to be so addressed, he did not show it. 'How do we know what is in any man's heart? For all I know, you could be an agent of Spain sent here to snatch me away. I have been called a coney and more, Mr Shakespeare. But could a fool have devised the perspective glass? If I am a fool, what does that make the rest of humanity?'

Shakespeare glared at him. He was about to say something harsh about Edward Kelley and angels and the exchanging of wives, but then thought better of it and laughed.

'You are right, Dr Dee. Accept my apologies. But take care. Resume your questing, but go nowhere without Oxx and Godwit. Do not stray from your purpose – and do not be led away by Ickman. You may have great knowledge, but I know the ways of men better than you, and I tell you, he is not to be trusted. If I left a sound horse in his care I would expect to find it three-legged on my return.'

Cole came into the dining hall as Shakespeare ate bread and eggs and drank milk. The steward bowed.

'His lordship wishes to speak with you, sir.'

'The earl is well again?'

Cole grimaced. 'He gets weaker by the hour. He knows he is dying.'

'I will go to him straightway.'

'There is something else I think you should know, Mr Shakespeare.'

Shakespeare was already up from the table and on his way to the great hall stairway. He stopped. 'Yes?'

'The Gentleman of the Horse has disappeared – and he has taken the earl's best stallion.'

Shakespeare hesitated. 'Mr Weld? I went to him yesterday, but he was not to be found.'

'Yes. I know you had wished to speak with him. The grooms told me he rode out sometime in the night. I looked in his room. His possessions were gone.'

'Call in the constable and the sheriff and raise a hue and cry. I want him apprehended.'

Cole shifted uneasily. 'There is more to it, sir. Some people say he was a Jesuit lay brother – and that he poisoned the earl in revenge for the death of Richard Hesketh, then fled. My own belief is that he has gone to offer his services to the Earl of Essex, as have several other retainers of Lord Derby.'

Shakespeare looked closely at Cole, but saw only the nervous caution of a retainer trying his best to hold things together when everything was falling apart. The man was bathed in sweat and his starched ruff had flopped with the damp about his neck.

'You had better tell me more,' Shakespeare said.

'There was a Jesuit priest in these parts. It was said Mr Weld spent much time with him.'

'Father Lamb?'

Cole's eyes widened in surprise.

'You know he is dead, Mr Cole?'

Cole nodded. His voice became reverentially low. 'Yes, I heard. The carters from Ormskirk brought the news.'

'You were, I think, familiar with Father Lamb. He lived here, did he not?'

Cole said nothing.

'And yet you did not consider *that* worthy of my attention?'

Still Cole remained silent.

Shakespeare suddenly became angry.

'Mr Cole, if you think you will keep yourself out of trouble by sealing your lips, I must tell you that you are mistaken. If I find that you have been involved in anything unlawful, I shall see that you are brought to court. You know what that means. However, help me sort out what has been going on in this midden of a house, and I will do what I can to assist you and save your skin. And what is this other matter, of servants deserting this house and going to the Earl of Essex?'

Cole winced as though he had been hit across the face. 'I fear it is disloyal of me to say this, but I know there has been a great falling-out between his lordship and Essex. I think my lord of Derby blames Essex for speaking against him to the Queen, and that is why he did not get the chamberlaincy of Chester. In these past four months other servants have gone from here to Essex House, where they have found employment. His lordship believes Essex is luring them away out of some spite.'

'And the matter of Father Lamb?'

'He did spend some time here. I am no Papist and I understood the danger in harbouring such a man. Not just the earl was in peril, but everyone in this house.'

'Good. So this Walter Weld, this horse thief and possible Jesuit lay brother, was close to Father Lamb and may now have gone to Essex. But why would he poison the earl?'

'In revenge for the execution of Richard Hesketh. That is what some of the estate workers say.'

'Well, bring me some evidence, Mr Cole. Without evidence, it is nothing but tittle-tattle.' The same uninformed tittle-tattle that accused Dee of bewitching the earl. 'For the moment, I must go to my lord of Derby in his chamber.'

*Before he is dead*, Shakespeare thought grimly.

The earl was slumped in bed, supported by a bank of red velvet and gold braid cushions. His curiously disconnected eyes were open, staring one way and another into nothingness. His mouth, too, was open, drawing in shallow breaths.

He was still alive, but he had the pallor of death. Joshua Peace would have to arrive very soon from London if there was to be any hope.

The physicians were absent. Only the woman, Mistress Knott, was in the room. Her lips were moving, chanting soundlessly. She did not look at Shakespeare.

He cleared his throat to announce his presence, then bowed low to the sickbed. 'My lord, you asked for me.'

The earl slowly turned his face towards Shakespeare. His hair was lank and flat, his complexion sallow. His very bones seemed to protrude through his brittle skin. He tried to raise himself further up his cushions, but fell back.

Shakespeare moved forward, but the earl shook his head.

'I wish you to do something for me, Mr Shakespeare,' he said. His voice, though quiet, was surprisingly clear, like a small bell. 'There is a priest, Father Lamb. I would have you bring him to me, to perform the last rites.'

'My lord—'

'I ask you this because I know a little of your history, Mr Shakespeare. Your Papist wife, your disagreements with the late Mr Secretary over his methods concerning seminary priests. I do not wish to ask this of my own good wife, for she must not be endangered. Everyone else in this house is afraid. I had thought *you* might grant me this one dying wish.'

'My lord, I cannot.'

'I beg you, Mr Shakespeare.'

'Forgive me, my lord, I must impart sad tidings. Father Lamb is dead.'

It seemed for a moment that the earl went even paler. He gasped and then his breathing ceased, before starting again after a few seconds.

'I could try to find you another priest. It may be possible.'

'Matt is dead? How?'

'Shot.'

'But who . . . who would do that?'

Shakespeare approached the earl and stood by the bed, close to him.

'Do not spare me, Mr Shakespeare. Soon, I will hope to meet our Lord. There is no place for dissembling in what little remains of this life. Though my suffering is great, he sends us nothing that we cannot endure.'

Shakespeare told him, briefly, of his encounter on the road and of the provost marshal, Pinkney.

'Pinkney?' The earl's voice was barely audible.

'He insisted he was recruiting men on your authority. I had thought it strange for men to be pressed for Brittany so far from the Channel ports.'

'I do not know the name Pinkney.'

'As Lord Lieutenant, have you authorised a muster in the area in recent days?'

'No, Mr Shakespeare.' The earl's voice was becoming weaker. 'It is two or three weeks' march to the southern coast. Our Lancashire levies are always for Ireland or Scotland.'

So Pinkney was indeed a liar, and a murderer. Or was there something else to the man?

Shakespeare brought to mind a picture of the provost and his plough-horse of a companion. They were most certainly soldiers, for they had the garb and bearing of men-at-arms. But why were they here, in this far northern county? And why had they taken and killed a Jesuit priest – one who had acted as chaplain to the Earl of Derby? It could be no mere coincidence. And yet if they were pursuivants – state enforcers – they could have simply arrested Lamb, questioned him about his contacts and brought him before a court of law, where he would have been sentenced to die as a traitor. There could be no reason for summary execution on the road, as though he were an army deserter.

There must be more to this. Someone had to be behind this, someone powerful, someone who did not wish Father Lamb to talk, perhaps.

'My lord of Derby, I know how weak you are, but I feel as though there is much I would ask you, while . . .' His voice trailed away.

'While I yet live, Mr Shakespeare? I think that is what you were about to say.' The earl closed his eyes momentarily, as though sampling eternal darkness. 'My death is of no account. But I do desire the comfort of the Holy Sacrament in these last hours. Ask your questions, as you must, Mr Intelligencer, and then find me a priest.'

He opened his eyes again and Shakespeare searched for a glimmer of light at their fading core.

'Please, sit here on the edge of the bed, for it fatigues me to look up at you.'

Shakespeare sat down. The stench, close to the earl, was almost overwhelming. He looked him in the eye.

'My lord, who do you believe has poisoned you?'

'As surely as I believe in the Lord's salvation, so I believe that I have not been poisoned but beguiled. There is no doubt in my mind. None.'

'Humour me, my lord. Your food is tasted by Mr Dowty, is it not?'

'Yes, that is so. Those who advise me thought it safer, after Mr Hesketh's attempt to ensnare me.'

'You believed Richard Hesketh was trying to trap you?'

'I know it, sir, and so do you. He was not sent by Cardinal Allen nor anyone else from the Church of Rome. He was sent to test me by the government for which you work. He was their man, though he did not know it. The letter did not come from Prague or Rheims or Rome, but Islington-next-London. And from whom? Why was Hesketh there at the White Lion and who gave him the letter?'

'I confess I do not know, my lord. I was not at his trial.'

'There was no trial. He was shown the rack and made his confession. He was a tragic fool. I wish I could have sent him on his way with his ears boxed and told him to look to his own family. Yet I could not. If I had not handed his letter to the Queen – and condemned him as a traitor – then I would have been denounced for treason myself and taken to the scaffold in his place. I would have done anything to save poor Mr Hesketh, but I could not. It was not in my power without condemning myself and my own family.'

Shakespeare could not argue. The letter might well have been a trick to put the earl's loyalties to the test. *Shades of the late Mr Secretary Walsingham and his subtle entrapments.*

'It was not even enough for me to denounce Hesketh to the Privy Council,' the earl continued, becoming agitated. 'I had to take the information directly to Her Majesty, for if I had not, there are those on the Council who would have dripped lies into her ear, like bitter syrup.'

Shakespeare knew enough about the dog-pack that was Elizabeth's court to realise the truth in this. When one courtier lost favour, the others descended on him like feral beasts.

'Who do you believe sent Hesketh to you, then?'

The earl tried to laugh, but only coughed up a thin trickle of blood and grasped at his frail chest and throat.

The woman in the corner was immediately at his side with a beaker of some liquid, which he sipped, and the coughing eased.

'My lord?'

'Who knows? Your master, little crookback Cecil? His father, the serpentine Burghley? Essex, whom I once counted my friend? Heneage? Or perhaps the King of Scots himself? He would happily see all other claimants to the throne eliminated. Perhaps *you* had a hand in it, Mr Shakespeare.'

'I vow to you that I did not. Nor do I believe my master was involved.'

'I think you truly believe that, Mr Shakespeare. I have already told you that I trust you, as I love your brother. I also trust Mr Dowty. He has tasted my food and wine faithfully. If I am any judge, then I think him a true servant. The proof is that I am sick and he is not, so I have not been poisoned, for he has tasted every morsel of my food.'

Shakespeare had many questions to ask, but the earl was wasting away before his eyes; time was short.

'You know why I am here, my lord?'

'Alice told me that you were sent to protect Dr Dee and take him to Kent. I do not claim to understand what you are about, nor do I wish to. I have my own feelings about the doctor, and yet he has been a friend to my family, so he must be a welcome guest under my roof.'

'Some say he is the cause of your sickness, that he consorts with the devil and has bewitched you.'

'Dr Dee says he converses with angels, not demons. We are much alike, both questing for something unseen, both cast out . . .' The earl attempted another laugh. 'I think he will struggle to love Lancashire if he is consigned to the Manchester church.'

'And the Bohemian woman – Lady Eliska?'

For a moment, the earl's eyes lit up. 'So you have met her?'

'Is she an old friend of yours?'

'No, no. She wrote with letters of introduction. Few enough have come to this palace these past six months, so she was very welcome. Anyone who does not shun me in these days is welcome . . .' He paused, his thin breath rattling in his throat. 'Every day, another servant or retainer leaves and goes I know not where . . .'

'Yet many stay, my lord. Many love you.'

A ghostly smile crossed his lips. 'I thank God for them. I thank God for my players. Their visit was arranged many months ago. I know that lesser men than your brother would not have come. I beg you, thank them on my behalf. Their play excelled and Alice was a marvel.'

'We were talking of Eliska. When she sent letters, did you not think it strange that she hailed from the troubled city of Prague? The possible connection to Richard Hesketh could not have escaped you, my lord. And what of Dr Dee? He was in Prague some years ago. He knew Hesketh from earlier days and would have known many of those in contact with him.'

The earl's eyes closed again and he slid down the wall of cushions, into the depths of the bedding. Shakespeare realised his barrage of questions had beaten the man down, and he was almost spent. Yet he could not give up.

'My lord, one last question. There is the master of your stables, Walter Weld, now missing. While some say Dr Dee has bewitched you, others say Mr Weld is the cause of your present sickness.'

There was no reply from the Earl of Derby. Shakespeare gazed on him, sunk in the bedding. Only the flickering of an eye and the occasional soft, rasping breath gave evidence that life remained. A fly buzzed over the bed, as if awaiting the mortification of the flesh.

Shakespeare rose. There was no more to be learnt in this room at this time. He went to the woman in the corner and handed her a coin.

'Bring me news, Mistress Knott, of any improvement or worsening of his condition.'

She took the coin and nodded.

'I will give you more money if you bring me information of the truth behind the earl's sickness.'

She said nothing, but returned to her silent chanting. Her lips moved, but no sound came.

Shakespeare strode to the door. His hand was on the latch when he heard a whisper from the bed. He turned back.

'Did you say something, my lord?'

'Closer,' he said faintly. 'Come closer.'

Shakespeare leant across the bed so that his ear was near the earl's fetid mouth.

'The name of the man who gave the letter to Hesketh at the White Lion,' he breathed, his clammy, gaunt hand grasping Shakespeare's. 'Hesketh told me who it was. His name was Ickman, Mr Shakespeare. Bartholomew Ickman . . . Now for pity's sake find me a priest.'

## Chapter 14

SHAKESPEARE MOVED FAST. He found the steward Cole in the kitchens with Dowty. Both men seemed startled at his approach.

'Mr Cole, Mr Dowty, you look very much like conspirators.'

'We were discussing the bill of fare, Mr Shakespeare,' Cole said.

'Come with me, Mr Cole. I have a task for you.'

Shakespeare led Cole outside. In the lee of the battlements, he lowered his voice. 'I wish you to bring a priest – a Roman Catholic priest – to the earl. I pledge that this will not be held against you.'

Cole was taut. 'I have told you, Mr Shakespeare, I am not a Papist. The only priest I knew of was Father Lamb.'

'Someone here must know of a priest. The place is overrun with Catholics.'

'I cannot help you. In God's faith, I cannot.'

Should he ask Dowty? No, that might not be good for anyone's health. He had another idea. He clenched the hilt of his sword.

'Get me a horse, Mr Cole, saddled and fresh.'

Dee was on horseback, walking slowly across the boggy land-scape that stretched from Lathom down to the sea. He was accompanied by two diggers on foot and by Oxx and Godwit, both mounted. They reined in as Shakespeare cantered up.

'Mr Shakespeare?'

'Where is Bartholomew Ickman?' Shakespeare demanded.

Dee hesitated.

'I am in a great hurry, Dr Dee.'

'He did not arrive at our meeting place this morning. I am continuing without him. I am hoping the map will prove sufficient even without his powers of divination.'

'Where is he?'

'I do not know. It is most unlike him to absent himself. Perhaps he ails.'

'He said he had lodgings in Ormskirk. Is he at the inn?'

'Yes, the Eagle and Child.'

'Dr Dee, when you agreed to deal with Mr Ickman, did you know of his connection to the case of Richard Hesketh and the Earl of Derby?'

Dee hesitated a moment too long. 'No, Mr Shakespeare, what connection?'

'I had not taken you for a liar, Dr Dee. A fool, yes, but not a liar. Think carefully how you answer me. Did you know that it was Bartholomew Ickman who gave the incriminating letter to Hesketh, the letter he brought to the earl and which cost Hesketh his life?'

'I had heard such a whisper, yes. But I paid it no heed.'

'You know, Dr Dee, the simplest thing for me now would be to take you into custody for further questioning; that would keep you safe from any Spaniard who would abduct you – and it would enable me to get to the truth about what you do or do not know. I feel as if I have stepped into a fetid sewer in this county.'

'Take me into custody on what charge? That I know a man who was named in a court case? You would be laughed at, Mr

Shakespeare. Do you not think that Mr Ickman would have been arrested long before now if the Privy Council had given any credence to Hesketh's testimony? Hesketh brought the letter from the Jesuits in Prague, Mr Shakespeare – he brought it from Prague himself. His tale of being given the letter by Mr Ickman at the White Lion was devised to save his skin. And it failed. Meanwhile, poor Mr Ickman has been traduced!'

*Poor Mr Ickman.* There was nothing unfortunate about Bartholomew Ickman, nor any of his clan, except they had brought it on themselves. Shakespeare turned to the guards.

'Mr Oxx, Mr Godwit, you will take Dr Dee back to Lathom House now. There will be no digging for treasure this day. Keep him confined to his room, whether he wishes it or not.'

From the corner of his eye, he caught the satisfied smirk on the faces of the two diggers, but he did not look back nor wait for Dee's protests. Instead, he pulled his mount's head around, kicked the horse into a canter and rode for Ormskirk.

Andrew Woode was shaking. He stood in the hall of St John's College, Oxford, and looked up at the wall behind the top table. The picture of his sovereign, Elizabeth, gazed down at him with an accusing eye.

'Well, Master Woode?' the college president, Ralph Hutchinson, said.

He tried to speak, to say that it was not him, but no words would come. He shook his head.

'You do not speak, I presume, because you have no defence against the charges laid before you. Look at your gown, sir, your hands. They are red. You have, in the most literal sense, been caught red-hand.'

'No.' Andrew blurted the word. He had been dragged to a cell and locked there. Now this. He stood before Hutchinson and the Fellows, a boy alone, accused of a heinous crime.

Hutchinson's eyes went once more to the red of his hands and the splattered red of his gown. 'I fear you will have to do rather better than that, Master Woode. And I must say that I am sorry that your presence at St John's has come to this, for I know you to be here at the personal request of Sir Robert Cecil. From what your tutor told me, I know you had some difficulties, but I greatly hoped that you would become a fine scholar.'

'I didn't do it, master. It wasn't me.'

'Then you must explain to me the red of your gown and the red of your hands.'

Andrew could scarcely catch his breath. He looked from one to another of the dozen men ranged before him. Their eyes were stern and unforgiving, their minds already decided against him. He was thirteen years old. He was tall, big for his age, and strong, but he felt very small here in this hall. Tears pricked at the back of his eyes.

'Weeping will not help you, Master Woode. I must say to you now that this is more than a college matter. It is a felony. You will be taken from here to the town gaol and will there await your trial. May the Lord have mercy on your soul, young man, for I am certain that the law will not.'

Shakespeare found Goodwife Barrow with little difficulty. She lived close to the town square in Ormskirk, in a modest stone-built cottage.

She answered the door with two small children at her skirts. 'Why, Mr Shakespeare.' She smiled with evident good nature.

'Goodwife Barrow, a word . . . I need a Romish priest.'

'Indeed, and there was me taking you for a Protestant gentleman, sir.'

'The Earl of Derby is gravely ill. There must be a priest in the neighbourhood. Tell him I will guarantee him free passage to the earl. I will not inquire after his name, nor question him in any way. He will merely come, say his words, then leave, unhindered. Can you do that for me, Goody Barrow?'

She hesitated. 'I think I know one who would do that for his lordship, yes. Though I cannot speak for him with certainty.'

'Tell him to make haste, for there may not be much time.'

She nodded, genuine sadness in her eyes. 'I am sorry to hear that, sir. While some seem to hate his lordship, there are many in the district with cause to love him, and I count myself among them.'

'Thank you, Goody Barrow.' Shakespeare handed her a sixpence coin. 'Buy cakes for your children.'

She took the coin. 'I will do that. Thank you, sir.'

'One more thing. I believe the attorney Thomas Hesketh has offices in Ormskirk.'

Goodwife Barrow seemed to stiffen. 'Indeed, sir. It is the great building that fronts the north of the market square.'

Shakespeare recalled that the Countess of Derby had spoken disparagingly of the wretched Richard Hesketh's brother Thomas. It seemed Goody Barrow did not have much time for him either. Well, it would be convenient to meet him this day and make up his own mind. But first he had track down Bartholomew Ickman.

Ickman was not at the Eagle and Child in Ormskirk. The surly landlord shuffled uneasily from foot to foot and said that, yes, there had been a curious young gentleman of that name staying there, but that he had left in the night, without paying for his room or his food.

'Take me to his room,' Shakespeare demanded.

Begrudgingly, the landlord led the way to a cramped cell of a room with a small, hard cot, scarcely big enough for a child. Apart from that, it was bare.

'How long was he here?'

'Ten days, master. Paid straightway for a week, but these last three days he has had free of charge, the devil flay his hide. A fart in his face, I say.'

'Did anyone come to him here?'

'Tried to bring a whore here one night. I kicked her out. Not having that sort under my roof.'

'Who was this whore?'

'How should I know? Some vagabond slut. Never seen her before. Won't see her again. She'll be in the next county by now.'

The room smelt of sweat and stale tobacco smoke. Shakespeare tore the stinking blanket from the bed, then overturned the thin mattress. There was nothing here.

'If he comes back, bring word to me up at Lathom House, landlord. There will be a shilling in it for you.'

'If he comes back, I'll slit him open and spill his entrails. No man leaves my inn without paying.'

Thomas Hesketh was poring over a vellum scroll, his ink-stained index finger pointing to the written words, one by one, like a child in the schoolroom. He did not look up as Shakespeare pushed past a servant and entered the room.

'Mr Hesketh?'

'Come back later, whoever you are,' Hesketh said sharply, still not looking up from the bulbous folds of his well-fed face. 'Can you not see I am busy here? Go away.'

Shakespeare reached forward, lifted Hesketh's fat finger and removed the scroll from beneath it.

Hesketh looked up. His jaw was slack and descended into a series of chins. 'Give me that back, damn you.' As he spoke, his protruding lower lip quivered.

'I wish to talk with you, Mr Hesketh.'

The lawyer leant across his table and lunged for the document. Shakespeare held it out of his reach with ease.

✝ 127 ✝

'What is this? Why, it is a contract of leasehold. It seems a great deal of work has gone into it. And you have a fine fire burning in your hearth . . .'

Hesketh glared at him, then reached down beside him and pulled up a pistol. He pointed its muzzle at Shakespeare's heart. 'This is primed and loaded for just such a one as you. Return my contract, leave my chamber or die here.'

'And how will you explain that to the justice?'

Hesketh's finger tightened on the trigger of his finely orna-mented wheel-lock. 'I am the law in this town. I have the power of the Duchy and will answer to no man for my actions.'

'Then how will you explain it to Sir Robert Cecil?'

The muzzle of the gun wobbled. Hesketh's grim expression did not change but slowly he lowered the weapon and laid it on the table, within reach of his right hand.

'So you're Shakespeare. I had heard you were here.'

'Good, then we can talk, which is why I have come to you today.'

Shakespeare tossed the dense scroll back to Hesketh, who caught it with his left hand.

'Just because I have heard of you does not mean I have anything to say to you.'

'I will decide that. You will answer my questions.'

Hesketh had the look of a judge who has eaten too many fat-basted fowls, drunk too many casks of good Gascon wine and sentenced too many felons to be whipped and hanged. An unwelcome vision came to mind of avarice and greed oozing from his skin like pus.

Shakespeare sat down on a three-legged stool and put his booted feet on the table. He looked about.

'A well-appointed room you have here, Mr Hesketh. Fine panelling, good plasterwork . . .'

'If you have a question, ask it.'

'Yes, I have a question. I want to know about your brother Richard and the Earl of Derby. Some might wonder whether you desired vengeance for his untimely death.'

'What is this gibberish? I am a busy man.' Hesketh clapped his hands and a servant hurried in. 'Bring me brandy.'

The servant hesitated, looking from his master to Shakespeare.

'One goblet, damn you. For me.'

The servant scurried away.

'Well?'

'Shakespeare, you know nothing of the way things are around here. Does Cecil know what you are about? Go back to London before you get burnt.'

'Are you trying to threaten me, Mr Hesketh?'

'I am warning you, not threatening you.'

'And are you saying you do not wish to avenge your brother's death? Vengeance is a powerful instinct.'

The servant hastened back and poured a large brandy for Hesketh and none for Shakespeare. Hesketh took a swig. 'Is it?' he said tersely.

'If it is not, then enlighten me.'

'Richard got what he deserved. He was one of the most stupid men that ever walked this earth. He took the blame for that landowner's murder, though it was none of his doing, then ran away to Bohemia, of all the world's most godforsaken places. There he fell into the clutches of the Jesuits – and took their treacherous letter to Lathom House! Insanity. He is no loss to the world and is better dead. So die *all* Papist vermin. He ceased to be my brother many years since – him and all the Romish Hesketh cousins. William, marrying the foul Cardinal Allen's sister Elizabeth, and William's son Thomas becoming secretary to him. They are all dirt beneath my feet, and Richard was the worst of them, a stain on our house. Doing for him was the one good thing Strange ever did in his life. But he'll be dead himself soon, from what is said about town, which will be no sorrow.'

'So you would wish the earl dead?'

'You understand nothing, Shakespeare. I never wanted to avenge Richard's death, but neither am I sorry to hear of the earl's destruction, for he is a Papist, too, and has treasonable designs on the throne. He crosses me at every turn as I attempt to crush recusancy in this county. I would issue a writ of praemunire against him and consign him to the Tower if the Queen would allow it. He maintains the Pope's supremacy. Everyone knows it. I told Walsingham often enough, and I have written to young Cecil in like wise.' He sat back in his fine chair and folded his dark, fur-trimmed robe round his proud belly. 'Nor would I be displeased to hear of *your* death, for are you not a Papist-swiving excuse for a man?'

Shakespeare was up from the stool in an instant. He rounded the table and gripped the lawyer's throat in his right hand, pushing his head back into the wall behind the chair. Hesketh's hand floundered for his pistol, but Shakespeare hammered down on his wrist with the rough edge of his bare fist. Hesketh yelped with pain and threw up his hand. Casually, Shakespeare released his throat and picked up the pistol.

'Learn some civility, Mr Hesketh, or I will teach you manners the hard way.'

Hesketh rubbed his throat and glared at Shakespeare. 'You think I seek vengeance for Richard's death? I tell you, more people have motives to kill Derby than a rat has fleas.'

Hesketh thrust his thumb in the air.

'One, the King of Scots, for he wants the throne of England for himself.'

His index finger joined the thumb.

'Two, the earl's own brother, for he will inherit his title and lands as the earl has only daughters. Three, the Jesuits for betraying my hapless brother, who was their tool. Four, any number of enemies at court including Essex, little Cecil and old Burghley. Five, the Puritans for his patronage of the play-houses. Six, other members of my family deluded enough to think Richard Hesketh sinned against. I could go on, Shakespeare: local people with a grudge, resentful servants in his household, Dr Dee or some other witch – for does Derby not believe himself charmed? Perhaps the earl's pretty wife has another man and wishes rid of him. You could put twenty men and women in a room and they would fight each other for the right to kill the earl. And then there is you, Shakespeare. Perhaps you would have him dead – perhaps you are Cecil's assassin. You tell me.'

Shakespeare was silent. All those the lawyer had mentioned had a reason for killing the earl, but did they have the means? And then there was the other matter . . .

'You have heard of the death of Father Lamb, Mr Hesketh. I ordered an inquest. Has it been held yet?'

'No, nor will it. Everyone knows how he died, so there is no call for further inquiry. He is buried in unconsecrated ground, where he belongs. I will have no deserter or traitor buried in a Christian graveyard in this county.'

'You take a great deal upon yourself, Mr Hesketh.'

'Well, if we waited on action from the Lord Lieutenant, *my lord of Derby*,' he said the words with scorn, 'we would be over-run by Popish hordes. Someone must act on behalf of the Queen and Council in Lancashire. You may have powerful friends, Shakespeare, but you are not alone in that. I have my friends, too. My informants tell me you were sent here to protect Dr Dee. I suggest you keep to your mission and leave the inquiry into Derby's *strange* sickness to others.'

'What of the villainous Bartholomew Ickman, then? If you

know all that goes on in Lancashire, you must know that he has been here.'

'Never heard of him.'

'He was lodged at the Eagle and Child. I suggest you have a word with the landlord if he is not passing on such information, for you must know that Ickman was linked to the affair that brought your brother to the scaffold. It was he that handed him the letter.'

'Nonsense. The letter came from the sordid seminaries of Prague and Rome.'

'And Pinkney? Provost Marshal Pinkney, supposedly scooping up men for the Brittany wars, here in your domain. Have you and the Duchy lost all control of these lands? Or perhaps you are in league with these men to harm the earl—'

'Good day, Shakespeare. I have had enough of your impertinent questions. You will not get another word from my lips.'

Hesketh unfurled the scroll and searched for the passage he had been studying when his visitor arrived. For a brief moment of madness, Shakespeare pointed the pistol at him and considered blowing his head apart. Instead, shaking with rage, he dropped it clattering to the floor, and strode from the chamber.

# Chapter 15

BOLTFOOT COOPER LAY asleep in the barnloft. His bed was hay, his sleep was deep, as though he had been drugged by juice of poppy. It was early evening, not even seven of the clock, but he could not stay awake. He had not meant to sleep, but the drowsiness had come over him without warning.

In his dream, he felt a violent quaking, like the shiver of a fever, but then he awoke and found his shoulder actually being shaken by Jane.

'Boltfoot, I brought you food.' She leant forward and touched his forehead, then frowned. 'You are burning up, husband.'

'A cold in the head, that is all.'

'You are not well. If this is the sweating sickness, you are in peril.'

'Not the sweat. It is a cold, Jane, a common cold. Leave me be.'

'I will bring you home.'

'No, I must stay here, with Ivory . . .'

'Boltfoot Cooper, your son wants a father to look up to, not a grave to visit.'

Boltfoot's bones and joints had been aching for a day. His back, still not healed properly from being badly scorched by fire a year past, caused him yet more pain. And he had this feverish cold. It was a slight thing, he was certain, but it fatigued him and slowed him down, and it would last a day or two. He needed rest. He felt nearer sixty than forty.

'Where is Mr Ivory?'

'He is here.'

Boltfoot looked around. Where was he?

'Perhaps he is outside, smoking his curious pipe. Even *he* is not foolish enough to light up here in a hayloft.'

'I did not see him, Boltfoot.'

'He won't be far.' He struggled to his feet.

'First take a drink. You need drink for a sweat, the old gossips do say.'

Boltfoot took the flagon from her hands and swallowed some of the ale. It did not taste good to him, but he said nothing, handed the flagon back to her and wiped his sleeve across his mouth.

Jane put down the flagon and the basket of food – two loaves, some cold smoked herring, butter, a pint of peas. She went first down the ladder from the loft, followed by Boltfoot, who was slower than usual. Each step on each rung seemed an effort.

They stopped at the ground floor of the old oak-framed barn. Boltfoot looked around. It was an echoing place, high with ancient beams, and littered with ploughshares, sickles, scythes and old wagon wheels.

'Mr Ivory!' he called. There was no response.

He and Jane went out of the gaping, double-doored entryway and looked about again. The barn was a few hundred yards from the farm cottage, which was easily visible across a flat field, new-sown with barley. They could see clearly in all directions in this wide landscape. There was no sign of Ivory.

'He may be a churl, but I hadn't taken him for a fool,' growled Boltfoot. 'He knows I've saved his life once and he'll need me again.' He spoke to convince her, though he had a churning in his belly. 'Was that sister of yours at home when you left?'

Jane shook her head. 'No.'

'Well, if we find her, we'll doubtless find him, too – and I'll have some hard words for him.'

'You're in no state to walk. It's three miles home. Farmer Cox will take us in his cart.'

Boltfoot sighed. He did not feel at all well. 'As always you are right, Mistress Cooper. That's what we'll do.'

Boltfoot and Jane arrived home in the farm cart soon after dark. The younger children were all in bed. Judith was at her sewing in a corner of the room. Jane strode up to her and shouted at her.

'Where is he? Where's Mr Ivory?'

Judith bristled, but averted her eyes and fixed them instead on her stitchwork. 'Why are you asking *me* where he is?'

'Because you've been like a vixen on heat with him, that's why. Now, where is he? Do you not know how important all this is?'

'I've done nothing.'

'Well, you look as guilty as a dog with a string of sausages.'

Boltfoot came up to them. 'Hush, Jane. I'm sure if Judith knows anything she'll tell us.' He smiled at the girl and lowered his voice. 'You wouldn't want anything to happen to him, would you?'

She looked up from her sewing. Her mouth was turned down. It occurred to Boltfoot that she had been crying. Jane saw it, too.

'What is it, Judith? You must tell me if something has happened.'

'She won't tell anyone,' their mother said from the far side of the room, where she was knitting a cap for one of the children. 'Been like a dumb mule since she came in an hour ago. I don't like it, Jane.'

Jane knelt beside her sister and put an arm around her shoulders. 'Has he done something to you, Jude?'

Judith fell forward, sobbing, into her sister's arms.

'There, there, little sister.'

Boltfoot saw a spare stool by the fire and went to sit on it. He leant forward and rested his elbows on his thighs. Women's tears were a thing he found hard to cope with at the best of times, but in his present condition, it was beyond him.

'I had thought he loved . . . *liked* me. But he only wanted me for one thing.'

Tom Cawston stood up from the seat where he was drinking his evening beer. He shook his fist and beer slopped from his tankard. 'I'll kill him. Never mind Cecil or the Council, I'll have his balls for pig fodder if he's used a girl of mine dishonestly.'

'Oh no, it's nothing like that, Father. I know what you're thinking and it's not that.'

'Then what, Jude?' Jane said gently.

'Oh I feel such a fool, Jane. He asked me to come to him quietly and show him the tavern over in Sudbury where they have the games, the ones the constable knows nothing about, or pretends not to. The Black Moth—'

'How do you know about that place, young woman?' her father demanded.

'Some of the boys go there, when they have a few pence. I got ears, Father. Soon as I got him there, he just walked in and left me outside.'

Boltfoot was already up from the stool, his hand gripped firmly around the stock of his caliver. 'I'm going there now.'

'You can't, Boltfoot,' Jane said. 'You're sick.'

✝ 136 ✝

'I'll be sicker still if anything happens to that stoat of a man.'

Shakespeare was sweating and dusty when he entered the bed-chamber at Lathom House. He glanced over at Dee, who was studying some book or map, and looked up, unsmiling. Shakespeare nodded to him in acknowledgment, then sat on a stool and pulled off his boots.

Dee rose from the table and stood to his full height. He was a tall man, with an elegant bearing.

'Mr Shakespeare,' he said with as much hauteur as he could muster. 'I have been restricted to this room all day long, a pris-oner, held by the two men who are supposed to protect me.'

'Good. They have done their job well.'

'This is not to be tolerated!'

Shakespeare undid his doublet and lay on his mattress. He closed his eyes, hoping for some sleep. It seemed to him he had seen most of south-western Lancashire in his riding this day. From Ormskirk, he had travelled south to Knowsley, a few miles inland from the small harbour town of Liverpool. It was at Knowsley that the earl had been hunting when his illness struck. The house there was shut up, manned only by an aged retainer and his wife. They would say nothing and had closed the door in his face.

Near by, he had found a clergyman walking with a dog along a country lane. The cleric had grumbled about the impossibility of his work and the number of Catholics in the area.

'Some Sundays there's only half a dozen in church. They laugh at the recusancy laws, for who will enforce them?'

Shakespeare ignored his complaining. He was interested in other things, particularly what he had been told by the woman who chanted in the earl's bedchamber.

'There is talk that the earl has been bewitched, reverend sir,' he said to the vicar. 'He even believes it himself. Have you heard word of witches or cunning men in these parts?'

'Jesuits, seminary priests, witches, they're one and the same to me. All do pray to the dark side.'

'It is said there is a woman resides in the woods near here, one that lives wild and consorts with birds. Have you heard of her? Can you point me the way to her?'

The vicar looked at Shakespeare doubtfully. 'Who am I talking with, sir?'

'My name is Shakespeare. I am an officer of the crown, inquiring into certain matters. Your cooperation will be looked on most favourably. When next I dine with the Archbishop, I will be pleased to inform him of your assistance.'

The vicar considered this for a few moments, then nodded gravely. 'Very well. I have heard such talk, too. I have never seen the woman, yet this is no surprise for they flee at the sight of a cross or a vicar of God. How can a witch be discovered when she can turn herself into corbie-crow or mole-warp at will?'

'Which wood is she said to inhabit?'

'Sceptre Wood, the other side of Knowsley House, where the earl hunts.'

Shakespeare bade him goodbye and spent the next four hours walking and riding through the wood, to no avail. There was no woman there, no house of twigs, no waxen images or giants, nothing to be seen. All he got for his efforts was a raging thirst and briar-scratched hands and face. Returning to Lathom House, he felt a pang as he noted that his brother and the players had departed, leaving only flattened grass where their tents had been. It felt like the end of something, a coming of winter at a time of year when summer should be blowing in.

Now he lay on his mattress, vaguely aware of the cold animosity radiating from Dr Dee.

'I must get back to my treasure digging, Mr Shakespeare,' Dee said, his tone a little more conciliatory. 'You cannot know what this means to me.'

'You can return to it when you are safe,' Shakespeare mumbled, his eyes still closed.

'And when will that be?'

'When I say you are safe, Dr Dee. Anyway, we will be gone very soon. It seems there is much ill-feeling towards you here. People believe you have cursed the Earl of Derby.'

'That is preposterous!'

'Indeed it is. Now if it please you, I would like to sleep a little . . .'

Shakespeare turned over, his face away from the doctor. His breathing eased as sleep took him.

Boltfoot knew Sudbury well enough. In one of the meaner alleys, he quickly found the drinking den known as the Black Moth, though there was no sign to inform the passing stranger. He tethered the horse to a ring set into the wall, then lifted the latch on the low, anonymous, door. It did not open. With his fist, he knocked lightly, twice, paused, then once more, as Judith had instructed him.

From inside, he heard the muffled sound of loud voices and barking. He waited. Eventually, he heard a bolt being pulled back. A small opening appeared, a crack of light that promised a glowing, welcoming interior.

A voice came through the crack, though no face was visible. 'Who's there?'

'The name's Cooper. Boltfoot Cooper.'

'Do I know you, Mr Cooper?'

'I'm not the bloody law. I'm new around here and I heard

you have good ale and a game or two of primero. Just let me in and give me a drink.'

'Who told you of us?'

'A gambling man in Stowmarket.'

'Very well. But one wrong step and you'll leave here with more bones broken than whole.'

The door opened wider and Boltfoot stepped into the room. The landlord, a big fellow with a beer belly and an ill-kempt beard that made him look no different to ten thousand other innkeepers, eyed Boltfoot up and down, assessing him. Boltfoot lowered his gaze. The man seemed jolly enough, but Boltfoot did not like the look of the bared teeth displayed by the mastiff that the landlord held, straining, on a leash.

'Well met, stranger,' the landlord said, proffering a hand to be shaken. He had a firm grip that crushed Boltfoot's knuckles. 'And I see you are well armed, which is a fine thing for any man out after dark. But while you're in the Black Moth, you'll leave your gun and sword with me.'

Reluctantly, Boltfoot unslung his caliver and handed it to the landlord, then took his cutlass from his belt and held it out on his palms.

'Look after them, landlord, I went halfway round the world and back to get those.'

'Aye, you look like a seafarer. You're a long way inland.'

'Served under Drake when he circled the globe. I'm here visiting kin.'

The landlord looked at him closely, almost with respect, and his suspicions seemed to ease. 'Well, I'm pleased to make your acquaintance, Mr Cooper. If you served with Vice-Admiral Drake, then the first gage of booze is on me. You'll be Jane Cawston's man, I reckon, for I know she married one of the *Golden Hind* mariners.'

'That's me.'

'Then you're famous in these parts. Here, take back your weapons.' He handed back the caliver and cutlass.

Boltfoot took the arms and nodded his thanks.

The landlord's response worried him. He had come to this remote region of eastern England because he wished to be obscure, not famous. Looking around the room, he was painfully aware of the many eyes that studied him. He smiled and nodded. Some of the men nodded back, others looked away, as though ashamed to be caught in such company. There were half a dozen tables, all with men playing at cards or dice, drinking great tankards of ale and beer. There were also several serving girls, with low-cut chemises and ale-stained kirtles, who looked very much as if they would serve up more than strong drink for a few pennies more.

The landlord sent his dog on its way with a pat on the flank, then strode over to the keg and drew a tankard of bitter beer, which he handed to Boltfoot.

'There you are, Mr Cooper. Now tell me, what is your game of choice? We mostly play primero and dice, but there's bowling to be had at the back and on Saturdays we have cockfights. I have to charge an entrance fee for that.'

Boltfoot packed tobacco into his pipe and cadged a light from a tallow candle, then looked around the room once more. There was no sign of Ivory, damn his scrawny hide.

'You have other tables than this, in another room?'

'Why, what's wrong here? The constable's taken care of, so you've no worries on that score. No need to hide away. No one's going to come barging in, and any goodwives that try to drag away their husbandmen feel the toe of my boot.'

'It's not that.' He lowered his voice to a whisper and moved closer to the landlord's ear. 'In truth, landlord, I'm looking for a man, a particular man, known as Ivory, though he may be here under another name.'

The landlord stiffened. 'No one here of that name. And if you can't see him, he's not here.' He studied Boltfoot more closely, the friendliness in his eyes suddenly gone. 'Nor do we like people snooping to find other fellows.'

Boltfoot drew deep on his pipe and blew out a stream of smoke as he considered how much to reveal. The smoke tasted foul, and his throat ached. He was aware that the men in the room were looking at him again, envious of his tobacco, most like.

'This is Queen's business,' he said at last. 'Mr Ivory is in danger and I must protect him.'

'Aye, well, I'll look out for him. Tell me what he looks like. If I see him, I'll send him to you. Now I'm afraid I must ask you to drink your beer and leave. Though I salute you for your sea ventures, I cannot abide a man who comes a-spying. Nor can any man here.'

Boltfoot's left hand held his pipe in his mouth. His right hand cupped the hilt of his cutlass. 'He was here, I know that much, for he was brought by Judith Cawston not three hours since.'

The landlord eyed Boltfoot's weapons, evidently wishing he had not returned them to him, and seemed to consider his options.

'You seem hard of hearing, Cooper,' he said irritably. 'I tell you again that if he was ever here, I would have seen him, for none gets in without being admitted by me and my dog. But if you don't believe me, look around. I'll show you every room in the house if you wish.'

'I promise you a hammerweight of trouble if I do not find him safe. If you think your constable will save you when the pursuivants march you away, your racked body will tell you otherwise.'

For a brief moment the landlord hesitated, then spat in the

sawdust at Boltfoot's feet. 'Take your threats and get out of here, you filthy cripple.'

He thrust out his fat belly and pushed Boltfoot with it.

Boltfoot stumbled back, but kept his footing. The gamblers were all up from their stools, some clutching daggers. The dog was growling, not two yards from him, its yellow fangs dripping saliva. He put his smouldering pipe in his jerkin pocket and raised his wheel-lock caliver. Its ornate octagonal barrel swivelled back and forth across the room. He was disconcerted to see that his hands were shaking. His hands had never shaken, however hot the battle. It must be the fever. He was aware, too, that he was shivering. He was in no state for a fight. He had to get out of here, fast.

He backed away towards the doorway.

'Come on, why don't you shoot me?' the landlord sneered. 'Shoot all of us!'

Boltfoot was painfully aware that the weapon wasn't loaded, and these men were ready to descend on him like wolves. He nestled the gun in his left arm while his right hand fumbled at the doorlatch behind him.

'Scared of a few farmboys, Mr Cooper?' The landlord spat again. 'All them stories we heard about you fighting battles to the death with savages and Spaniards in the Indies and Peru, all lies, were they? Jane Cawston must have been desperate indeed if she lifted her skirts for you. She's welcome to you – and your mangy foot.'

The door opened. Boltfoot slid out, his eyes still on the candlelit scene inside. He caught one man's eyes and saw a smirk of loathing. And then he slammed the door, slung the caliver over his back and hobbled as quickly as he could towards the horse. The animal was small, no bigger than a pony, but tough. He untethered it and threw his good foot up and into the saddle. The landlord, his dog and half a dozen other men were standing in the street now, laughing and jeering.

Boltfoot shook the reins and rode away with their shouts ringing after him. It was the first time in his life that he had fled from a fight. The humiliation cut deep into his soul. But there was something he had to do, and for that he had to stay alive.

# Chapter 16

I T WAS A moonlit night. Boltfoot was cold to the bone. His throat was thick and painful. His neck was stiff and aching, as were his arms, shoulders and chest. He fought to keep from coughing, but it was not easy.

He was well concealed, behind a low pigsty wall about twenty yards from the door of the Black Moth. Watching, waiting. The minutes turned to hours. He had to get this right. There would be one chance only.

The card players came out in ones or twos, presumably when their wages were gone or when they decided they really needed a few hours' sleep before dawn. He watched them and studied their faces by the moon, cursing his luck that he had caught this damnable ague.

The last watch had come by with his lantern at midnight, but still the muffled sounds of games came from the dismal alehouse. At about two of the clock, in the early hours, he saw him: the man with the smirk. He was alone. He bade the landlord goodnight and said something that made them both laugh. Boltfoot bridled, certain that he was the object of their ridicule.

The smirking man walked off down the street, away from the straggle of houses towards the countryside. Boltfoot eased himself from the pigsty and followed him, padding silently on bare feet. He had left his hard-soled boots by the horse, which was tethered in a spinney. He could not afford to be heard or seen.

From the way he walked, it seemed that Boltfoot's quarry had not been drinking heavily. Either that or he could hold his ale well, for he did not stagger or weave, but walked firmly and with purpose.

Twenty minutes later, just over a mile from town, the man turned right through a gap in the hedgerow and went down a farm track between two ploughed fields. Boltfoot would have to act fast. Up ahead he could see the dark outline of a small cottage – clearly the man's home. Any number of people could be there.

Boltfoot's foot dragged through the rutted path. He should have been in great pain, but he would not acknowledge it and drove himself on, faster, as silent as a cat. His caliver was in his arms, fully loaded and primed with powder. His finger was on the trigger. He was no more than ten feet behind the smirking man.

The man stopped, alert as though he had heard something. He twisted around and recoiled in shock. Their eyes met, then the man's eyes lowered and he realised he was staring into the muzzle of a gun. Boltfoot took two steps forward and pushed the gaping barrel full into his face.

'One word and you are dead,' he growled.

The man tried to step back and flee, but Boltfoot pushed forward again, smashing the stock into his nose. The man grunted, fell backwards, into the ploughed earth, gasping for breath, clutching at his bloody broken nose. Boltfoot was on him, his gun full on the man so that he could not move nor yell without bringing on his own demise.

'If you cry out, it will be my pleasure to kill you.'

'I—'

'Say nothing. I will ask questions. You will give answers. I saw the way you looked, back at the Black Moth. You know what happened to Mr Ivory. Where is he?'

'I don't know—'

Boltfoot smacked the barrel of the gun into the side of the man's face. More blood spilt from a gash, just below the ear.

'Speak. You have little time.'

'He was a bastardly cheat. Got his deserts.'

Boltfoot hit the man again, on the other cheek, with the butt of the gun, making him gasp with pain.

Boltfoot raised the caliver so that the butt hovered over the man's head. 'The next blow will crush your face deep into your miserable brain.'

'I'll talk. I'll talk, Mr Cooper.'

'Is he dead?'

'No. No – I don't think so. I pray not . . .'

'Take me to him.'

Boltfoot pulled the man to his feet and began pushing him back along the track, the gun in his spine, prodding him forward.

'He's a-ways from here.'

'Then you had better walk fast and hope to God my finger doesn't get an itch.'

Ivory was lying on his back at the bottom of a dyke, six feet deep with steep sides. He was still, his head to one side, his limbs at strange angles.

'You better hope he's alive, or I'll see you hanged for murder. Now, how are we going to get him out of there?'

'You'll have to go down and get him, Cooper.'

'We'll need a rope. Hoist him up.'

'I got no rope, so you're out of luck.'

The horse stood quietly by. They had gone to the spinney to

get it on the way here. Their trek had been about three miles, skirting the town. The smirking man – who said his name was Stonebreaker – had become increasingly defiant. It occurred to Boltfoot that he perhaps did not believe he would use his gun. Either that or he saw how slow and weak Boltfoot had become.

'No, Mr Stonebreaker, it's you that is out of luck. Take off your clothes.'

Stonebreaker folded his arms across his chest and jutted his chin forward. He was a brawny farmhand, with a face weathered by a life lived in the outdoors. His eyes were brutish. Boltfoot felt pity for the man's wife. He shrugged his shoulders and took out his razor-edged dagger.

'Your life hangs by a very thin thread, Mr Stonebreaker. You will remove your clothes, alive, or I will remove them, dead.'

The man looked at Boltfoot's caliver, slung casually in his left arm, pointing directly at his belly, and at the deadly blade in his right hand, glinting in the moonlight, and suddenly lost his confidence and courage.

'All my clothes?'

'You may keep your under-breeches if you have any.'

Slowly, he began to undress. First his rough cassock coat and the narrow cord that tied it, then his shirt and undergarment and nether-stocks. He stood shivering at the edge of the ditch, arms folded across his broad, hairy chest.

'Now, down into the ditch.'

'I'm not going down there.'

Boltfoot lunged forward and pushed him. Stonebreaker was taken by surprise and lost his footing. He tumbled backwards into the long, narrow trench, landing awkwardly in the thin puddle of mud and water that lined the bottom of the ditch. He yelped with pain.

'See if you can wake Mr Ivory while I make a rope, which you will attach to his arms.'

Boltfoot began to cut the man's clothes into strips, which he wound and tied with secure sailors' knots until he had a rope fifteen or sixteen feet in length. He looked down into the ditch.

'Well, how is he?'

'Alive, Mr Cooper. But he does not move.'

'Are his bones broken?'

'I cannot tell.'

'I'm going to throw down one end of the rope. You will loop it under his arms. If you do that faithfully and assist me to raise him, and if he survives this night and regains his mind, then I promise you in the name of Christ that you will live, too. You know the alternative.'

Boltfoot tossed down his makeshift rope, holding one end back, looped tight around his wrist so that no sudden tug should let it slip from his grasp. Stonebreaker raised Ivory's head and fed the rope under his arms.

'Be careful with him,' Boltfoot ordered sharply.

'I am being as careful as I can, Mr Cooper.'

'Now put a good knot in it, as if you were tethering a farm beast. A knot that won't slip.' He looked down at Stonebreaker's work. It was dark in the trench and difficult to see much, even by moonlight. 'Is that strong?'

'Yes. Strong enough.'

'Lift him to his feet, like a sack. Then the horse will drag him up.'

'What about me?'

'You stay down there till I tell you otherwise.'

Boltfoot attached his end of the rope to the horse's saddle strap, then drove it forward. Ivory came up from the trench easily and lay, still, on the grassy verge of the ditch. Boltfoot went back to him and listened to his breathing. Even in this dim light, he could see that he had been badly beaten. His face was swollen and bruised, his eyes puffed up. Blood crusted around his mouth. Boltfoot's hand slid across Ivory's ribcage and felt the comforting tubular mound of the perspective glass. It seemed to be intact. Thanks be to God. What was it John Shakespeare had said before sending him on this mission? *Do all in your power to keep the glass safe and Ivory alive. But remember this: the instrument is more important than the man.*

Boltfoot undid the cord from about Ivory's armpits and shoulders. He held a flask to his lips and poured a little clean water into his parched mouth. Ivory groaned, but his eyes did not open.

Stonebreaker was trying in vain to scramble out from the ditch. Boltfoot stood and watched him as he slid back down the slippery sides, bringing a tumble of mud cascading down with him. Boltfoot laughed, though it hurt his throat.

'I would leave you there, except I have one more task for you. Here.'

He flung the end of the rope to him, then led the horse forward again, pulling Stonebreaker up.

He lay on the earth, panting.

'Get up. I want you to put Mr Ivory over my horse.'

Stonebreaker stumbled to his feet. 'Why should I do that?'

'You have been a sound man thus far, Mr Stonebreaker – like a mule and almost as clever. Don't do anything foolish now and make me spill more of your blood.'

Stonebreaker wiped his bare arm across his damaged face where Boltfoot's gun had struck him. 'It wasn't just me, you know.'

'I do realise that, Mr Stonebreaker, but, in faith, I care not.'

'There were six of us. He cheated us all, took our money by trickery.'

'I'm sure I would have done the same to him myself. I am not judge, nor jury. But whatever he has done, I must have him back, for reasons that I am not at liberty to explain. Now put him on the horse and be done with talking.'

Stonebreaker grumbled, but his eyes never left Boltfoot's formidable array of weapons and he did as he was told, lifting Ivory like a sack and slinging him over the horse. There was no smirk on his face now.

'You're as strong as your name, Mr Stonebreaker. Well done. But I fear I shall now have to ask you to stand against yonder tree.'

Once again, he did as ordered. Boltfoot tied him securely, but not so tight as to hurt him. 'You will doubtless be found soon after daybreak.'

'God blind you, Cooper.'

'And you will see that, unlike Ivory, I am not a cheat, nor a thief, for I have left you bound with your own clothes. A little sewing should fix them well enough.'

# *Chapter 17*

'ARE YOU NOT wearied by this tedious place, Mr Shakespeare? Since your brother left, there is no amusement, no diversion. The gloom of death hangs heavy over the house, like a shroud.'

Shakespeare did not answer her. He had barely had time to think these past days as he questioned the estate workers and household retainers. Most seemed scared, but that was not surprising. Most believed the earl bewitched and they were not slow in accusing Dee.

Eliska lounged on a cushion-spread settle, her full gold and silver dress splayed out around her, with her monkey perched on the board near her head, its little hands clasping a nut kernel to its mouth. The rain had returned and they were sitting closeted in the withdrawing room with Dr Dee after a supper of roast waterfowl. A fire in the hearth spread fragrance and warmth around the small, candlelit room.

'And you, Dr Dee?' she demanded. 'What do *you* do all day?'

Dee shot a glance at Shakespeare. 'I read, my dear Eliska. And write a little. In my chamber. I agree with you, Lathom House has lost its lustre.'

Shakespeare had pressed Dowty again, and had talked at length with the grooms and other staff members. They insisted they had nothing more to tell him. He had searched Walter Weld's room but everything was gone. The hue and cry had been to no avail. Both Weld and the horse had disappeared without trace.

Shakespeare had ridden out to Knowsley once more and had tramped for hours through the dank woods, but still could find no proof of the existence of a wild woman, nor any clue to the sickness of the earl. But he had discovered one piece of information, from Cole: before coming to Lathom House, Richard Hesketh had gone home to his wife, a day's journey to the north. Any man would have done the same after years of exile, but Shakespeare's curiosity was stirred. He wished to speak to Mistress Hesketh.

If time dripped slowly for Dee and Eliska, it raced by like a storm for Shakespeare. In his few quiet moments, late at night, he studied the original copy of the Lamb letter. If it was encoded, he could not see it, but such things were not his skill.

He badly wanted to get Dee away from here and make his way south but he could not leave until Joshua Peace arrived and cast his expert eye over the earl. He knew well that Cecil would expect him to stay until this was resolved. If only Joshua Peace would come.

'How fares my lord, the earl?' Dee said now, as if reading Shakespeare's thoughts.

'He is alive. That is all I can say.'

'I pray to God he survives.'

Shakespeare looked at him. 'Do you, Dr Dee? Do you, indeed?'

'Why, yes, Mr Shakespeare. The earl is my friend. What are you suggesting?'

'I wonder about your connection to this place, that is all.'

'Please explain yourself.'

Shakespeare shrugged. 'Very well, I will. You come to Lathom saying you have an interest in the living at Manchester collegiate church, which you believe may be offered to you. You also have a treasure chart that, in itself, is of no interest to me. But your choice of companion in your quest intrigues me greatly: Mr Bartholomew Ickman, who has himself disappeared. And then there is the fact that you were once a close friend and colleague of Richard Hesketh, the man brought to his doom by a letter handed to him by Ickman to be delivered to the earl. Now, do you not think that a mighty curious set of intertwined circumstances? Like a wild briar, so entangled that it is impossible to sort the stems from the main plant. I might even suspect a conspiracy to poison. Would it not suit you and Ickman to destroy the earl in revenge for your friend Hesketh's death?'

Dee spluttered as if he would explode. 'Mr Shakespeare, this is a calumny! You condemn a man because he knows people. This is egregious absurdity, sir.'

Eliska clapped her hands. 'Well said, Dr Dee. You could have been a lawyer.' As she applauded, her monkey clapped its little hands, too.

'Then tell me about Richard Hesketh,' Shakespeare said. 'Was he a traitor or a dupe?'

Dee was up from his settle now and pacing. He stopped and faced Shakespeare, then shook his head. 'Richard was always rash and headstrong, but the answer is that I do not know. I would like to think that he was a dupe, carrying a letter in all innocence, but I cannot say that with confidence. The court said he had confessed to being a traitor . . . but which of us knows the true heart of man?'

And which of us, thought Shakespeare, would not confess to anything – even at the cost of life itself – when faced with the rack? *Put your hand to this paper or we will subject you to pain*

*beyond enduring and we will destroy your manhood. You will sign*
*in the end, after much pain, or you can sign now, without pain.*
Some choice.

Alice, the Countess of Derby, had looked in on them during
dinner and had apologised for the poor performance of her
duties as a host. She had touched Shakespeare on his shoulder
and said quietly in his ear, 'A priest came to my husband.
Thank you, Mr Shakespeare. It has brought Ferdinando
comfort. He would like to see you again, too.'

'Shall I go to him now?'

'Later. He is sleeping.'

Now, in this withdrawing room, the air suppurated with
dread. Waiting, impotently, for the death of a young man,
one of the noblest and must cultured of this age. Dee
gazed out of the leaded window into the wind-lashed rain.
Eliska studied her fingernails. Shakespeare stared into nothingness, trying to unravel the intricate knots of this tangled
affair. As one knot came free, so another seemed to form.
Motives and suspects. He had those a-plenty. But no evidence, no proof. No certainty, even, that a crime had been
committed.

The door opened and Cole stepped in. 'Mr Shakespeare,
your friend Mr Peace has arrived.'

Shakespeare was up from the settle instantly. This was what
he had been waiting for. There was no man better versed in the
science of the body than Joshua Peace.

Cole stepped aside and Peace stood in the doorway. He was
drenched and muddy. He saw Shakespeare and they strode
towards each other and clasped hands in salutation.

'Thank God you're here, Joshua. Never have I needed your
services and knowledge more.'

'Do I have time to dry myself and take victuals before we
talk?'

Shakespeare smiled. 'Half an hour. No more.' He looked towards Cole. 'Please find Mr Peace a chamber, fresh clothes and whatever he requires to eat and drink.'

Andrew shivered in the cool, damp, evening air as he stood outside the gatehouse of St John's. His wrists were bound behind his back. He was tethered to the iron latch of the door like a beast.

A maniciple, or college servant, stood stiffly to attention, watching over him. 'Well, Master Woode,' the maniciple said, 'the outlook is bleak for you. I think they will take you from the assizes and hang you by the neck.'

Andrew ignored him. He had seen the man about the college but did not know his name. He was unremarkable, of middle years with thin hair and a flattened nose.

'A right shame, I call it. Young lad like you, going to meet almighty God before your time. The tipstaff will be along any minute to collect you, then you will be taken to the town gaol to await your fate.'

'But I haven't done anything!'

'Caught red-hand, they say. Caught red-hand in a diabolical felony.'

'It wasn't me.'

'Tell that to the judge then. He won't listen, you know. Judges are there to ensure the guilty are convicted and the innocent hanged.'

All the while he was talking, the maniciple was behind Andrew, tugging at the ropes that bound him. Andrew shied away at his touch and the man laughed. Suddenly Andrew realised he was loosening the cords.

'Now then, Master Woode,' the maniciple said at last, standing back and grinning. 'It looks to me like they should have bound you better before delivering you to me. I'm going to get my ale from my table. There's a big world outside these doors. I suggest you make haste to discover it. If you're still here when I return, there's nothing more I can do for you.'

'Thank you,' Andrew said, rubbing his released hands together.

'Oh, don't thank me, young master. Your troubles are only just beginning. Go on, lad. Get you gone.'

Shakespeare and Joshua Peace, the Searcher of the Dead at St Paul's, London, stood together inside the earl's chamber. The earl's eyes were closed and he lay deep and small in the bedding, which was stained with stinking blood and vomit. His breathing was shallow and infrequent.

Peace approached the bed. His gentle hands felt the earl's brow. With his fingertips he opened the eyes and looked closely at them. He smelled the earl's breath and brushed his fingers across the thin, dry skin. Picking up a stained silver bowl, he examined the contents, the paltry blood-dark liquid that the earl had most recently brought up. There could be little left inside him. He was so wasted, there seemed to be little of him left at all.

The three doctors had been dismissed by the earl, never to return. Only Mistress Knott remained, her mouth still moving but no sound emanating. Joshua Peace went over to her and clasped her hands. He spoke to her quietly.

'Can you tell me what you have given his lordship?'

'Herbs. Good herbs. Spleenwort and feverfew, as I told Mr Shakespeare, but also meadowsweet and willow bark, to soothe and ease his suffering. There is no magic here.'

'No. That is good. And I am told the earl believes himself beguiled.'

'I think I am losing the battle, master. The spell is too powerful for me.'

'Well, do what you can, Mistress Knott. I believe your presence can only help.'

Peace gripped her hands once more, then nodded to Shakespeare. They stepped from the room.

'The smell, Joshua. I swear it is worse than your crypt beneath St Paul's. I never understood how you endured the stench of rotting corpses.'

Peace laughed. 'It does not offend me, John. It is naught but nature, doing her work.'

Shakespeare studied his old friend. Though his circular rim of hair seemed thinner each time he saw him, he looked hale and strong. Joshua had to keep his health to carry out his duties, examining bodies for signs of crime and its causes. It was a difficult task, and one that became no easier in these cruel days of conspiracy, famine and plague.

They went to Peace's chamber. A glass flask of brandy had been left with small glasses. Peace poured them each a measure.

'Ah, that is a fine spirit,' Peace said as the brandy slid down his gullet. 'Most welcome.'

'I called on you because I could think of no finer mind. The physicians here were dolts.' Shakespeare paused. 'Perhaps I was wrong to send for you. It must seem strange to you to examine a man while he yet lives.'

'Not so strange. Death is but the blow of a candle's flame. The candle still looks very much the same whether lit or not. However, I do fear the earl is soon to be snuffed.'

'Can you do nothing to save him?'

Peace shook his dead decisively.

'What of bezoar stone?'

'You obviously think him poisoned, John.'

'Don't you?'

'It seems a likely cause, yes. But would I think it if the man were not a premier earl with a claim to the throne of England? I am not so sure.'

'But he is so close to death – surely it is worth trying anything? If we could find bezoar . . . it is said to be the antidote to all poison.'

'Have you heard of the French physician and surgeon Paré?'

'No.'

'Twenty years ago, Ambroise Paré experimented with the stone. He gave it to a criminal who had agreed to be poisoned rather than face the hangman's noose. The stone made no difference at all. The poisoned man died, just as he would have done without the bezoar. He would have had a quicker, less painful death on the scaffold. Unfortunately, there are still many coneys who believe in the bezoar's efficacy. The sort of person who buys relics and believes in astrology.'

'So you call me a coney, Joshua.'

'I apologise. That was not what I meant. It is just that I believe in what I can see, or what I can prove. And the bezoar has been disproven.'

'Well, what I can see – but not prove – is that the Earl of Derby is very likely poisoned. I would to God there was something we could do for him.'

'But there is not. He is a mere breath from death.'

Shakespeare poured the brandy down his throat.

Peace sat on the edge of his bed. His eyelids drooped and he tried to stifle a yawn. 'I must sleep now, John. I am so tired, my senses are closing down.'

'One more question. Can you tell me which poison, if any, might have caused this? Is it arsenic, belladona?'

'Has the earl been lucid all these days?'

'He has. At one stage he seemed cured. Everyone rejoiced and he joined in a festive occasion. Then, before the evening was out, the deadly pain and vomiting returned.'

'There could be many causes. Had it been later in the year – autumn – I might have suspected a lethal mushroom such as Death's Cap. Only a small amount needs to be ingested. It has a pleasant scent and flavour and is easily mistaken for a good eating mushroom. It takes a week or two to kill and the victims retain their wits throughout. They also go through a stage when they feel themselves cured, and give thanks to God, only for the sickness to return, yet more horrible than before.'

'But it is not autumn.'

'And so there are no Death's Cap mushrooms to be had. But, John, I must tell you straight, that the mushroom – or any other poison – is but one possibility. From what I have seen there really is no reason to believe this is other than a natural rupture of the entrails. I swear such ailments of the gut kill more people than warfare, plague and famine combined – and they strike young and old with equal ferocity.'

Shakespeare nodded. Peace spoke sense, but his words solved nothing.

'I will let you sleep now, Joshua. Let us talk more in the morning.'

He bade his old friend goodnight, then slipped from the room and headed, on silent feet, for Eliska's chamber.

# Chapter 18

S HE WAS NOT alone. Her coachman was standing to attention just inside the door. He stared at Shakespeare, barring his way, until Eliska said something in her native tongue, then he turned and bowed to her before departing, without a word.

'I was not expecting you, Mr Shakespeare. Solko has quarters in the east wing, but I am beginning to fear that no one in this house is safe so I asked him to stay with me.'

He had noted that the coachman was a powerful, good-looking man. It was no business of his, so he did not pursue the question of what might or might not pass between them.

'You have no need to explain to me, my lady.'

'Then why are you here?'

'I want you to help me.'

She smiled. 'Indeed?'

'I must visit Richard Hesketh's widow. She lives a day's ride from here at a place called Over Darwen. I want you to come with me.'

'Well, that would be a pleasant diversion, but why me?'

*To keep an eye on you, as I have been commanded*, he thought.

'I think a soft woman's voice might draw more information from poor Isabel Hesketh,' was what he said. 'She has clearly suffered greatly from her husband's misdeeds.'

'How can I refuse, Mr Shakespeare? When do we leave?'

'At first light.'

'And how shall we pass the hours until then?'

She moved towards him and snaked her slender arms around his waist. He was aroused, by the closeness of her body and the heady scent she exuded. She nestled into him so that their forms blended: her lips kissing his throat, her belly pressing against him.

He ran his hands across her shoulders and down the sides of her well-fitted bodice. He tilted her head up and kissed her.

She kissed him back. Her lips and tongue were sweet, as though she had been eating soft, ripe fruit. Her hand slid down and caressed him, then she stepped away, smiled and looked at her large, canopied bed.

He reached down and pulled up the skirts of her gown. His hand was on her smooth calf, then her inner thigh. He was so close, he could almost catch her true scent.

She moaned and moved herself closer to his fingers. 'Mr Shakespeare . . .'

He sought her mouth to kiss, but she pulled back, a strange smile on her lips. Suddenly, she pushed him away and laughed. 'It seems we have a long journey tomorrow. We must sleep tonight. Go to your chamber.'

He did not know what to say. His blood pounded in his loins. There had been no doubt that she wanted him, that her need was as great as his. And now this . . .

'Oh, Mr Shakespeare, do not look so despondent. I am sure you can see to yourself.'

For a moment he stood there, unsure. Then he realised she was serious. He felt a fool, stranded. But what could he say? He bowed his head sharply, then turned and, without a word, left the room. Outside, the coachman stood to attention and paid him no heed. Before the door closed behind him, he heard her husky, foreign voice.

'Until dawn, Mr Shakespeare. I will see you in the hall at dawn.'

Janus Trayne played a poor game of primero and lost money steadily. He was unconcerned. He had come to the Black Moth because he knew that if Ivory was in the vicinity, he, too, would come here soon enough.

Trayne had been to the house in Dowgate where Boltfoot Cooper lived and worked in the service of the government secretary John Shakespeare. But he was not there. He said he was an old seafaring friend and wished to reacquaint himself with Cooper, for he had something of value to him. The Dowgate servants would say nothing to him and sent him on his way.

From there, he travelled downriver to Blackwall, to the shipyards, where he had a contact. This man knew a little of Boltfoot Cooper. He was married to a woman named Jane, whose family hailed from somewhere near Sudbury in Suffolk. It seemed a reasonable guess that this might be where Cooper and Ivory would have gone. It was the sort of place he, too, would choose if he wished to lie low.

The hours ticked by, but there was no sign of Ivory. Was there another game of cards to be had in town? The landlord said no; this was the only game for ten miles in all directions. Take it or leave it.

And so he waited and played by candlelight. And then, almost on the call of ten of the clock, a tall, slender man with flowing hair and a long grey-flecked beard walked into the bar. He was puffing on a pipe – an ornate, long-stemmed pipe that Janus Trayne had seen before. Some sort of native pipe from the Indies. There could be only one of them in the whole of England. It was Ivory's pipe.

The man smoking the pipe was not Ivory, but he must know where he was.

Before daybreak, Shakespeare went to the chamber of Joshua Peace and woke him. Peace rose from the bed in a single movement.

'What is it, John? Has the earl—'

'No. As far as I know he still lives. Forgive me for waking you so early, but I must leave you this day. Try to see the earl again. Try to divine how he was poisoned – if he was poisoned – and how it might have been administered. For God's sake, find a remedy if you can. Go to Dr Dee if you need assistance or merely company and stimulating conversation. He is under the guard of two men named Oxx and Godwit. I have instructed them to grant you admittance. And here, study this if you will.'

Shakespeare handed him the letter he had taken from the lining of Father Lamb's jacket. Briefly he told him the story of their meeting on the road – and Lamb's death.

'What am I looking for?'

'I don't know. I have seen many such letters from seminary priests and Jesuits to their masters in Rheims and Rome. I would think it unremarkable, except for the circumstances here at Lathom House – and the warning Father Lamb begged me to convey to Lord Derby. Perhaps I have missed something in the letter. Perhaps there is a hidden code. I have sent a copy to Cecil; this is usually Frank Mills's work.'

'The only ciphers I have ever broken are those contained in the human body.'

'But you have the mind for it, Joshua. An analytical mind. Show it to no one else.'

Peace ran a hand through his thinning locks. 'I think you know me rather better than that, John. One other thing—'

'Yes?'

'Has it occurred to you to wonder whether Sir Robert Cecil – or anyone else on the Privy Council for that matter – would really *want* you to investigate the possible poisoning of the Earl of Derby?'

'As I said, Joshua, you are still the cynic.'

Shakespeare clasped Peace's hand, then left the room, stepping quickly and quietly down to the hall. Eliska was there, dressed in a riding cape and skirt, with a safegard to protect her clothes. As he gazed at her, he wondered whether he was being honest with himself: was he really taking her along to keep her under observation or did he, perhaps, have a baser motive?

Her monkey was sitting on her shoulder, and her coachman, Solko, was at her side. Shakespeare ignored him, but nodded to her coldly and pointed to the monkey.

'Do you think it a kindness to bring the poor creature on this journey? The roads will be rough, no more than farm tracks and rocky moorland paths. The weather is foul.'

She smiled warmly, as though the events of the previous evening had never happened. 'My monkey loves to be with me. She enjoys the fresh air of England.'

Eliska turned to the coachman and said something in the Bohemian language. The man clicked his heels, bowed and departed.

'There now, Mr Shakespeare. It is just me and you – and my little friend here.' She stroked the spiky fur on the monkey's head.

'Then let us ride. Our horses await us.'

Andrew Woode crept forward through the forest into an open field. His hands and gown were still stained red. He was not certain where he was, nor how he came to be here. It was all a terrible dream. One moment he had been asleep between the fetid sheets of his college bed, then he was held and accused. Now he was in the woods, running and hiding. He still could make no sense of it: neither the charge laid against him, nor his escape.

A hawk circled above him, then fell into a sharp stoop. The boy's eyes followed it as it struck its prey.

He watched for a few moments. The bird's great wings enveloped the animal like a monk's hood. Its head moved, pecking. Ripping flesh and eating.

Andrew rushed at it, shouting, waving his arms. The bird dropped its prey and flapped away in its languid manner, trying to rise once more into the air.

Like a scavenger, Andrew fell on the new-killed prey. It was a coney, a young rabbit. It lay still, its neck broken by the force of the hawk's attack. Andrew tore his nails through the fur and skin into the flesh. With all his energy, he ripped away strips of warm red meat and stuffed them into his dry mouth. Barely waiting to chew, he swallowed the flesh and drank the hot blood.

Wet through after four hours of riding, Shakespeare and Eliska stopped to eat at a wayside post-house, the Sheared Fleece. They had already begun the climb up into fell country and the going was hard for both the horses and their riders. The journey could only grow worse.

'Well, Mr Shakespeare, here we are, working together to unravel a mystery,' Eliska said, shaking the rain from her hair as they awaited their food in a dark booth that stank of tallow candles and unwashed farmhands.

Her good-humoured remark lightened his mood. 'But are we really on the same side, madame? Am I right to trust you?'

'The answer to both questions is Yes.'

'I asked you before about your connection to the Gentleman of the Horse, Walter Weld. I saw you together and you seemed close.'

Shakespeare was still angry that he had not managed to speak with the man before he disappeared.

'Mr Shakespeare, you clutch at air. The only time I spoke with Mr Weld was concerning horses. One of my geldings was lame. When you saw us in the hall we were going to the stables together to inspect the animal.'

Shakespeare stared searchingly into her eyes. She did not blink.

At last she sighed. 'Must I explain myself further? There is nothing to say. I have saved you once, from those two hangmen. And I showed you the earl's secret chapel. Were those the actions of an enemy? Why should you *not* trust me? I have also shown you my letters of pass, signed by Lord Treasurer Burghley. What more would you like to see?'

Shakespeare said nothing. He supped the beer and waited for the promised hotpot of mutton and kidneys to be brought from the bakestone.

'But I forgot,' she continued. 'You have already seen that, have you not?' She formed her lips into a kiss. 'And you didn't want it. But now you do. How fickle you are.'

# Chapter 19

ISABEL HESKETH WAS slicing the head from a large capon.
Clad in a bloody apron, she stood at a wood block at the
back of her large manor house. Clumsily, she cut the last gristly
tendon, then let the fluttering bird fall to the ground, where it
raced around the muddy yard, headless, blood spurting from
its neck.

The dark irony was not lost on John Shakespeare. *Did the
headsman work as inefficiently as this woman when his axe
relieved her husband of his head?*

He sat at a short distance on his black steed, Eliska at his
side, watching Richard Hesketh's widow at her housewifely
task. At last she noticed the two strangers and put a hand to her
ample bosom in surprise.

Shakespeare doffed his hat. 'Mistress Hesketh? I am John
Shakespeare and this is Lady Eliska ... Lady Eliska
Nováková.'

The woman wiped her hands and knife on her linen apron
and looked bewildered.

Shakespeare dismounted and walked towards her. The ride
to Over Darwen had become even slower and more arduous
across the high fell tracks, picking their way past bogs and
rocks along craggy, barely discernible paths. At last they had
come to the edge of Darwen parish and the steep descent to the

village began. The rain had gone and they were drying out as they reined in at this bleak place.

The woman shied away from him, holding the knife defensively in front of her.

He smiled to reassure her. 'I am not come to harm you, mistress. I just require a few words, if you would.'

'Who are you? Are you from the Duchy? Is this about the rents?'

'No, nothing like that.'

Even as they rode up to this hard, cold, stone-built house, he had noted signs that all might not be well. It was an uninviting building, though clearly important locally. There was dilapidation – gatepost timbers rotted, stones cracked and fallen away, gardens untended. The four children he had encountered at the front – aged from about six to twelve, he guessed – were in shabby clothes that looked as if they had been handed down through the generations. They had been startled by Eliska's monkey, but when they were assured it was harmless, they clustered around, begging to touch it. Eliska let them stroke the animal, then asked about their mother. They said she was around the back, killing a chicken for supper.

Something was amiss. The lady of a large manor would never despatch her own fowl. Such tasks were the work of kitchen drabs. And yet Isabel Hesketh, with her well-rounded figure and her bloody apron, looked more like a farmwife than a member of one of the most important families of the North-West. If this house had servants, as anyone would expect, they were not in evidence.

Mistress Hesketh's eyes kept flitting from Shakespeare to the animal that sat on Eliska's shoulder.

Shakespeare smiled at her again. 'It is a monkey, mistress, a creature from the New World. See how like a Capuchin friar she looks. She is safe enough.'

The woman looked doubtful.

Eliska stroked the animal to show that it was, indeed, merely a pet.

Isabel Hesketh adjusted her shoulders and bosom, as though standing on her dignity. 'Well, you can scare me all you like with such things, but I tell you we've got no money. It's all gone. There are mortgages on the property and estates. We have nothing left – you have it all.'

'I am not from the Duchy, Mistress Hesketh. Please, we have ridden a great distance to see you today. If we could perhaps go inside and talk to you a while . . .'

The knife lowered and became less threatening. She was a short woman with a large belly and heavy breasts, her face lined with worry. Shakespeare wondered whether she had smiled these past five years.

The capon had stopped running and lay dead, close to the block where it had lost its head. Isabel Hesketh picked it up by the talons.

'You had better come indoors then . . . whoever you are.' She pointed at the monkey with her knife. 'But that stays outside. I'm not having godless beasts and gargoyles in this house.'

The inside of the building was spacious and surprisingly well tended, despite the obvious lack of servants. Mistress Hesketh might have lost her husband and her wealth, but she retained her pride. Eliska left the monkey tethered to the saddle and followed Shakespeare and Mistress Hesketh into the kitchen.

'We are brought so low, this is where we spend most of our time,' she said, with a sweep of the hand to indicate the pots and old crockery that remained. 'That way we need only the one fire. And all because my fool of a husband brought disgrace and ruin upon us.'

'That is what I wish to talk to you about, mistress.'

'He always had more kindness than sense, but I loved him

so. And I know that he loved me. Why did he not stay with buying and selling of cloth, which was what he knew? Always had to get involved with someone else's business, and look where it brought him. I do pray that he did not suffer too greatly. Well, it's over now.'

Shakespeare looked at her and suddenly realised that she was not so much fat as big with child.

She caught his glance. 'Another two months. I know the date well enough, for Mr Hesketh was here only three nights. It was between the twenty-second and twenty-fourth of September last.' A tear appeared and she dabbed at it with the corner of her blood-stained apron. 'It's the babe I feel for, waiting to come into the world when his father has already left it in disgrace. He'll have no father, the poor mite. Nor have any of the others, only the scorn and jeering of their fellows. I do not know what's to become of us, for no one wishes to be seen to help us, stained as we are with Richard's treason.' She breathed deeply, trying to regain her composure.

'Can you tell us about your husband's last days here in Lancashire?' Eliska asked.

Isabel Hesketh was taken aback by her husky accent.

'Lady Eliska is from the eastern lands,' Shakespeare said by way of explanation. 'She is my companion today. I am here on behalf of the Privy Council investigating certain matters pertaining to your husband and his tragic dealings with my lord of Derby. I promise you, there is nothing to alarm you in any way. Anything said here today is private, between the three of us. Your husband has paid his penalty and no more is required of you or your family.'

'So you're not sent by that brother of his?'

'Thomas, the attorney? No, we are not sent by him. I say again, I am John Shakespeare, an officer of the crown, in the service of Sir Robert Cecil.'

A look of distaste crossed her mouth. In other, less cruel times, her lips would have been generous and warm. Now there was an edge of bitterness that might never be erased.

'There was no love between my Richard and his brother, nor any of the other Heskeths. You will find a Hesketh in most every parish of south-west Lancashire, but none came forward on behalf of my husband, God rest him.'

Shakespeare let her expend her quiet bile, then questioned her further. 'Tell me, you must have been surprised when he turned up last September, for he had been gone four years, had he not?'

'No, Mr Shakespeare, I was not surprised, for Mr Hesketh was always a loving husband and communicated with me often by letter. He told me he was coming. My only wish is that he had never gone away to Prague and those filthy, hateful places, but had remained with me and kept away from all the troubles he always fell in. Fighting court battles over property, arguing over cattle, then that murder of Thomas Hoghton, which he swore to me was none of his doing but which drove him into exile.' Her eyes misted again. 'He was my third husband, you know, but the only one I ever loved.'

'Some time in late September, he did return to you. Was he alone?'

'No, by no means. I am certain it must have been said at the trial: Trumpeter Baylie was with him.'

'Baylie?'

'Trumpeter Baylie – Richard Baylie, a soldier lad, discharged from the Low Country wars. My Richard met him in Canterbury on his return journey and took him as his servant.'

'What sort of man was this Baylie?'

'I liked him. We both did. He was fair and strong and honest.'

'So they came from Canterbury together. What was their route?'

She proceeded to pour three small measures of wine from a flagon on the sideboard while she pondered the question. The last one was merely a trickle. She turned the flagon upside down to get the final drops.

'I don't know, Mr Shakespeare,' she said at last, handing him one of the fuller beakers. 'We did not talk of it. There were more important affairs to discuss: the children's tutoring, the court battles over my inheritance. We still cannot get title to Ambrose Hall up by Preston, and I fear we never will, though it should be mine by rights. Everything fell into a bad way when Mr Hesketh went into exile in that dirty foreign land.'

'Do you believe he came here directly from Canterbury?'

'In God's faith, I do not know. But I tell you this, he looked mighty thin and gaunt. I just wanted to feed him up and get him in my bed, and that's about what I did do. He brought a smile to this house, and now look at the place . . .'

She nodded to the dead fowl lying on a slab.

'And that's the last of the capons. All we've got now is laying hens, so there'll be no more chickens in the pot from now on. We cannot even afford to keep the eggs for ourselves but must sell them.'

'What date did your husband leave here?'

'The morning of September the twenty-fifth. He went on horse with Trumpeter Baylie. And that was the last I ever saw of Mr Hesketh.'

'Did he tell you where he was going, or why?'

'Yes. He said he had to go to my lord of Derby and present his passport and letters, saying he was not wanted for the murder of Mr Hoghton and was a free man.'

'Did he show you these letters?'

'No, but I know he had them, for he was promised them

before he came back to England and received them at Sandwich when he landed.'

'And who signed these letters and this passport? It must have been someone in the Privy Council.'

'I do not know that.'

'Did he mention anything about a letter he was given at the White Lion in Islington, the one he was to take to the Earl of Derby, the one that was said to concern the royal succession?'

Mistress Hesketh shook her head quickly, agitated. 'No, though I have since heard of it. That was the letter that brought the trouble upon him.'

'Indeed. And do you know the name of the man who asked him to carry the letter?'

'No.'

'Bartholomew Ickman. Have you heard that name?'

'No. No, I don't know anything other than I have told you.'

Eliska was listening to the exchange in silence. She sat on a hard wooden settle ranged against a cold stone wall, watching with keen eyes.

'Did you hear nothing of the trial or your husband's confession?'

Isabel Hesketh put her hands over her ears and closed her eyes and shook her head with great agitation.

Eliska rose and touched Shakespeare's sleeve with the tips of her fingers. 'I think she has said enough for the present.'

'No. I want to get this over with. Mistress Hesketh, are you a Roman Catholic?'

'No, I am not.'

'But Mr Hesketh was?'

'One day he was, one day he wasn't. I told you, Mr Shakespeare, he was a fool. If he was with a crowd of Catholics, I believe he would be a Catholic; if he was with a throng of murderers, he would be shouting murder. That's how he was

‡ 174 ‡

always getting into the mire. But when he was at home with his family, he was the kindest husband and father a family could ever have – and that's the only way we ever saw him.'

'Did you hear from your husband again? Did he write to you after he left?'

'There was one letter before he was captured.'

'Do you have it? I would like to see it.'

'It was taken from me, along with other correspondence, but I can recall what it said. He wrote it from Brereton Hall in Cheshire on the second of October, when he was with the earl but before he was arrested. It was brought to me by Trumpeter Baylie. Mr Hesketh wrote that he could not come home as quick as he had hoped because the Earl of Derby had taken a great liking to him and wished him to go with him to court. He also asked me to provide lodging for Trumpeter Baylie until next he came.'

Shakespeare's jaw tightened. He knew what had happened next. Hesketh had, indeed, accompanied the earl to court – but soon found that his 'great liking' was nothing of the sort, but a trick to get him to accompany him south where he could show Hesketh's treasonable document to the Queen and have him arrested. Instead of being fêted as the boon companion of a premier earl, the Lancashire cloth merchant had been taken to a dungeon, and the grim proceedings were set in motion that would end at the scaffold.

Eliska sat down beside Isabel Hesketh and put a comforting arm around her shoulders. 'And that was the last you heard?'

Mistress Hesketh breathed deeply before she was able to continue. 'No. There was another letter, sent from St Albans the night before he died. He commended his soul to God and wished his love upon the family. And he said we would be provided for well by a noble gentleman.'

Shakespeare leant forward, alert. 'And have you been

provided for?' He gazed around the dismal surroundings, which spoke of impending poverty.

'No, sir, we are still waiting for alms from the noble gentleman. Mr Hesketh was certain gold would come to us, but we have not seen it yet. You are not the one bringing it to us, are you?' She suddenly looked hopeful.

'I fear not, mistress. Tell me, who is the noble gentleman? Did your husband name him?'

Her face fell as quickly as it had lit up. 'I cannot say, sir.'

'Cannot – or will not?'

'I do not know his name and the letter said I must never inquire, or it would bring yet greater trouble on me and the children.'

Shakespeare and Eliska looked at each other. A noble gentleman had promised to pay for the family's upkeep. It was blood money – money to be paid in exchange for a confession that would silence Hesketh for ever. Yet it had not been paid, and for a very good reason. To pay such a debt would in itself be seen as an admission of guilt.

'Mistress Hesketh,' Shakespeare persisted, 'this is important information. I must tell you that the Earl of Derby is mighty sick and likely to die. There are those who believe he has been poisoned in revenge for your husband's execution. You must not withhold any evidence that might have a bearing on that.'

She was wringing her hands and shaking her head wildly. 'No, I will say nothing further.'

Eliska reached out to comfort her again, but Hesketh's widow pushed her away.

'Is it the Earl of Derby?' Shakespeare demanded, his tone no longer coaxing, but urgent and stern. 'Did he promise to pay you to buy remission of his sins?'

The woman appeared bewildered. She shrank from them.

'Or do you, perhaps, know of any plot against the earl? Have you or your husband's family sworn vengeance for the earl's betrayal?'

Suddenly she lunged for the knife that she had used on the capon. She held it at arm's length in front of her, pointing first at Shakespeare's throat, then Eliska's. 'Get out. I know nothing of any poison. Get out of my home!'

Eliska stepped towards the woman, smiling. 'Mistress Hesketh, there is really no need for this. We will go if you wish. But you must understand that we are here to seek the truth, and to help you if we can.' She took out a purse from beneath her riding safegard. 'Here, there is a little gold for you.'

Isabel Hesketh's knife wavered, then with her left hand she snatched the gold and the knife fell from her grasp. She clutched the purse of gold to her bosom, then broke down and fell to her knees, gasping for air as great, choking sobs came from her throat. Eliska knelt beside her, saying soothing words.

'I beg you,' Shakespeare said, 'tell us what you know.'

Eliska looked up at him and shook her head softly. 'She says she does not know the name, John.'

Shakespeare studied the woman. She was untying the strings of the purse, pouring its contents into the palm of her hand. Counting the money. She was a simple soul, brought to the edge of the abyss by great, cataclysmic events. There was no more to be gained from her.

He nodded to Eliska. It was time to go.

## Chapter 20

THEY HAD RESERVED a chamber at the Sheared Fleece, the post-house where they had taken their midday repast. With evening upon them, they reined in there once more, handing their mounts into the care of ostlers for feeding and stabling for the night.

It was a large but modest inn. Riders with horses and clothes of such quality as those belonging to Shakespeare and Eliska were rare. The innkeeper had seemed overwhelmed by their presence earlier in the day. Now, when they asked to be shown to their rooms, he bowed so low in their honour that his nose might have scraped the sawdust floor.

'It is a fine chamber, your worships, a very fine chamber.'

'We will need two—' Shakespeare began.

'One will be enough. Show it to us,' Eliska said.

The landlord bowed again and stepped with short little strides to the room, turning every two paces to smile ingratiatingly at his especial visitors and make sure they really were still with him. He opened the door to the room and wrung his hands. It was large, with a goodly sized curtained bed, and smelt of lavender.

'Why, this will suit us perfectly, landlord,' Eliska said. 'Have supper and your finest wines sent to us. And bring fruits and nuts for my little friend.'

'There are no fruits, save one or two old apples, well past their best.'

'She'll eat those. And a few raisins if you have them. Perhaps a small songbird's egg . . .'

'As you wish, my lady.'

The innkeeper backed out of the room. Shakespeare looked at Eliska questioningly. She shrugged her slender shoulders and smiled. With much ado, she took her monkey to the coffer and perched the little creature there, tethered by a three-foot leash, linked to her bejewelled collar. The monkey sat quietly and watched them.

'We should have questioned her further. With time we would have prevailed.'

'No,' Eliska said. 'I do not believe we would. She was terrified. I doubt whether the threat of rack or manacles would have torn the name from her lips.'

He was silent a moment, then nodded. 'Perhaps you are right.'

'Now, no more games, Mr Shakespeare. You spurned me once, I spurned you once. I think that is quite enough, don't you?'

They spent the evening drinking ordinary wine, eating hearty food and exploring each other's bodies with energy and joy. Her skin, softened over the years by lotions and bathing, was sensuous and responsive to his touch. She was well versed in the arts of desire. She understood how to arouse a man and hold him there, just long enough, before she released them both in a frenzy of bliss. In the moments when they were spent, between couplings, they laughed at the incongruity of their shared lust, here on the bleak edge of the dark moors, among shepherds and common huntsmen, and clerks and couriers trundling endlessly between Lancaster and the southerly towns. And lust it was, thought Shakespeare, sheer pleasure. No love. No questions or answers. No explanations or promises.

She bit his nipple and he pushed her down hard on the creaking bed and entered her again. The whole inn might hear them. Neither of them cared. They drank more wine, spilt it on their bodies and lapped it off.

Then they slept.

She woke him once but he feigned sleep. It was still dark outside. This time she was gentle and he let her go about her business. The only sign that he was awake was the growing intensity of his breathing. She climbed on to him, legs straddled across his hard belly, slipping his yard into her and working with exquisite slowness until he could bear the pretence of sleep no longer and turned her over and brought her to her climax. He kissed her mouth, then her cheek and discovered she was weeping. Salt, silent tears. He kissed them away, then turned on his side and drifted once more into oblivion.

He awoke to a screeching sound and a harsh chattering of teeth. There was light. It must be dawn. Then he realised it was the light of a lantern or candle. The screeching was the monkey. It was sudden, then it stopped. Shakespeare's shoulder was touching Eliska's breast. She was silent, but he could tell that she, too, was awake.

Someone else was in the room.

He tensed his body against hers to let her know that he, too, was awake. Where were his weapons? Their accoutrements were scattered across the chamber, flung off in the heat of passion.

The intruder was not moving, evidently alarmed by the monkey's noise. The seconds stretched into a minute, then the prowler moved. Shakespeare heard a rustling sound.

Whoever was in the room was rifling through their clothes. This was a thief, a common thief. An assassin would have done for them with blade or bullet by now.

Shakespeare kept his eyelids barely open so he could see enough, but might be thought asleep by the intruder. The lantern light was moving. The figure was coming closer. He could hear the breathing.

A face was peering down at him, studying him to make sure he was asleep. Shakespeare was conscious of his nakedness and the lack of bedding. There had been warmth enough in the hours gone past, and their sheets and covers were left in a tangle at the foot of the bed.

His hand shot up, as swift and silent as an arrow, punching at the throat. He felt his fist meet flesh and heard a grunt. The figure fell back. His fist had connected, but it had not hit home hard. Shakespeare twisted and rolled from the bed, on to his feet, crouching. He hit out again, lower this time, and made contact once more, a hefty blow to the belly. The intruder stumbled backwards, the lantern falling, clattering to the floor, extinguishing the light.

Shakespeare pressed forward, thrusting his fist at what he took to be a face, but missed. He lunged again and this time his body smacked the trespasser back against the coffer. The monkey screeched and chattered. The figure groaned and was still.

Eliska was up. She pulled back the shutters to let in what little light there was. Shakespeare scrabbled around the floor by the bed and found his sword. There was a knock at the door, a light tap.

'Who is it?'

'The innkeeper, master.'

'Open the door, slowly.'

The door opened. The landlord was standing there in a long

nightgown and nightcap, holding a candlestick, which threw a yellow light into the room.

'What is it, master? What is happening here?'

'An intruder.'

Shakespeare nodded towards the prone figure on the floor by the coffer. It was a thin, short, beardless man in a dark green fustian jerkin and hose. Hardly even a man, a youth. Maybe eighteen years old. Clear-skinned and slight of frame.

Eliska knelt down beside him and put her hand to his throat. Suddenly, the youth's hand shot up and grasped hers, then he was on his feet, crouching, stumbling towards the doorway. He ducked under the innkeeper's arm, knocking his candle to the floor, and was gone.

Shakespeare, still naked, pushed past the innkeeper into the darkness. He could see nothing. He heard the sound of foot-falls below him in the taproom. Clutching at what he took to be the banister, Shakespeare stepped tentatively forward. Quickly, he ran downstairs. A door was open. He ran out. By the gloomy, pre-dawn light he could see the young man throw-ing himself up into the saddle of a horse. Shakespeare ran across the yard and lunged just as the rider kicked his mount in the ribs. Shakespeare's hand caught the intruder's foot, but it slipped from his grasp. He cursed and stood a moment, scarcely conscious of his bare body in the open air, watching the direction where the horse had gone. But he had already lost him in the gloom.

Turning on his heel, he returned to the chamber. The innkeeper was still there. He had lit candles.

'Who was that youth, innkeeper?'

The innkeeper shifted from foot to foot. 'I don't know. Didn't get a good look at him.'

'You seem uncertain.'

'I'm certain. Never seen him. It's not the type of thing you expect in the middle of the night in these parts.'

'At first light, you will fetch the constable and try to find out who he is.'

'Look at this,' Eliska said.

Shakespeare saw a glint. She was picking up a long-bladed knife from the floor. Perhaps the young man had not been a mere burglar after all. Maybe he had wanted more in this room than a few shillings for food. In the candlelight he had seen the youth's fingers as he grasped Eliska's wrist. They were blackened.

Suddenly Shakespeare realised that he and Eliska were standing naked. No wonder the innkeeper looked so ill at ease.

'Prepare some breakfast food for us, innkeeper. We will be gone as soon as the constable has been. Do you understand?'

The innkeeper nodded and backed away.

Boltfoot felt like an impostor. The sickness, such as it was, amounted to nothing more than a streaming nose, a raw throat that made good food taste like ship's galley slurry, and a slight fever. Jane, however, would not allow him up from his couch of straw in the hayloft of the barn. With the help of her mother, she tended to the needs of both Boltfoot and Ivory, bringing them beef and herb broths and ointments.

Judith refused to come along to help with Ivory. 'I never want to see him again, let alone nurse the maggoty bastard.'

'Judith Cawston, I will not have such unholy language in this house,' her mother said.

Ivory had woken on the ride from the ditch to the barn, strapped over the back of the Cawston family nag. His head and upper body were mottled by dark bruises. He could not recall much about the attack, but he complained constantly about his aches and the loss of his New World tobacco pipe.

Now, in this hayloft, fussed over by women and watched over by Boltfoot, who kept his caliver loaded, he was inconsolable.

'I'll do for them, Mr Cooper.'

'You'll keep your head down and stay alive.'

'I'm going back there,' Ivory growled. 'They've got property of mine and I want it.'

'You've got the perspective glass, Mr Ivory, that's all I care about.'

'The devil can take the glass, I want my pipe. I bought that from a savage at St Augustine on the Florida coast. It's been halfway round the world with me, and I won't be robbed of it. One of them sheep's bollocks took it from me.'

'Well, perhaps you shouldn't have tried cheating them at cards.'

Ivory grumbled but said no more. Boltfoot watched him closely, certain he would try to give him the slip again.

Things could not continue like this.

'We cannot stay here now. It is too dangerous,' Boltfoot told Jane. 'That mob at the Black Moth will be wanting to give us both a beating. And who knows who they might tell about us. Word gets about.'

'So where will you go, husband?'

Boltfoot looked at her and said nothing. That was the problem.

Five miles away, a little south of the village where the Cawstons lived, a man in black doublet and hose reined in his bay palfrey at a crossroads. In his belt he had a wheel-lock pistol, damascened in silver and mother-of-pearl. His hand cupped the hilt of his sword. His journey had been long. He knew he must be close to his destination.

A milkmaid was walking his way, heavy pails slung from a yoke about her shoulders. He hailed her and asked her the way to the Cawston house. Smiling at the stranger, she pointed the way. He put his hand in his purse, took out a farthing and tossed the coin to her. She caught it, surprised by the man's generosity, for she had expected nothing. He shook the reins of the bay and kicked on.

## *Chapter 21*

THE CONSTABLE, WHO had three teeth visible – one loose brown peg on top, two below – studiously ignored Eliska and demanded to hear Shakespeare's story in full. In particular, he wished to know exactly who they were and insisted on repeating the questions four times. Each time he spoke, his teeth whistled.

'For the last time, I am an officer of Sir Robert Cecil,' Shakespeare said sharply.

'No, never heard of him. Is he from the Duchy?'

Shakespeare shook his head slowly, like a teacher exasperated by a child of slow wit.

'He is on the Privy Council. Apart from Lord Burghley, his father, he is the Queen's senior minister. He carries out the duties of Principal Secretary. Does news of such great matters not reach this far north?'

'Why should it? If he's not from the Duchy, he is of no importance and has no power in Lancashire. I'm not satisfied with your answers, Mr Shakespeare. Mr Hesketh will wish to know of this night's doings, I am sure.'

'Thomas Hesketh?'

'Indeed, sir, attorney and escheator for the Duchy of Lancaster. I know nothing of Cecils and Burghleys. Mr Hesketh is the law in these parts, in the absence of Chancellor Heneage, that is.'

'Well, we are guests of the Earl of Derby, your Lord Lieutenant. I think you will find he holds sway over Thomas Hesketh.'

'That's not how Mr Hesketh sees things. You ask him. Anyway, from what I heard, the earl won't be holding sway over anything very soon. Now tell me, Mr Shakespeare, this lady here –' he nodded in the direction of Eliska in an offensively casual manner – 'if she is your wife, why does she have a strange, foreign-sounding name? Why is she not plain Mistress Shakespeare?'

Shakespeare had to be careful. This was neither London with its bawdy houses, nor the court with its ladies of pleasure. Here, if a couple slept together and were not married, then the woman was a whore, and the man an adulterer, and they might be flogged in punishment.

'She *is* Mistress Shakespeare, constable. We are newly wed and are enjoying our honeymoon. She is not yet accustomed to her married name, that is all.'

The constable scratched his hairy belly, which protruded obscenely through his coarse, stained jerkin. 'I have to ask, you see, because we would not be wanting any lewd behaviour.' He glanced at the monkey and smirked. 'Perhaps you should have married the pretty, hairy one. She don't speak so strange.'

'Mind your mouth, constable, or I might stop it for you. A young man has attempted a most heinous burglary, armed with a deadly knife, and you talk of marriages!'

The constable stared at him, then at Eliska, with a disdainful, gimlet eye. 'Well, then. As you will. And you say you'd never seen the youth before?'

'No.'

'What do you suppose he was looking for?'

'Money, gems? What do burglars usually seek?'

'But why you – and why here?'

Shakespeare shrugged helplessly. Eliska tried to speak, but the constable hushed her with a wave of his hand. 'It is your husband's business to speak for you. Know your place, mistress. Mr Shakespeare, speak up. What was he looking for? Why you?'

'Pure bad fortune. It could have been any traveller. We just happened to be the ones here last night.'

'There will have to be an inquiry.'

'I had thought that was what we were engaged on now. And if you ever manage to discover the boy and need witnesses, then you will find us at Lathom House near Ormskirk. We will both be happy to tesify to what has happened here. Now, if you have asked your questions, we have paid the reckoning for our chamber and wish to be on our way. Good day to you, constable.' He took Eliska by the arm. 'Come, Mistress Shakespeare.'

Together they strode out to their horses. Shakespeare leant towards Eliska's ear. 'He was right about one thing – the monkey is prettier.'

She elbowed him in the ribcage, hard. 'I think you owe my little friend an apology. You have been most uncommon rude towards her, and yet she saved our purses with her screeching, perhaps our lives.'

They mounted up and rode out. A few hundred yards down the track, Shakespeare stopped in the shade of some trees.

'I am going back there. I have a few more questions for our host the innkeeper. I am certain he knew the youth.'

'Yes. I agree.'

After a few minutes, they saw the constable striding off towards the village. They rode back to the inn. The landlord was in the cellar, rolling in a new delivery of ale casks. He seemed shocked to see Shakespeare looking down at him through the open trap-hatch.

'A few more words, innkeeper,' Shakespeare began as he descended the ladder.

'I told the constable all I know.'

Suddenly the innkeeper's obsequious manner had turned defensive, almost belligerent. He was an unremarkable-looking man, yet there was something familiar about him. His face was square-set with thick features and a heavy brow.

'He was satisfied with my answers.'

'What is your name?'

'Why? What business is it of yours?'

'You will find out soon enough when I have pursuivants sent to arrest you – if you do not cooperate with me.'

The cellar was dusty and stank of rat droppings. Shakespeare put his hand to his poniard irritably.

'Barrow, the name's Barrow.'

Barrow. That was why the face was familiar. The constable at Ormskirk was called Barrow. This man must be closely related. Shakespeare took a stab.

'I know your brother.'

The innkeeper shifted uneasily, but said nothing.

'The constable at Ormskirk. He *is* your brother, is he not?'

'What's my brother got to do with this?'

'It is interesting that you have such a close connection with Ormskirk. How far is it from here, twelve miles, fifteen?'

Again, the innkeeper was silent.

Shakespeare took the poniard from his belt. He moved a step closer. Their eyes met briefly, then Barrow looked away. Shakespeare reached out and gripped the man's shoulder, twisting him so that he had to look at him.

'You knew that youth.' His thumb rubbed the honed edge of the blade, with menace.

'Get your hand off me. I never saw him before.'

'That lad was no vagabond. His clothes were almost new.'

'Maybe he stole them. You said yourself, he was a burglar.'

'And did you note his hands?'

'Hands?' Barrow's voice was full of disparagement now. 'Why should I note his hands?'

'His fingertips were ink-stained. He worked with inks. That does not sound like a common thief or rogue to me.'

The innkeeper shrugged his shoulders dismissively and averted his eyes again.

'God damn you, Barrow, you will answer my questions or pay a heavy price. A boy has attempted burglary, perhaps murder, and I want to know why – and who sent him. It was remarkable how quick you were to the door of our chamber, like a ferret down a rabbit-hole. You knew all along that he was there because you sent word to his master in Ormskirk – and when the boy arrived at the inn, you let him in. Now tell me his name.'

Ignoring Shakespeare's poniard, Barrow leant his forearm across the keg he had just deposited. 'You, Mr Shakespeare, can stick your questions up your southern arse. You are not the law here and you are not welcome. Come for me with pursuivants, will you? You couldn't raise a band of pursuivants anywhere west of Manchester. Now get out of my inn. I've got men upstairs will be glad to scrape out your eyeballs and replace them with your bollocks if you try anything. Understood?'

Shakespeare laughed. 'You have already told me everything I need to know, Mr Barrow. Good day.'

He turned his back and climbed the ladder from the cellar.

'Come,' he said to Eliska. 'Let us ride hard. I have business to attend to.'

Near Ormskirk, they stopped at a crossroads beneath a sycamore.

'I must take the left fork, into town,' Shakespeare said.

Eliska leant across and embraced him, then kissed his cheeks. 'It is time for us to part. I am leaving this place. I have a wedding to attend, which I greatly prefer to funerals. I cannot abide them.'

'I understand.'

'You would be wise to leave, too, Mr Shakespeare.'

'Indeed, my lady.' He smiled at the formality of her address. He tried to kiss her again, but she pulled back from him.

'Let us not delude ourselves. It was a fine diversion, nothing more. A little cheer in a barren landscape. Farewell.'

She squeezed his hand, then withdrew her fingers, shook the reins and kicked on, alone, towards Lathom House. He waited a few moments, watching her retreat. He imagined her galloping across England in her carriage with her monkey, accompanied by her loyal coachman. He had never met anyone like her, nor ever would again, he fancied. Briefly he wondered about her tears in the night, then wheeled his horse and trotted the last two miles into town.

The market square, so busy on his last visit, was almost deserted. He went to the magnificent chambers of Thomas Hesketh and hammered at the door. A servant opened it almost instantly.

'Take me to Hesketh.'

'He is not here, master.'

Shakespeare pushed past the man into the dark-wood interior and went to the room where he had last seen Thomas Hesketh. It was empty.

'Where is he?'

'At Lancaster, master. He will be there some few days.'

'When did he go?'

'This morning, early.'

'But his boy did not go with him?'

The servant said nothing.

'His scribe, man. He did not go, did he?'

'I believe not,' the servant said cautiously, a dark note of suspicion in his voice. 'Might I inquire why you ask, sir?'

'Because he tried to kill me last night, in an inn a few miles from here.'

The servant blanched. 'Parfitt did this?'

'Yes, indeed. Tell your master, Mr Hesketh, when you see him next. Or, better yet, send him a messenger. Tell him John Shakespeare told you this. Tell him his hireling Parfitt – if that is his name – found nothing.'

Shakespeare turned and strode from the building into the market square.

He had a tight, uncomfortable knot deep in his belly at the thought of what he would find at Lathom House. The portents did not seem good, not good at all. His fear was well grounded.

Tumult awaited him.

# Chapter 22

D EATH HUNG OVER the great house. The pennants fluttering across the battlements were lowered. It was midday but the sky was black. The threat of thunder menaced the air. As Shakespeare approached, he knew that Ferdinando, the fifth Earl of Derby, a man who might have been king, lay dead.

By the time he had entered the great palace, the gloom was utterly pervasive. He dismounted and went into the great hall. Cole was there, issuing orders and responding to questions. A clergyman was talking to him.

'Yes, my lord bishop, he will be buried in the family chapel at Ormskirk, with his forebears. We will organise everything from here. You need only be there for the service.'

'I should stay with the body, Mr Cole. It is only right . . . I must pray for his eternal soul.'

'The countess wishes to make her own arrangements in that regard.'

Bishop Chaderton scowled. 'She is bringing in a greased priest, is she? Thomas Hesketh will hear of this, as will the Privy Council.'

Cole scratched in a ledger and did not look up at the cleric. 'No, there will be no Catholic priest. The earl will be buried according to the rites of the Church in England, just as his father before him. And I am sure that your services will be required yet again.' Cole looked up, unsmiling.

The bishop glared at him for a few moments, then sidled away, muttering.

Shakespeare approached. Cole met his eye, his countenance grim.

'My lord died a few hours since, Mr Shakespeare. It was peaceful at the end. He said last night that he was resolved to die and would take no more remedies nor suffer any liquids to pass his lips, for he wished to fly swiftly into the arms of Christ, lightly, on eagle's wings. Those were his very words.'

Shakespeare nodded. 'Where is the countess?'

'She is with the children.'

'And the bishop? How did he arrive at such speed?'

'Mr Chaderton arrived last night, meaning to bring comfort to the earl, but the earl would not see him. I believe he also intends conversing with Dr Dee about the wardenship of Manchester collegiate church. There is talk that Bishop Chaderton will be translated to another see in the near future.'

'Thank you. Keep me informed. I am going to my chamber.' He began to walk towards the stairway.

'Mr Shakespeare—'

He stopped. 'Yes, Mr Cole?'

'There have been other developments. The searcher, Mr Peace, has had his room rifled. I believe some of his property is missing.'

'Is he hurt?'

'He was not in the room at the time, but with Dr Dee. There is yet more news. A messenger has arrived from court. A commission of inquiry is to be sent here, for the Privy Council already fears the worst. It is said the Queen's rage is tempestuous that a man so great as the late earl, her well-beloved cousin, should be beguiled and brought to his deathbed in such a manner. She insists the witch who cursed him be caught and made to face the full and terrible wrath of the law.'

'Who are the commissioners?'

'Sir Thomas Egerton and Sir George Carey. Sir Thomas has local connections. He is Chamberlain of Chester. He is also well known to the family, having served as an adviser to the earl and his father in earlier times. I think they will be here within the week. I have already sent messages that his lordship has died.'

Egerton. An interesting choice. As a lawyer, his star was rising, newly appointed Master of the Rolls in the Court of Chancery. Perhaps he was helped by the severity of his Protestant faith. He was a scourge of Catholics, having prosecuted the Jesuit priest Edmund Campion, Mary Queen of Scots and the Babington plotters. He spoke of Catholicism as 'the devilish doctrine of Rome'. How closely would he inquire into the death of an earl suspected of being a crypto-Papist? He had been pleased enough to see Mary of Scots lose her head. And yet, if he had been close to this family in his earlier days, perhaps he would wish to see justice done.

Carey was a lesser known quantity, an administrator and diplomat – a man who went wherever he was ordered in the service of the Queen, and dealt with matters to her satisfaction.

'What of the earl's brother, William – the sixth earl as he must now be known – does he know what has happened?'

'Word has been sent to him on the Island of Man. The weather does not look good for the sea crossing, I fear.'

'No. Indeed not. Well, I am sure he will take up his inheritance in due course. Now, where is Joshua Peace?'

'You will find him in his chamber. And I have here a letter for you, brought by messenger this very hour.'

Shakespeare took it, surprised to see it bore his brother's seal. He stuffed it inside his doublet to read later and went in search of Joshua Peace.

Peace's door was open. He went straight in and clasped the searcher's hand.

'Joshua, I have heard—'

'I am well, John. But I am mighty glad you have returned. This place has been in turmoil. Wailing, shouting, heavy footfalls as servants and retainers run hither and thither. Not only that, but I have been robbed, my belongings turned upside down, my clothes torn to shreds.'

'The Lamb letter?'

Peace sighed. 'Safe. I am sure that is what they were after. But I had it about my person.'

'Joshua!'

'I applied gentle heat to it. You were right to think there was more to it. I revealed secret writing – lemon juice or some such ink.' Peace grimaced. 'It still does not mean much, not to me. The secret writing itself is like a riddle or puzzle. A riddle within a riddle.'

He fished in his doublet and held up a scrap of paper on which he had scrawled a few words.

'*The killing birds wait in line. The hawks edge nearer, even as golden eagles under soaring eyries dive. Malevolent dove, evil nightjar, baleful ibis and twisted hoodcrow toss overhead, preying on insects, shrews or newts. Let dogs fester, orphans rot, ere rooks lay down and die.*'

'God's blood, Joshua, what is this about?'

As he spoke, it occurred to him that whoever Cecil had assigned to the decoding of the letter would not have discovered this hidden writing from the copy.

'I have no idea of the significance. I will keep that copy. You take the original.'

Joshua delved once more into his pockets and produced the Lamb letter, wrapped in waxed paper for safe keeping.

Shakespeare took it. The secret writing was quite clear where the heat had revealed it.

'The Earl of Derby's crest has an eagle and child. It is everywhere. Even the inns are named after it. This is about Derby.'

'But what exactly can we learn from it?'

Shakespeare read it again. It meant nothing to him.

'All I have learnt is that it is mighty important to someone – important enough to ransack your chamber.'

*And perhaps mine, too. Was that why the boy with the knife was in his room at the inn?*

'Well, I will continue to study it,' Peace said. 'But my work here is done. I must be away, to London.'

'I know, Joshua, I know – and I thank you for your trouble in coming here. Before you go, however, I must ask you to examine the body of the earl, as a searcher rather than a physician.'

'Very well.'

He looked at his old friend closely. Joshua Peace was normally imperturbable, but he seemed shaken. The evidence of the attack was all around – ripped clothing and bedding, a broken chest. Shakespeare could understand why he would wish to return to London. Summoning servants to help, the two men put the room to rights as best they could before Shakespeare set out for his own quarters, pulling out his brother's letter to read on the way.

The letter was but three lines long and shook him to the core.

'*John, I have grave news. There has been an incident at St John's. Andrew is missing, accused of a most shocking crime. Come to Oxford immediately. Your loving brother, Will.*'

Shakespeare stopped in his tracks, scarce able to take it

in. He felt his heart would stop with fear. It changed everything. He raced back to Joshua Peace, threw open his door and thrust the letter towards him.

The searcher read it quickly, then looked up into his friend's eyes.

'I cannot wait a moment longer,' Shakespeare said. 'I must go and I must take Dee with me.' He took a deep breath and began to regain his composure. He pushed the letter back into his doublet. 'Joshua, I must ask you to stay here on my behalf. Carry out your duties as Searcher of the Dead. Examine the earl's body, then report to the commissioners, Egerton and Carey – and to me.'

Joshua Peace looked uncomfortable, but nodded in resignation. 'I will stay and do what I can.'

'I must go to Oxford.' Shakespeare clasped him to his breast, then stood back. 'I am sorry to involve you in this. Forgive me. I will bring you a gallon of French wine when next we meet, but until then I *must* leave you.'

Within the hour, he was mounted in the outer courtyard. Dr Dee came at last, shuffling along reluctantly in his rich alchemist's gown, accompanied by the powerful figures of Oxx and Godwit. Shakespeare turned to the guards.

'Mr Oxx, do you have a sharp knife?'

'Indeed, I do, Mr Shakespeare.'

'Then use it to cut off Dr Dee's beard. And you, Mr Godwit, demand a suit of apparel – a common jerkin and hose – to fit the doctor.'

Dee looked horrified. 'What is this?'

'Dr Dee, if you think I am riding through England with you attired like some latter-day Merlin, you are sorely mistaken. I might as well light beacons along the way to herald our advance!'

'Very well. I will change into other clothes. But not my beard.'

'You can grow another when this alarm is over. Now hurry, for we have no time to lose. You are coming with me to a safe place.'

Oxx and Godwit marched Dee into the house while Shakespeare sat and waited. Within the hour they returned. Dee's face was clean shaven with a few flecks of blood. He wore the clothes of a working man.

'You look a good deal more handsome, Dr Dee.'

'This is an outrage!'

'Ten years younger. Your wife and children will not recognise you. I assume the clothes belonged to a carpenter or groom. A little tight in places, but they will suffice. Now let us ride, gentlemen.'

*Away from this benighted county.* Shakespeare's first duty was to Andrew, his adopted son. Any man's priority must be his family.

As they trotted out of the great crenellated walls of Lathom House into the open countryside, Shakespeare spotted Mistress Knott, the chanting woman from the corner of the earl's death chamber. Her hair was awry and a bright, tattered shawl was clutched around her large bosom. She was waddling towards him, trying to catch his attention.

'Mr Shakespeare, I beg you—'

He did not stop, but kicked on into a canter. The air seemed clearer now. The thunder and dark clouds had passed eastwards. At last spring, real spring, was upon them. In two or three days' riding, they would be in Oxford. He would find secure lodgings for Dee. And then he would set about finding what had become of Andrew.

# Act 2
## To Oxford

# Chapter 23

Andrew Woode awoke on a bed of long-dead leaves in forest undergrowth. He had lost track of time. He had drunk water from streams and foraged for food. Exhausted, he had crawled into this place and fallen into a dreamless, animal sleep.

The sleep had been broken by noises close by. Voices. He held still. He did not move nor make a sound. He listened.

One of the voices was a young woman or girl, a few yards away. She was angry.

'He won't have it. He will not have it, and he'll pigging do for you if you try it. More than that, *I'll* not have it!'

'Oh, I'll break you, dell. Don't worry about that.' The man's voice was hard and full of scorn. 'I'll break you like the wild hawk that you are.'

There were sounds of a struggle. They were closer now and Andrew could see them. A slim girl in peasant tatters, a man in a blue velvet doublet. He held her arm and was ripping at her chemise with a farmhand's sickle. She wrenched herself away.

The man laughed. He lurched forward, as though drunk, and grabbed at her skirts. 'What's in there is mine . . .'

Andrew's heart was hammering at his breastbone like a woodpecker's beak boring oak. He knew he should stand up and help her, but that would give him away; that would mean his own death, either here or on the scaffold.

The attacking man grunted with sudden pain. She had kicked him between the legs, hard.

'Bitch slattern!' He lashed out with his sickle but missed. She fell back, sprawling into the brambles.

The man stumbled backwards, swearing oaths, groaning as he clutched his balls. The girl was scrabbling away from the man, trying to get deeper into the thorny undergrowth.

Though he was doubled up, the assailant tried to kick her with his booted foot, but he could not get at her. Still clutching himself, he picked up a rock the size of a brick and flung it at her. It hit her leg and she yelped in pain. She shrank back further into the slashing brambles, thorns tearing her flesh.

'I'll have you – and then I'll slit your throat!' The man groaned again, then staggered away into the forest.

For a few moments the woods were silent. Then the girl moved, trying to free herself from the cruel, tangled briars. Gently picking away every thorn, she edged forward.

Andrew slid out from his hiding place.

The girl gasped with surprise at his sudden appearance in front of her and backed once again into the long, twisting spikes.

'I'll help you,' he said. 'Don't be afraid.'

He thought of a trapped kestrel he had once freed. He found a stout stick and used it to lever the brambles up and away. At last she was out. She stood up and began dusting herself down, removing thorns from her skin, applying spit to the little cuts that decorated her arms and legs, ignoring Andrew.

He stood and gazed at her. She was fair-haired, slim – perhaps a little too slim – and underdressed, given that the day was not warm. She looked up from her grooming and seemed surprised to see him still there.

Andrew suddenly felt incongruous in his torn and filthy scholar's black cap and gown, and his mud-caked town shoes.

'Who are you?' she demanded.

'Master Woode – Andrew Woode.'

'Well, why didn't you pigging help me?'

'I did – I pulled the brambles away.'

'When Reaphook was trying to do me, why didn't you help me then? You must have seen everything.'

Andrew hung his head. He couldn't tell her he was scared for his life in case she summoned an officer of law.

They were in a small glade. Light dappled through the ancient oak and ash. Andrew, not far off six foot tall, was seven or eight inches taller than the girl, though she was obviously several years the elder. She had no fear of him.

'Why you dressed like that? You look a fool.'

'I'm a scholar.'

'What's that? What do you mean?'

He shrugged his shoulders. 'You know. . . a scholar.'

'Well, don't try anything, or I'll kick you in the pigging offals, like I done to Reaphook. What you doing here?'

He said nothing.

'You a prentice, hiding from your master? Perhaps you're a murderer hiding from the justice. You got anything to eat?'

His belly hurt with hunger. Worse than the hunger was the thirst. His throat was parched, though he had licked rain from his cupped hands before the sleep took him. He shook his head.

'How old are you?' she demanded. 'Seventeen? Come with me.'

She reached out and clasped his hand. Her fingers were small and delicate to look at, but the palm was hard and callused.

'Pig it, your fambles are like a pigging babe's bum,' she said. 'What are you, a frater? A fingerer?'

'I told you, I'm a scholar. But if you have food or drink, I would be grateful.'

As he spoke, he was painfully aware of his measured London tones and the grammar-school precision of his words. The girl looked at him strangely. From her clothes – a tattered cheap kirtle and a stained rag of a shirt – it seemed likely to him that she was some sort of farmworker.

'Are you a dairymaid, a shepherdess?'

She frowned a moment, then burst out laughing. 'Oh, Lord, oh dearie me, I seem to have lost my bleating cheats. Are they here in the ruffmans, hiding behind a bush?' She smacked him on the face scornfully. 'Do I look like a pigging shepherdess?'

Andrew felt his face heat up and knew his humiliation was there for the girl to see, crimson all over his cheeks and forehead.

'I just meant . . . I just wondered who you are, that's all.'

'I'm Ursula, who did you think I was? Queen of England? Mort of Rome?'

'I don't know. I don't even know where I am.'

'You're in Ursulaville, my kingdom. How old did you say you were?'

'Thirteen. I'm on the run, hiding. Something happened at my college, and they blame me. They'll hang me if they catch me.'

'So you're one of us then, a felon and a vagabond. What was it – thieving, horse-prigging, cutting purses? Big lad like you should be earning a fair crust of bread by now.'

He shook his head. 'No, I'm no thief. I don't want to say.'

'Well, that's your business.' She reached out, cupped his face in her hands and peered into his eyes. 'Can you read?'

He nodded.

She seemed impressed. 'Good, that'll help you get a living. Forging licences and warrants is the thing for you. You got to have a living. Do you know anything else?'

'I know Latin . . . and Greek.'

'Well, that's going to help us, isn't it?' She shook her head in exasperation. 'As for what you done, that's your business. Just say you're running from the beak. No one'll question that, because we're all on the run from the gallows. And don't ask too many pigging questions, or you'll wake up with your throat cut.'

He nodded.

'Come on, come to the Dogghole and meet the Upright Man. If he likes you, you'll sleep with a full belly tonight. If he don't like you, then get running. Whatever else you do, stay away from Reaphook – and don't let on that you saw what happened. You may be a big lad, but he'll slit you up and spill your guts like a sheep at the shambles.'

The Dogghole was a dilapidated cowshed, close by a tangle of overgrown stone rubble that had once been a farmhouse. All it had to recommend it was that it had some of its roof intact. Half a dozen ragged men were standing outside, picking at bits of meat and drinking.

'Here we are. I met you on the road, right? I'll say it again – don't get in a brabble with pigging Reaphook.'

'Who *is* Reaphook?'

'He's the Curtall – next in line to the Upright Man. All you need know is that they hate each other.'

'What is this place?'

'It's a boozing ken.' She sighed and patted his cheeks, a little too hard. 'And it's called the Dogghole because it's as appetising as a mastiff's arse.'

At the gaping entranceway, a thin one-eyed man sat in the dust. He wore rags. His bony legs were covered in sores and his scrawny hand was stretched out, grasping for coins. The girl kicked him and the beggar cowered. She turned to Andrew.

'He's a dirty palliard, don't give him nothing.'

'Palliard?'

'Burns them sores into his legs with ratsbane, dug his own pigging eye out with a stick. Now no more questions.'

They had walked two miles through the forest, then across fields to get to this place. At times, when she spotted someone, they had crouched out of sight. As they hid, he stole a glance at her and realised that she was strangely beautiful. She was thin and her face was lean, her nose almost too sharp and a little pinched, like the undernourished children he had seen begging on the streets of London and Oxford. She caught him looking at her on one occasion and punched his arm.

'Here, what you looking at?' she had demanded.

'Nothing,' he replied.

'Well, pigging don't,' she said.

A heady brew of smoke and steam billowed out from the Dogghole. Stepping inside the low-ceilinged drinking den, Andrew decided he had entered the devil's inferno. It was packed with men and women, drinking, smoking foul-smelling leaves in nutshell pipes, shouting to be heard above the din. One man had his hand up a woman's skirt and she had her hand in his breeches, both of them groaning lasciviously. Andrew averted his eyes.

Above it all was the fragrant aroma of woodsmoke and the smell of roasting pig. Andrew's mouth watered.

'There should be a keg at the back, I'll get ale.' Ursula said. 'Got any coin?'

'I have a groat.'

'Give me the groat. Got a cup?'

He shook his head while fishing into his pocket for the coin. 'No.'

'You can share mine, but if you filch it, I'll find you and poke a scythe-handle up your arse. You know what *filch* is, don't you? Then we'll find Staffy – and before you ask, he's the Upright Man.'

'Did someone say my name?'

Ursula recoiled. A dark presence loomed over her. Andrew stood rigid, rooted like a tree. The newcomer towered over him and everyone else. He was six inches over two yards tall by anyone's reckoning, and his head scraped the remains of the ceiling. His beard was thick and dark, with flecks of grey. His eyes were deep and searching. He had a long ash staff, which he propped against the wall while he put his enormous hands around Ursula's tiny waist and picked her up as though she were a doll. He frowned as he studied her.

'Someone been cutting you, Ursula Dancer?'

'Brambles. I got caught in pigging brambles running from a bull.'

'Is that so? Is that so, indeed?' He kissed her on the lips and gently put her down. Then he noticed Andrew. 'And what is *this* maggot?' he demanded with a deep-throated growl. 'What has my cat brought home this time?'

'This here's Andrew Woode. He can read.'

'Can he now? Can he so?'

'But he's as pigging daft as a plank of wood.'

'He'll have to pay his due whatever his brains.' Staffy thrust out a hand. 'Sixpence. And *you* owe me a shilling, Ursula Dancer.'

'We've got no coin, but we're going sharking. I'll get some. I pledge it.'

Staffy stared at her doubtfully. 'You better had, lest you want my belt about your arse.' He prodded Andrew with his staff. 'Will he bring trouble down upon us? That is no ordinary apparel he wears.'

'I'll make sure he don't.'

'Then he is your responsibility, Ursula Dancer. You look out for him, and make sure he brings no harm to the band.' The big man put one of his ham-sized hands on Andrew's shoulder, almost crushing it. 'And *you*, Mr Andrew, had better not try putting your paws or anything else on my Ursula. Because if you put your grubby fingers where you shouldn't, I shall snap them in two. And then I'll crack your spine. Do you understand?'

Andrew wasn't at all sure that he did understand, but he nodded obediently.

Staffy looked around the room. Andrew noticed that all eyes were on him, as though he were their king.

'And the same goes for any man,' he boomed so all could hear. 'I'll break any man touches my Ursula Dancer!'

*Chapter 24*

BOLTFOOT COOPER CLIMBED the ladder up to the hay-loft. Ivory was sitting on a bale, playing with a pack of cards.

'That's what brought you to this state in the first place, Ivory. I should burn them if I were you.'

Ivory ignored him. His face was still blue and yellow from the beating, but his hands were unharmed. His fingers skipped like mayflies as he shuffled the pack, fanned them out, took a middle card and held it up. Knave of Hearts. He shuffled the cards again, pulled the top card from the deck and, yet again, it was the Knave of Hearts. Six times in a row he did it, taking the card from top, bottom or middle at will. Boltfoot squinted to see the secret, but could not work out how he did it.

'I can't say I blame them in the Black Moth for tanning your miserable hide,' he muttered.

'That's because you're a lame, good-for-nothing speck of flotsam, Cooper, and know nothing of art.'

Boltfoot felt himself bristling. He didn't, in general, mind when folks laughed at his club-foot. It had not been easy as a child, but he had grown a skin as tough as oxhide since then and usually managed to pay no heed to such comments. But coming from this dog Ivory, it was another matter. One day, he'd teach him a lesson in respect, but not now. They had to be on their way.

'Come on, Ivory. I've got horses. We're going. West of here. Warwickshire. I know a place there. It'll be safer. Mr Shakespeare will know where to find me.'

'And there will be dice there? And a game of primero?'

'Certain to be.'

'You always were a lying, worthless cripple, but I suppose I've got no choice.'

'No. You got no choice.'

Ivory rose from the haybale and nonchalantly stowed his card-pack in his jerkin pocket. Boltfoot climbed awkwardly back down the ladder and watched Ivory follow him.

He heard a sound. Instinct kicked in and he turned, going down on one knee. In a swift movement, he unslung his caliver, which was loaded and ready to shoot.

He relaxed. It was only Jane, standing in the doorway.

He dropped the muzzle of his gun. 'We're on our way.'

'I'm not alone, Boltfoot. There's a man here for you.'

Boltfoot raised the caliver again and trained it on the entranceway behind Jane.

A man in black doublet and hose appeared from the daylight and stepped past Jane. His damascened pistol glinted in his belt. What little was left of his hair was white and he had an open, generous face. He bowed almost imperceptibly. After so many years in service to Lord Burghley and now Sir Robert Cecil, it was his way to show due deference to all men.

'Mr Cooper . . .'

Boltfoot breathed a sigh of relief and stowed his caliver. 'It is a great delight to see you, Mr Clarkson. I was beginning to wonder whether we had been forgot.'

'Indeed not.' Clarkson turned to the other man and bowed

again. 'Mr Ivory, I have come here with orders to take you elsewhere.'

'About time, too. Where we going – London?'

'I'm afraid not. All I can tell you is that you are to be given an assignment. Your especial talent is required, Mr Ivory. And you, Mr Cooper, are to accompany us and continue your watch.'

'Boltfoot,' Jane said, tears pricking her eyes, 'I don't think I can bear much more of this.'

He went over to her and held her clumsily. 'It'll be over soon. You'll see.'

Ivory shook his head and strode out from the barn. 'I can't stand this henhouse a moment longer. Let us go, Clarkson. Cooper can follow when he's done with the wailing.'

Boltfoot's hand went to his cutlass, but Jane stayed it.

Ivory laughed. 'Look at that – she's even telling you when to draw your sword. Who's the cock and who's the hen in your house, Cooper?'

Boltfoot ground his teeth. He was beginning to wonder whether he might kill William Ivory before the Spanish had the chance.

Shakespeare was glad to have Oxx and Godwit with him. The road south was hazardous at the best of times, but with a man such as Dr Dee in tow, the going was slow and they were vulnerable. As they travelled close to towns and villages, they were assailed by the clawed hands of beggar children, the unmistakable evidence of famine. Everywhere they went, they kept watchful eyes open for outlaw bands.

Drawing close to Oxfordshire, they stopped at an inn and noted that men shied away from them. Shakespeare ordered ale from the landlord and asked him what made the people so fearful.

'They think you're soldiers, pressing men for Brittany. There's already been one company through here, like locusts they were, sweeping up our men.'

'Did you see them? Did they come here?'

'Aye, they did. Took my son-in-law, poor fellow. Their captain was a man named Pinkney. Had a face so ravaged it seemed the devil himself had torn at him with his claws.'

*Pinkney*, thought Shakespeare. It was as if the man was dogging his every step.

Andrew felt Ursula's eyes boring into him. He very much wished to be away from this place. Everyone here looked as if they would kill him without blinking.

'If you want to stay alive, you'll have to learn quick,' she said, reading his thoughts. 'Staffy's put me in charge of you, so you'll do as I say. Have you got more coin?'

'No, the groat was all I had.'

'You're pigging useless. Luckily, I got a penny of my own, so I can hire me a fine gown. Let's go a-sharking.'

With Staffy's permission, Andrew and Ursula had eaten their fill of the roasted pork. Now they walked out from the squalor of the Dogghole. It was early afternoon. Two ponies, thin and uncombed, stood gnawing at a poor patch of grass between the drinking den and the woods. Ursula kicked the beggar once more and demanded to know where Maud was.

'I'd tell you if you didn't kick me.'

'I'll kick you the more if you don't.'

The beggar looked at her sullenly through his one, watery eye. He knew better than to cross her. 'She's round the back.'

Ursula pulled back her foot as though she would kick him again. He shied away, but she just laughed and stepped past him.

'Pigging blind cripple,' she said. Then, to Andrew, 'Come on.'

They found Maud on the other side of the old cowhouse. She had a hastily erected table built of staves and an old door. Various items were laid out: jewellery, knives, pans, crockery, a pair of old shoes, a torn calico jerkin, caps, white kid gloves, songbird eggs, horsebread, unidentified flesh.

'Best market stall in the shire, this, Andrew. You name it, Maud's got it or can get it.'

Andrew looked at the array of goods with wonder. He suddenly had a horrible thought. 'Is it stolen?' he said, his voice barely more than a whisper.

She rapped her knuckles on the side of his head. 'Stolen? What a pigging, dirty little boy you are to think such a thing.'

Andrew was not convinced. 'If it was stolen, you – we – could all hang just for knowing about it. It's a felony.'

'Well, it's not. And, anyway, so pigging what? From what you say, you'll already hang for whatever it is you've done. We could all hang or die of the pest or leprosy or a thousand other causes. Not worth worrying about.'

She approached the stallholder, who had leathery skin, wild black hair and a clay pipe hanging from the side of her mouth.

'Maud, I need a fine gown, just for today. I got a penny piece.'

Maud looked her up and down, assessing her size. 'Got just the thing, Ursula,' she said, without removing the pipe. 'Come with me.'

Ursula followed Maud into the woods. Andrew was about to go after them, but Ursula stopped him.

'You stay here and keep your dirty pigging eyes to yourself.'

Andrew stood alone. Men and women with cups of ale and liquor milled around. An old woman came and prodded his costly black gown.

'What you wearing? You look like a justice.'

He towered over her, yet he was rigid with fear.

Suddenly, a few yards away, he noticed the man who had been attacking Ursula in the woods, the man in the blue velvet doublet: Reaphook. He could see him clearly now. He was strong and menacing. His brown hair was cut short and combed forward straight down his forehead, so that its ragged fringe covered his eyebrows. His beard was no more than a tuft in the cleft of his chin and his lips were slightly parted, revealing teeth that protruded like a mule's. A sickle was thrust into his belt.

Reaphook looked at him and their eyes met. Andrew immediately looked away, but the contact was made. Reaphook strode over and stood before him. A thin youth was at his side.

'What are you?' Reaphook demanded of Andrew.

He did not know what to say. Reaphook moved his face closer so that their noses almost touched.

'Well, boy?'

He stepped back. 'My name is Andrew Woode.'

Once again, he was conscious of his soft-bred London voice and the desperate inadequacy of his reply.

'I didn't ask your bloody name, I asked what you are.'

'I'm a fugitive. I've run away. From the law.'

Reaphook raised his hand in a fist. Andrew flinched but, instead of being hit, the dirty, broken-nailed fingers unfurled and Reaphook flicked them twice, indicating that he wanted more information.

'I'm a scholar. At St John the Baptist College in Oxford. I am accused of a felony. They will hang me if I'm caught.'

'Oh, we're a scholar, are we?' Reaphook imitated Andrew's educated voice, then returned to his habitual rasp. 'What you doing here?'

'Seeking refuge, sir.'

'We might hang you for spying on us. Who sent you? Who told you of the Dogghole?'

Andrew didn't know what to say. He looked desperately towards the wood where Ursula had gone with the stall-woman.

'You'll find no answers there. Who was it told you of us? You sent by the headborough or the justice? I'll cut off your bollocks and send them to town cooked in a pie.'

The thin boy at his side laughed.

Suddenly Ursula was there. 'I brought him.'

She was wearing a gown of embroidered yellow and crimson worsted. Andrew could not believe the transformation. Her hair had been disentangled and she looked a lady of breeding, but for the scowl on her face.

'And he's got Staffy's let to stay. So you nor no man can pigging say otherwise, Reaphook. Anyway, Staffy's been looking for you. He wants his due. You owe him more than a mark, last I heard.'

'I've had my fill of giving him coin. His days are numbered.' Reaphook scowled.

'Got a plan, have you? Going to do something dirty? Never stand up to him man to man, would you?'

'You mind your tongue, Ursula Dancer – or one day I'll cut it from your mouth.' He looked her up and down scornfully. 'Don't you look the fine lady. You off to nip a bung?'

'That's my business. Just leave the boy alone.'

He raised his fist again, but Ursula glared back defiantly and spat into the dust at his feet.

The fist hovered, undecided.

'Touch me and I promise you, you'll die, Reaphook. Staffy's in the Dogghole.'

The thin boy stepped forward now, reached out and clasped Ursula's breasts. She pushed him away.

'And you, Spindle.'

'Take on the both of us, will you?' the thin boy said.

'Staffy could kill the both of you with one hand, and you know it.'

Andrew hadn't paid much heed to the boy, but now he noticed that he was astonishingly thin and wiry. His mouth was set in a smile that carried more than a hint of sneer and threat. He reached out again towards Ursula's breasts. This time Andrew stepped forward and pushed the other boy's hands away.

'He's hit me, Mr Reaphook!'

'So he has, Spindle. So he has. What you going to do about it, boy?'

'I'm going to kill him. No one assails me!'

'Pig off, Reaphook. He hasn't hit no one. Just protecting me.'

'We'll see about that.'

The thin boy was squaring up to Andrew. Ursula pulled him away.

'Come on, let's get out of here.'

A group of tattered children had gathered around them, all craning to see and hear, hoping for violence.

'Oh, your boy has done it now, Ursula Dancer,' Reaphook said. He turned to Andrew, raised his hands, fingers apart like bearclaws, and growled.

'Come away, Andrew Woode. Don't listen to him. He's all talk and no prick.'

Reaphook's rotted mouth creased into something akin to a smile, then he spat at the dust where Ursula had spat, and strode away, laughing, the thin boy at his side.

Andrew was shaking. The children looked at him, pointing and laughing.

'Who was that?' he asked.

'The thin one? That's Spindle. So thin he don't get wet in the rain. But just because he's skinny as a stick, don't go picking a fight with him. He's as strong as a badger.'

'I'm not going to fight him.'

'No? He might have other ideas.'

Suddenly she began laying into the children who still clustered around. She beat them with her fists and kicked them with her new-shod feet. They backed away, grumbling and laughing in equal measure.

'Pig off, the lot of you.' She turned to Andrew. 'Come on. We haven't got much time.'

# Chapter 25

THE LAST OF the livestock was being removed from the pens, spring lambs to the slaughter, laying-hens to new owners. It was the end of market day.

In the main square of the small town, well-to-do yeoman farmers talked prices with wool factors, chapmen drank with common herders, all crowding the taprooms around the market place. Much strong liquor had been taken during the day and some of the men wouldn't get home tonight.

Andrew and Ursula stood on the north edge of the square. She put her small, callused hand to his lips.

'Just keep your mouth shut. Watch and learn.'

Three men emerged from a tavern on the east side of the market. The early evening sun lit them. They stopped and gulped in the fresh air. They were well dressed in the staid garb of merchants or town burgesses, but that was the only sober thing about them. They were drunken and loud.

They shook hands with each other. Two tottered off southwards, the third ambled north. Ursula squeezed Andrew's hand.

'Sharking time. Stay here. Don't run. Do nothing but watch.'

She stepped forward and began walking down the street. Andrew was amazed by the way she moved, decorous and elegant, as though she had been born into the gentry. She walked past the drunken yeoman, then stopped, turned back and tapped him on the shoulder. He stumbled back a little and tried to focus on her. She threw her arms around his neck.

'Uncle Jack!' she exclaimed, then kissed him on both cheeks and pressed herself to him.

The man looked bemused but happy to be embraced so. Ursula stood back from him and smiled, pushing out her small breasts provocatively. Then her eyes widened in seeming horror and she put a hand to her mouth.

'Oh, in the Lord's name, I am sorry, sir,' she said, aghast. 'A thousand apologies. I thought you were my uncle. Can you forgive me?'

'There is no injury, young lady. No injury at all, so nothing to forgive.' He grinned inanely and proffered his bearded face. 'You may kiss me again if you so wish.'

He tried to take her back into his arms, but she stepped away, like a demure young woman, mortified by her error. She lowered her head in shame and walked on. The drunk watched her go, shrugged his shoulders, then resumed his stumbling walk until he disappeared into one of the side streets.

A minute after he had gone Ursula was back at Andrew's side.

'That's lesson one. Now, let's leave town directly but slowly. If you run or walk fast you will arouse men's notice, and their suspicions. That's lesson two. A fair day's work. A pigging fair day, I do say.'

Bewildered, Andrew went where she went, walking at her side at a steady pace back out of town into the countryside. Only when they were deep in woods, on a well-trodden path, did she stop. She fished a goatskin purse from inside her skirts and held it up.

'How much do you reckon?' she said, weighing it with her hand.

'Where did that come from?'

'That came from Uncle Jack – he gave it to me. And all for a kiss.'

'You cut it from him!'

Ursula lifted her eyes to the heavens and shook her head in exasperation. She loosened the ties of the purse and poured the contents into the palm of her left hand.

'Now what have we here?' She counted the coins. Eight of them. Then she held up the prize. 'A gold sovereign. Look at that, Andrew Woode! We'll eat for two months on that alone. And a noble, an angel, three crowns and two groats. Did you ever see such pigging bounty!'

'But you've stolen it. You can't just take money from people.'

'Why not? What's the world ever done for me? We've all got to live.'

'Well, I want none of it.'

'Suit yourself. Go hungry. Starve if you want.' She counted the money again.

Andrew stared at her and wondered how something so beautiful could be so rotten. Still clutching the purse, she put her hands on her hips and glared back at him. Without a word, he turned and set off back the way they had come, towards the town. He had no idea what he was going to do, but there was no future with this girl or her villainous friends. She ran after him and stopped him.

'Pig's arse, Andrew, you're stubborn and stupid,' she said. 'What do they teach you at that pigging school you go to?'

'That theft is a mortal sin.'

'And if you got no money and no food, what then? Are you supposed to starve?'

'No. You work.'

'And if there's no pigging work to be had because the crops have failed, if your parents are dead, if you've got no trade, if the commons are enclosed and the headboroughs drive you away, what then? You supposed to lie under a hedge and die, is that it?'

He didn't know what to say.

'Well? Why should I die? I'm seventeen years of age. Why should I lie down and pigging die? And you, what have you done that's so bad you deserve to have your neck stretched? Haven't killed anyone, have you?'

He shook his head. 'No.'

'Anyway, you're a fine one to go all holy book on me. You're already a receiver of stolen property. You ate that pork at the Dogghole, didn't you? You drank that ale? Where do you think that pigging stuff came from? Do them rogues and beggars *look* like pig farmers or brewers to you? Think they got that food and drink legal?' Suddenly her voice softened a shade. 'The Upright Man has told me to look after you, so you better come with me, otherwise he'll take it out on me.'

He reached out and grabbed the hand that held the stolen purse. 'What are you going to do with it?'

'Eat and drink.'

'Why don't you at least do something good with it? Buy yourself a stall at market – earn an honest living.'

'Because the whole world's spoken for, that's why. And I'm not part of it. They'll never let a girl like me in my tatters set up stall. If I went to the burgesses and asked for a stall, they'd have a good laugh, then whip me at the cart's arse for impertinence.'

'Well, at least buy that dress you're wearing. You look something in it – like a lady.'

'I can't go round every day dressed like this! This is work

clothes, for sharking and getting of bungs. You've a lot more to learn, Andrew pigging Woode.'

'Well, you do.'

'What?'

'Look like a lady.'

She was about to say something sharp, but she paused, pulled back her shoulders and held her head at an angle. 'Do I?'

'Yes. You look like a London gentlewoman . . . or a duchess.'

She hesitated a moment longer, then shook her head and pushed him in the chest. 'You're daft as a pig. Come on. It's getting late and I've got to feed you and tell you what's what. No pigging horsebread for us this night!'

With strong, gentle hands, Joshua Peace turned the frail body of the fifth Earl of Derby over on to its front. He began to examine every inch of the bony back, starting at the nape of the neck and working down. The skin was a pallid, mottled blue. He did not expect to find any clues to the noble earl's death, but Peace was painstaking in his work.

He looked up as the door to the chamber opened. A stranger stood there. He wore a sober doublet of black and silver and his hair was cut close to his head.

'Mr Peace?'

'Yes.'

'You are to come away from this chamber. Immediately.'

'I have been instructed to examine this corpse.'

'The instruction is rescinded. Please come with me.'

'And who, might I ask, are you?'

'I am the Earl of Derby's steward. The *sixth* earl's. He wishes you to be out of Lathom House within the hour.'

Peace frowned. 'But I had thought Mr Cole was steward here.'

'He has been dismissed. Now, if you please. Make haste or I shall have you removed.'

'But the commissioners, Egerton and Carey, they will require my report.'

'Indeed they will not. The matter is decided. The late earl was beguiled to his death and they will have him prodded no more. He will be allowed to rest in peace before he is taken away for burial. Good day, Mr Peace.'

The stranger turned on his heel and was gone.

## Chapter 26

FIVE MILES NORTH-WEST of Oxford, John Shakespeare stopped and considered the position. Where could they lodge in the city to garner least attention? He looked closely at Dr Dee. On the journey down here his disguise, such as it was, had been secure enough. But there were likely to be those in the colleges of Oxford who recognised him, for he had been among England's leading men of learning for decades.

It seemed he had four options: take Dee to the town gaol and have him held secure there; enlist the aid of the mayor or local justice and lodge him in their house; take him to a nearby great house or manor where the lord or lady of the estate might be glad of the opportunity to be of service to Cecil and the Queen; or go anonymously to one of the large coaching inns and keep Dee incarcerated under the watchful eyes of Oxx and Godwit.

None of the options was perfect, but the first three seemed the most flawed, for they involved entrusting secret information to new people. He had already done that once, in Lancashire, and had felt uncomfortable, even though Oxx and Godwit had proved themselves stout, reliable men. He did not want to increase the peril in a town like Oxford, where tittle-tattle would be rife.

Dee had been sullen and disconsolate the whole journey,

complaining at regular intervals about being taken away from his treasure hunting and bemoaning the leaving of his precious books and other possessions at Lathom House. Yet it was the loss of his beard and dazzling gown that most irked him.

'You will be my servant in Oxford, Dr Dee, along with Mr Oxx and Mr Godwit. We need a cover story in case anyone should question us.'

Dee said nothing, but looked at Shakespeare with indignation.

'Do you understand?'

'Mr Shakespeare, I see straightway what you are getting at and I consider your proposal outrageous. Your ruse might work with a lesser-known man, but putting me in workday clothes and cutting off my beard will fool no one. I am acquainted with many of the Fellows and senior members of the Oxford colleges.'

Shakespeare laughed. 'I doubt one of them will ever have seen you clean-shaven or in other than your alchemist's robes. They will not be expecting you, Dr Dee, especially in the role of a servant, carrying my bags and tending to the horses. Besides, you will be confined to our chambers most of the time.'

'Tending horses! Carrying bags! I am sixty-seven years old!'

'And as fit as a fighting dog.'

Dee gritted his teeth and looked away with studied disdain.

Shakespeare sighed and shook the reins of his horse. They rode on. He began to survey the fields and woods and farmhouses in vain hope of spotting Andrew. They kept well away from the main road, travelling along farm tracks to ensure they were not followed or watched. They saw shepherds and tillers in the fields and peasant women in the farmyards, but no one else. The countryside was rich with burgeoning crops, fresh green leaves and wild flowers.

An hour later, the four men rejoined the main road. A multitude of church spires loomed in the near distance: Oxford. Soon they entered the busy city, finding their way through the wagon-clogged streets to the Blue Boar Inn. The large stableyard was a din of noise and movement. The hammering of blacksmiths' hammers on anvils rang through the warm summer's air; the smell of horse-dung was all-pervasive. An ostler took their tired mounts and Shakespeare strode into the inn. Dee struggled behind him under the weight of a pack-saddle, with Oxx and Godwit at the rear, carrying the bulk of their baggage.

'You could not have found a more public place in all of England, Mr Shakespeare,' Dee said angrily as they settled into a large room looking out over the yard at the back. 'I believe this place must have thirty or more chambers.'

'Easier for us to get lost in, and not be found.'

'I suspect you were never a scholar of Oxford or Cambridge, sir, or you would have a better grasp of logic.'

Shakespeare ignored the barb. 'As my servant, I should command you to go now and order food for us, but it is probably more circumspect if Mr Oxx or Mr Godwit were to carry out that task. And remember, you will refer to me as master. Like a true and faithful servant. I must give you a name. Mustard, I think. Yes, I shall call you Mustard, for I am certain you will serve me keenly.'

Dr John Dee, Master of Arts from the University of Cambridge, adviser to the Queen, communer with angels and reckoned by many to be the most eminent man of science and letters in England, hesitated a moment. At last he sighed and his shoulders fell.

'Well, I suppose if we are to do this, we must do it properly.'

'Indeed.'

*

'Here you are. That'll make you fall over.'

Ursula passed Andrew a flagon. He sniffed it and grimaced.

'Just drink it!'

Andrew sipped the liquor. His face creased up with disgust.

'Now then, let's put you straight about a few things. First thing you got to know is, you're a vagabond now, and you're in a vagabond band. There's a hundred of us or more at the moment. More you have in a fraternity, the stronger you all are, because it makes it harder for the villagers and farmers to drive you away. But it also means you're more visible. Gets harder to do your business, because doors get locked and purses get hid. If the band accepts you, you'll be looked after. If not . . . well, you don't want to know about that.'

Andrew nodded. He looked around. They were deep in the woods in an area of thick bracken. Ursula had told him they would be staying the night there. He had accepted this without demur, for he knew of no other place to go.

'So, listen, you need to know a few more things,' Ursula continued. 'As Upright Man, Staffy has rights over every rogue and every doxy. No man may break a dell – that's a maiden to you – until the Upright Man has had his turn. What he says goes. No man argues with the Upright Man. Got that?'

Andrew nodded again. He had no intention of arguing with Staffy, nor anyone else. He took another tentative sip of the liquor. He gasped and his eyes widened.

'Next after the Upright Man is the Curtall – and in this band that's pigging Reaphook, like I told you. He's a mean one and wants to be the Upright Man, but Staffy's bigger, stronger and meaner still. Except with me, that is. Staffy's always looked out for me, and I've been with the band since my mother died when I was in swaddling clothes. And he hasn't broken me, though I couldn't say why. There's times I wish he would, just to get it pigging over and done with.'

'Is he your father?'

'No. Does he look like my pigging father?'

Andrew shrugged his shoulders. 'I don't know. I just wondered. He seemed to treat you as if he was.'

'Well, he's not. So stop asking daft questions and just listen. He protects me, that's all. He protects me from Reaphook and Spindle and anyone else who wants to try getting bawdy with me. But that don't mean he's not tough with me, too, because he is. He demands his due in coin and he'll cuff me or beat me when he's in his dark mood. So I keep on the right side of him. Like you will.'

'Why didn't you tell him what Reaphook tried to do?'

'Because I can look out for myself. Anyway, Staffy would get madder than a baited bear, and that's not good for no man. And I don't want to push him because I know that he'd throw me out if I ever threatened the band. But first he'd blame you and throw you out – or do for you.'

'But why are you all here – out in the wild like this? Why aren't you all in villages and towns, living in houses?'

Ursula sighed. 'You can read but you can't think. There's four reasons people become vagabonds. One, they lose their land and grazing rights to the pigging lords and ladies. That's Staffy. The common land he farmed was enclosed and given over to bleating cheats or lowing cheats or some such, so he beat up the landlord's bailiff and ran away to find work. No one wanted him, so here he is. Two, they're born to it – and that's me. My mother was a vagabond so I am, too. Three, they choose thieving and begging because they don't like pigging work. Four, they're on the run from the hangman – that's you, and that's Reaphook.'

'What happened to your mother?'

'Died having me. Staffy says she danced and that she was named Ursula like me.'

'Did he love her?'

'I suppose he must have done, otherwise he'd have had nothing to do with me. All I know is he found a mort as had lost her own babe and gave me to her as a wet-nurse, until she got hanged.' She punched him. 'You got me talking all pigging soft.'

'Tell me about Reaphook. What did he do to deserve hanging?'

Her voice lowered. 'He *says* he killed a man in a knife fight in London town.'

'He's a murderer?'

'The worst sort. I know the true story. He killed a whole family – father, mother and three children. They caught him rifling their house. He was armed with his sickle. Slashed their throats one by one with his sickle until the house was drenched in their blood. Always has his sickle; that's why men call him Reaphook. But I don't like to think on that. Come on, let's have another drink and couch a hogshead. You've worn me out with your pigging daft questions.'

Andrew woke to a bright, warm morning. Above him, the canopy of trees looked friendly for the first time in the days since his flight from Oxford. For a few minutes, he simply lay there, hands behind his head, looking up at the blue sky and the fresh green leaves of this ancient woodland. From a few yards away, he could hear Ursula's light snoring.

Suddenly the snoring stopped. A second later, she was standing over him.

'Let's get moving. Don't want to be here when foresters or huntsmen arrive.'

He had been trying to plan his next move. He needed to find

a way to London or to Stratford. But with no money, no food, no horse, no weapons and no idea of the way, he was helpless. He was very aware, too, that the presence of another person had brought a feeling of safety in the night. He would not go. Not just yet.

# *Chapter 27*

S HAKESPEARE STOOD IN the hall of St John's College, the evening sun slanting in from the west. At his side was the college president, Ralph Hutchinson. They were gazing at a blank space on the wall behind the top table. It was clear from the lighter colouring of the limewash – a square that had been exposed to neither sunlight nor woodsmoke from the hearth – that a picture had once hung there.

'That space, Mr Shakespeare, is the reason for your boy's disappearance,' Hutchinson said.

'I do not understand. What has happened here?'

'Come with me.'

Hutchinson, an intelligent, energetic man with an engaging and commanding manner, led Shakespeare through to a store-room leading off from the hall. A small window allowed in some light.

'Over there, gathering dust.'

In the gloomy light, Shakespeare could not make out what he was supposed to be looking at. Then he saw it, carelessly propped against a cupboard door: a picture, turned so that the image faced inwards and could not be seen. He looked at Hutchinson, who nodded. Shakespeare picked it up and carried it from the room into the light. It was in a heavy, dark-stained frame. He turned it round and put it down against a stone wall, then stepped back and gazed at it. It was a portrait of the Queen, painted in the early years of her long reign. It was one of the better pictures of her that Shakespeare had seen: less flattering than most and more accurate. It seemed to capture more of her stubborn will and less of her supposed beauty.

But that was not what caught his eye. It was the four words scraped across it in red paint, like blood, that held his attention and brought a chill to his bones.

## THIS IS NO VIRGIN

The words were written in a large script, in capital letters, and ran from the bottom left to the top right, covering her magnificent golden gown, her pale, determined young face and her golden hair. The paint of the lettering was thick and had clearly been applied over and over to ensure it could not be removed easily or covered up in any way.

'God's wounds . . .'

Hutchinson sighed. 'Your language, Mr Shakespeare. I know such profanities are common currency at court, but I must insist that you do not use coarse oaths within college bounds. The scholars would be whipped for speaking thus.'

'Are you saying that my boy is responsible for this outrage?'

'Yes, I'm afraid he is. There can be no doubt. He was caught with red hand. There was even red paint on his gown.'

'I cannot believe it.'

'Indeed. I wish it were not so, for we had great hopes of young Master Woode. For his age he had good Latin and Greek, and I am told he was not given over to some of the excesses of the other boys, such as football, playing of cards and . . . other things.'

Hutchinson adjusted his sober clergyman's gown as though

the very thought of the scholars' extra-curricular activities made him hot.

'But which of us knows what demons lurk within the human heart?'

'I know him enough to be certain he did not do this.'

Hutchinson smiled helplessly. 'I fear that your understandable faith in the lad will not save him.'

'I need to know more. Who found the painting like this? Who discovered the paint on Andrew's hand and gown? I also need to know more about his time here and his acquaintances. Please show me to his rooms.'

Hutchinson moved closer to the painting to examine it. He dropped to his knees and narrowed his eyes in contemplation for a few moments.

'We are trying to discover whether there is any way to save the work. Can the writing be removed or painted over? My inclination is to believe it ruined. The artist is long departed from this world.'

'I will find the money to cover the costs. If a replacement is to be commissioned, then I shall pay for it.'

Hutchinson stood up again. 'That is not the point, I'm afraid, Mr Shakespeare. Not as far as the boy is concerned. You must know the severity of this matter.'

Shakespeare bit his teeth together, hard. He understood the implications all too well.

'Can this be kept a college disciplinary affair? At worst, send him down . . . if he be guilty, of course.'

Hutchinson shook his head. 'It is too late for that. This is already a case for the town courts. Your son stands accused of conspiracy against the person of Her Majesty, which is a felony. A charge has been laid and there is a hue and cry for him. When he is arrested, he will be arraigned before the court, tried and hanged.'

'He is a child!'

'Mr Shakespeare, I wish I could ease your distress. What I can say is that Evensong is about to begin and I must be there. I trust you will join me, and go down on your knees in supplication. All that is left is our prayers. If man's justice is unbending in this world, we can at least pray that the Lord will bestow forgiveness upon the boy in the next.'

The room stank of sweaty, seminal adolescence. It had little enough in the way of comfort: books, black gowns and caps hanging from hooks, quills and ink on an otherwise bare table, a full-sized bed, which housed a truckle bed poking out from beneath, boxes of meagre belongings and sweetmeats brought from home but eked out so long they had gone to mould. And over it all, that stale, unwholesome whiff of boy.

Shakespeare paced the room under the suspicious gaze of James Fitzherbert, a Fellow of St John's and Andrew's tutor. He hoped Mr Fitzherbert would prove more enlightening than the time spent at Evensong in the college chapel. He had not enjoyed the excessive display of prayers, Bible readings and sermonising.

'Is this his box?'

A flicker of acknowledgment crossed Fitzherbert's small red mouth. Shakespeare opened the wooden chest, picked up a small silver box and opened it. He stiffened at the sight of a lock of Catherine's dark hair and snapped it shut again.

'Where did he sleep, Mr Fitzherbert?'

'Two or three would use the truckle bed, one or more would share mine.'

'How many scholars share this room?'

'Apart from Master Woode and myself, there are three others: Penn, Talbot and Lebrecht. Master Woode was the youngest.'

Shakespeare examined the black-clad Fitzherbert. He guessed he was in his mid-twenties. He had smooth skin, save for a covering of chin fluff that a good housewife would most likely try to dust away. His eyes were stern and joyless. He stood erect and still, like an underfed guard dog. Shakespeare understood: this was his territory, his little realm where he was king. He did not like strangers intruding.

'Tell me what happened.'

'In what respect, Mr Shakespeare? I am not sure I understand the question.'

'The mutilation of the painting. Who discovered it? How did Master Woode become implicated?'

'One of the college manciples found it at first light when he went to prepare the hall for the morning repast.'

Shakespeare looked out of the leaded window on to the quad. With the fading of the light, the rich honey colour of the sandstone walls had turned to drab grey. Scholars in black gowns, black nether-stocks and buckled black shoes walked about briskly. They did not stop to talk or fight or kick a ball as boys of their age were wont to do.

He had been told that after their supper of beef and oatmeal they were made to do a little exercise before their evening studies. How had Andrew fared here? Hutchinson said he was a good scholar, but this cheerless regimen would test the best of boys. Though scholars in the quad held their heads high and seemed alert, yet he could not quite get a picture out of his mind of the prisoners at Bridewell, milling endlessly, their heads hung in misery. Worst of all was the enclosed world of this rank and stuffy room.

'And then?'

'And then, naturally, an inquiry was set in motion. But the identity of the culprit was already clear, for the paint about Master Woode's person was spotted as soon as he rose from his slumber. The other boys and their property were all examined but he was the only one at fault. He had paint on his hands and on his gown. He had pigments and oil in his box.' Fitzherbert nodded sharply towards the wooden chest.

'Not very clever for a boy noted for his reasoning powers, wouldn't you agree, Mr Fitzherbert? I think a village idiot could have covered his tracks better.'

Fitzherbert said nothing. His closed little mouth clenched tighter.

'So he was apprehended, red of hand. Did he confess?'

Fitzherbert hesitated a moment, then shook his head, almost imperceptibly.

'Did he protest his innocence, Mr Fitzherbert?'

'Yes.'

'But no one believed him.'

'Why should we? We had conclusive evidence to the contrary.'

'But you had him in your custody. How, then, did he escape?'

'Is there any point in all this, Mr Shakespeare? You are like the Inquisition—'

'I don't wish to remind you who I am, Mr Fitzherbert. Just answer my questions.'

Fitzherbert's neck stiffened. 'Very well. He was held here for three days while the President and Fellows discussed the matter with the proctor and decided what to do.' Fitzherbert's tone was crisp, irritable. 'One or two Fellows wished the affair to be treated as a disciplinary matter within the college, but they were greatly outnumbered. This was an attack on the Queen of England, Mr Shakespeare, not just on the college. In days past, as a boy who could read well, Master Woode would have had benefit of clergy and would have been tried at an ecclesiastical court. But nowadays, as you must know, such benefit is applied only *after* conviction. It was determined that the offence was so grave that the town authorities had to be brought in.'

'And then?'

'He was to be taken to the Oxford gaol. Somehow, as he awaited his escort, he slipped the cords that bound him and ran away.'

'Who was in charge of him while he was being escorted to gaol? Was it someone from the college – or a tipstaff?'

'A college servant was with him awaiting the tipstaff. He has been questioned and reprimanded. It seems he left the boy for no more than a few moments to bring him a cup of ale. When he returned, the boy was gone.'

'Just the one man?'

'I believe so. Master Woode was bound. A scholar of thirteen would hardly need a squadron of men to take him the short distance to the gaol.'

Yes, he was but thirteen years of age. But for all that, thought Shakespeare, Andrew was tall and fleet of foot; he doubted very much whether *he* could catch the boy in a race.

A thought struck Shakespeare, born of years working in the devious underworld of intelligencers and assassins. Perhaps someone untied the cords for him. He would need to talk with the college servant.

'Had you noticed any changes in Andrew in the days and weeks leading up to this event?'

'Changes? What exactly do you mean?'

'Was he withdrawn, melancholy? Had he become less attentive to his studies?'

Fitzherbert frowned. 'This is a university college, Mr Shakespeare, not a nursery. Which of us is not afflicted by melancholy at some time or other? I am not a nursemaid. I cannot pay heed to such things.'

Shakespeare looked at Fitzherbert with scorn. The Fitzherberts were an old family who had courted much controversy in recent years, splitting like a cleft log between the causes of Catholicism and the new Protestant Church. Where did this man's heart lie – and to which branch of the family did he belong?

'Mr Fitzherbert, you may not be a nursemaid, but you were put in a position of trust and so I would know more. The names Thomas and Nicholas Fitzherbert must hold meaning for you . . .'

Shakespeare peered closely into the tutor's eyes to see what reaction the names might invoke, for both men were Catholic exiles and deemed traitors: Nicholas was a member of Cardinal Allen's household in Rome; Thomas was a paid adviser to King Philip of Spain.

'They are my cousins. Would you hold that against me? I disown them. Is that enough for you? Have you no cousins that *you* would wish to disown?'

Shakespeare stepped forward with menace and the tutor backed off. 'They are more than mere cousins, Mr Fitzherbert; they are traitors. You cannot cast them off so easily.'

Fitzherbert hunched into his bony shoulders and turned side on, like a cur that has seen the whip. 'I am of the new Church, Mr Shakespeare, the true English Church. I despise the scarlet whore of Babylon and all its acolytes.'

'Indeed?'

Something in this cringing man made Shakespeare want to strike him. Instead he turned away. He was unsatisfied. The man's answers were sound enough, if a little glib, yet the thought of Andrew being in his care made revulsion well up within him. He would have to investigate Fitzherbert in more depth, when Andrew was safe.

*

Janus Trayne lay still in the undergrowth watching the house. He had stayed there twenty-four hours, barely moving a muscle. The occupants of the house came and went. It looked like any other rural cottage. The chickens and pig were fed, vegetables were watered, children played in the muddy yard, the man of the house walked off to his work. There was no sign of Ivory or Cooper. Either they were not here, or they did not leave the house, even for a moment.

It occurred to him that they might be hid near by, in an outhouse or byre. On the second day, one of the young women of the house walked out in her Sunday clothes, carrying a basket. He followed her from a distance and observed her as she went to the market, bought meats and bargained for a kitchen pot, then returned home.

By the end of the day he knew for certain that his quarry was not here. And yet they must have been here or hereabouts, otherwise Ivory's pipe could not have been at the Black Moth in Sudbury.

He watched a little longer. He needed to ask some questions and get some honest answers, at the point of death if need be. The master of the house, a man in his fifties, strode out in the early evening. Trayne guessed he was going to the alehouse and trailed him through woods. The man slowed down and stopped, as though considering which path to take. Trayne lunged forward. In a rush he was upon the man, thrusting the muzzle of his wheel-lock pistol into the side of his head.

'Mr Cawston? You are Mr Cawston, I believe.'

Tom Cawston stood back from the pistol. 'What if I am?'

'This is loaded and will kill you if you do not answer me straight.' Trayne noted a lack of fear in the man's eyes and pushed the muzzle forward into the middle of his face. 'Do not think I jest.'

'Ask away then.'

'I am looking for two men, William Ivory and Boltfoot Cooper. I know they are here.'

'Friend of theirs, are you? Well, you've missed them. They were here but they've gone, and they didn't tell me where.'

Trayne was taken aback. He was accustomed to see the fear in men's eyes. 'Are you not afraid of me?'

'Afraid of you? In God's name, why would I fear you? I go to church and I say my prayers and live in peace with the Lord. If this is my last day, so be it. You can pull the trigger and I'll know nothing about it, or you can go on your way and leave me to live out my days.'

'Or I could cause you much pain and force you to reveal the whereabouts of those I seek.'

Suddenly, Tom Cawston threw back his head and laughed out loud. 'You must think me an ignorant country fellow. Indeed, you must think us *all* ignorant country doddypolls. Look around you, Mr Pistol, look around you.'

And he laughed even louder.

Trayne swivelled his head. Ahead of him and slightly to the right was a man with a bow, its string drawn, an arrow set and pointing directly at him. And then he saw another archer, to the left.

'Did you think we weren't expecting you? Did you think you could trawl these parts, hiding in woods and bracken, asking questions in towns and villages and not be noted? Shoot me if you like, but you'll have two arrows in you before I hit the ground.'

Trayne had the weapon in his left hand. His right arm was still weak and painful. He realised the gun was shaking. He began to back off. The two bowmen advanced. Trayne stumbled on a branch but kept his footing. With his damaged right hand, he grabbed out and caught Tom Cawston by the lapel of his jerkin. The pain in his wrist was excruciating, but he pulled

Cawston forward roughly. The archers hesitated. It was just enough for Trayne. He pushed Cawston away, turned, ducked low and ran into the depths of the wood. An arrow brushed past his temple. Another stabbed into a tree at his side. Behind him he heard laughter and footfalls.

Deeper and deeper into the wood he ran. Slowly the noises of his pursuers faded, then died. Somehow he had escaped. He crossed himself and thanked God, then cursed, for it seemed he was no nearer his quarry than he had ever been.

# *Chapter 28*

Andrew and Ursula did their best to keep away from Reaphook and Spindle. It was a situation that could not last.

The evening was warm. Staffy was not around. Ursula and Andrew were at the Dogghole, cooking pigeon at the fire. A gaunt young man, newly arrived, was playing a tune on his wood whistle, hoping to get a bit of food for his pains.

Ursula repeated her refrain, 'Don't give him nothing.'

Suddenly, there was movement behind them.

'Well, well.'

They turned to see Reaphook and Spindle standing over them.

'Pig off, Reaphook.'

'I wondered where you two had got to.'

'Do you want Staffy to know what you been trying?'

'Staffy ain't around.'

'But he will be.'

Spindle moved forward and stroked her hair. She shook him off. He laughed.

'Word has it that you got coin, Ursula Dancer,' Reaphook said. His hand was on the haft of his sickle. 'Did some good sharking on market day. I don't believe I've had my share.'

Ursula jumped to her feet and faced him aggressively. 'The

only one gets a share is the Upright Man. And Staffy's had his coin from me. You get nothing.'

'How about a kiss?' Spindle said. He tried caressing her waist, but she brushed his hand away as she had done before.

Andrew leapt to his feet. 'Why don't you leave her alone?'

'Oh dear, why don't you leave her alone, Mr Spindle,' Reaphook said, imitating Andrew's refined vowels once more.

'And you leave *him* alone. Come on, Andrew Woode, we're going. It stinks of dog turd around here.'

'Not so fast.' Spindle had grabbed her by the skirts. 'We're having your coin.'

Andrew lunged forward and pushed the thin boy away.

Spindle clutched his chest in feigned horror. 'Why, Mr Reaphook, he has hit me again. That's twice now.'

Reaphook grinned, his mule's teeth splayed across the lower part of his face. 'There's only one way to settle this, then. There'll have to be a challenge fight. Only way to settle a feud in the band. Staffy's own rules, I do believe.'

'That's it,' Spindle said. 'I want a challenge fight. Tomorrow morning.'

Ursula shook her head. 'He hardly touched him. You got no cause for a fight.'

'The challenge is made. That's it. Even Staffy can't break it.' Reaphook eyed Andrew up and down. 'Good fighter, are you? You better be, because you're fighting young Spindle here. Vagabond law. You hit him – you fight him. One hour after daybreak. Be there or begone. He'll enjoy doing for you, won't you, Spindle?'

A mere fifteen miles away from Andrew and Ursula's wood-land lair, Shakespeare stood in the gatehouse of St John's

College. He was itching to get away, to hunt for Andrew, but there was no point in going before dawn and he had business here before leaving.

He examined the manciple's face for signs of nervousness or guilt, but could detect nothing. The college servant was in his late twenties or early thirties. He was squat and bent, but looked strong enough to hold a boy of Andrew's age.

'How did he make his escape, Mr Porter?'

'Slipped his ropes. Here –' he picked up a length of cord from the table – 'this is the very one used to tie the boy. I believe Tutor Fitzherbert tied him, so blame him if the knots were too loose.'

'But you left him – and that's when he got away?'

'Aye, the tipstaff was a long time coming. Poor lad was dying of thirst. So was I! Never occurred to me that he'd work himself free of the rope.'

'Did you see Andrew Woode run? Did you see what direction he went?'

'No. When I came back with the ale he was gone. No idea where he went. But the justice's men will find him soon enough, I'm certain. Is that all, Mr Shakespeare? I have work to do.'

'For the present, Mr Porter.'

Shakespeare walked through the streets of Oxford. Even this late in the evening there were people about, going in and out of the various alehouses, brothels and taverns. Had Andrew made for one of these dens? Had he tried to find lodging – or did he, perhaps, have a friend in the town who had given him a space in a room? It seemed unlikely. Shakespeare guessed that Andrew's instinct would have been to get out of Oxford as quickly as he could and make straight for the countryside. He would start his search at first light.

At the Blue Boar, he found Dee in the company of Oxx and

Godwit. Shakespeare sent the two guards out for a break, their first in many days, and told them to be back by midnight.

'And what of me, Mr Shakespeare?'

'We will stay here together. I wish to hear your thoughts.'

Shakespeare proceeded to tell the old alchemist all that had passed at St John's, along with the conversations with the college president, Hutchinson, James Fitzherbert and the manciple, Mr Porter. At last he was silent.

'Your first instinct is that Andrew is innocent of this charge, Mr Shakespeare?'

'Yes . . .' He hesitated. 'But I know, too, that the boy is angry. And he tends towards papism. His family has suffered grievously these past years. His mother died young, his father died after being tortured for his faith. If he has committed this madness, he has reason enough, though no excuse.'

'Let us go with your first instinct. Let us say he is innocent. And if that is the case, then it means someone else is guilty. And that someone has deliberately laid the blame on Andrew.'

'Yes.'

'Had the painting been protected – guarded – in any way?'

'I don't believe so.'

'Then I imagine almost anyone in the college – scholar or tutor or servant – could have inflicted the damage.'

Shakespeare nodded. 'That must mean well over a hundred, perhaps two hundred people would be suspect.'

'But we can narrow it down,' Dee continued, putting his thoughts in order. 'Not everyone would have access to the boy's room. How many are lodged there?'

'Besides Andrew? Three boys and their tutor, Fitzherbert.'

'So any one of those four, or their servants, could have put paint on the boy's gown and placed the pigments in his box?'

'Again, yes.'

'But we can narrow it yet further. There was paint on his

hands, too. That would have had to be done during the night, stealthily, while he slept. Are there any servants lodged in the room?'

'No.'

'Then it had to be one of the other boys – or the tutor.'

Shakespeare listened carefully to Dr Dee's analysis. It was clear and logical; his own mind had been a fog.

'What of the other option: that Andrew is guilty?'

'You say the boy is clever. Why did he implicate himself so? Why did he wait to be caught instead of making good his escape straightway? There is no logic there, Mr Shakespeare.'

'Indeed, not.'

'And even if, for argument's sake, he *is* guilty, then it would be reasonable to assume that he had already organised his flight from England to France or Rome, and would most likely be on his way there already. In which case, your decision to search in this area would be futile.'

'But we have agreed that it is more likely that he is innocent.'

'Yes, Mr Shakespeare. I think we are agreed on that. Yet in running from the college to save himself from the noose, he has done the cause of his defence no favours. Fleeing justice will always make a man seem guilty.'

What Dee said was harsh but true.

'So you must do two things, Mr Shakespeare. You must not only find the boy, Andrew, but must also discover the true culprit.'

Shakespeare nodded. Yes, he would do that. And he could not but wonder at the timing of this grim event. It was almost as if someone had done this thing intending to draw him away from his inquiries in Lancashire. If so, then they had succeeded. But that was something to be investigated another day; finding Andrew must come first.

He sat at the table, dipped one of Dr Dee's quills in an

inkhorn and began to write to Sir Robert Cecil. The letter said simply:

'*Sir Robert, I have urgent business in Oxford concerning my son. This may take some little time and I beg your indulgence in the matter. Suffice it to say, my charge is safe and will remain so. I will report to you again as and when I may. Your faithful servant, John Shakespeare.*'

He handed it to Dee. 'Ask Mr Oxx to find a messenger in the morning.'

'Cecil will not be happy.'

No, Shakespeare knew that. His letter would not be at all well received.

Close by the Dogghole, four fence posts had been driven into the ground and a rope strung around them to form a square, ten feet by ten feet. A crowd of the dispossessed was gathered around it, perhaps eighty strong. They were noisy and riotous. Drink was already being taken, despite the early hour. Men, women and children had appeared from their secret sleeping places in barns and copses. They smoked pipes of woodland leaves and clasped beakers of strong liquor and ale. They cheered and barracked the empty square, and had brawls of their own as they waited expectantly for the entertainment. There would be blood and broken bones here this day. Perhaps a death. That was worth waiting for.

The embers of last night's fire had been stoked up and those fortunate enough to have food were cooking it: songbirds or their eggs, young hedgehogs, skinned weasel, rabbits, broth, potage of foraged leaves, roots and rancid meat found on the forest floor. Others were busy placing bets on the fight. The bets were not on the outcome, which was reckoned by all a certain win for the thin and wily Spindle, but the duration of the fight and the nature of Woode's injuries.

'Ten to one a busted arm! Four to one a gouged eye!'

'Even money a broke nose!'

A short distance away, inside the Dogghole, Ursula slapped Andrew's face. It hurt, and he sat back with a jolt.

She laughed. 'You look pigging awful. I never saw a boy so cup-shotten as you last night.'

'My head. I can't fight.'

He was sitting on a three-legged stool, his shoulders slumped.

'Well, if you don't, you'll have more than the catchpoles and constables to run from. Get out there and do your best.'

She pinched his nose to make him open his mouth, then pushed in a hunk of bread. She held a beaker of ale up to his face. 'Drink. Wash it down. It'll stop your shakes.'

He wanted to be sick again, but tried chewing as ordered, then took a sip.

'That's not so pigging bad, is it? Now remember what I told you. Spindle will fight dirty. He'll trip you, stamp on your balls and gouge your glazers. He might be pike-thin but he's a mean, slippery gullion. You're a strong lad, too, though, and you're bigger than he is.'

Suddenly the doorway darkened. Staffy was ducking in, then rose to his immense height. 'Is he ready, Ursula Dancer?'

'Ready as he ever will be. Don't let Spindle hurt him too bad, Staffy. He's like a big pigging baby and I doubt he's ever had a fight in his life before.'

'It's out of my hands. The challenge has been made. You're the one who let it come to this, Ursula Dancer. If he wants to stay with us, he's got to see it through.'

'You're wrong, Staffy. This isn't my doing.'

'Maybe so, Ursula, but you should have steered clear of Reaphook. He'll use anything to stir his followers. Well, I'm going to have it out with him, and soon. That'll be the next challenge fight. There isn't enough space for both of us in this fraternity.'

Andrew was only half listening. He grimaced and chewed. His head and body ached, but he was clear about what was happening. He should be up and running, not sitting around waiting to be mashed. But if he didn't have the strength to run, how was he to fight?

'What if I don't *want* to stay with you?' he said weakly as he managed to swallow the last bit of bread. 'If I go now, you'll have no more trouble on my account.'

Ursula shook her head. 'If you go now, you'll have handed victory to Reaphook. Anyway, how you going to survive on your own? You can't feed yourself and you can't even steal. If you don't have a band around you to look out for you, teach you what's what, you'll be swinging from a tree within a week.'

'I told you. I've got to get to London. That's where I live. My family's there. They'll look after me.'

'And it'll be the first pigging place the law looks for you. If you've done a hanging felony, they'll send a catchpole up to London to bring you back.'

A cheer went up from outside the filthy, crumbling building. Staffy nodded sharply. 'That's enough talk. Spindle's arrived. Get your boy out there, Ursula.'

Spindle was weaving from side to side, parrying and ducking imagined punches. As Andrew and Ursula approached the fighting-square, the crowd murmured, but Spindle did not turn to look at them.

All the eyes in the audience were on Andrew, sizing him up. Was he worth a wager? Could he spring a surprise? Their scornful faces said No.

'Fight for your life, Andrew Woode,' Ursula whispered

urgently in his ear. 'Even if you're down and bloody, show your courage.'

Andrew stumbled forward as if in a waking nightmare. Suddenly, the rope was held up and he was pushed under. He was in the fighting-square. He turned and tried to crawl back out, but half a dozen hands pushed him in again.

Ursula looked on with trepidation. Suddenly Reaphook was at her side, leering. He grabbed her arm.

'We can stop this now, dell. It's your choice.'

Ursula recoiled from the harsh voice in her ear and the iron grip of his hand. She tried vainly to shake him away. 'Pig off, Reaphook.'

He pulled her to him. His breath smelt of ale and meat. 'Open your legs, give me what's mine and I'll save your young friend. I laid the challenge, I can stop it.' His other hand went to her skirts, grabbing at her through the coarse tatters.

She shied away from him again. She had a knife in her hand, and thrust its point at his belly. 'Reaphook, I swear I'll do for you.'

He laughed and pressed his belly into the point of the knife. 'Then he'll die in there. Your choice. Watch Spindle do for him. He's got my orders: no quarter. Only one gets out alive.'

Staffy was now in the middle of the square, his enormous bulk dominating his surroundings. He had his six-foot ash staff gripped in his right hand. He didn't have to hush the crowd. They went quiet at the mere sight of him. Even Spindle turned round and ceased his shadow-fighting.

'You know why we're all here,' Staffy boomed. 'We've got a fight, called by young Spindle. He reckons he's got a quarrel with a newcomer named Andrew Woode. There's only one way to settle it. I'm the Upright Man of this band and I say the fight is over only when *both* boys agree it's over. Now let's see if Woode is as hard as his name. Fight on. Nothing barred.'

An old woman screeched, 'It's like putting a week-old chick against a fighting-cock.'

Staffy ducked under the cord and out of the square. As he moved towards Ursula, Reaphook pulled away from her and slunk off.

The two boys were alone in the fighting-square, facing each other over a distance of five feet. Spindle had rags wrapped tight around his fists and around his feet. Andrew looked incongruous in the remains of his black college gown, spattered with mud and a few remaining daubs of red paint. Spindle began weaving his shoulders again, grinning that endless grin, as though his mouth had been permanently frozen in the shape of an upturned horseshoe. He swaggered towards Andrew, winked at him, then punched him in the stomach. Andrew doubled up, winded.

'Go down on your belly, lick the dirt off my feet and I might let you live.'

Andrew gasped for breath. 'You win. I never wanted this fight.'

'Well, you got it. And I win when I say I've won.'

As he spoke, he wheeled on the balls of his feet and lashed out backwards with his right foot, cracking hard with his heel into Andrew's shin. Andrew yelped and fell backwards against the rope. Spindle hadn't stopped turning. He came around with his fist, which caught Andrew's temple a crunching blow. The older boy's knee jerked up and smacked hard into Andrew's balls. Andrew howled and crumpled to the dusty ground.

The crowd roared approval. 'Cut him, Spindle. Cut him and cook him.'

Spindle put his foot on the side of Andrew's head, wedging it against the stony earth. He put all his weight on it and twirled around, grinding the head down, wrenching Andrew's ear.

✠ 253 ✠

Ursula turned to Staffy. 'Make him stop.'

'I can't.'

Spindle was dancing around the square, feinting punches and kicks. Andrew was lying still on the ground, blood seeping from his torn ear. Spindle went back to him, knelt at his side, grasped his balls and squeezed them with a grip like a smithy's vice.

'Do you like that?'

Suddenly Andrew lashed out with his elbow and tried to scrabble away. The blow didn't hurt Spindle, but it caught him by surprise and he loosened his grip. Andrew crawled to his knees, his face twisted with pain. Spindle jumped to his feet with the agility of a cat, then kicked upwards, hitting Andrew an uppercut blow to the chin with his bony, bandaged foot. Andrew sprawled backwards, his head smacking down with a juddering crack.

The blood-hungry crowd laughed and jeered.

Spindle was angry now, enraged by Andrew's blow. The lurid cries of the onlookers intensified his bloodlust.

'I've had enough of this game,' he said.

Across the square, Ursula locked eyes with Reaphook. He was smirking. She could bear it no longer and moved forward, pulling up the rope to the fighting-square. If Staffy wouldn't put a stop to it, she would. But Staffy's enormous hand grabbed the back of her ragged chemise and dragged her back.

She struggled to get free, but he was too strong.

'No, Ursula Dancer. I've protected you these many years, but not this. You can't interfere in a challenge fight. If it's his time to die, so be it.'

Spindle had produced a knife. It was long and narrow with a dull blade but a bright, honed edge. He was pulling Andrew's hair back and the blade was at his exposed throat. His voice was hoarse, quiet and gloating in Andrew's bloodied ear.

'Used to work at the shambles, didn't I? No difference between bowelling a sheep and a man. I'll drain your blood and cut you into joints, ready for the pot.'

The crowd hushed in taut expectation. The gamers who had wagered on this outcome kept a close watch on those who had taken their bets to be sure they didn't run.

'One little slice,' Spindle said.

His raised his eyes and looked towards Reaphook for a signal. Reaphook nodded. Spindle grinned back.

'One little slice and a rush of lovely blood . . .'

## Chapter 29

A PIERCING WHISTLE shrilled in the morning air. The frenzied shouting of the crowd ceased instantly, leaving only an alarmed murmur. Eyes turned away, scouring the landscape. In the distance, they could hear dogs barking.

The vagabonds knew what it meant. The whistle had been blown by their lookout. The townsfolk, farmers and their hired hands were coming to drive them on. They had been expecting this for many days.

Spindle's blade hovered like a dragonfly over Andrew's tender skin, but the audience was already dispersing.

'I think I'll save this pleasure for another time.' He slid the knife away and thrust it into the waist of his breeches, then pulled Andrew to his feet. 'Arm yourself.' He pulled one of the fighting-square posts from the ground and flung it to Andrew.

Instinctively, Andrew caught the pole. Ursula was at his side now, looking at his injured ear.

'You'll live,' she said. 'Come on, come with me.'

Spindle was curling the fighting-square's rope around his shoulder and gathering the posts to hand out.

Staffy banged his staff on the side of a crate. All eyes turned to him. 'Order now. We've got the men, but we must have order.'

'We're standing and fighting, yes?' Reaphook snarled.

'Mr Reaphook, shut your mouth and listen. We fight if I say so.'

'Only—'

'Mr Reaphook, if you say another word, I will push my staff down your gullet until it comes out your arse. Now go – take the eastern flank and wait for my word. I'll hold the centre and the west. As soon as I know their numbers I'll flag the signal. Black, we fight; white, we disperse.'

Reaphook was about to say something else, to protest, but Spindle touched his arm and shook his head. Together, they turned away and began rounding up men. Spindle glanced at Andrew, as if wondering whether to include him in his squadron, then looked away.

This band of men, eight-strong, spread out towards the rising sun with the blue-velvet figure of Reaphook in the centre, sickle in hand. They had staves, old billhooks, knives and clubs. One man powdered an arquebus and tried to light the match as he followed them at a fast trot. They were a ragged company in a strange assortment of clothes. Some looked tough, some frail. The rest of them, men, women and children, gathered close around Staffy.

'Get up on the roof, Ursula Dancer. Tell us what you see.'

Staffy held out his enormous hands as a stirrup for her foot, then raised her to the broken, perilous roof of the Dogghole. Nimbly, she scrambled up. Standing with one foot on an exposed rafter, the other on the top of the wall, she shielded her brow with her small hand and looked northwards from where the barking seemed to have come.

'What do you see?'

'Men, mastiffs on leashes. They're stretched out across the field. Coming this way.'

'How far are they?'

'Two furlongs, moving fast. I see bows and pikes and bills. Hagbuts, too. Half a dozen hagbuts, I'd say. Some men riding. More dogs at their hoofs. Archers, six archers.'

'How many all told, Ursula? How many?'

'Twenty-five . . . no, thirty-five. Six, seven horsemen.'

Staffy banged the empty keg again. The attackers were too well armed; the vagabonds would be overwhelmed. He tied a grubby white kerchief to the end of his staff and held it aloft, waving it.

'Bills and pikes are one thing,' he said to those around him. 'Bowmen and mounted shot are another. We retreat. Go your own ways. We'll meet at the white horse, where I will decide our next move. Good fortune to you all.' He turned back to the roof and helped Ursula down. 'Come on, Ursula Dancer, we got to go and quick. You take the boy. Look after yourself, girl.'

She looked at Andrew, and his bruises and cuts, and shook her head in resignation.

'At least tell me you can run, Andrew Woode.'

He grinned. 'Oh yes,' he said. 'I can pigging run.'

Walter Weld stood on the strand at Deptford and looked about him. His hand rested on the stock of his pistol. This was all familiar territory. He felt at home here with the caw of the gulls, the swoop of the cormorants, the slap of the sails, the bustle of a war machine under construction. He believed he knew every inch of the dockyards from here eastwards – Blackwall, Woolwich, Gravesend. This was where he needed to be. If Trayne did not manage to lay hands on the perspective glass first, then it would pass through these ports and quays. And with the war in Brittany coming to a head, he rather suspected it would be here very soon.

He turned away from the river and walked towards the

Royal Docks. Time to lay the ground. He knew exactly what needed to be done.

'I trust you realise how valuable I am to this realm, Cooper? I tell you this: I have brought more gold to the Queen's coffers than all your Drakes, Frobishers and Raleghs.'

'Is that so, Mr Ivory?' Boltfoot said.

'You may scorn me, but I tell you it is true. More gold from my blue eye than ever your London merchants or pirate venturers could bring in.'

They were on horseback. Ivory, Boltfoot and Cecil's man Clarkson, moving southwards through Essex farmland at a pace slow enough to shame a side-saddled nun. Clarkson was a few lengths ahead. Boltfoot kept at Ivory's side, his hand always close to his loaded caliver and his cutlass. From time to time he urged Ivory to go faster, but received nothing in return but derision.

'What's the haste? I like the countryside. Don't worry, they'll wait for me. They need me; that's why little Cecil sends his best man for us.'

Boltfoot gritted his teeth in frustration. Ivory had been increasingly talkative since recovering from his injuries; Boltfoot wished to God he would return to his old, taciturn ways.

'So where did all this fabled treasure come from, Mr Ivory?'

'King Philip of Spain himself.'

'You had better tell me about it, then. For I would be glad to hear such a faerie story. Let us hear your tall tale!'

'Very well, then, Mr Cooper. I shall tell you. Do you know what this instrument is that I carry? This perspective glass?'

Boltfoot nodded, warily, not certain how much he was supposed to know. 'My master has told me something of it.'

'I first had use of it in the summer of 1592, two years past. I was keeping watch atop the mainmast of the bark *Dainty* as she patrolled west of the Azores looking for the plate fleet.'

'I know the *Dainty*. A fair ship.'

'Aye, fair enough. Day after day I was up there, observing the horizon through the glass. Then, on the third day of August, I caught sight of a speck of dust on the ocean's rim. At first, I turned the strange instrument around to check whether a mote or splash of spray had polluted the glass. It was clear. Peering through the tube again, straining my bright eye, I began to realise that I was looking at the sails of a wallowing carrack of enormous dimensions, like a sea monster.'

'I've seen a few sea monsters myself,' Boltfoot said, eyeing him wryly. 'In truth I do believe I am looking at one now.'

Ivory ignored the barb. 'Descending the rigging in haste, quick as a monkey, I alerted the captain, Thomas Thompson. A good man, that. A fine ship's master. He did not waste a moment. Straightway, he ordered the crew of the *Dainty* to battle stations and commanded the helm to drive the bark forward with the wind to intercept and attack the approaching carrack before its own master had any chance to turn and flee or run out the guns. They didn't even know we were coming for them until we were almost upon them, so great was the advantage afforded by my work with the perspective glass. So what do you think, Cooper?'

*I think I have never heard you string together so many words, and that I preferred your sullen silences.*

'You tell *me*, Mr Ivory. You tell me, for I am sure you will.'

'Only the bloody *Madre de Dios*, wasn't she! Only the largest ship the world has ever known – seven decks high, one thousand six hundred tons in weight, and with cannon enough to take on a whole flotilla of royal ships! Did that scare Captain Thompson and his crew? It did not. The *Dainty* may be no more than four hundred tons, but she is nimble and fleet – and full of courage. We pressed home the advantage and moved to engage the great carrack. Like an English mastiff against a Spanish bull, we came to close quarters and held on to the *Madre de Dios*, snapping at her with a constant barrage of gun-fire until the rest of Frobisher's ships could catch up with us and enter the fray. But it was *we* that held her, *we* that did the damage. The *Madre de Dios*'s decks ran with blood and we had our prize for Her Royal Majesty.'

'I'm amazed and astounded she didn't bestow a knighthood on you for uncommon valour, Mr Ivory.'

Ivory was too busy talking to listen.

'The treasure we captured was enough to take a man's breath away. Thousands upon thousands of rubies, chests full of dia-monds and pearls, gold in such abundance the royal coffers could not hold it, silks and calico, camphor and perfumes, spices and ebony. All that and four hundred blackamoors that the Spaniards had taken for slavery. We did set them down upon an island of the Azores, but I could not say what became of them. It was the treasure we all had eyes for; no room for slaves. I heard Ralegh did say later that it was all reckoned at five hundred thousand pounds, which is a number I never even heard of before then. *That* was the worth of my blue eye to the Queen and this realm, Cooper. Think on that if you will. That's why you will show me the respect I deserve.'

Boltfoot had had enough. He kicked on a little way ahead. He looked around him constantly. Every time they passed a horseman or wagon, he expected to see a man in a voluminous cape with a wheel-lock pistol. That wounded wrist must be healed by now. He was out there somewhere . . .

Joshua Peace woke early at his chamber in the Eagle and Child in Ormskirk. His first instinct on being dismissed from Lathom House had been to leave immediately for London. Yet his loyalty to John Shakespeare and his irritation at being evicted so peremptorily by the sixth earl and the commissioners had made up his mind. He would stay a little longer and keep his ears open.

He lay on the bed and wished himself anywhere but here. The room smelt stale, of smoke and sweat. But he would rise from the bed soon and venture out. He wished to find Cole, if he was still in the area after being dismissed as steward of Lathom House, and he wanted to talk with Mistress Knott.

There was a rap of knuckles at the door. He jumped up, smoothed his nightshirt to ensure he was decent and opened the door.

A surly youth stood there, scowling insolently. 'Are you Peace?'

'*Mr* Peace. Yes, I am.'

'You're to come with me.'

'Who are you?'

'Parfitt. Attorney Hesketh demands your presence.'

'Tell your master that I shall be happy to attend his offices later this morning, after I have broken my fast.'

'Now. He wants you now.'

'Well, Master Parfitt, you can tell him I shall see him in two hours' time. Good morning to you.'

He began to close the door, but Parfitt's foot was already there.

'You can walk across the square with me, Peace, or I shall drag you through the mud and horse-dung. Which is it to be?'

Peace sighed heavily. 'Wait one minute. I will clothe myself and come with you.'

Thomas Hesketh leant back in his richly carved oak chair.

'You know why I have summoned you here, Peace?'

'No, Mr Hesketh.'

'Because you are in possession of a letter, a traitor's letter, which should have been handed to me when first it was discovered about the person of the boy-priest Lamb.' Hesketh stretched out his fat hand. 'Give it to me now.'

'I have no letter.'

'Where is it?'

'I have no idea what you are talking about, Mr Hesketh. And I do not much care for your manner of asking.'

Hesketh turned to his assistant. 'Search him, Parfitt. See what you can find. If it's not on him, search his room at the Eagle and Child.'

'By what authority—'

'My own.'

Parfitt was standing in front of him, unhooking the buttons of his doublet. Peace struggled, but the boy, though lean, was powerful and tore the garment from him. He proceeded to feel every seam, paying particular atttention to the padded fore-parts and sleeves. The boy took a poniard from his belt and slid it through the stitching, then pushed his ink-stained fingers up into the gaps, pulling out wool stuff. Peace looked on in horror.

When Parfitt discovered nothing in the doublet, he turned his attention to Peace's shirt, then his hose, upper stocks and nether-stocks, patting the searcher most intimately. Thomas Hesketh, attorney to the Duchy of Lancaster, watched all the while, his moist eyes half hidden in the folds of his overfed face.

'Nothing, Mr Hesketh, sir. It's not on him.'

'Go to his chamber then.'

'This is an outrage!'

Hesketh glared at him. 'I don't know what you think you are doing in Lancashire, Peace. But I want you away from here by nightfall. If you are not gone by then, you will be arrested and charged with necromancy, for men have seen you consorting with the dead, casting spells over bodies, bidding them to rise. Am I clear, Mr Peace? Am I clear? Now get out of my sight – and do not return to the inn. Any possessions found there by Parfitt will be burnt.'

Gathering up his pack-saddle and sword, Shakespeare strode out into Oxford's morning sunshine. The day was already warm and would be hot.

He looked about him. Who here might know the truth of Andrew's flight from justice? What would he, Shakespeare, do in the same circumstances? Where would a boy alone head for? His first instinct, surely, would be to run wildly and then, when he had time to consider his options, to try to head for Stratford or London. Yet, at the front of Shakespeare's mind there was still the fear that this had all been planned, and that Andrew might already be making the crossing to France, assisted by the underground network of Jesuits and seminary priests so active in England these days. Then he would follow the long trek south to the Catholic colleges of Rheims or Rome.

Shakespeare rode northwards and westwards. A mile outside Oxford, he turned left along a track, starting a tight circuit around the city, anticlockwise. He would do a circle at a time, like the rings on a target, calling at every village along the way, and speaking to every man, woman and child he encountered.

At a fork in the path, he spotted a group of farmhands sitting at the side on a grassy bank, eating their bread and drinking their cider. He stopped.

'I am seeking someone, a runaway boy. A tall, strong lad. He would be dressed in black like a scholar.'

The men looked at each other blankly and shook their heads. He thanked them and rode on. Again and again he hailed passers-by and workers, asking each the same question. Some thought for a while, made suggestions as to where he might have gone, but none was convincing and Shakespeare stuck to his planned route. He followed the track around Oxford in this tight circle, then again in a wider circle, stopping every person he saw and constantly sweeping his eyes across the woods, fields and lanes for some sign of Andrew. It did not seem a hopeless mission; someone must have seen him. He must be somewhere.

# Chapter 30

PANTING FOR BREATH, thirst raging in the early afternoon heat, Andrew and Ursula threw themselves down to rest, high up on a broad slope in the curve of the folded hills. They lay on their backs in the tough downland grass. Laid out before them, England seemed to stretch for ever. Above them, a solitary cloud drifted by.

As his breathing subsided, Andrew turned to his companion. 'We're first here.'

'You were right. You *are* pigging fast.'

'Is there any water left?'

'We'll get some.'

'Where?'

'I don't know. Watch and learn. Think I've survived seventeen years on the road not knowing how to get pigging water!'

He laughed and saw her bristling. 'I'm sorry,' he said. 'I wasn't laughing at you.'

'You better pigging not be.'

'Do you think everyone got away?'

'Don't know. Annis Jolly is eight months gone. Not easy for her to run, nor one or two of the old ones. But they're all good at hiding and probably found a hole in the woods somewhere. Tell you this, though. Reaphook won't be happy. He wanted to stand and fight. Too stupid to see we'd all have got killed or rounded up and hanged.'

'If he hates Staffy so much, why doesn't he just leave and go somewhere else?'

'Go where? This band is his home. You still don't understand. It's home to all of us. You don't just run off because you've got a brabble with someone. You have it out with them.'

Andrew listened and tried to make sense of it. It seemed to him the trouble between Reaphook and Staffy was a little more serious than that.

'Why did Staffy tell you to look out for me?'

'He does that when new ones come in. Same way as he has always looked out for me. That's why I stay with the band. And that's why you should, too. You don't stand a hope without the band. Whatever else you've done, the burgesses and justices will take you and whip you at the post until you bleed – just for being a sturdy vagrant beggar. And then they'll put a halter around your neck for thieving – even if you haven't been caught stealing nothing. *That's* why you need friends. Stand together, you got some strength. Go on your own, you're nothing, lower than pig slurry.'

'But I *can't* stay.'

She raised herself on her elbows. 'You going to cross England like that? In your black gown? You look like a big bear cub dressed for its own funeral. We'll *buy* you a jerkin,' she said with undisguised disdain. 'I've got money.'

'So we won't steal it – just use stolen money? That will make it legal and moral, will it?'

'It will, yes. You're learning fast, Andrew Woode. Now let's have a better look at your ear.'

Roughly, she pushed his head down to examine his injury, then proclaimed him sound.

'Would he have killed me?'

'Spindle? I don't know. He's a strange one. Does pretty much what Reaphook tells him. He might just have been trying to raise a laugh by making you piss yourself.'

Below them, in the vale, they heard a distant sound, carried on the warm air: the beat of a single drum. They raised their heads and gazed down. In the west, coming in their direction, they saw a column of men, perhaps twenty or thirty, marching slowly through the valley.

'Who are they?'

'Soldiers.'

'Are they the ones that attacked us?'

'No, those were townsfolk and villagers. These are soldiers, pressing men for the war. I heard they been around here a couple of days. Steer clear of them, Andrew. No good can come of them.'

As the column of soldiers passed by, their eyes turned right in the direction of Andrew and Ursula.

'They're looking at us. Should we run?'

'They're looking at the pigging white horse, you fool.'

He laughed. Of course they were. The giant chalk white horse carved into the grassy hillside where they lay.

Joshua Peace walked disconsolately towards the stables where his horse was liveried. His doublet hung from his shoulders in tatters where Attorney Hesketh's boy had cut its seams. He felt defeated; he had failed his friend John Shakespeare. There was nothing left for him here now; he had little gold left in his purse and no possessions apart from his mare.

He felt a hand on his shoulder and turned. It was the curious woman from the corner of the earl's chamber. She seemed agitated, her hair awry.

'Mistress Knott—'

'Come with me, quickly, before we are seen together.'

Peace hesitated but she tugged at his sleeve and pulled him.

'What do you want of me?' he asked.

'You are a friend of Mr Shakespeare's?'

He nodded.

'Then say nothing, just come with me. You will see.'

They walked out of Ormskirk, south and west, for two or more hours, deep into the countryside, until the sun was high in the sky. They came to a wood and the woman stopped. She looked at Peace questioningly, as though doubt had suddenly seized her.

'Are you a man of God, Mr Peace?'

Was he? Perhaps not in the way she meant it. He said nothing.

'This is Sceptre Wood. There is darkness here. Turn away now if you wish.'

He shook his head. He had come this far; he would go on.

At first the wood was dappled and light, with well-spaced oak and ash, but then it became more dense and overgrown, thick with broken, dead trees and briar.

She stopped and lifted her chin, pointing ahead with her face.

He tried to see what she was looking at. They were at the edge of a clearing. And then he saw it, hidden in a tangle of sticks and vines and leaves. A squat cabin or shelter, built of branches and mud, and so constructed that it was part of the very forest itself.

Mistress Knott pushed him forward. 'Go in,' she said. 'You are expected.'

'No, you go first.'

'I cannot go in. It is an ungodly place.'

Joshua Peace wished more than anything to turn and run, but he was as rooted to this course of action as the trees that surrounded him. He stepped forward. There was no door to the cabin, just a gaping entranceway, with a step that went down into the earth.

A grey-haired woman was sitting on her haunches. She was thin and bent and her face was lined. Their eyes met. She smiled.

'Welcome, master, welcome,' she said, her voice as thin as her small, sunken frame.

He looked away from her and surveyed the interior of the shelter. There were earthenware pots and glass vials all around. She followed his eyes.

'I have love philtres and charms, remedies for the ague and pox and a hundred other ailments. I can rid you of the stone or the gout or turn a falling prick to oak. Tell me what you wish, master.'

'I was told you were expecting me. Mistress Knott . . .'

As he said the name, he looked closer at the old woman. Though she was very different, though she exuded malevolence, yet he could see clearly now: she was Mistress Knott's kin. No, more than that; she was her mother.

'Indeed, yes indeed. I have the very thing. I gave it to one who came before you, but you shall have it, too.'

She laughed, an unearthly sound like birdsong in water, then began scraping at the earth close to her feet.

Peace watched her in ghastly fascination. Her quill-thin fingers scratched at the mud until they clasped something about the size of a large pebble. Then he saw that it was a glass vial. She rubbed it against her long black skirts to clear away the earth, then offered it to him. He touched it and tried to discern its contents. There seemed to be something dry and dull-coloured, grey or brown, in the little bottle.

He tried to take it but she snatched it back and held it to her breast.

'Two marks. I want two marks. The one who came before gave me a sovereign.'

Peace knew he had no more than ten shillings in his purse. It was all he had to get him back to London. He shook his head.

'I do not have it.'

'Then give me your knife and a lock of your hair.'

Every part of him told him this was superstitious nonsense, yet he was fearful. What would she *do* with his hair? More powerful yet was the sense of duty he still felt he owed to John Shakespeare. He took the knife from his belt and cut a lock from the thin ridge of hair that was all that remained encircling his pate. He handed the hair and the knife to the woman. She placed the vial in his hand.

He took out the little wooden stopper and put his nose close to the opening. He immediately caught the faint whiff of rose petals and went cold . . .

Parfitt knocked at the door to Thomas Hesketh's room and went in. His master was there, with the slender young man from London.

'Well, Parfitt,' Hesketh said. 'Did she take him to the old woman in the woods?'

'She did, master.'

Hesketh turned to his guest. 'Then we must act, Mr Ickman.'

'Indeed,' Bartholomew Ickman said. 'It is time to tie up the loose ends of this entanglement.'

## Chapter 31

IN THE EARLY evening, soon after beginning his third – and yet wider – circuit of Oxford, Shakespeare came to a village alehouse a few miles west of the city. He handed his hired bay mare to a sullen ostler and told him to feed it well with oats, water it and wash it down.

The taproom smelt of sweat, smoke, ale and farmyard manure. He ordered food and settled into a corner booth to rest an hour. The food was poorly seasoned and the beer was indifferent, yet he barely noticed. His mind was elsewhere. After eating and paying, he spoke with the landlord, asking him the same questions he had asked all day. The words tripped from his tongue by rote.

The landlord was curt. 'Got more than enough fugitives in these parts without your boy. Vagabonds and rogues. They been around here for weeks, thieving. No house is safe while they are about.'

'Where are they?'

'They had their camp in the woods around an old cowhouse four miles from here, towards Faringdon. Three of their women came into this village one day, begging, trying to sell wildflower posies for farthings and clutching babes that they said would die without food. Well, I gave them horsebread and some oats and told them to clear off. When they had gone, a

‡ 272 ‡

bridle from my stables was missing, the devil damn their dirty hides. What's more, the washing from Mistress Crispin's line had been filched. No guessing where that all went. But with luck they'll have gone for good now, with broken bones and cracked skulls to speed them on their way.'

'Tell me more.'

The landlord scratched his balls, then belched. 'Some farmers and their men were getting an armed band together against them, to drive them off. I'd go further than that, though. Hang them all, every last vagabond in the land, I say. Why don't Her Majesty the Queen take care of these enemies at home rather than fighting her foreign wars in Belgia and Brittany? Get the militias in against them . . .'

Shakespeare listened to the grumbling and managed to get a clearer idea of where to find the vagabonds' camp. He considered the hour. It was getting late and he was tired from riding all day. Still, he wanted to see this camp.

The ride took him an hour over fields and lanes. The only people he saw were farmworkers in their smocks, trudging homeward with the tools of their trade. He was in a hurry, but still he stopped and spoke with each one he saw, both to ask whether they had seen a boy like Andrew and also to ask if he was on the right route to the vagabond encampment.

The sun was dipping low when he arrived. He found a desolate, ghostly place. He tethered the mare and walked about. It had clearly been occupied recently, for the earth was either muddy or scuffed by many feet. An old cowhouse had been broken apart and burnt to the ground. Spirals of smoke ascended from charred rafters. Yes, people had been here recently, that was certain. But it was deserted now. The farmers and their men had done their work well in sending this lot of vagabonds on their way.

Wandering into the woods, he found evidence of small

campfires and beaten-down ferns where people might have slept. There were a few abandoned belongings – a cup, a child's carved doll – but no sign of Andrew.

Exhausted, Shakespeare built a bed of ferns and lay down, close to the horse. There was nothing for him here. Sleep came instantly.

'We cannot fail in this, Sir Thomas. The Spaniard must not be allowed to seize Brest. Does Her Majesty understand that?'

It was late evening. They were in Sir Robert Cecil's private rooms.

Heneage nodded his handsome head. 'I think she does understand now. Norreys has been persuasive. She will give him the men she needs. About time, too.'

'Indeed. And no risk of Essex taking over command . . .'

'No, thank the Lord. We need a soldier, not a peafowl.'

There had been rumours around court that the Earl of Essex would replace Norreys in command of the English army in Brittany for the final push to secure Morlaix and the Fort of El Léon on the Crozon peninsula. It had been a moment of panic for the Cecils and their allies, but Elizabeth was having none of Essex. Too much was at stake in Brittany. Essex had failed in Normandy; she needed a successful, battle-hardened general for this operation. That man was Sir John Norreys.

Cecil had sighed with relief at the news, but his comfort was short-lived. The truth was that Norreys and his army could do only so much. The two men in this small, cool room, away from the hubbub and listening ears of court, knew that there was more to this battle than a good general and an adequate complement of men. Their reports on the fortress of El Léon suggested it was all but impregnable.

Cecil handed a paper to Heneage. 'This arrived within the hour. It is a letter from John Shakespeare.'

Heneage read it quickly and looked up at Cecil in dismay. 'God's blood, the man has midsummer madness.'

'I rather fear so. What do you suggest?'

'Well, it is certain that we need him for this operation. We are agreed on that. A great deal of work has already gone into preparing his path. It would be impossible to replace him at such a late stage.'

Cecil nodded. More than that, Shakespeare had the guile, the skill, the courage and the command of Spanish required. Most importantly of all, he had a huge working knowledge of England's intelligence network. No, there was no other man.

'You must send a squadron of men to Oxford,' Heneage continued. 'Bring him back, by force if necessary.'

'We need his cooperation, not his enmity. Everything I know about him tells me that he would not comply if we did such a thing. He will put his family first. That was how he came to part company with Mr Secretary Walsingham.'

'Can we not threaten him?'

'With what? No court would consider it a felony to refuse to undertake such a mission. He is not subject to military law.'

On the far side of the table, there was a soft clearing of the throat. Both men looked across at Lady Eliska.

'If I may say something, gentlemen . . .'

'My lady?'

She held up the letter. 'I do believe that you are both looking at this from the wrong angle. In my opinion, the letter from Mr Shakespeare is most opportune. Used with subtlety, it might just help us to persuade Mr Shakespeare to play his part with great willing.'

Cecil smiled. 'I think I begin to understand.'

'The missing boy should not be seen as a bar to our plans,' Eliska said, 'but as the key to securing his father's cooperation.'

*

Shakespeare rose at dawn, wakened by an earwig crawling across his nose. He looked around once more, just to be certain there was nothing more to be learnt, then untethered the horse and rode back towards the village to resume his meticulous quest.

Just before the first house, he stopped beside a man of middle years and began questioning him.

The man put up his hand to interrupt. 'I *heard* there was someone around asking questions.' His tone was gruff and he was clearly accustomed to being heard and obeyed. 'Who are you?'

'My name is John Shakespeare. I am a government officer, looking for a boy, a scholar, who has gone missing from his Oxford college.'

'That's what I heard. Tell me more.'

Shakespeare described Andrew in detail.

'Why?' he said eventually. 'Have you seen or heard of such a boy?'

'There would be some money in it if I had, wouldn't there? A scholar boy on the run, there'd be gold in that, I reckon.'

'It is possible.'

'He'd be worth gold to others, too, then. Reward money for bringing a fugitive to justice.'

Shakespeare rested his hand on the hilt of his sword. The man had the satisfied, well-fed look of a yeoman farmer. But more than that, he had, too, the brutish eyes of an employer who habitually drove his workmen hard and drove commercial deals harder.

'What are you saying? Have you seen such a boy?'

'I would need to know a bit more. Who is this scholar? Son of a nobleman, perchance? In trouble with a girl, is he?'

Shakespeare leapt down from the horse and pulled out his sword. He drove its tip into the ground, with menace.

'You don't need to know more, nor ask any questions. If you know something, you need to tell me without delay or suffer the consequences.'

The yeoman farmer glared back, his chest puffed out. 'Scare me with your sword, will you? I'm a justice in these parts and I'll have you strung up.'

Shakespeare raised his sword, its tip to the man's large chest. 'I do not use my sword to scare people. I use it to kill them.'

The farmer hesitated, then backed off gingerly, his hands up, palms towards Shakespeare. 'Hold on now. Hold on. I didn't say I *did* know anything about a boy. Just wanted to know what it would be worth if I found anything.'

'There would be a little silver in it, for information leading to his discovery – his *safe* discovery.'

'Because I know all the farmers and most of the tradesmen in these parts. And the worst sort come before me in court. I could ask about for you, if there was something in it for me . . .'

Shakespeare lowered his sword, slowly. 'Do so. If you hear anything – anything at all – bring word to me or my servant, Mr Mustard, at the Blue Boar in Oxford. Meanwhile, I will be travelling these ways around the county until I find the lad.'

'And the reward?'

'We will discuss that when you have something to tell me, Mr—'

'Trungle. Farmer Trungle.'

'Where can I find you?'

'Church Farm.' He nodded westwards. 'Or at my horsemill, where I'm headed now, a half-mile further on from the ale-house. I'll ask around for you, Mr Shakespeare. As to the silver, no offence wished upon you, sir, but a man's got to make a living the best way he may in these hard times.'

Shakespeare said nothing. He slotted the sword into its sheath, remounted and rode southward on his next circuit of Oxford. He was beginning to feel like a man on an ever-enlarging treadmill. He could end up in the sea and still find no word of the boy.

Clarkson swept his arm around the room. 'Mr Cooper, Mr Ivory, you will wait here. This house is to be your hiding place until you are called upon. I cannot tell when that might be, but I am leaving you well supplied with money, powder and shot to protect yourselves and the perspective glass. Is that understood?'

Both men nodded. Boltfoot's face was set and grim. He could not have been less happy.

'A woman will come in each day to bring food and to clean,' Clarkson continued. 'Sir Robert Cecil is most anxious that you be well looked after, for he understands that there may well be arduous times ahead. The woman's name is Mistress Winter. She will arrive an hour after first light each day and will give three knocks and then a double knock at the door. She has been instructed to ask no questions, nor to reveal your names to any man. She will, however, endeavour to bring you news of the outside world so that you do not feel cut off.'

'What about our needs – our *bodily* needs?' Ivory demanded.

Clarkson eyed him sceptically. 'I am sure that two men who have spent months, even years, on the ocean wave without the company of womenfolk, will have no problem there. Sir Robert quite understands, though, that to stay healthy you will need fresh air and exercise. Your horses will be kept in livery in the village. I will take them there now, when I leave. If you wish to ride, Mistress Winter will have them brought to you, ready saddled. You are only to ride inland, northwards into

Essex, and no more than five miles, returning the same day. You must never be away from this house for more than three hours and you will always go armed. These are tight restrictions, and I pray they will not be necessary too long. As my other duties permit, I shall make an effort to visit you to keep you informed. Is that all clear?'

They nodded again, but said nothing.

'Then I shall take my leave of you.' Clarkson bowed, then shook them by the hand. 'I have faith in you both, as does Sir Robert. He knows how deeply felt is your desire to work in the interests of England and Her Royal Majesty. Good day to you.'

With another, slightly deeper, bow, he turned and walked from the house where he had brought the two men.

'Well, we shall have a merry time here, Mr Cooper, I do believe.'

'Do you so, Mr Ivory?'

Boltfoot was certain his time in this house would be utter misery. The house was a mile from the northern banks of the Thames, in a village two miles to the west of Fort Tilbury and its river crossing. From the back, the marshland swept down to the endless vista of the estuary.

'In truth, I do not like this Thames marshland,' he said, half to himself, half to Ivory. 'It is unhealthy.'

He stretched his aching back. The pain was raw from his old injuries. He had bad memories of this stretch of water.

'It's a good enough place. Better than your goodwife's rotten farmyard cottage. Here, we are but a boat ride from Gravesend. Taprooms, bowling alleys, games of chance, bawdy houses. What more could a man want?'

'You go nowhere without my let, Ivory.'

Boltfoot understood well enough why they had been brought here. It was close to the naval dockyards, so that Ivory could be embarked upon any man-of-war leaving Gravesend, Deptford or Blackwall in haste. But it was the very proximity of a place such as Gravesend that worried him; if Ivory went there to the gaming rooms or brothels, there could be mariners who might recognise him.

'You have tried to get away from me twice. If you vanish from this house in quest of some trickery or wager, then I will blow a hole in your head and look after the glass instrument myself.'

Ivory laughed. 'And I suspect you wish to God you could do that, Cooper. Well, put aside such thoughts, because we both know well that you cannot.'

At eight o'clock, Shakespeare was halfway through his fourth circuit, some seven miles out from St John's College. He was south and east of the city, near the London road. A wooden sign hammered into the ground beside a milestone told him there was a post-house no more than a mile and a half away. It promised a welcome, good food and a bed for the night. More to the point, thought Shakespeare, there would be men there to question – men who had travelled this road and might have seen or heard tell of a boy heading towards the capital.

Two men rode up behind him, passed him, then stopped a little way ahead. One of them wheeled his horse and came back to Shakespeare, reining in as he halted his own mount.

'Are you Mr Shakespeare?' the man asked. 'The Shakespeare who has been asking hereabouts for a boy?'

'Yes.'

'Well, your fortune's in, Mr Shakespeare. I do believe I know where he is.'

Shakespeare's body tensed. 'Where?'

'If I am correct, he's in a village near here, Haseley Talmage.

It is said he has been taken in by a widow of the parish. The talk is that she is feeding him like he was her own lad and that he is as happy as a cock in a hencoop. Your lad, is he?'

Shakespeare looked the man in the eye. The eye was smiling, and the teeth were bared without guile. He was twenty-four or twenty-five, in a good leather jerkin and a cap over his brow. Shakespeare's gaze travelled to his companion. They were of an age and wore similar working clothes.

'What are you men?'

'Timbermen. Been foresting not far from here.'

'And do you live in Haseley Talmage?'

'No, but we've been lodging there. We've been given our wages this day. We're off to the post-house to spend a little.'

Shakespeare hesitated. Mr Secretary Walsingham would have told him to trust his first instinct: there was something wrong here. Yet he so badly *wanted* to believe it, and it was a sound enough story.

'How far is it to Haseley Talmage?'

'Just over a mile. We'll take you there. Never met the widow, but I know where she lives. Little cottage with thatch almost to the ground, like a fine manchet loaf.'

'I thank you for your kindness, but I could not allow you to break into your well-earned evening of pleasure. Point me the direction if you would.'

'No, no. We'll take you. We can go the short way, through the woods where we been working and over the fields. It would be our pleasure to see you and the boy brought back together. That would be the greatest joy a man could have, nor would we ask for a farthing's pay.' He turned around to his companion. 'Are we agreed? We'll take Mr Shakespeare to his boy.'

The other man grinned and nodded.

'No,' Shakespeare said decisively. 'I thank you once again for your assistance, but I am continuing on my way. I will go to Haseley Talmage on the morrow. Alone.'

The smile slowly vanished. 'Why do I get the impression that you do not trust us, Mr Shakespeare? Are you suggesting we might harbour some villainous intentions towards you?'

Shakespeare's hand had never strayed far from the hilt of his sword. The men were armed with visible daggers but that was nothing strange. There could, perhaps, be other weapons, concealed. He tried to smile, but knew it was not convincing. Yet he did not care whether they believed him, or took offence at his refusal to be taken to the woods and be robbed by them.

'I have already given you my gratitude. Now let us all go our ways in peace. Ride on. I am sure you have a hotpot and a game of cards awaiting at the post-house.'

'There is an insinuation in your tone. We have made you a generous offer. I would consider it an affront to be refused. We are two men, you are one. Do you consider it wise to insult and cross us?'

Shakespeare sighed heavily. His hand now cupped his sword-hilt. It was a small movement of his fingers, yet the eyes of the man followed it, then fluttered up and their eyes locked. Shakespeare shook his head, almost imperceptibly. 'It is your decision, good friend – your life,' he said quietly. 'Preserve it. Ride on, and enjoy it, for death is the shadow that hangs over us all.'

The man was about to say something else. His own hand hovered near his dagger. He was weighing the odds. Two against one was powerfully persuasive – and yet that one was an unknown quantity and did not lack confidence.

Of a sudden, the man grabbed up the reins, wheeled the horse and kicked the barrel of its chest.

'Come. Let us leave this place.'

The other man glared briefly at Shakespeare, but said nothing. In a stamping of hoofs, they spurred on their mounts and galloped away, throwing up a cloud of dust.

Shakespeare rode on at a sedate walk. A quart of beer, a trencher of roast beef and a fine down mattress would serve him well this night. And in the morning? He would ride to the village of Haseley Talmage, if it existed.

# Chapter 32

T HE SOFT FOLDS of green around the enormous chalk horse carved into the top of the downs was dotted with Staffy's camp of vagabonds. Andrew and Ursula had a little fire going, using dead wood collected in a nearby spinney. They were in the white horse's eye. Staffy was just below them, beside the hindleg, beating his staff noisily against a wooden handcart to call the band to gather around him.

Staffy nodded to Ursula. 'Do a head count, Ursula Dancer. See how many we got.' He turned to the crowd and his voice rose. 'We're here because we didn't have the arms to fight the men who were coming at us,' he boomed. 'We're here so we can live – and fight – another day.'

'We ran like craven dogs.'

There was silence.

Staffy pointed his staff at Reaphook. 'Another word from you, Mr Reaphook, and I shall stop your mouth for good.' He paused. 'I shall deal with you in a while.' He glared a moment, then turned back to the crowd. 'You all know why we had to disperse. There was nothing craven in what we did. We made our escape because we would have been blown to dust if we had stayed. I want to hear no more of it. We have to think where we're to go now. We can't stay here. So, do we go back to the Dogghole – or do we move on? And if we move on, which path do we take?'

'We can't go back to the Dogghole, Mr Upright Man,' Reaphook called out, with heavy, sarcastic emphasis on the word *Upright*. 'It's not there!'

Staffy had had enough. 'Begone!'

Reaphook would not be stopped. 'It's not there, Mr *Upright* Man, because the villagers burnt it down while *you* turned and ran! Our drinking hole went up in smoke and flames! And what have *you* done about it? Have you burnt down *their* drinking hole in revenge? Or will you leave that to a *man*?'

Staffy began striding towards his challenger. It would have to end, here and now. Reaphook stepped backwards. He was strong and agile but he was only two-thirds the size of Staffy and no one here was going to intercede on his behalf. Spindle, the only one who had not backed away from his side, looked uneasy.

'Brave enough now, Mr *Upright* Man?' Reaphook spat.

Staffy growled and swung his heavy rod, but he hit only air. Reaphook ducked down, then turned. Staffy swung again, the bone-crushing staff cutting the air in a great arc. Reaphook skipped back on his heels, then turned and ran. He ran down-hill, away from the camp. Staffy began to go after him, but realised it would do his authority no good to be seen to give chase, yet fail to catch the man. Instead, he stopped and let Reaphook run. From the brow of the hill, he watched him stumble and tumble, then drag himself back to his feet and stop a few hundred yards away, a distant insect, skulking.

Staffy turned back to the band of vagabonds, who were mur-muring uneasily, yet went silent at his scowl. 'I think we know which one's the runner now!'

Uncertain, the crowd muttered approval. Some clapped and cheered. But it was less than conclusive. Staffy's authority had been challenged – and he had failed to finish off his challenger.

'Anyone want to go with Mr Reaphook, go now. And if you do go, don't never show your face in this band again lest you wish me to wrap my staff around your head.'

No one moved.

'That's that then.'

Spindle stepped forward. 'I'm off. You're finished, Staffy.' He turned and sauntered away down the hill towards Reaphook.

'Any more?' His gaze swept the assembled vagabonds. Men and women shook their heads when they met his eyes.

'This isn't over,' Ursula said quietly to Andrew. 'I know of at least five others will go tonight. They think Staffy's lost his power. He should have done for Reaphook. Should have done it long ago. This can only end one way. One of them – Staffy or Reaphook – has to die. And I pray for our sake, you and me pigging both, Andrew Woode, that it's Reaphook as goes down. Because if Staffy dies, we're done for.'

John Shakespeare overslept. He felt more tired than he had expected. He had eaten well at the post-house, which was as good a place as the signpost had promised. He had also caught sight of the two men from the road, drinking in the taproom. Their eyes had met, but they looked away. Shakespeare had bolted his door during the night.

In the morning, he took his time over bacon and fried eggs, then rode for Haseley Talmage.

He had not seen the two men watching him at the stables as he mounted up, but he saw them now, on the byway to the village. He was not surprised. They had clearly singled him out as a fair prize and wanted his purse. Well, let them try to take it.

He rode up to them and stopped. 'I had thought that you

might have had some common sense. But you won't learn, will you?'

'Hand it over.'

'My purse? I do not believe I will. Take it from me.' Shakespeare unsheathed his sword and held it across his lap.

'Fine swordsman, are you, Mr Shakespeare?'

'Good enough. Try me.'

'No.' He pulled a pistol from his belt. 'You try this.'

Shakespeare had already seen the weapon. Even as the pistol came up, his own sword flashed like a viper's tooth and sliced the man's forefinger – trigger finger – from his hand. The pistol spun into the air and seemed to hang suspended before falling and clattering down to the hard, dusty path beneath his horse's hoofs. Blood spat from the man's hand where the severed finger hung, limp, by a mere tendon and strip of skin. Shakespeare's gaze turned to the other man.

'And you? Do you want my purse? Will *you* take it from me?'

A look of terror crossed the second man's face. He kicked his spurs into his horse and rode away. The man who had lost his finger clutched his hand to his body. Shakespeare threw him a kerchief.

'Tie this around it.'

The would-be robber looked up astonished and did as he was bidden, stemming the bloodflow as best he could. Then he grabbed the horse's reins to ride away.

Shakespeare already had the man's reins. 'No. You're going nowhere until you have answered a question or two. How did you know who I was?'

'What?'

'You heard me.'

'It was the talk, that's all. Everyone in the villages has been talking about the wealthy stranger and his lost boy. You were as easy to spot as a swan among ducks.'

'Wealthy?'

The man looked with meaning upon his fine city clothes, his gold and brown embroidered doublet. Yes, thought Shakespeare, it must have been quite obvious that he was not a local man.

'Who sent you to do this? Who gave you the pistol?'

'No one. I swear it. I am sorry. If you will let me go, I give you my word I will change my ways.'

'If I had time, I would take you into Oxford and have you arraigned for highway robbery. You would be hanged. Instead, I will ask you one question: you have heard much talk about me. What do men say about the boy I seek?'

'Nothing. I have heard nothing.'

Shakespeare raised his sword to eye level and squinted along its shining length to the point, which was at the man's throat.

'In God's name, I swear it!'

Shakespeare's sword, blood lining its sharp edge and point, remained absolutely still as he considered. After a few moments, he lowered the sword.

'Very well. Give me your powder and shot. A sword is clearly not enough on these dishonest roads.'

The man handed over his bag of bullets and his powderhorn, fishing awkwardly about his person and saddle with his uninjured hand. It was shaking with terror and etched with the blood from his other hand.

'Now go. If I were you I would get that tended to by a good surgeon. Say you cut it with your timbersaw . . .'

As the man rode away as fast as his nag would take him to join his fellow on the rim of a nearby mound, Shakespeare dismounted nonchalantly and picked up the pistol. It was a plain thing, not well made, but it might be useful. He thrust it into his pack-saddle with the balls and powder, and rode on.

*

During the night, six men slipped away from the vagabond camp to join Reaphook and Spindle. Though no one was sorry to find them gone in the morning, an air of despondency hung over the band. All felt uneasy. This was not over. Reaphook was planning something.

Staffy had the eye of an enraged and cornered bull. All were too afraid to talk to him. Early in the morning, he wandered off alone with his ashwood staff, striding across the downs. No one knew where he was heading or when he would be back.

Andrew and Ursula shared bread and cheese in silence. Finally, she stood up. 'Let's go, Andrew Woode.'

'Where?'

'Sharking.'

'I'm not going stealing.'

She shrugged her shoulders. 'As you will. I'll see you when I return. If you're a good lad, I might even bring you some food – or that jerkin and hose you need.'

'I don't want anything. If you gave me something, I'd know you had stolen it. Is it any surprise that the villagers and towns-folk want to whip you and kill you? You all deserve to be beaten and pilloried the way you carry on.'

Ursula gave him a strange look. 'I thought I had been pig-ging good to you, Andrew Woode. Took you in, squared it with Staffy, gave you food and ale. What more do you want?'

'Honesty.'

'Well, pig off back to Oxford and tell the justice you're wanted for a felony. That would be honest and you can be honestly hanged! You're on your own, Andrew Woode. Is that honest enough for you?' She kicked him viciously, then marched off without looking back.

He stayed at the camp all day. He should have simply walked away, headed for the road to Stratford or London, where, God willing, he would be given safe haven. But he was infected by the same inertia that afflicted so many in the band. They were all waiting for some decision from their Upright Man, for none of them could make a decision on their own. This band was all they had, their only comfort in a world that considered them vermin, lower than rats.

Ursula returned in the afternoon. She barely glanced at Andrew but went off and joined a family group. Then, in the early evening, Staffy came back, his face clouded and brooding. He said nothing and sat apart, drinking ale and chewing on a hunk of black bread.

In the evening, Staffy sauntered over to Andrew with a beaker of ale and half a loaf of black bread.

'Here, have this. Keep your strength, because you'll likely need it.'

Andrew jumped to his feet at the Upright Man's approach. He took the proffered food and drink and thanked him profusely.

'Sit down, sit down.'

Andrew descended to the grass. Staffy squatted beside him.

'Where's Ursula Dancer?'

'With a family over there.' He nodded in the direction where he had last seen her. 'She is not talking to me. I fear I offended her.'

'Then you're a fool. I knew no good would come of you being here. I'd have thrown you out straightway, were it not for Ursula speaking up for you. You can stay tonight, but you'll leave at first light. You have no place in this band.'

Andrew nodded. 'I understand.'

'Do you so? Do you understand? I do not believe you do understand what our life is, nor how dangerous. You sit on this greensward in summer and think yourself a rogue and a free man, but you wait until the barren midwinter sets in, when there is no food nor shelter, when a man may lose his fingers and toes to the cold, and babes freeze to death in their swaddling tatters. Then you'll know why we huddle together. Then you will know what it is to be an Englishman spurned by his own countrymen.'

'I did not choose this life, sir. It was forced upon me by circumstances. I have been wrongly accused. I thank you for the hospitality you have given me and I will trouble you no more after this day.'

Staffy looked at him. His angry eyes seemed to mellow. 'Very well. So be it.' He supped at his own ale and made no attempt to move away from Andrew's side. 'You're not like us,' he said at last. 'Are you high born?'

'My father was a merchant. He is dead. So is my mother. I live with my adoptive father. I am not of the nobility, but neither am I lowly born . . . I have never gone hungry.'

'No. I can see that. Something in you calls to mind Ursula's mother. You have a little of her wit, though she was more than you will ever be.'

Andrew wanted to know more. He sat quietly and drank the ale and gnawed at the bread.

'I loved her, you know. Only woman I ever loved, that's why I look after her girl, Ursula.'

'But you are not her father?'

'No. Her belly was already beginning to swell when I met her. Her family had thrown her out for getting with child, unwed as she was. They were yeoman farmers in the shire of Cambridge. Harsh Puritans. She had no choice but to take to the road. She had no money nor home nor family. Her sin? To lie with a man – the son of a neighbour, I do believe, though he wanted no more to do with her – and bring life into the world. What family would throw away a daughter and a grandchild for that? But their loss was my gain. For a few months she was mine. She danced, her skirts swaying with her hips, so that no man could watch her and not be beguiled. In the firelight by night, she danced, and in the glow of the sun across a wild-flower meadow by day. There was magic in her movement that summer. Then the fall of the leaf came and her belly swelled too great to dance. She died with the birth of her child; one life ends, another begins. The priests say it is the natural way of things, yet it did not seem so to me. I could not forget her, nor forgive her leaving me so.'

'Does Ursula know her history?'

Staffy ignored the question and carried on. 'Even now, the pain eats at me like a toothed worm in my entrails. And the sight of you with your well-born tones and your bright face brings it back. I cannot bear to set eyes on you no more.'

Andrew looked at the giant of a man and was astonished to see tears streaking his cheeks. He turned away, ashamed that his gaze intruded in such a terrible way on another man's grief.

Staffy sat there a while, saying nothing. It occurred to Andrew that he had never encountered such a lonely, solitary man. He might have the strength and commanding presence of a lion, yet he was close to no one.

At last, as the camp fires dimmed and died all around, Staffy rose to his feet without a word and walked away into the night, back to his own palliasse. Andrew curled up on the ground and imagined Ursula dancing in a green meadow, her skirts swirling and swaying as once her mother's had done.

The woman was cowled and veiled, swathed in gowns from her head to the toe of her delicate shoe. It was dusk. She descended from her exotic carriage in a side street, looked about her, then walked a quarter-mile along the darkening alleyways.

The guard outside the French embassy stood to attention, his halberd sloping over his shoulder. The woman approached him, held back her cowl so that only he could see her face and spoke a few words. He seemed to recognise her and bowed low, bidding her enter with a flourish of his rich-liveried arm.

Inside the opulent hall, the assistant secretary was waiting for her and ushered her towards the tranquillity of the garden.

'We will not be overheard here, my lady. I take it you were not followed.'

'Do you not trust me, monsieur?'

He bowed again, as though mortified at the very suggestion. 'A thousand apologies. I had not meant to doubt you but there are those here who do not share our loyalties. And we are watched day and night.'

'Which is why I come with my face covered.' Eliska drew aside her cowl and veil and smiled. 'Let us talk, quietly.'

'Indeed, my lady.' His voice became little more than a whisper. 'Mr Weld told me to expect you. He said you had advised him to leave Lancashire.'

'The climate was a little warm. I judged it unsafe. But there are other ways . . .'

The assistant secretary was a good-looking young man, with dark, oiled hair and smiling eyes. 'He said as much. We can leave the matter of the instrument in his capable hands, I think. But there is the other prize to discuss. The question of you and Cecil's man. Are you still certain that this can be achieved?'

Eliska reached out and clasped the assistant secretary's smooth, warm hands in her own. 'More certain than ever. Fear not, I bring the news our friends in the Escorial have been anticipating.'

'Then you have made progress?'

'John Shakespeare is as good as ours, monsieur. All is in place, as I promised.'

# Chapter 33

THEY CAME AN hour before dawn when the camp still slept and snored. Thirty soldiers, armed with longbows and arquebuses and pikes. They had the camp surrounded before anyone even knew they were there.

Provost Pinkney stood in the first rank. He nodded to his drummer boy and a slow drumbeat began to sound in the still morning. Then the trumpeter blared forth. In an instant, the camp stirred to frantic life, like a nest of ants poked with a stick. Some tried to run but were caught. Others huddled together. One vagabond man picked up a stave to defend himself and was immediately singled out for attack. Another swung out wildly with a pickaxe and was killed by the hack of a military short sword to the neck, then a thrust to the belly.

At Pinkney's side stood Reaphook, smirking in the eerie twilight, his eyes surveying the encampment for his prizes. His honed sickle dangled, menacingly, from his right hand.

'There he is,' Reaphook said.

Staffy had risen to his full height. He stood in the centre of his people, ash staff in hand, facing the commanders of the armed group that surrounded them.

Andrew looked on in horror and dismay. He tried to pick out Ursula, but there was no sign of her.

Staffy took a pace forward. 'Come and get me, Reaphook.

Come to me and I will crack your head open like a filbert between stones.'

A petronel fired harmlessly into the gloom, its fire, smoke and boom bruising the crisp air.

'Wait!'

It was Pinkney who had fired the warning shot and who now spoke. 'You don't need to die this day. I will give sixteen shillings' coat and conduct and a three-shilling pikestaff to any sound man who joins me for the wars. The infirm, small children and women will be left here, in charge of Mr Reaphook. I will hang any man who defies me. Martial law.'

'I defy you,' Staffy said. He began to stride through the cowering groups of vagabonds, sweeping his staff before him.

Suddenly an arrow sliced into his neck, then another ripped into his chest. He stepped forward a pace or two, then stopped. He looked down at the arrow protruding from his chest, then looked up. A third arrow hit him in the left thigh. He crumpled at the knees.

As he buckled, men descended on him from all sides, just as a wolf pack falls on its prey once it can no longer run. Spindle was there, so was Reaphook, along with the other men who had deserted the camp. They all had knives – daggers, poniards, kitchen blades, axeheads – and they slashed and chopped at the body of their fallen chief, cutting the very life from him. He made no sound, no howl of pain, nor let out any scream for mercy, but bled to death as stoutly and as silently as he had lived.

Just as the first speck of sun appeared on the horizon, golden and bright, Reaphook stood up from the body, and held the dead man's dripping heart aloft in one hand and his bloody sickle in the other. His lips were drawn back fully from his mule's teeth and he roared with the potency of triumph.

'I am your Upright Man now!'

*

'That one is to be pressed, and that one.' Pinkney eyed the assembled band of vagabonds, all ranged before him in lines. 'You may take that one and that, Mr Reaphook.'

He was walking along the lines examining the men as a horse trader might look over young colts at the fair. Pinkney ran a hand down the shot-pocked scar that ravaged half his face. One by one, he selected the soundest of the men and let the halt and lame be. He came to Andrew.

'How old are you, boy?'

'Thirteen, sir.'

'Consider yourself a pressed man. You are a soldier now.'

'No,' Reaphook said. 'I want that one. I wish to hang him.'

'Indeed? What is his crime?'

'He offends me. You agreed that I could hang one, Mr Pinkney.'

Pinkney looked askance at Reaphook, then turned and counted the men he had set aside. 'There are only eight there, and not all those likely soldiers. You promised me twelve good men, Mr Reaphook.'

'I will find you another four, but I want the boy.'

Pinkney tugged at his bristled chin. His cold expression did not change and neither did he look at Reaphook. 'As you will. But I want sound men. Those that remain would not scare a Frenchie, let alone one of the Spanish troops in Brittany. Find me the men or I'll have *you*, Mr Reaphook. What of that one?' He pointed to Spindle. 'He looks strong enough.'

Reaphook hesitated a moment, then shook his head decisively.

'No, he's mine, one of us. But fear not, Provost Pinkney, I agreed twelve. You shall have twelve.'

Reaphook grasped Andrew by his black gown and pulled him out of the line. He pushed him towards Spindle.

'You have unfinished business with this thing. Take it. We shall hang it one hour from now, to cheer the company. In the meantime, I want Ursula Dancer. Where in God's name is she, Spindle? Take men and find her for me.'

Pinkney's drummer boy beat out his death-slow time with a single stick. Andrew stood with Spindle and Reaphook and the other six men who made up the core of his band. The boy's arms were bound behind his back. Ahead of them, at the edge of the spinney, a rope and noose hung from the stunted branch of an ancient oak. Below it there was a box, on which the condemned would stand before it was kicked away to leave him swinging.

'It is time.'

Andrew did not bother to struggle. There was no point. He had seen a hanging before and he knew what was to become of him. A few minutes of panic and pain and then it would all be over. If there was a God, he would ascend to heaven and be once more in the comforting arms of his father and mother and with Catherine Shakespeare, whom he had loved as a mother. He had to believe in this, otherwise there was nothing in the world or in the universe beyond. Endless nothingness.

'Afraid?' Spindle rasped in his ear.

Andrew ignored him. His lips moved only to mouth the Lord's Prayer. He looked straight ahead at the rope.

'Get on with it,' Pinkney said. 'I want no tormenting of souls. This is martial law. We are royal soldiers, not barbarians.'

Reaphook nodded to Spindle. The youth stood behind Andrew and began to push him forward towards the rope, at the edge of the dark wood. Suddenly a figure appeared, ghost-like, beside the rope. She stood there, then her hand reached up and took the rope. She climbed up on the box and put the noose about her own neck.

No one moved. All eyes were on Ursula Dancer. What was she doing? Would she kick the box away and kill herself by hanging?

She smiled, then removed her neck from the noose. She was wearing the gown she had worn when she and Andrew went to rob the man in Faringdon market. She was beautiful. She walked forward towards the assembly of soldiers and vagabonds. Without hesitating, she went up to Reaphook.

'Unbind him. He is a boy. Give him to the soldiers. It is not his death you want, it is my maidenhead.' She put her hands around Reaphook's neck and kissed him on the lips. Then she smiled at him, as a bride smiles at her new-wed husband. 'Will you let him live?'

Reaphook nodded, dumbfounded.

'Say it.'

'Yes, I will let him live.'

Ursula looked towards Pinkney. 'You heard that? The boy Andrew Woode is now your soldier, to take to the wars or wherever you will.'

Pinkney signalled to his lieutenant. 'Bring the boy here. He'll make up numbers. That will leave just three to find.'

Ursula put her hand in Reaphook's. 'Come, sir, come with me to the woods.' Gently, she pulled him forward, bewildered and disbelieving, 'I have a bed of leaves there. Come and I will be yours, body and soul.'

Reaphook looked at her, then all about him. He was no longer the killer of men, but a gauche and callow fellow, unsure of himself, uncertain that he would rise to the occasion. He stepped forward, looked about him and grinned self-consciously with his protruding teeth.

'Come, sweet Mr Reaphook. Leave your blade here and come with me.'

She took the sickle from his belt and dropped it to the

ground, then squeezed his hand and led him away from the crowd. Two soldiers laughed.

Their coarse laughter and jests were drowned by a howl. It came deep from within Andrew's throat and it seemed to split the air. Just the one word – 'No' – carried long and piercing across the downs, like the cry of a dying animal through the warm scented morning.

*Chapter 34*

J OHN SHAKESPEARE HELD a sealed paper in his hand. He
    had lost track of time. How many days had he been along
these endless paths? How many miles had he trod and how
many people had he questioned?

Every two days, he sent a message to Dr Dee in Oxford
and, invariably, a message came back saying all was well.
Shakespeare gazed at this latest message, brought by Godwit
to a tavern in the market town of Wantage. The message was
thicker than the usual missives from Dee. Taking his poniard,
he broke the seal. Inside, the message was simple: '*This was
sent to you, your faithful servant, Mustard,*' followed by Dee's
own signature, the Greek letter $\Delta$. Inside this message was
another paper. Shakespeare unfolded it. This second message
was written in a different hand. It said, '*Mr Shakespeare, I
have information for you. Bring two pounds in gold to me.
Trungle.*'

Shakespeare recalled the yeoman farmer whom he had been
inclined to run through. Well, he had better seek him out.
Without delay, he took horse and rode for the village where he
had met the man. The journey took him an hour and a half,
riding north-eastwards on the main track.

At the village, he asked about Farmer Trungle.

'He'll be at market in Faringdon this day,' the landlord of

the alehouse said. 'Always goes there on market day with his meal and flour from the horsemill.'

Shakespeare allowed his horse a pail of water and took a cup of ale for himself, then rode off again, heading westwards towards Faringdon.

On the outskirts of the town, by a crossroads, two corpses hung from a gibbet, their deadweight bodies swaying in the light breeze, rope creaking against rough oak. He stopped and gazed at them. The faces were purple, their death agony frozen in their staring eyes. One of them was old with long white hair that obscured his face; the other was as thin as a stick. He looked away and rode on.

He found Trungle in the market square, hands on hips, ordering his men to load jute sacks of flour on to carts for distribution.

Shakespeare dismounted, tethered his horse and walked over to him.

'Mr Trungle, you said you had information for me.'

'Ah, yes, Shakespeare. So you've come. Have you got the gold? Two pounds, not a penny less.'

'I have the gold if you take me to the boy.'

'I'd want ten pounds for that. But I have information that should help you find him. It's up to you what you do with it.' He held out a flour-dusted hand. 'Put it there, Shakespeare, put it there.'

Shakespeare took out his purse. It was a great deal of money that Trungle was demanding – half a year's wages for an unskilled working man. He counted out the coins and put them in the proffered hand. Trungle's fingers curled around them tight.

'There. Now tell me. If this is some trickery, I will have my gold back and give you sharp steel in its place.'

'No trickery, Shakespeare. I'm an honest dealer.' Trungle

put the coins in the pocket of his tight-fitting doublet, then pointed across the market square to a squat stone building. 'That's the town gaol. There were a couple of thieves in there. I'm Justice of the Peace here and they came before me in court these four days past. I sentenced them to be hanged. You probably saw them swinging at the Gallows Lane crossroads on the way into town. They knew your boy.'

'How do you know that?'

'Because I have kept my word to you. I have asked every man I met whether they have seen such a youth as you described. The two thieves told me they knew him. What's more they told me his name, the name you mentioned: Andrew Woode. They offered to tell me more if I saved them from the rope, but I was having none of that. Great Henry had the right way to deal with rogues. Hanged three score and twelve thousand of them in his reign, so we are told. Would that his daughter's justices had such stomach, for these vagabonds are vermin along the length of her realm.'

Shakespeare swallowed his distaste. 'What use is any of this to me if they are dead?'

'Because there was another one with them – and she is still alive.'

'Where is she?'

'You will see her presently.'

'Who are these people? How do they know Andrew?'

'The hanged ones called themselves Watson and Spindle, but they may well be invented names. I do not know their true identities, nor do I care. They will now be in hell where the devil can sort out who they are.'

The crack of a whip broke into their conversation. On the street, a cart was being pulled along by an old horse, driven by an equally old-looking man. A young woman, naked to the waist, was tied by the hands to the back of the cart. Behind her a broad, strong man in a leather jerkin raised a lash and brought it down across her pale-skinned back. She cried out in pain and stumbled forward, through mounds of horse-dung, trying to keep pace with the nag that dragged her. A small crowd watched and jeered. Some spat in her direction, others flung stones.

'There she is. You can speak with her when her punishment is done: whipped around the square at the cart's arse.'

'God's wounds, is this necessary?'

'Aye, it is. She is a vagabond. Same band as the two swinging. They've caused havoc in these parts with their thieving, begging and burning of barns. These three came into town with an eye to cutting purses, but we were ready for them. Pretty little thing. I'd have hanged her, too, but I liked the look of her. She could be put to work. Maybe I'll take her on as a dairymaid. Not the other two; villains and murderers through and through.'

'What has she told you?'

'Not a thing. The insolent hussy will not say a word to me. But the lash will open her mouth wide enough.'

'I want to talk with her. Let her loose.'

Trungle put up his hand. 'When she's been flogged.'

'Now.'

'Be very careful the way you talk to me, Shakespeare. I will not be ordered about by you. I know, too, that the boy you seek is accused of a heinous crime, for I have friends in Oxford—'

'In that case, as an officer of the courts, why have you not taken this information to St John's College or the city justices? I know why, Trungle: the glint of gold. You are as corrupt as worm-eaten fruit. Now release that girl.'

'Who *are* you, Shakespeare?'

'I think you know that, too, Trungle. If you have friends in Oxford, I am sure you are well aware of who I am. In which case, I am sure you would not seek to antagonise a senior officer to Sir Robert Cecil.'

Trungle scowled, then called over to the man with the whip. 'Release her and bring her here.'

'She's only had the two stripes.'

'Just do it, Josh.'

The whip-man looked disappointed, but he unbound the girl's ties and pushed her across the square towards Trungle and Shakespeare. She tripped on a loose cobble and fell at their feet. Shakespeare saw the livid red lash marks angling across her naked back. He bent down and gently pulled her up by her elbow.

'Cover yourself, mistress,' he said.

Slowly and with painful care, the girl pulled up her chemise, sliding her arms into the sleeves and anxiously arching her back so that the linen material did not touch her fresh and bloody wounds. She closed the garment around her small breasts and fixed the stays.

'What is your name?'

'Ursula. Ursula Dancer.'

Shakespeare turned to Trungle. 'I wish to speak with this young lady alone.'

'She is a common trull, a grubby vagabond! If that is a lady, then I am the King of England.'

'Come, mistress. We will repair to the tavern.'

'You'll have her back in gaol before the hour is out, Shakespeare.'

Shakespeare fished in his purse and took out a crown. He tossed it towards Trungle, letting it fall short so that it clattered to the cobbles at his feet.

'That will buy her freedom. She is in my care now. Begone, Trungle. I wish never to see your face again.'

*

The tavern-keeper was unhappy about letting the girl into his taproom, but a sixpence from Shakespeare put a halt to his grumbling. They were given a booth away from the eyes of the drinking men.

'You must be hungry, Mistress Dancer.'

She looked at him with contempt. 'I know what you pigging want and you're not having it. You won't buy me with pie and ale.'

'I have no wish to buy you. I want information from you. About a boy named Andrew Woode, whom I believe you know.'

She looked away, towards the leaded window. 'Never heard the name.'

'A lad in a black scholar's gown. Aged thirteen, but big and strong.'

'Means nothing to me.'

'He was with your vagabond band, with the two men hanging from the tree outside town: Watson and Spindle. They knew him.'

'Well, ask them. You'll get no more out of me than you will out of them.'

Shakespeare sighed. 'Do you want money? If you know where he is, I beg you tell me. I am desperate to bring him home.'

She said nothing. Shakespeare signalled to the bar wench, who came over and, with a sidelong glance at Ursula, took an order for food and ale.

'I ask you again, Mistress Dancer. Tell me what you know of Andrew. I wish you no ill.'

'Who are you?'

'I'm Andrew's father. His adoptive father. He was in some trouble and ran away from college in Oxford. I wish to get to him before the law officers do.'

'How do I know you're his pigging father? You could be anyone.'

'So you *do* know him?'

She stiffened. 'I didn't say that.'

'If you are trying to protect him by maintaining silence, I thank you. But I beg you to trust me. I swear to you that I am his father. We live together in London, but he is presently gone up to Oxford to study.'

'Swear on a Bible – in a church. Then I'll believe you.'

'Very well.'

'First I want my pie and ale. Then we'll go to the church. And I say just this: if I did know anything – and if I did tell you – then you'd have to promise me you won't let them whip me more, nor put me back in their verminous, pigging gaol.'

'I pledge it.'

The church of All Saints was in poor repair. It had clearly stood for many hundreds of years, but it had not fared well in recent times. Shakespeare swept his hand in an elegant invitation for the girl to precede him through the doorway. She held back.

'I've never been in a church before.'

He smiled. 'There is nothing to fear. God will look kindly on you.'

'I've done things . . .'

'I do not wish to know and neither, I am certain, does the Lord. Follow me.'

Shakespeare led the way. A young curate was at prayer but looked up.

'Good day, reverend sir,' Shakespeare said. 'Do you have a Bible that we might borrow?'

'I will fetch it for you.'

He returned swiftly with a large, much fingered and torn

tome, which he placed on the plain table that served as an altar.

The girl was looking about the building in awe. 'It's pigging huge. I knew they looked big from outside, but inside it's amazing. What do they do in here?'

'Converse with God, pray to him for all our needs: bread . . . forgiveness.'

She nodded towards the great book. 'Is that it, then, the Bible?'

'Indeed, it is.'

'Go on then. Swear on it.'

Shakespeare placed the palm of his right hand on the book. 'I swear by Almighty God that I am the adoptive father of Andrew Woode and that I am looking for him to save him, and not to do him any harm.'

'That's it, is it?'

'Yes. Unless you wish me to say anything else.'

'Say this: let God strike me down if I am lying.'

Shakespeare smiled. 'Let God strike me down if I am lying.'

'I suppose I had better believe you, then. Yes, I know Andrew Woode. Daft as a pig, but I liked him.'

'Has anything ill happened?'

'He was with our band. Now he's been pressed and taken for a soldier.'

Shakespeare's heart sank. 'But he is only thirteen years!'

Ursula bristled, feeling herself under attack, as though this man blamed her for allowing the boy to be taken.

'Well, he's pigging alive, isn't he? At least he has a chance with soldiering. It was either that or be hanged.'

Shakespeare paused before speaking. He needed her help and he needed it quickly.

'Tell me when this all happened and where he might have been taken. Help me and I will help you. Tell me everything

– with honesty – and I will protect you and see you right. Do you understand?'

She laughed. 'Honesty! That was his favourite pigging word! And look where it got him.'

# Chapter 35

BOLTFOOT WAS PISSING in the backyard when he heard the sound of a door closing. Quickly, he adjusted his dress and hobbled inside. Mistress Winter had long since departed from her daily chores; that could only mean Ivory had gone from the front door.

He muttered an oath, flung open the door and looked about. In the distance, he saw him – loping along like a wolf, southwards towards the river and the ferry.

'Come back here!'

Ivory thrust two fingers in the air without turning round and increased his pace.

Boltfoot cursed, went indoors, collected his cutlass, caliver, powder and shot and limped out after Ivory. He was surprisingly nimble, despite his club-foot, but he was nowhere near as fast as his quarry. He dragged his foot along the dusty road towards the river, arriving just in time to see the ferry leaving the quayside, with Ivory waving to him merrily from the stern.

Boltfoot grabbed the grey-bearded mooring man. 'How long until the next ferry?'

'Half an hour. Why the haste?'

'Is there a tilt-boat here? Is there a fast rower will get me across before the ferry is landed in Gravesend?'

'How much you talking about?'

'Two shillings?'

'Half a crown and you've a deal.'

'You'll take me?'

'No, but my boy will. He has a small wherry-boat. William!'

A strong-armed lad came running.

'Want to earn two shillings for you and sixpence for me, William? This gentleman wants to cross the river in a hurry. Wants to beat the ferry. Can you manage that?'

The lad, who must have been eighteen, looked out at the wallowing, heavily laden ferry and the churning waters of the turning tide in this narrow stretch of the Thames.

'Aye, Father, I reckon I can.' He looked Boltfoot up and down uncritically, then walked down the water-stairs to his little wherry. 'Do you need assistance embarking, master?'

Boltfoot smiled. He could have said, 'I've jumped in more cockboats and wherries than you've had herring dinners,' but instead he merely followed the lad down and shuffled himself into the boat.

'Fine weapon-of-war you have there,' the rower said, looking appreciatively at Boltfoot's caliver, as he untied the mooring rope and pushed off.

'And a fine strong arm you have, lad. Now show me how good you are at rowing.'

'With a will, sir. With a will.'

The rower was as good as his father's boast. He pulled hard against the encroaching tide and undertows, to far greater effect than the ferrymen, who were weighed down by a wagon, two oxen and a dozen or more passengers. As the little wherry caught and passed the ferry, Boltfoot gazed across at Ivory and put up two fingers in salute.

Boltfoot was waiting on the quay when the ferry docked. He had his caliver in his arms, primed with powder and with a heavy ball thrust down the muzzle. Ivory's face was clouded with wrath as he jumped ashore and, ignoring the weapon, strode past Boltfoot, shouldering him aside. Boltfoot stumbled sideways, but did not fall.

He turned and stabbed the butt of the weapon into Ivory's back. Ivory lost his footing and fell to his knees on the grey slats of decking. Boltfoot stood above him, the muzzle now pointing downwards, pressed into the nape of his neck.

Ivory shook the cold steel off his neck and rose to his feet. He turned and faced Boltfoot.

'If you think you can fright me with that, you are mightily mistaken, Cooper. I have been your prisoner too long. Today, I will have a game of cards and a turn with a woman, and I will not be stopped by a monstrous cripple with a Spanish gun and a pirate's cutlass. Indeed, I will not, for I know you have orders to keep me alive and will not use it.'

Boltfoot pressed the muzzle into the man's throat.

'You know only part of my orders, Ivory. It is true I have been told to keep you alive, but above and beyond that I have been ordered to keep guard over the instrument you carry. They don't want you to die, but if it is a choice between you and the glass, then they are quite clear about which must take precedence.'

'Then shoot away, or shove your gun-muzzle up your arse, for I am off for some merriment at a little alehouse I know hereabouts. Come and watch me play at cards if you like, Cooper. I'll buy you a gage of beer and you might even learn a trick or two.'

Boltfoot sighed and shrugged his shoulders in seeming resignation. He pulled the muzzle of the caliver to one side, but instead of putting it out of harm's way, he swung it back with numbing force into the side of Ivory's head.

*

'This arrived for you less than an hour since,' Dee said, handing Shakespeare a letter.

He recognised Cecil's seal, hesitated, then opened it. He read it quickly, then looked up at Dee in surprise. 'He says he understands my predicament and feels great sorrow. He offers to do what he can to help and protect Andrew.'

'Then he is a better man than I had imagined, Mr Shakespeare.'

'There is more . . .'

Shakespeare read the last two sentences again, to himself.

*'But I must urge you to make haste with your inquiries, John, for I have great need of you here in London. There is a mission that I believe can be entrusted to you alone. Do this for England and all indiscretions will be washed away like dust in a summer rain.'*

Shakespeare sighed. It was a condition. Come to me, carry out this task I have for you and I will use all my considerable power to save your boy.

'Mr Shakespeare?'

He shook his head. 'It is nothing, Dr Dee . . . nothing more than I would expect.'

'What will you do now? From what you say, you seem certain that Andrew has been pressed into service by this provost Pinkney.'

'There can be no doubt. The girl's description fits him precisely. They must be on their way to Brittany, or perhaps they are already there. Anyway, that is the way I must go. We will rest tonight and ride for Kent in the morning. Come, prepare yourself. We have a fair ride ahead of us. The girl will come with us. So will Oxx and Godwit.'

They were in their rented chamber in the Blue Boar. Oxx guarded the door, while Godwit had taken Ursula to the ordinary for food.

'Do you not have unsettled business here in Oxford, Mr Shakespeare?'

'I do not have the time to deal with it.'

'I have been thinking about Mr Fitzherbert, the tutor.'

Shakespeare sighed. 'I did not like the man, but does that mean he is a felon? He is related to traitors, Catholic exiles who lend assistance to Philip of Spain and the Pope. But as he pointed out himself, that does not make him either a Papist or a traitor.'

'I still believe he warrants investigation. There is another Fitzherbert, Tom Fitzherbert, who occasionally rides with Richard Topcliffe and his vile band of priest-hunters.'

'Indeed, yes, I have encountered him in past years, Dr Dee. I believe he considers priest-hunting a better sport than chasing deer.'

'Well, *that* Fitzherbert is not a Papist.'

'Indeed not. But what of it?'

'Mr Shakespeare! I have heard it said that Topcliffe bears a blood-grudge against you. If he had some power over Tom Fitzherbert . . .'

There was no doubt that the white-haired old torturer Topcliffe would happily see the entire Shakespeare family go painfully to their graves. Their paths had crossed many times, for Shakespeare loathed Topcliffe's delight in torture and Topcliffe despised Shakespeare for marrying a Catholic and for what he saw as the Papist sympathies of some in his family. But a link between Topcliffe and the tutor James Fitzherbert? To a plot against Andrew?

'God's teeth, Dr Dee, there is no shortage of Fitzherberts in England. They are a large family with roots back to the Conquest.'

'Yet it is not such a long shot . . .'

Shakespeare pondered a moment. There was time enough

this evening to pay a visit to St John's College. He strapped on his sword, then picked up the wheel-lock pistol he had acquired from the highway robber and thrust it into his belt. He clapped the old alchemist on the back.

'Thank you, Dr Dee. You are a more clear-thinking man than I had given you credit for.'

'Ah, Mr Shakespeare.' The college servant at the gatehouse welcomed Shakespeare like an old friend. 'Have you found that lad of yours?'

Shakespeare eyed the man and wondered again what part he might have played in Andrew's escape. He shook his head.

'Not yet, but I have hope.'

'I pray he will be well, master. I do indeed.'

'Thank you. I am here to see Mr Fitzherbert, my boy's tutor.'

'Then I fear you have had a wasted journey, sir, for he is gone.'

'Gone where?'

'No one knows, Mr Shakespeare. He just disappeared, along with his belongings, like a will-o'-the-wisp. The day after you were last here, it was, if I recall right.'

Clarkson was at the house in Tilbury when Boltfoot arrived home with Ivory. Cecil's retainer looked at Ivory's bandaged head with dismay.

'How did this injury come about?'

Boltfoot grunted. 'He can tell you himself.'

'Well, Mr Ivory?'

'He hit me with his caliver. This shambling ruin of a man could have killed me, Mr Clarkson. I would have been better served being guarded by a dog than this wretch.'

'Is this true, Mr Cooper?'

'Wish I *had* killed him.' Boltfoot looked away.

Clarkson removed the makeshift bandage and examined Ivory's head carefully. It was bruised and there was a small cut. The blow had clearly dazed the man, but he seemed otherwise hale.

'I think you will live. And I take it the perspective glass is equally safe?'

'As close-fixed to me as my prick but not so highly esteemed.'

'Then let us go. A ship awaits you.'

Boltfoot said a silent prayer of thanks.

'You, too, Mr Cooper.'

Boltfoot glared at Clarkson with sudden loathing. 'If Ivory is to embark on a ship, then my work is done. I will not be needed there.'

'I am afraid that is not how Sir Robert Cecil sees it. He is most impressed by your work so far in protecting Mr Ivory and the glass, and he wishes you to remain with him still. It seems you are both to undertake a mission of great importance to this realm. Your services are considered more vital now than ever, Mr Cooper.'

'No. My seafaring days are done. I am a married man with a small child. I work for John Shakespeare and I must go to him.'

Clarkson touched Boltfoot's arm as if they were old comrades. 'I am sorry, Mr Cooper, but this is not being *asked* of you – you are *ordered* to do it, in the Queen's name.'

Boltfoot ground his feet into the straw-strewn flooring like a stubborn colt that will not advance. 'No. Unless I hear it from my master himself.'

Clarkson's hand lingered on Boltfoot's shoulder and gripped it. He made him meet his eyes.

'Sir Robert is your master's master, and Mr Shakespeare is engaged on other business . . .'

He paused. There was nothing to be gained in telling Boltfoot that that business concerned Andrew Woode.

'I can tell you that this voyage you are to embark on with Mr Ivory may well be the most hazardous part of your mission.'

Boltfoot looked at Ivory and saw he was smirking. 'A plague of Satan's hornets on you, Ivory.'

Clarkson affected not to hear and continued with his instructions. 'You will be posted aboard a royal ship, under the command of Sir Martin Frobisher. His fleet sails from the Thames on the morrow. You are to embark this evening. There is no time to be lost.'

Ivory burst out laughing. 'Frobisher! He'll love you, Cooper. Once he hears you were a Drake man, I say ten shillings to a mark he'll have you striped at the mainmast by week's end!'

# Act 3
## To Brittany

# Chapter 36

S HAKESPEARE REINED IN and looked down at the fine manor house at Chevening in Kent. John Dee came to a halt on his left; Ursula Dancer, riding bareback and astride her gelding in the way of a gypsy rider, stopped at his right hand. Oxx and Godwit rode a little way ahead.

The journey here had taken two and a half days, cutting south by the western approaches to London town. It seemed to Shakespeare that his whole life these days was spent in the saddle. His thighs were like leather, beyond chafing.

The day was still. Not a breath of wind. A herd of fallow deer grazed beneath trees in the lee of the ragstone-built manor. It was the country home of Thomas Digges, one-time student under Dee and his joint deviser of the perspective glass.

'Here we are, Dr Dee,' Shakespeare said. 'This is to be your home until it is decreed that you are no longer in danger.'

He signalled to Oxx, who kicked on ahead. Shakespeare and the others followed him, descending through the parkland and causing the deer to drift away as they passed.

They were stopped before they reached the stables by a man with a pair of pistols. Oxx had his own weapons primed and poised. Shakespeare shook his head to indicate to both men that there was no danger and rode up to the man with the pistols.

'Good day, Mr Shoe.'

'Ah, Mr Shakespeare. Can't be too careful, sir.'

'Quite so. It is good to see you so diligent.'

Jonas Shoe was an unprepossessing man – short, squat and bald. He worked for Francis Mills, Shakespeare's associate in the service of Sir Robert Cecil. His very ordinariness was one of his great strengths, for he could meld into any crowd without remark.

'Is Frank Mills here?'

'He is indeed. Shall I convey a message to him, sir?'

'Tell him I am here with Dr Dee. Tell this also to Mr Digges, if you would. And send a groom for our horses. They are in great need of drink, as are we.'

Thomas Digges clasped Dee in an embrace that would have done credit to the bears of Southwark.

'Let me look at you, my wondrous mathematical father. It is too long since last we met.'

'Far too long, mathematical son and heir, far too long. And I had heard you were unwell.'

'Oh, that is nothing. The sunshine cures all ills. But pray, what has happened to your resplendent beard?'

'It is my disguise. It seems you and I are the most wanted men in England, though I wish it were reflected in the weight of my always empty purse.'

'Well, thanks be to Pythagoras and Archimedes that you are here at last, for I was going mad with this fellow.' He nodded towards Mills. 'I am told he is the cleverest intelligencer in Cecil's employ, and can disentangle the most complex of codes. Yet when I try to converse with him on the flaws of Ptolemy and the true movements of the celestial spheres, his eyes cloud like an old man's. Talking to him is like trying to teach new tricks to a dying dog.'

Mills, tall and stooped, ignored the insult and, turning to

Shakespeare, drew him aside. 'It is a pleasure to welcome you, John, but I must tell you that Cecil is most anxious to see you. There is work he wishes you to do.'

'So I understand. Have you any idea what he has in mind?'

'Only that it involves the perspective glass and Brittany. The war there gathers pace. If we cannot secure Brest from the Spanish, the outlook for England is bleak.'

'Is there word from Boltfoot?'

'He is safe, but I know no more than that.'

Well, that was some comfort. If only the same were true of Andrew.

They were all in the withdrawing room of Digges's manor, taking refreshment. Ursula had been sent to the kitchens with Oxx and Godwit to be fed and found lodgings within the house.

'I am told by Jonas Shoe that there is some ragged vagabond girl with you,' Mills said.

'I am indebted to her, yet do not know what to do with her. For the present, she must stay here.'

And yet he could see the difficulties. The girl was an inveterate thief. On the ride here, she had filched a tankard from an inn and he had caught her trying to remove coins from his own purse. He had promised to protect her, but he feared no good would come of it. She would likely make off with the family silver.

'But I promise I will return for her.'

Shakespeare told his story over supper. Digges, a large man who looked older than Dee, although he must have been at least ten years the younger, listened attentively. He hammered his fist on the table.

'It is what I have been telling Her Royal Majesty for years. We need to model a new army – a professional standing army.

With respect to your lad, Mr Shakespeare, what use is a terrified boy of thirteen? Or an ancient drunken vagrant? Pressed men are the dregs of our land, gentlemen – and a hindrance to military endeavours.'

Shakespeare knew a little of Digges's history. Though not a fighting man, he was acknowledged a master of the art and science of war. He had written on the great siege guns, the proper building of fortifications, military formations and mining. As a follower of the late Earl of Leicester, he had been both mustermaster general and trench-master in the Low Countries campaign of '85.

'How is Captain-General Norreys to protect the port of Brest with such men sent to him? And if the Spaniard snares Brest, we shall all be saying Hail Marys before the year is out. A professional army of well-trained English soldiers is what we need. They would be a match for any army Spain could muster and, I believe, would save money, too.'

'Save money, Mr Digges?' Mills demanded, heavy scepticism in his tone.

Digges eyed Mills with distaste. 'You have never been to war, sir, or you would understand the way things are. Fraud, sir, fraud! It is a greater menace than enemy fire or God-given flux. And always it is the bawdy-house captains who are to blame. My lord of Leicester knew it – and Black John Norreys knows it but connives at it. Too many captains go to war to fill their purses, not fight for Queen and country. They are petty princes, more concerned with swiving the camp followers than campaigning. I tell you, many of them withhold their men's pay until the clamour becomes too great – and then they send them out to skirmish with little hope of survival. Dead men's pay, gentlemen. Dead men's pay! With *my* army, we would have live soldiers and dead Spaniards.'

Shakespeare's jaw tightened. The conversation threw the

bloody horror of what Andrew faced into stark relief. Shakespeare could not be concerned about reorganising the army. Leave that to another day; he had to deal with matters as they were. He had to find Andrew and haul him out of the line of fire before some Spanish sword or ball cut him down.

The talk turned to old times and alchemy. Shakespeare took the opportunity to speak quietly again with Francis Mills.

'Give me the truth about the war, Frank.'

'Bad. The Spanish have completed their fort at the spit of land known as Crozon, on cliffs overlooking Brest roads. It is clear they have the cannon-power to control all shipping in and out of the harbour. It cannot be long before they take the town of Brest itself.'

'How strong is this fortress?'

'Exceptionally so. The walls are built of stone up to thirty-seven feet thick, above two-hundred-foot cliffs. It was designed by the engineer Don Cristobal de Rojas who, I am told by Mr Digges, knows as much about military fortifications as any man living. He was responsible for the fortification of Cadiz and Lisbon and Águila's main Brittany fort at the mouth of the Blavet river.'

'Then the news is all bad.'

'Well, at least Her Majesty now sees the danger. She has recalled Black John to court and has assured him that he will have everything he needs. He returns to the war with new levies any day. There are three thousand men being recruited from eighteen counties.'

'Not Lancashire?'

'No. Only southern counties. They are being removed to Brittany with great speed. Norreys is supported by a fleet under Frobisher. The new levies are to be embarked at ports all along the south coast, as far as Plymouth. The fear is that this will all be too late.'

Shakespeare listened intently. Andrew would be in one of those levies – but at which port would they embark? From Oxfordshire, Provost Pinkney would likely take the recruits directly south towards Portsmouth, or perhaps further west towards Poole, Weymouth or Plymouth. Certainly not to the naval dockyards east of London on the Thames. There was nothing for it: Shakespeare would have to trawl through them. He just prayed he was in time to find the boy before he crossed the narrow sea to war.

Men and equipment thronged the muddy banks of the Thames. A tangle of humanity, iron, steel, tar and rope, wrought for killing.

Four great royal ships, their sails furled, were anchored in midstream along with three armed merchantmen. Three more merchantmen and a fifth royal ship, the *Vanguard*, were moored against the long quayside. Loading of barrels of powder and biscuit was constant. The river teemed with traffic – cockboats and wherries, taking men and supplies in all directions. Cries of salute, the stench of fresh-applied pitch, the creak of cables, the splash of oars – the sounds and smells of the river.

Treadwheel cranes of oak swung out their jibs, hoisting the great siege guns inch by inch towards the decks of the merchantmen. One crane was set aside for embarking the beasts: warhorses suspended in cradles, pigs in netting, chickens in closed woven baskets.

The panoply of war was immense, from the might of cannon to the commonplace: thousands of bricks to build ovens, hundreds of frying pans, lanterns, mortars and pestles, funnels, taps and tap-borers, great bundles of firewood, tallow for light, bells to summon the men to meals, weighing scales and fishing nets. The men carried their weapons and packs, with all they would need on the march: powder, lead, knives, porringers and cups.

Among this brutal bustle of a war machine preparing to depart, few would have noticed the three men disembarking from a wherry. Clarkson walked beside Ivory, with Boltfoot limping behind as they made their way from the water-stairs towards the Treasurer's House beside the Royal Docks.

Boltfoot cradled his primed caliver. His grip was tight, his finger on the trigger. His eyes moved constantly, looking for the face in the crowd that stared too long, or the man who was out of step. His eyes were sharp and had been trained for this by his years in service with John Shakespeare. Ivory might have the best eye in the realm, but Boltfoot could not think himself far behind.

Frobisher was in the Treasurer's House. He glanced at the newcomers without interest, then turned back to his conversation with one of his lieutenants.

'All powder is accounted for, Mr Millwater? Two hundred thousand pounds for cannon, fifty thousand for hagbuts and calivers. All dry and tight?'

'Yes, Sir Martin.'

'None skimmed?'

'No, Sir Martin.'

'How many desertions?'

The lieutenant looked uneasy.

'Speak, man, before I remove your brains from their housing!'

'Three hundred and fifteen. Twenty of those recaptured and thrown into gaol. Morale is low . . . the delays.'

'God's blood, what sort of men am I dealing with here? Does Norreys have no control?'

'He has been drilling them relentlessly, but they are mostly poor soldiers. He is as unhappy as you, Sir Martin. This lack of wind—'

'We will have a fair breeze in the morning. What of my marines?'

'All accounted for. Two thousand fighting men.'

'*Real* fighting men.'

Clarkson approached him. 'Sir Martin, if I may interrupt. I have Mr Ivory, and his companion, Mr Cooper.'

Frobisher nodded to his lieutenant. 'Be so good as to leave us now, Mr Millwater, and mark all I have said. You will assume command of the *Quittance* with immediate effect, then return here as ship's master at Morlaix.'

'Yes, sir.' Millwater bowed in salute and marched out.

Frobisher turned to the newcomers and studied Ivory from head to toe. 'I know that rogue. Still not been blinded for your cheating, insolent ways, Mr Eye?'

'Still not been hanged for piracy, Sir Martin?'

'No, but I'll hang you as soon as I no longer need you. And I am happy to see from your bandaged head that someone else has been knocking you about.' He turned to Boltfoot. 'And what is this woodlouse? Why is he armed with Spanish shot and steel?'

Boltfoot lowered his ornate caliver, which had, indeed, been captured from a Spaniard, and bowed his head in deference. 'Cooper, Sir Martin. Boltfoot Cooper.'

'Formerly of Drake's service,' Ivory put in.

Frobisher raised an eyebrow in scorn. He was powerfully built with a chest that filled out his slashed gold and damson doublet. An eyeglass dangled from a cord about his neck and his large hand never strayed far from the hilt of his sword. His hair was cut short and curled back from his forehead, and his red-brown beard descended into a fine starched ruff.

'Drake, eh? Well, you'll have learnt nothing of seafaring from that worthless dog. Are you a fighting man?'

'Aye.'

'Good, because we'll need all we can muster.'

'His mission is to afford constant protection to Mr Ivory and the instrument in his possession,' Clarkson said. 'He has succeeded in keeping him alive thus far. I know my master has told you all this, so I will leave them in your hands to use to best advantage. God speed you.'

'Thank you, Mr Clarkson. Always a pleasure. And send my compliments to Sir Robert, if you will. Now then,' he said to Ivory and Boltfoot. 'You two weevils will both be on the *Vanguard* with me. Go aboard now and find berths. The master is expecting you. Have you been told aught about this mission?'

'No,' Ivory said. 'But I was hoping for a game of cards and a woman before sailing.'

'There'll be none of that. I have been delayed too long. We sail for Brittany on the morning tide. I will give you full details of what is required in due course. Now be gone. I have work to do.'

Not far from the Treasurer's House, Janus Trayne lounged against the doorway of a tavern, a tankard of beer in his hand. He had seen Ivory, Clarkson and Boltfoot while they were still in the boat, hoving towards shore. Even with his head bandaged, Ivory was unmistakable. That whiskery grey beard, those sharp, questing eyes.

Trayne allowed himself a smile and carried on drinking as, now, they emerged from the Treasurer's House and walked towards the *Vanguard*. So, he had found his quarry again. And now he knew that Ivory would be aboard Frobisher's ship. He knew because he had been told by Weld. It could not have worked out better. He could almost feel the perspective glass in his grasp, almost smell its hide casing. Ivory's companion was hobbling; was that Cooper, the man who had stabbed him at

Portsmouth? Well, he'd do for him, too. Make him pay for the injury to his wrist and for the humiliation in the woods near Sudbury.

In the morning, before leaving Chevening, Shakespeare told Mills of the events at Lathom House in Lancashire, culminating in the Earl of Derby's death.

'Very convenient,' Mills said.

'Indeed, there are many who might have wished my lord of Derby dead. But that is not my concern now. It is in the hands of a commission of inquiry – Sir George Carey and Sir Thomas Egerton.'

Mills raised an eyebrow. 'Not your concern, John?' he said doubtfully.

'You are right. It still preys on my soul.'

'What is your instinct?'

'Poison. But how and by whom? So many had motives, so many had the opportunity.'

'Well, I should be careful if I were you. Leave it to Carey and Egerton.'

Shakespeare fished into his doublet. 'Here, Frank, something to occupy your mind while you wait in this house, keeping company with these mathematical men.'

He handed the missive found in the lining of Father Lamb's doublet to Frank Mills, who read it quickly, along with the secret writing that had been revealed.

'Well, one is a straightforward letter from a seminary priest to Rome or Rheims. But what is this other gibberish? "*The killing birds wait in line. The hawks edge nearer, even as golden eagles under soaring eyries dive. Malevolent dove, evil nightjar, baleful ibis and twisted hoodcrow toss overhead, preying on insects, shrews or newts. Let dogs fester, orphans rot, ere rooks lay down and die.*"'

'You tell me, Frank. You are a man who loves to unveil the secret of a cipher. I sent a copy of the original to Cecil, but at that time I had not discovered the *hidden* writing.'

'Are you sure you *wish* to know what it means?'

'I will take the risk.'

'Will you now ride to court and Cecil?'

'I cannot. Tell him I will come to him as soon as I have found the boy. But if I discover he has already crossed to Brittany, then I must follow him there.'

Mills closed his eyes and stretched his tall thin frame as though wondering how to say something, and how much to reveal.

'Frank?'

'There is more, John. Let me just say this . . .' He chose his words with care. 'Cecil will not be unhappy if you make your way to Brittany.'

'Is that so?'

'I don't know any more, just that. Whatever the mission he proposes for you, it is over there.'

'Are you suggesting Cecil is somehow behind all my troubles?' Shakespeare felt a sudden chill of fear.

'Indeed not. No, no. The fact that you are likely to go to Brittany anyway is merely fortuitous. But we both know how the Cecils like to seize on fortuitous events and use them to advantage.'

Shakespeare relaxed a little. It seemed that whatever diversion he took, his road would always ultimately converge with Cecil's planned path. Well, if Cecil wished him to go to Brittany, he had every intention of obliging him on his own account. Cecil could reveal his hand there.

He thanked Mills. He was almost warming to the man. Their relationship over the years since first they worked together for Mr Secretary Walsingham had always been difficult and tempestuous. Perhaps they were learning to live together, like a couple forced to marry who discover after ten years together that they quite like each other after all.

'Thank you for dealing straight with me,' Shakespeare said. 'And do what I suggested to you long ago: be done with that wife. You are looking less melancholy than I have seen you in months now that you are away from her.'

Mills uttered a small, sad laugh. 'In truth I find myself remarkably cheered by my absence from the adulterous slattern. I no longer dream of slitting her throat. Well, not so frequently, leastwise. But no, I fear I will not leave her. Death will us part.'

# Chapter 37

I N THE STABLES of Thomas Digges's manor house, Shakespeare appraised Ursula in her new clothes. Her tatters had been replaced with a plain worsted gown belonging to Digges's wife, Agnes. She looked respectable.

'How does that feel?'

'Like nettles and hedgehogs. It's going to be hot today. I'll die in this.'

'Well, you'll have to deal with that as it happens. I can tell you that you look a great deal more comely than you did. No one would take you for a thief dressed like that.'

'They'd be pigging wrong then, wouldn't they.'

'There is to be no more stealing. You are staying here in this manor and you will be in the charge of Mr Mills. He will ensure you are fed properly and I have told him I want you to have some education. He will arrange that.'

'I don't want no learning. I want to come with you. You're going to pigging France.'

Shakespeare ignored her plea. 'If you are caught stealing again, then you will be sent away from this place and your chance of a decent life will be gone. Stay here, try to learn your alphabet and some writing, and I pledge that, when I return, I will find a position for you in some household. I believe you to be good. This is your one chance to prove it.'

'You're worse than Andrew pigging Woode.'

The groom brought out Shakespeare's bay gelding, saddled up.

'And if you are permitted to do any riding while you are here – and that is down to Mr Mills and Mr Digges – you will use a saddle. For if you do not, you will be marked down as a vagabond wherever you go. Try it – you might grow to prefer it. You might also find that townsfolk treat you with a great deal more respect.'

Ursula turned her face away. For a moment, Shakespeare wondered whether she was about to cry, but then realised it was a preposterous thought. This girl had lived through harshness that a seasoned soldier might never see. What was left in life to bring tears to her eyes?

Shakespeare mounted his charge. Without another word, he patted the horse's neck, then shook the reins and rode out.

Marching. Endless marching. Andrew had always had strong legs and a good heart. He had been the fastest runner of all his friends. But nothing could have prepared him for this daily, gruelling slog, through the summer heat as the ever-changing band of recruits threaded its way down through southern England. Along the way, they picked up new pressed men and lost others to desertion and, in the case of one persistent offender, the sting of Provost Pinkney's summary justice.

Andrew kept his head up and marched. He did not complain about the exhaustion, nor the poor food of oatmeal and rotting salt beef. The only comfort was the ale, which was bought or requisitioned from alehouses and taverns along the way.

They were camped near Weymouth when Reaphook approached him. 'I'm going tonight, slipping away. Come with me.'

Andrew gulped down the remainder of his cup of ale. 'Why would I want to go with you?'

'It's our last chance. Together, we can get away. Help each other . . . It's got to be better with two.'

'You're insane, Reaphook. I'd rather dine with the devil than go with you. Anyway, he'll hang you.'

'Not if he doesn't catch me he won't. I'm not going to no war. Only sheep walk willingly to slaughter. And for what? Eightpence a day they're supposed to pay us, which is paltry enough seeing that they take half of it for the muck they call food. And even the fourpence left over we never see. Whose purse do you think that goes in?'

'Stow you, Reaphook. Do you ever stop complaining?'

'There's a great deal to complain about. My feet are nothing but blisters so that my feet squelch with blood and pus.'

'Wish you were still with Staffy, do you? Should have treated him with respect. He was twice the man you are.'

Reaphook snarled. 'He wasn't so bastardly clean. You didn't see the worst of him.'

Andrew laughed. 'Well, he put up with you until you betrayed him. Being in his band was worse than marching with the militia, was it? You should have seen how the vagabonds all laughed when Provost Pinkney pressed you into service. Just like you betrayed Staffy. Serves you right, Reaphook.'

'I'll kill you one day, boy. I'll pluck out your eyes with my sickle and tread them into the dust.'

Andrew's fear of Reaphook had been replaced by anger. 'You're a dirty turd of a man. You're less than a man for the way you treated Ursula.'

'Well, I had her, boy. She's a grubby little drab, but I had her first.'

Andrew considered pushing his fist into Reaphook's nasty face for talking of Ursula in such terms. Instead, he arched his aching back. 'I'm tired of listening to this. I'm going to lay out my palliasse and sleep. You can piss off into the night if you want to, but I'll be laughing when Pinkney whips you and strings you up.'

Reaphook looked at him with loathing. 'Spindle should have done for you when he had the chance. There'll be another time, though. I'll make sure of that.'

The monkey leapt through the rigging with crazy abandon, as though she had returned to the freedom of her jungle home in the Americas. The mariners fell for her instantly, could not take their eyes off the little animal.

Boltfoot sat on the deck beneath the bulwark, watching the antics with half an eye. Mainly he watched Ivory, who had climbed higher up and stood alone in the maintop, keeping lookout.

After days without wind, the *Vanguard* was out in the open seas, tacking east towards Cape Margate and Foreness Point, before the long turn into the narrow seas and the run westwards. The sea was racing with white-flecked waves. If the wind held, they should be in Brittany within three or, at the most, four days. The sooner, the better, for Boltfoot. The crew and fighting men on this vessel seemed to have been dredged from the gaols of London. He trusted none of them.

Boltfoot had heard that Captain-General Norreys was confined to his cabin, seasick. The monkey was what most men talked of, though – that and its exotic owner, a great and beautiful lady, travelling with Norreys. No one knew who she was, though someone said she was a Frenchie, for they had heard her speak with a strange accent. Most believed her to be Black John's whore.

Frobisher stood by the helm or on the poopdeck. He was restless, ever-present. Two years away from the sea, ashore at his Yorkshire home, had made him hungry for the churn of the ocean, and even hungrier for action. Men who had served under him before knew to avoid him when he was like this. His energy could be brittle.

A shadow came across Boltfoot. A young gentleman officer stood in front of him in a black and gold doublet, as though he had come direct from the royal presence. Boltfoot looked up, but did not move.

'Get up, man,' the officer ordered. 'There is work to be done.'

Boltfoot rose to his feet. 'I am not here as crew, master,' he said with due deference.

'I say who is crew.' He nodded over towards some loose ropes. 'Stow those cables, then fetch me brandy.'

'No, sir, you have no authority over me.' Boltfoot could see that this man was new to the sea and that he had no idea either what he was doing or what needed to be done. 'It is not my task.'

'Damn you, man.' The officer raised his hand to strike Boltfoot. Suddenly, Frobisher's hand clasped the wrist.

'What is this?' he growled. 'Why are you raising your hand to this man?'

'He disobeyed an order, Sir Martin.'

'Did he now?'

Frobisher raised his gold-inlaid wheel-lock pistol, but instead of threatening Boltfoot, he battered the stock into the officer's head and shoulder, clubbing him down to the deck. Frobisher stood over him with contempt, then turned to his lieutenant.

'Remove this man to his quarters. He will remain there until I decide what to do with him.' He turned to the other officers. 'For those not acquainted with my methods, let this be a lesson: I alone administer discipline aboard my vessels. My men will be treated with respect, as will I. And I am to be addressed as admiral at all times.'

Above him the monkey had leapt down through the rigging and was sitting on the yard-arm watching the proceedings. Frobisher ignored her.

'As for you, Mr Cooper, I see you attract trouble. Are you, also, a thief like Drake?'

Boltfoot was standing stiffly. 'No, admiral, I am not. In truth, Drake stole from me as he steals from all men. He stole gold from me and Will Legge.'

'Well, as long as you bear hatred towards Drake, you may yet turn out to be a friend of mine. At ease, Mr Cooper.'

Boltfoot tried to relax, but could not. He was being sent off to war in Brittany! What was that godforsaken spit of land to do with him? Why should he die and leave a widow and orphan just to protect some poxy Frenchies from rampaging Spaniards?

'Thank you, admiral,' was all he said.

'You'll find me harsh but fair. But I tell you this: I need Mr Eye and his infernal contraption. Make sure they remain safe.'

'I will do my utmost.'

'Good man, Mr Cooper.'

Frobisher resumed his pacing of the deck, but Boltfoot did not feel reassured. If the would-be assassin from Portsmouth or any confederate was still seeking Ivory, they would be here. But how could he be spotted among a ship's complement of hundreds of men?

John Shakespeare looked out over the port and bay of Weymouth in Dorset. Seagulls screeched and swooped overhead. In the harbour entrance, waves broke and foamed.

It was mid-morning and the fish market was closing for

business. The day's trades had been made; cod, haddock, John Dory and herring bought and sold.

Shakespeare stopped a porter and asked about soldiers.

'Talk to the mayor,' the man said curtly, pointing at a building that looked out over the port. 'That's his counting house.'

Shakespeare's progress here along the coastal roads had been swift. First Portsmouth, then Southampton, then Poole, now this wide bay. Along the route, he had sought soldiers. Mostly, he had found stragglers and deserters, who ran from him as though he were a provost sent to round them up. He also encountered companies of recruits in the towns, one of a hundred men, another of thirty. He was told that most men had now gone to join Captain-General Norreys at Paimpol in Brittany.

A couple of recruiting sergeants said they had heard of Pinkney, but had nothing to say about him other than that he was a Low Countries veteran. They had no idea where he might be.

Now, at Weymouth, the mayor studied Shakespeare suspiciously.

'Aye, there was a company here,' he said at last. His eyes swivelled from Shakespeare to the doorway, as if expecting to be set upon by robbers. 'New-pressed recruits by the look of them. Shabby, villainous lot, they were. They are all embarked for Brittany now. Why? Who wants to know?'

'I am John Shakespeare, an officer of Sir Robert Cecil. I am on urgent business.'

'Cecil, eh? Well, they left with the tide, crowded aboard a couple of old fishing hoys. No bark would take them. The hoy masters didn't want them, but even less did I want men-at-arms remaining in town, plundering food, strong liquor and our womenfolk. They had been here three nights and were becoming ever more lawless and drunk, waving their pikes and pricks about. The Lord knows how many bastard babies will be born here in nine months' time. We have had levies through here before, so we know that soldiers will forage, but this was worse – this was pillage. I feared for the safety of all. In the end I twisted the hoy skippers by the arm, called in favours and paid them out of my own coffers. If you work for Cecil, as you say, then you can tell him I want my money back and Her Majesty should pay, as it's her war. Will you do that for me, Mr Shakespeare?'

'I will pass on your message. In the meanwhile, do you know anything about the men – who they were?'

The burgess smelt of fish. He scratched the inside of his ear with the rough-hewn nail of his forefinger. 'They were commanded by a provost marshal named Pinkney. If you need to know more, there is one as may tell you – one we picked up for thieving a silver cup from my house. Pinkney wanted him handed over so he could mete out justice himself, but I wasn't having it. The felon's in the town gaol, on short commons until he returns my cup or is hanged.'

'Thank you.'

Shakespeare left the mayor to his business. Outside, he untethered his horse and walked it to the stone-built prison. The keeper showed him to the cell, where the miscreant was shackled to the floor in a small space he shared with rats, fleas, lice and a dozen other men awaiting trial or punishment. Shakespeare held his kerchief to his nose. He recognised the man immediately. It was Pinkney's lethal companion on the road to Lathom House in Lancashire.

'Well, well, what have we here?' Shakespeare said. He could scarce believe his good fortune.

The man looked up at him through dull eyes. He was thinner and less powerful than he had been; his muscles seemed wasted, the bull chest shrunken. He did not appear to recognise Shakespeare.

'Remember me? You were trying to hang a priest in Lancashire.'

The man grunted non-committally.

'So now *you* are the one to be hanged.'

The man spat at Shakespeare's feet, but his mouth was dry and his aim fell short.

Shakespeare did not move. 'I would talk with you.'

'I have nothing to say to you, whoever you are – unless you give me ale and food and spare me from the rope.'

'I cannot do that. You are on short commons by order of the justice and will be convicted by a court of law – if you are guilty.'

'Then I will not talk.'

'I recall Pinkney calling you Cordwright. What are you to Pinkney? His sergeant?'

The man spat on the ground again, closed his eyes and leant back against the dripping stone wall. He was clearly in pain.

'Why were you in Lancashire? There could have been no levy for Brittany that far north. My understanding is that the pressing of men was confined to eighteen southern counties.'

The man laughed, suddenly interested. 'Oh, yes, you'd like to know about Lancashire. I'm sure you'd like to know the truth of that. Aye, that would send a shiver down your spine. Let us just say that when we are not a-soldiering, Provost Pinkney and me do little tasks for a certain great personage, a man whose word is his bond. As is Mr Pinkney's.'

'What tasks?'

'Clearing of hornets' nests, scourging of vermin. We are scavengers, clearing up the foul messes of other men. But I have told you the price. Food for my stomach, ale for my gullet and no rope for my neck. It would be worth it to you, though.'

Shakespeare left the villain in his dungeon, with the lice and ordure, and returned to the mayor's counting house.

'The man has information I need. He will talk only if his life is spared and he has more food and some ale.'

'Well, he won't get that.'

'What if I got the money you want from Cecil for the transport vessels?'

The mayor looked at him questioningly. 'Is that possible?'

'Yes.'

'It's forty-two marks. Do you have it?'

'That is a great deal of money. I had thought a crossing to France was reckoned at two shillings a man.'

'Sheep's bollocks, Mr Shakespeare. Two shillings a man may be true of Dover to Calais, but Weymouth to Brittany is more than a hundred miles and the coast there has some of the most treacherous waters you could care to encounter. Forty-two marks, sir.'

'Well, I do not have that amount here. But I will bring it to you.'

The mayor hesitated, then shook his head decisively. 'I'll have the money first – and my silver cup. Then I'll do a deal over the prisoner. Come back to me when you have forty-two marks in gold, Mr Shakespeare. If you're quick about it, you may yet find the prisoner alive when you return.'

# *Chapter 38*

PROVOST MARSHAL EDMUND Pinkney was in a dark humour. It had been a long and difficult sea crossing, in which three men had disappeared overboard, probably trying to swim to the English shore. At last, the fishermen from Weymouth dropped anchor off a wide expanse of beach, which, they said, was two miles from Paimpol, the English-held haven where all levies were supposed to muster. It was late at night, and dark. There were no town lights and no landmarks. Pinkney remonstrated with the hoy skippers, but they were insistent.

'Can't take you into port. Rock shoals, undertows – we'd need a local pilot. It's a two-mile march from here to Paimpol, nothing more.'

Reluctantly, Pinkney agreed to disembark his remaining thirty-eight men. They waded ashore, carrying their meagre equipment, arms and provisions through the surf. A two-mile march come morning would be nothing, but Pinkney felt uneasy. Something was wrong.

At first light, they started a slog through mudflats, sand and rock. After an hour, he realised Paimpol was a good deal further than two miles; after another hour, he became certain they were nowhere near the port. The hoy skippers had tricked them deliberately, in retribution for the trouble caused in their home port. God burn their miserable souls.

All day, they marched westward. Finally, in the distance, they spotted a fortified town and the men's hopes rose. Pinkney was less happy. By now he was certain they had been landed a great distance from Paimpol.

Nor could they gain any information from the local people they saw. All fled at the sight of their armed column. They cornered an old man, whose feet would not carry him fast enough. At the point of a sword, he put them right.

'*Paimpol? Non, c'est St Malo!*'

Pinkney cursed. He wished very badly to kill the hoy skippers and their crewmen, but they were long gone. Well, he would not forget their treachery. He *never* forgot a bad turn. For the moment, though, he had to make the best of a bad situation.

If the fortified town was St Malo, he gauged from his crude chart that they must be eighty to a hundred miles east of Paimpol, and the going would be slow. At the best of times, a company of men could not march more than twelve miles a day, and these were mostly raw conscripted men, unused to marching. The march would be a great deal more difficult because caution would be necessary; the lines here were blurred between royalist French and Catholic French. Some of this country was held by the enemy, either the Duc de Mercoeur's Catholic League French forces or their Spanish allies. Each step of the route had to be measured and thought through; that meant avoiding defiles, river valleys or any terrain where they could be surprised. There would be rivers to cross and towns to pass. It was a march that would take all his soldierly skill. In truth, he doubted very much whether they could manage it.

He looked at his troops with scorn. They were the most incompetent, ill-disciplined rabble he had ever commanded. Simply getting them to understand commands such as 'Charge your pike' as an order to prepare for an attack on enemy infantry had been difficult enough. To go further and make them understand the order 'Charge your pike against the right foot and draw your sword' – for defence against cavalry – had been nigh on impossible. Matters had been made considerably worse by losing Cordwright, his quartermaster sergeant, to the Weymouth gaol.

By nightfall, they were camped outside a small market town, just inland from the coast and a few miles from St Malo. The French townsfolk had welcomed them with loaves and wine, but Pinkney had fought too many wars in the Low Countries and Normandy to be deceived by such shows. They would be off to tell the nearest French soldiers of the English presence as soon as night fell. These people greeted you with one hand and stabbed you with the other.

'You two,' he ordered Andrew and Reaphook. 'Take the first watches at the southern corners of the camp.' He handed halberds to them both. 'If you sleep, I will shoot you dead.'

These two vagabonds seemed to be among the better recruits. At least they were reasonably strong and able. He didn't trust the one with the sickle, though, not since his attempt at desertion while they awaited passage at Weymouth. Pinkney had caught him quickly because a local smithy had spotted him hiding in his backyard. 'Twelve stripes with the cane,' Pinkney had ordered. That seemed to suffice. He had made it very clear that if there was another such attempt at desertion, he would be hanged.

Pinkney looked at the man now with amusement. He called himself Reaphook and carried a sickle in his belt; he thought himself a hard man, and thought he could do a deal to win the captaincy of his vagabond band in return for twelve pressed men. Pinkney suddenly laughed aloud at the memory of the man's bewildered expression when he had decided, after all, that he, Reaphook, should be one of those pressed into service. That had taken the shine off his afternoon of carnal pleasure with the vagabond girl.

The sun was about to set. Pinkney wondered, could they hold this camp for a few days? These men were in desperate need of training. No more than three of them could fire an arquebus and he had only four archers left. The remainder were poor creatures who would scarce be able to defend themselves in an alehouse knife-fight, let alone survive a battle. The two small wagons they had were packed with supplies: two barrels of ale, one of beer; salt beef; peas; two sacks of oatmeal; a keg of fine-corned gunpowder; six arquebuses; thirty pikes; twelve bills; six halberds; twelve longbows; two hundred arrows. It was little enough if they had to survive in this country for more than four or five days without resupply. They would be easy meat for a well-armed and battle-hardened enemy.

He had a cup of ale in his hand and drained the last drop. He looked into the young sentry's eyes. 'What do you do if you are approached, Mr Woode?'

'Demand the watchword, sir,' Andrew replied instantly, stiffening his shoulders and standing to attention.

'Good man. We'll make a soldier of you yet.'

The man sidled up to Ivory as they stood in line for their food in the ship's galley. 'How about a few hands of primero, Mr Eye? The lads say you like a game.'

Ivory looked around. Boltfoot was being served his food. He was out of earshot and did not seem to be watching him.

'When?'

'Second dog-watch. Lower gun deck.'

'No, that's too early. End of the first watch, beginning of the middle.'

'As you wish. We'll still be playing then. My name's Trayne.'

Ivory moved forward away from the man. A porridge of oatmeal was slopped on to his tin trencher and a quart of ale was poured into his jug. It would taste better today than it had in a long while.

An hour before midnight, Boltfoot tapped the dead embers from his pipe and gazed at the sleeping form of William Ivory, curled up close to the bulwark. The *Vanguard* rose and fell with the swell. Though Boltfoot had had his fill of seafaring, he was still soothed by a racing wind and the roll and dip of a well-built ship.

Ivory snored loudly. A deep, unpleasant, pig-like sound emanated every few seconds from the back of his throat. Around them, soldiers and marines slept, packed like pilchards in a Cornish pie. Boltfoot put his pipe in his jerkin and lay down on a tarpaulin, so close to Ivory that he could almost feel his breathing. He closed his eyes. Sleep came readily.

Ivory opened one blue eye, then two. At the stern, the ship's lantern swayed and guttered. Above them, a half-moon and the starry heavens lit the billowing sails. Clouds scudded past. He watched Boltfoot, certain he was asleep. Silently, Ivory rose to his feet. Instinctively, his hand went to the pig-hide tube strapped inside his jerkin against his chest, then to his money pouch. He felt a sudden surge of irritation that he no longer had his beloved tobacco pipe and thought bitterly that some peasant in Suffolk might even now be puffing at it. He looked about him warily. The watch was nowhere to be seen. Stealthily, he moved through the ranks of militia being transported to the war.

At the top of the companion way, he glanced about once more. No one was watching. He descended the ladder quickly to the gun deck. Among the guns, balls and powder kegs, there was scarcely room for a man to stand, yet men slept, curled into whatever space they could find or push into. The game would be in a quiet corner, between casks, lit by a single lantern. He had enjoyed many such games over the years, in ill-lit corners of decks. He narrowed his sharp eyes in the dim light.

He thought he saw a lantern and stepped carefully between the sleeping gunners, his gait rolling with the ship. Somewhere up here, towards the bow. The game must be hereabouts. Surely they would have waited for him, certain that they could relieve him of his money; how little they knew.

The blow came as if from nowhere. A gnarled hand clutching a six-pound cannonball descended and connected with a skull-splitting strike. Ivory crumpled and fell without even realising he had been hit. His head cracked against the decking, but by then he knew nothing.

Boltfoot looked at Ivory's prone body with horror. He lay on a wooden board in the surgeon's cabin, his face covered with blood. His jerkin had been cut open and his chest was bare. The pigskin tube was missing.

'I rather think the bandaging that was already around his head saved his life,' the surgeon said. 'It softened the blow somewhat.'

Frobisher bristled with anger. 'Didn't save the bloody instrument he carried, though, did it? Will he ever wake up?'

'He has already woken, admiral, but so far he hasn't spoken. He is merely sleeping now. We do not know yet whether there is permanent damage.'

'Well, I may still have some use for him. Keep him alive, sir.' He turned to Boltfoot. 'What in God's name was he doing on the gun deck, Mr Cooper? And where were you?'

Boltfoot did not rise to Frobisher's bait. 'He seemed to be

asleep, admiral. I was at his side. I do not know why he was below decks, though I could hazard a guess.'

'Yes. I know all about Mr Ivory and his taste for games.'

'The attacker must still be on the ship, admiral.'

'What do you want to do about it, Mr Cooper? We dock in one hour. We cannot hold Norreys and his troops back while every man is searched.'

'No, I understand. But there might be another way, admiral.'

Frobisher turned to the surgeon. 'Keep Mr Ivory under close guard at all times.' Then, to Boltfoot. 'Come to my cabin. We will discuss these matters further.'

In the woods, when he was running from Oxford, Andrew had felt alone and terrified. The trees harboured sounds and shadows that threatened him. He had seen wolves, though reason told him there could be none. He saw snakes and ghosts, and felt his throat burning for lack of water. Yet his fear and thirst then were as nothing compared to this terror.

Here, in this outlying post some fifty yards from the camp, reason could not tell him that the threats were only imaginary, because he *knew* that they were there. There were enemy soldiers out there: hard, merciless men who slit throats without blinking. What was this company? Nothing but a lost, isolated band, poorly trained, ill equipped and surrounded on all sides in a small pocket of France. What good would his halberd be against an arrow or musket-shot? What if a man crawled on his belly through the grass with a short sword to thrust up into his throat? This danger was horribly real.

He felt – or heard – breathing. He wasn't sure which. It was behind him. He stood back, then swung his six-foot halberd in a great arc, at knee level. He heard a low laugh.

'Good man, good man.'

He breathed a great sigh of relief. It was Provost Pinkney.

'Watchword?' Andrew demanded, suddenly recalling what he had been told.

'Even better, Mr Woode. The word is Agincourt.'

'Sir.'

Pinkney moved on into the night, to check on the other watches. Andrew's blood pulsed through him as if he were a hunted hare.

Boltfoot stood on deck at the top of the ship-to-shore ropeway. At his side were two marines, armed with drawn swords and loaded pistols.

One by one, Norreys's soldiers trooped off the ship, down the perilous gangway on to the bustling quayside. They went in orderly fashion, clattering muskets, shields, helmets and pikes as they went. Each had his right sleeve rolled back to expose the wrist and forearm. Boltfoot grasped each arm and examined the wrist, looking for the wound-scar caused by his knife on the harbour-front in Portsmouth.

Then came Sir John Norreys himself, with his exotic consort on his arm. He looked about at the scene on land, where thousands of men milled about and formed into companies, with their mass of equipment. This was his army preparing for battle, not just another of the inconclusive skirmishes that he had fought in the past four years. No longer was he the forgotten general. At last he had the numbers of men necessary to take on the Spanish armies.

On these ships, he had two thousand soldiers, with more in transit from the ports of southern England. In all, there would be more than five thousand four hundred men, and not just unblooded recruits. His most valuable asset was the thousand-strong detachment of hardened fighting men from the Low Countries. And the siege train; that would stay with Frobisher for the time being. He could carry it quicker by sea, and land it where and when required.

Boltfoot bowed to him deferentially.

'Don't you wish to see *my* arm?' Norreys said, thrusting it forward.

'Thank you, general.'

Boltfoot bowed again. He understood why Norreys had acted thus; it meant that none of his gentlemen officers would have an excuse to refuse.

'And mine,' the woman said.

'Thank you, my lady, but that will not be necessary.'

'What do you seek? The mark of the devil?'

Her accent was foreign and she had a chattering monkey on her shoulder.

Norreys laughed. 'Come away, my dear Eliska. This is a serious business. Let the man do what he must do.'

'Perhaps he would like to examine my monkey's little furry arm, though she might give him a bite if he tries.'

Boltfoot watched them proceed past him with their retinue, all of whom made a great show of baring their forearms for him. Frobisher approached him.

'No sign of your scarred man, Mr Cooper.'

'No, admiral. Perhaps he is among the members of your crew.'

'Then we had better examine them.'

Boltfoot gazed at the wound-scar on the man's wrist. It was still red and new. He looked up and met the man's steady gaze. 'Name?'

'Able Seaman Trayne.'

He nodded to the marine guards. 'Search this man.'

Trayne held his arms in the air and the guards began to pat him down.

'No,' Boltfoot said. 'Remove his apparel. Search every inch of his body.'

'What are we looking for, Mr Cooper?'

'You'll know if you find it. Send two men to search his berth and belongings.'

# Chapter 39

'SHOULDER YOUR PIKES and march!'

Pinkney's small company broke camp at dawn and headed westward across the farmland and lanes of northern Brittany. The troops marched in file, rank abreast, with a space of three yards between each pair.

'We will spread the target in case of attack,' Pinkney had rasped. 'If one man goes down or cries out, you will turn and form into a wide circle.'

They marched without drumbeat. A corporal held the van, his arquebus ready for action with powder, ball and glowing match. In his belt was a pistol. At his side was the ensign with colours flying. The rearguard was a pike corporal. He was immediately preceded by Andrew Woode and Reaphook with their six-foot halberds. Both had learnt fast: the lower ends of their poles were three feet from the ground, sloping towards the right ham of the pikemen in front, as prescribed by Provost Pinkney. Some of the other new recruits were less well drilled; their pikes, bills and halberds swayed and clattered against those near by.

Pinkney watched angrily. He would dearly love to beat these men into shape, but his priority was to get them to Paimpol and rendezvous with the English army, for he was desperately short of food and munitions.

Their progress was interrupted by constant halts as they tried to gauge the lie of the land against ambush. They sought directions from the few French peasants who did not run into the woods at their approach. Pinkney discovered that Andrew Woode was the only man with more than two words of French, and he brought him close to him in the ranks, so that he might interpret. Yet as they moved further westward, they found that almost no one they met spoke French, only Breton, and communication became more difficult. Andrew was reduced to saying 'Paimpol' – or '*Pempoull*' as the Bretons pronounced it – and watching to see which way the peasant pointed.

As they marched, Pinkney engaged the boy in conversation. 'What are you, then? It seems you have had learning,' he said as they skirted a town.

'I have been at grammar school,' Andrew replied cautiously. He had seen the savage beating meted out to Reaphook, and knew Pinkney was not a man to be gainsaid or lied to.

'Well, I'll hold that against no man if he has courage. You have the makings of a soldier. You have the height to be a pikeman, which is the heart of any army. Survive this campaign and you could one day be corporal on good pay. Half a mark a day or more.'

'Thank you, Provost Pinkney.'

'Have you ever shot with a hagbut?'

'Yes, sir, and a pistol. My father taught me.'

'Indeed. You are a most uncommon vagabond. I must assume you were fleeing home for some reason.'

Andrew said nothing.

'And from your voice, I would say you were London born and bred.'

'Yes, sir.'

'What is your father? Schoolmaster? Lawyer?'

'He has been both, but not now.'

'Tell me more, Private Woode.'

'He works in Her Majesty's service, sir.'

'Is that so? What is he, a scribe?'

'No, sir, he is an assistant secretary, in the office of Sir Robert Cecil.'

They marched on in silence for a few more yards. Pinkney handed Andrew his ale flagon. 'Have a quaff of that, lad. It'll fortify the bones in your legs.'

'Thank you, Provost Pinkney.'

The day was bright with few clouds. The terrors of the night were long gone. They could see for miles across fields. In the distance, to the north, the sea shimmered and there were white flecks of sail; they should be safe enough if the terrain could stay like this, and if they kept the sea to their right and visible. There was birdsong in the air. Andrew swigged the ale and gasped with satisfaction. It was good and quenching.

'Assistant Secretary Woode? I have not heard the name.'

'No, sir, that is not his name. His name is Shakespeare. He is my adoptive father.'

Pinkney did not break his stride, but he looked left and glanced at Andrew's profile. 'Indeed. Now that *is* interesting, lad.'

'Yes, sir.'

Pinkney thought back to a lonely lane in Lancashire. 'Yes, that is very interesting indeed.'

A dozen viols filled the *grande salle* with music. Sir John Norreys held the centre of the floor with the lady Eliska. They danced apart from each other, yet in time. He moved forward a step, she moved back. His shoulders were stiff and proud, her slender body mirrored his. As if suddenly tiring of this peacock display, his right hand went to the front of her exquisite skirts, clasping the busk of her corset in most intimate fashion; the other hand gripped her hip, just above her buttock. She pushed forward at his touch, moving closer to him so that their lips almost kissed, then as one they turned and sprang into the air, like doves taking flight.

The two hundred revellers crowding around the rim of this modest town hall burst into appreciative applause, then flooded forward to join their captain-general and his mistress in the volta.

Above the music, the din of laughing and cheering made it clear that this was an army with its blood up. They would drink and love their fill this night, for on the morrow the hard business of killing or dying began. There would be no more soft flesh to comfort them and the only music would be the martial beat of the drum and the shriek of the fife. At last they were being sent to win a war.

Most of the men here in this hall, in a square close to Paimpol Harbour, were English, but there were, too, officers of the French royalist army of Marshal Aumont.

John Shakespeare stood dripping in the doorway and watched with astonishment. For a moment he did not recognise the woman with Norreys. Then his eyes widened in disbelief. What in God's name was Lady Eliska doing here in Brittany? And with Sir John Norreys, too?

A serving man passed by with a tray of goblets. Shakespeare took one and poured fine French wine into his mouth, followed immediately by another. The wine was dry and smooth and very welcome to his parched, salty throat. He had arrived in Paimpol less than half an hour earlier, having been delayed interminably at Weymouth. In the end he had ridden back to Poole to find a boat willing to make the crossing. Now, standing at the edge of this revel among smartly attired soldiers and exquisite young women, he realised he must look out of place. He was drenched with brine from the rough voyage across the sea. His salt-thick clothes stuck to his skin as though coated in wet sand. He had not even had time to find lodgings.

He strode into the mêlée of officers and their young women. Norreys and Eliska had ended their dance and were making their way back to the edge of the hall, where his senior officers were gathered. Shakespeare recognised the heroic Sir Anthony Wingfield, whom he knew slightly and recalled to be a great friend of Norreys; Sir Thomas Baskerville, too, his boots and clothes thick with dust as though he had hurried here from battle.

Something made Eliska turn. She came face to face with Shakespeare and a curious look crossed her beautiful features.

Shakespeare bowed stiffly. 'My lady Eliska.'

'Mr Shakespeare.'

Their eyes searched the other's for some meaning to this encounter.

'Is it really you? You have no idea how glad I am to see you.'

'Indeed? That sounds as if you were almost expecting me, my lady.'

'I always expect the unexpected. But tell me, I assume you have been sent by Cecil?'

'In a manner of speaking. But how would *you* know of that?'

She at last managed to compose herself and smile, then leant forward for a kiss on her cheek. He did not oblige.

'It has been my most fervent wish to see you here,' she said. 'But look at you, John. You are like a barnacled sea-monster just stepped from the depths. Your hair is a tangle, your apparel is drenched. You look wretched.'

Norreys had turned now and glared at the newcomer. He was not as tall as Shakespeare, but he had a powerful military bearing, a thick head of hair curling back from his forehead and a well-trimmed spade beard. 'Lady Eliska?'

'This is Mr Shakespeare, Sir John.'

'Ah yes, Mr Shakespeare. Come to spy on me, have you?'

Shakespeare bowed. 'Sir John.'

Norreys laughed. 'Fear not, Mr Shakespeare. I know exactly why you are here.' He downed his drink and looked at Shakespeare dispassionately. His mouth was as flat and unsmiling as the horizon. 'Very well, Mr Shakespeare. Let us remove ourselves to somewhere quieter, and we will discuss our next move.'

They moved to a side room. It was stark and cheerless, some sort of civic office with a table and nothing else.

'Sir Robert informed me that you might not be fully acquainted with his plans for you, Mr Shakespeare,' Norreys said. He sipped a goblet of good wine. 'So I am to brief you. Sir Robert Cecil desires you to undertake an operation of great daring and extreme danger.'

Shakespeare listened in silence.

'We must take Fort El Léon to save Brest from the Spanish hordes. All our intelligence suggests it is practically impregnable, and is so well provisioned and manned that it would take a year or more to succumb to siege. That leaves us one option. We must take it from the inside.'

'I assume Sir Robert has devised some method by which this miracle is to be achieved?'

Norreys shook his head and looked at Eliska. 'No, but this lady has. And I can tell you that it all depends on the famed perspective glass – and you. It seems, Mr Shakespeare, you are to betray your Queen and country and become a traitor.'

Eliska came to him at three o'clock, when most of the revellers slept. His lodging was in a stable attached to Sir John's own quarters, which was the largest house in Paimpol.

He was already awake, thinking of Andrew. Norreys had

been unable to shed any light on the boy's whereabouts, but said that Pinkney was expected with a hundred men. He knew the provost marshal well from the wars in the Low Countries. He was a hard man, but a good soldier.

Eliska broke into his reverie. She was about to touch his cheek with her fingertips, but he reached up and gripped her slim wrist.

'Hush, it is only me.' The candle that she carried lit up her fair skin so that it glowed.

'I know your name. Now I think it is time to discover exactly who you are. You turn up in the most curious of places.' Shakespeare pulled himself to his feet. He had been curled on a borrowed palliasse. She kissed him, her lips lingering a few moments on his. He stood back from her. 'Well?'

'I will tell you everything, but first things first.'

She put the candle down on the flagstone paving of the stall.

He kissed her and took her in his arms and laid her down on his thin palliasse.

# Chapter 40

THE WEATHER BROKE. Storm clouds rushed in with the Atlantic. The five-hundred-ton royal ship *Vanguard* was anchored just outside the Brest roads, in the lee of the western coast. Through the slanting rain, they could see the squat fort of El Léon, sitting like a malign toad atop the cliffs of the Crozon headland. It looked impenetrable and menacing.

Frobisher's small fleet had swelled to nineteen ships: his five royal vessels and six armed merchantmen had been joined by eight Dutch warships, laden with gunpowder and cannonballs. A flotilla of six Spanish galleys had fled at the sight of them and the English now had total control of the sea coast outside the harbour entrance.

The *Vanguard*'s cannon roared. Fire flashed from five black muzzles protruding through the gunports and sent seventeen-pound balls of iron flying across the water. All but one smashed into the cliff face. Only one reached the lower edge of the fortress wall, but caused no damage. Frobisher smiled to himself. He knew from intelligence that the fort's walls were almost forty feet thick in places. He knew, too, that the ship's guns could not elevate sufficiently to hit the seaward defences at any height, let alone breach them. Yet it was necessary to let the Spanish defenders know that they were here and that they could make life uncomfortable. No longer could the fort be provisioned by sea.

Below decks, Boltfoot Cooper was eating broth. The boom of the cannon and the violent shaking of the vessel made him spill the stew from the spoon over his chest.

Ivory puffed on a pipe from the right side of his mouth. A young midshipman held the implement in place for him.

'Can't even feed yourself properly, can you?' Ivory said, slurring his words. 'You're less than a cripple, Cooper, you're about as useful as a hamstrung mole-warp.'

'Well, at least I can smoke a pipe of sotweed without assistance, Mr Ivory.'

'God damn you, Cooper. Where were you when I needed protection? Bloody asleep.'

'You placed your own self in jeopardy. That was none of my doing.'

Boltfoot studied Ivory with some indifference. He cared not a jot for the man, but he *was* worried about his slow recovery; Ivory might be needed still. The left side of his body was palsied; he could not raise his left arm nor use his left leg for walking.

'It is the stroke of God's hand,' the surgeon had said grimly.

Another cannon boom shook the ship. Boltfoot poured the remainder of the broth down his throat, then rose and made his way further below decks. A store-cabin near the galley had been emptied of kegs and turned into a makeshift prison cell for the man with the scarred arm. Boltfoot unlocked the door and stepped inside. For a few moments he looked at the hunched and bruised figure of Janus Trayne.

'Do you have anything to say yet, Mr Trayne?'

'Why am I being held here, Mr Cooper? What am I supposed to have done to be treated so? It has been days now . . . I have lost track of day and night.'

'You know very well why, Mr Trayne, or whatever your true name is. Your scarred arm identifies you and Mr Ivory has singled you out as the man who lured him down to the gun deck.'

'I wanted a game of cards, that is all. As for this scar –' he pointed to his injured arm – 'I tell you again, I got that injury in a knife fight in Chatham, attacked by a drunken Dutchman. I should be manning my cannon, not sitting in this filthy hole.'

'You have a confederate, I know it. Tell me who it is and your life may be spared.'

Trayne sat back against the wooden bulkhead and sighed. 'My only confederates are my fellow gunners, whom I should be assisting right now to pummel the enemy. Not rotting here.'

Boltfoot was certain Trayne had not acted alone. Yet he would not budge, would not reveal anything, even after a beating on Frobisher's orders. A search of his hanging canvas bed and his small chest had been fruitless. The whole of the gun deck and beyond had been thoroughly investigated in the days since the *Vanguard* sailed here from Paimpol by way of Morlaix. Now they faced the narrow strait of Le Goulet, only a mile wide and overlooked by the high cliffs that dominated Brest roads.

It occurred to Boltfoot that perhaps the pig-hide tube might no longer be on the ship. Perhaps a soldier had managed to get it ashore when Norreys's army had disembarked at Paimpol. Or one of the men could have taken it when the siege guns were landed at Morlaix. But he could not be certain of that, so he had to assume that Trayne had a confederate and that he was still aboard. He could not afford to let his guard drop again.

Frobisher appeared at Boltfoot's side. 'Is he still not talking? I believe it is time to try some stronger medicine, Mr Cooper. What say you?'

'I agree, admiral. I think it is.'

'Do you swim, Mr Trayne?'

Trayne shifted uneasily. 'What do you mean?'

'I mean,' Frobisher said, 'that I am considering releasing you. You can swim ashore to join your Spanish friends at the fort of El Léon.'

'I . . . I cannot swim.'

'Then it is a good time to learn, Mr Trayne. A very good time. Perhaps you will spy a sea unicorn, as I have done in the far northern oceans.' Behind Frobisher stood two marines. 'Take this man on deck,' he ordered them. 'Then throw him overboard. I have seen enough of his face and will waste no more food on him.'

The marines stepped forward and dragged Trayne to his feet. He kicked and tried to fight them, but they overpowered him easily and marched him from the cell.

'I leave him in your hands, gentlemen,' Frobisher said and strode off towards his cabin, one hand on the hilt of his sheathed sword.

'You can't do this!' Trayne yelled. 'I'll die.'

Boltfoot said nothing, nor did the marines. They half carried, half dragged him up the companion ways to the main deck and, without further ceremony, the marines threw him over the side into the churning grey sea. For a moment, they watched him floundering and spluttering, and then he was gone, beneath the waves.

Boltfoot turned away. He felt sick to his soul. He had thought it was a threat, that they would hang the man over the bulwark by his feet and terrify him. It had not occurred to him that they would really do it.

Andrew and Reaphook hid in undergrowth close to a remote farm. Reaphook stroked the tuft of hair in the cleft of his chin. For more than half an hour they watched the farm and detected no sign of life other than the pecking of chickens and the snorting of pigs.

'It's deserted. This'll do.'

'Wait,' Andrew said. 'There must be someone indoors, or working near by.'

Reaphook dug his elbow sharply into Andrew's side. 'It's Sunday. They're at church, all of them. That's what these people do early on a Sunday morning. We've got to get food, you maggot. Pinkney will flog us at the post if we don't.'

'But they may have left someone at home ... We don't know if it's safe.'

'I've got a short sword, a pistol and my sickle. You've got a sword and a dagger. We're soldiers. We're safe. Come on, there are a dozen chickens and there will be grain or meal in the store. It's now or never.'

Reaphook rose to his haunches, looked about, then ran forward at a crouch. After a few moments' hesitation, Andrew followed him.

'I get the hens, you go to the barn,' Reaphook said, unslinging a large bag from his back.

The barn was light and airy, and filled with sacks and kegs. For a few moments, Andrew stopped and looked around, entranced by its simple beauty and peace. He lifted up one of the sacks and reckoned it at half a hundredweight. From the soft feel of it, he guessed it contained milled flour. He could carry two at most. He hoisted one over each shoulder and sagged under the weight. Outside, in the farmyard, there was a furious clucking as Reaphook slaughtered chickens with the grim thoroughness of a fox in the coop. He was quick and skilful at catching them and wringing them by the neck. Each one he killed, he thrust into his bag. He carried on until there was one left.

'We'll leave that for their pot,' he said, grinning.

'Let's go,' Andrew pleaded.

'No, I want some wine. Cheese, too. To go with my supper.'

He closed the neck of the bag with string, then left it with Andrew and walked through an open doorway into the farmhouse.

For a few moments there was silence. Andrew watched the old house with a fluttering heart. And then he heard a scream, a girl's scream. Without thinking, he dropped the sacks and edged towards the gaping doorway. He looked in and shuddered. A girl was cowering beneath a table in the kitchen. She was no more than sixteen or seventeen, about the same age and size as Ursula Dancer. Reaphook had his sickle out and was slashing at her as if cutting grass, trying to flush her out. She was desperately scrabbling away from him, holding a pan up like a shield to deflect the deadly arc of his curved blade.

'Leave her!'

Reaphook put two fingers in the air, but did not turn around. He was down on his knees and he made as if to crawl under the table after the girl. Andrew leapt on to Reaphook's back, tugged a handful of his jagged brown fringe with one hand and wrestled the sickle from his grasp with the other. Reaphook shook his head free of Andrew's grip and tried to hit out, but Andrew had him pinned to the dirt floor. They both tried to lunge for the hook, but it spun across the floor, out of reach. Andrew hammered his elbow down into the side of Reaphook's head. Reaphook grunted, momentarily dazed.

With a force born of rage and desperation, Andrew fought to wrestle the man's arms behind him. Ursula had warned him of Reaphook's vicious strength, but suddenly Andrew realised he could match this man. He could take Reaphook. Pulling himself back upright, he wrenched Reaphook up after him.

Reaphook wasn't done. He twisted sharply and freed his right arm, which immediately went for the short sword in his belt. Before it was unsheathed, Andrew pulled back his fist and landed a crunching blow in the middle of Reaphook's face. He followed up with a knee to the balls as he had once seen Ursula do to him. Reaphook fell back, clutching his broken, blood-dripping nose. The kick to the groin had not been as skilfully performed as Ursula's, but the blow to the face clearly hurt. Andrew dived for the sickle, but Reaphook got to it first. He lashed out wildly and nicked Andrew's hand with its honed blade. He slashed again and tore into Andrew's woollen cassock. He was coming forward relentlessly, half blinded by the blood that streaked his eyes and his smashed nose. Without warning, he screamed and stopped, his left leg crumpling as though hit by something.

Andrew did not understand at first what had happened, then spotted the girl, still under the table but now with a long-bladed kitchen knife in her hand, its point and edge streaked with Reaphook's blood. She had stabbed him in the leg. Her dark eyes were wide in terror at what she had done and what she now believed would be done to her.

Reaphook gripped his leg. 'She's dead,' he rasped. 'I'll kill the French bitch.'

'Come away, Reaphook. Come away now. Someone will return any moment.'

Reaphook glared through his bloody slits of eyes. 'First things first. I'm going to cut the trull's throat.'

'No.' As Reaphook turned, Andrew grabbed the back of his soldier's cassock with his own cut hand and pulled him back towards the doorway. 'We've got to get this food back to the men. Have you learnt nothing from the beating Pinkney gave you? Leave her.'

Reaphook turned around, his face etched in bewilderment, blood and pain. He looked at Andrew. Pinkney's name had really struck home.

'Shouldn't we kill her? She's seen us. She can identify us.'

'We're in France, you dawcock, not England. No one's going to arrest us. They might do their best to shoot us dead but they're not going to take us to court for stealing chickens. Now come away!'

Provost Pinkney looked in the sack and pulled out a pair of chickens.

'Not bad,' he said. 'Not bad.' With his knife, he cut open one of the sacks from the barn and dug his hand into the flour. He brought out a handful and let it spill through his fingers. 'Yes, that's fair foraging. But what's happened to you two? Taken on Águila and the whole Spanish army, have you?'

Andrew and Reaphook stood to attention in front of him. Andrew's hand was wrapped in a bloody cloth and his cassock was gashed across his chest. Reaphook had washed his face in a stream, but it was still caked with blood, and his nose was flattened and both eyes were bruised black. His leg was bandaged with the sleeve of his chemise, fastened with a thin strip of rawhide. He could barely stand on it.

'We were discovered by the farmer and his men,' Reaphook said.

'Kill them all, did you?'

'Yes, Provost Pinkney.'

Pinkney laughed, not believing a word. 'I'd say you broke your nose walking into Mr Woode's fist and got a blade in your leg from a farmwife. Is that not closer to the truth?'

Reaphook looked at Andrew to back him up. Andrew stared straight ahead and said nothing.

They were camped on the western side of a stone bridge across a river, sheltered in a group of long-abandoned farm buildings – a byre, a barn and some old pigsties. The buildings had no roofs and much of the walls had crumbled, but they would provide some defence in case of attack. Nearby was a well-trodden road that led westward from the bridge. It was open country, with clear views in all directions save for a dense wood to the north and a copse to the south of the buildings. They had been there twenty-four hours, resting and foraging.

'Well,' Pinkney said at last, 'I care nothing for your injuries. At least we shall eat well tonight. But I must tell you, Mr Reaphook, that we cannot afford to wait here any longer. I will not have stragglers. I do not know the state of your leg, but we have no help for you. On the morrow, you will have to march or we will leave you here. Do you understand?'

Reaphook nodded stiffly, his lips tight closed about his unwieldy teeth. But it was his eyes that caught Andrew's attention: there was fear in them.

All the men received a share of chicken and their last portion of the peas brought over from England. Pinkney took no more than any other man. The cook had made an unleavened bread, kneading the flour into a dough with beer and salt, then frying it in a pan with lard. It was appetising and the men devoured it with relish.

Reaphook chewed at the chicken with his ungainly teeth, yet he did not seem hungry. Andrew sat as far away from him as he could, but found himself looking across at him, wondering about the man. He was a vicious bully, but he was also a broken wreck.

Andrew turned back to his meal, but once again he looked up. Reaphook was wiping the sleeve of his coarse woollen cassock across his eyes. Andrew sighed heavily, put down his food and walked over to Pinkney, who sat with his trumpeter and ensign, drinking brandy and smoking pipes.

'Provost Pinkney, sir.' Andrew stood rigidly to attention.

'Yes, Mr Woode?'

'What if I were to try to find another cart of some type? A handbarrow or somesuch. Could we not carry Mr Reaphook on it, sir, like a bier?'

Pinkney packed some tobacco into his pipe. 'That is a fine notion, Mr Woode. We could do with another cart. If you find a cart of sufficient size, we would be able to carry more provisions. Are you planning to go alone to find this cart?'

'Yes, sir. When darkness falls.'

'Very well. Indeed, I do say again, you have the makings of a fighting man. I know you do not love Mr Reaphook, yet you put such feelings aside for he is your comrade-at-arms. It is the correct way. All we need discover now is whether your courage holds under the fury of pike and shot, and whether you have it in you to thrust hard steel into soft flesh. What you would do well to remember, Private Woode, is that the thing you kill is not a man, it is an enemy. And who is your enemy? That is simple – it is any person who would do hurt to you or your sovereign.'

# Chapter 41

L IKE A LONG snake, the five-thousand-strong army of Sir John Norreys trudged across the north-west of Brittany. At their head, the drums and fifes sounded the time and warned the everyday traffic of farmwagons and draycarts to make way or be cleared off the road.

John Shakespeare rode in the mid-division, a little way behind Norreys and Eliska. The army was heading for Morlaix to flush out the last of the Catholic League garrison and secure the north-west coastline, before moving on to the Crozon peninsula and the Fort of El Léon. Shakespeare knew that Norreys's big fear was that the war would drag on into another winter; he wanted decisive action. The fort had to be taken, and quickly.

A cold wind was blowing in, with a light, squally rain. Shakespeare ignored it and constantly surveyed the countryside they were riding through, hoping to see the promised reinforcements of pressed men emerge from the mists and woods, with Andrew among their number. He turned in the saddle and looked back along the endless line of men and wagons carrying military equipment. A rider on a grey stallion was approaching, galloping along the flank of the marchers. As he reined in, Shakespeare recognised him as one of Cecil's most trusted messengers.

'Mr Shakespeare, I bring you this from Sir Robert.'

The man was breathless as he reached into his pack-saddle and removed a waxed waterproof packet, from which he took a sealed paper. He handed it to Shakespeare, then wheeled his horse and was gone.

Removing his dagger, Shakespeare slid the blade under the seal and broke open the letter. He unfolded it and glanced at its familiar, neat hand. It was encrypted in a code known only to Sir Robert and himself. He read it once, quickly, and found himself smiling wryly.

'*John,*' the letter said, '*by now you should have had your instructions from Sir John Norreys. Put your trust in him. Summon your courage and fortitude and do all that he asks of you. I suspect you may still harbour doubts about the Lady Eliska, but I would ask you to trust her also. I am certain she has the best interests of England at heart.*

'*I know you will do your duty. In truth, I can think of no other man who could undertake this work. With this in mind, I wish to reassure you that the authorities in Oxford have agreed to look favourably upon the case of your boy, Andrew. All will be well with him. I can also tell you that your man Cooper has done all that has been asked of him in protecting the Eye and that, God willing, very soon his labours will bear fruit for England. God speed, John. Written in haste at Greenwich, your good friend, Robert Cecil.*'

Shakespeare smiled because he saw again the implied threat there. Do this and all will be well. Fail me and then . . . Well, the outlook is not so fair.

Taking out a tinderbox, he cast a flame, burnt the letter and scattered the ashes to the wind.

By the light of a hunter's moon, Andrew approached the village. Dogs barked and he stopped. Had they caught his scent on the air?

It was a large village of two hundred or more houses, mostly poor, but a fair number of good quality, including a blacksmith, a brewer, a tanner and other tradesmen. On a normal night, they would all be asleep, but he knew they would have one or more men keeping watch because of the English soldiers, six or seven miles distant.

The barking stopped and Andrew moved on. Close to the village, he slipped off his boots and carried them, walking barefoot for silence. He trod across the fields and skirted the village. He knew where he was going, for they had passed through this place two days earlier, marching boldly down the main street while the villagers slunk in doorways or watched from windows. Some had jeered, some had offered them bread and wine, but most eyed them sullenly and said nothing. They had seen too much warfare already. The sooner the soldiers were gone – be they English, French or Spanish – the better.

He spotted it quickly. It was easily the largest building in the neighbourhood. A wayside inn – an *auberge* – with a stable block. Pinkney had gone in there with two of his men for a midday repast, while the rest of the men huddled on the street outside, eating bread, oats and the rancid remains of the salt beef they had brought with them from England. Then they had moved on, for a town or village was never safe. Too many windows, too many rooftops, too vulnerable to ambush.

The dogs barked again, but they were further away now and Andrew did not heed them. He crept to the walled stableyard of the inn and saw straightway what he wanted: a two-wheeled cart with long handles that one man could lie on and another could pull with relative ease.

He knew the wheels would creak and rattle, so he had brought butter with him. Now he smeared it into the hubs of the wheels and every joint. He rolled the cart slowly, this way and that, listening for squeaks and creaks. Near by, a horse whinnied in its stall. He ignored it. At last, satisifed, he began to roll the cart from the yard, inch by inch. If he went faster, the iron-rimmed wheels would ring on the cobbles.

Once outside the stableyard, he dragged the cart away from the stone path on to the grassy verge of the field. He let out a breath of relief. He was away. Now all that remained was the long haul back to camp. Two hours it had taken him to walk here. It would be three or four hours on the way back, pulling the cart.

Half an hour before dawn, Andrew was almost asleep on his feet. His arms, shoulders and thighs were past pain and into numbness. He was exhausted from the long trek across country pulling the cart.

There was birdsong in anticipation of the dawn, but suddenly it was silenced and the stillness spooked him. He walked on, more cautiously now. Then he heard the crack-crack of musket-shots and the sinew-tautening blare of a trumpet. He stopped. The fatigue simply slid away from his body like a discarded skin.

He was instantly alert, his heart beating as though it would burst. The sounds were coming from the camp, less than a mile away. He dropped the handles of the cart and began running towards the commotion.

The sound of battle intensified as he came near to the bridge. He stopped again, trying to make out what was happening. A sudden thought hit him: he should run the other way. This place was death. He screwed his eyes shut and breathed deeply. How could he run? There was nowhere to go in this land of strangers. He was done with running. One boy alone could not survive and stay hidden long. He would be caught – and he knew well what happened when a common soldier was captured. The two ancients of the company had spoken of it in gory detail. Private soldiers who were taken would be slaughtered with cold efficiency and without mercy. Only the officers were kept alive, to be ransomed. It had ever been thus. Word had reached men-at-arms throughout England of the ambush two years past at Ambrières-les-Vallées, a few miles to the east of this place, when a hundred captured English soldiers had been butchered. Such tales served to make English blood hotter.

He had a vantage point behind a hedge and saw the backs of five men on the bridge, kneeling and using the parapet as a rest for their muskets. They were firing towards the farm buildings. He could see the glow of their matchlocks, then the flash of fire and the billowing of smoke each time they shot.

From the copse behind the farm buildings there were more gun-flashes in a wide arc, but how many? He tried to count them through the cloud of smoke, and reckoned no more than seven. That made twelve arquebusiers shooting. Were there more hidden away, waiting to attack? Archers and pikemen? It seemed almost certain. Cavalry, perhaps? Less likely. If there were horses, he reasoned, they must be well in reserve or they would have been heard by the English watches as they drew near. But it was bad enough as it was. The English soldiers in the camp were caught in a crossfire. At their backs was the river, which they could not traverse without being picked off at will. The only way out was the open road. If they broke cover and tried to run using that route, most would be cut down. They had little hope of escape.

What worried him was the thought of what was happening inside the camp. Were the men already dead or wounded? So far, he had not seen or heard any musket-shots from the old buildings. At that moment, he saw two flashes from the wreck of the byre, then three more. Thank God. They were becoming organised. But they were in the dark. They needed to know the deployment of the enemy.

Two of the men on the bridge picked up their guns and muzzle-rests and advanced at a loping run into the open ground, fifty yards from the buildings. They immediately drew English fire, but it was wild and speculative. They threw themselves down behind a mound. Andrew heard them laughing and could see them pouring powder into their weapons and pushing balls into the muzzles; they now had a far clearer shot into the heart of the camp, yet they were well protected by the mound. He watched them line up their sights. One squeezed the trigger, then the other. From the camp, two screams pierced the air.

The sun was not up, but its light glimmered on the horizon. The glow gave the old ruins a jagged, ghostly outline. It occurred to Andrew that his comrades would be in an even more perilous position in daylight, there to be shot like targets. If he was to help, he needed to act now. For the second time that night, he removed his boots, tying them to his belt. He checked his weapons: dagger and short sword. That was all he had. The shooting from the woods was growing more frequent. His first estimate of the number of guns there was way out; there were more like fifteen musket-flashes in the undergrowth at the edge of the woods, and they were shooting rapidly.

He dropped to his belly and began to crawl through the meadow grass, keeping close to the hedging to break the line of his form. He said a silent prayer that he would not be seen.

Thirty yards upriver from the bridge, he slipped into the stream. It was twenty-five feet from bank to bank. After he had taken two steps, the water was up to his chest, then he lost his footing. He had to swim a few strokes before his feet touched bottom again. Emerging from the river at the far bank, he lay in the grass and mud for a few seconds to make sure he had not been seen.

He crawled forward, towards the mound. Suddenly he shuddered. His hand was touching warm dead flesh. In the wan light he saw that it was the body of an English soldier, a quiet, dull-witted youth two or three years older than himself. His throat had been slashed and his belly ripped open. He must have been on watch.

Andrew searched his body for weapons. He had a long dagger and a pikestaff. He took the dagger, then moved on. He was twenty yards behind the two men at the mound. They were shooting and reloading constantly. Andrew knew the drill: first pour good corned powder into the barrel from your flask, just the right amount; too much would blow the muzzle apart, not enough would make the shot fall short; next, prime the pan with touchpowder from your secondary powderbox; finally take ball from pouch and drop into muzzle, followed by wadding, pressed home with a scouring stick. It was a laborious process, but he could see that these men were skilled and quick.

He came closer. Five yards away now, he hugged the meadow grass, certain that they must hear his heartbeat and breathing.

He counted. Between one shot and the next, he counted to twenty. But he knew they could not continue at this rate or their weapons would overheat. After eight shots, one of the men put his musket aside to cool down. The other man shot twice more, then he too stopped. Andrew's hands shook. He knew what he had to do. He crossed himself. 'Forgive me, Father,' he mouthed. He took his dagger from his belt and gripped it in his left hand, willing it to stop shaking. Then he took his short sword in the right hand. He breathed deeply and launched himself.

He went for the man on the left first, stabbing towards the face and neck. The man twisted aside, but Andrew's long dagger blade was quicker and went through the arquebusier's throat, impaling him to the earth. Before the second man had time to react, Andrew was on him with the short sword, thrusting at his chest. It glanced off his ribcage. The man groaned and squirmed away. Andrew thrust again and caught him in the lower back. The enemy soldier's torso arched in shock and pain. Andrew pulled back the sword. There was blood everywhere. His hands were thick with it, slipping on the ridged hilt of the sword. He grasped it in both hands to get more leverage, raised it above him and brought it down into the nape of the man's neck.

He felt the wind of a musket-ball, then heard the crack. Looking up, he saw that the men on the bridge had turned their fire on him and that he was exposed. He pulled the two dying bodies on top of each other as a protective bank. The light was improving all the time. He cut the men's powder-flasks and touchpowder boxes from their belts. Keeping as low behind the wall of corpses as he could, he primed and loaded both their arquebuses. He blew on the matches and was satisfied with their glow. He prodded the first one forward, squinted down the barrel sights and pulled the trigger as John Shakespeare had taught him to do on holidays out with the trainbands at Artillery Yard. He heard a cry. Had he hit a man, or was that from elsewhere? As the smoke rose and cleared, he saw that he had felled one of the three on the bridge. The other two were backing off, to a safer position on the far side of the river; they must have realised that they were as vulnerable to his gunshots as he was to theirs.

'Provost Pinkney!' Andrew shouted. 'This way – the way is almost clear!'

Even as he spoke, he heard a trumpet sound, then saw two dozen men emerge from the buildings with pike and shot. Pinkney was at their head, a pistol in each hand, charging straight for the bridge. The enemy arquebusiers were trying to reload, but they looked up in panic and realised the English would be on them before they could shoot. They threw down the guns and ran. Pinkney loosed off a shot, but missed.

There was a shout from the woods. '*Avancez!*'

Pinkney put up two fingers in the direction of the enemy, strode across the bridge and picked up the two dropped fire-arms, then returned, walking towards Andrew. Hands on hips, he stopped, looked at him and shook his head. Stragglers were emerging from the English camp. Pinkney turned towards them and ordered them into line, pikes and bills at the front and centre, arquebusiers at the flanks.

Andrew watched in astonishment. The provost marshal seemed as calm as though he were organising a game of football between villagers. Last of all came Reaphook, hobbling on a stick. Pinkney stared at him dispassionately.

'We will march from here in an orderly fashion,' Pinkney said when his men were all gathered in order. 'If the Frenchies are foolish enough to follow us, which I doubt, we will turn and fight and we will kill them all. Any man of you who breaks ranks and runs will be shot by me.'

At that moment, the French soldiers from the woods arrived at the farm buildings. Andrew could see that there were about twenty of them. They had more guns than the English, but they were outnumbered man for man, and they no longer had the English trapped. They held back, suddenly lacking confidence, for they had lost their advantage of position and surprise. Pinkney took two steps forward, raised his arm, took aim down the muzzle of his wheel-lock pistol and pulled the trigger. The Frenchmen scuttled back into the cover vacated by the English. Pinkney laughed, casually reloaded one of his pistols, then turned again to his men.

Andrew did not move. His blood-wet sword hung from his blood-red arm. The stench of blood clogged his nose and his mind. He was dumbfounded, unable to take in the horror of what he had done. He made the sign of the cross over each of the corpses in turn and mouthed the Lord's Prayer. It brought him no comfort.

'About turn!' Pinkney said sharply. 'Ensign take point. Double your ranks by line. Open order. Shoulder pikes and march!' He glanced at the motionless figure of Andrew. 'That includes you, Private Woode.'

# Chapter 42

JOHN SHAKESPEARE REINED in his mount and unfolded the chart they had been given. It was a battle to hold it flat in the constant wind. It seemed to him that the Crozon peninsula jutted out into the Atlantic like a trident with splayed tines. Soon, they could be encountering Spanish troops, early-warning outposts for the Fort of El Léon.

'My lady, we have no more than fifteen miles to ride. Are you certain you wish to see this through?'

Eliska brought her monkey down from her shoulder and caressed its wind-swept fur, feeding it a nut from a leather purse. She raised her eyes and they met Shakespeare's. 'It is not that I wish to; I *have* to.'

'There is still time to turn around and ride back to Morlaix. Solko will be waiting for you there; he will protect you. I can go alone. The ride from here is rocky and rough.'

'Rougher than the high fells of Lancashire, Mr Shakespeare?'

'The risks in this enterprise are greater. Too great, perhaps.'

'You know what I must do.'

'But this is your life . . .'

Not for the first time Shakespeare found himself wondering about her true loyalties. Cecil trusted her, so did Heneage and Norreys. But Shakespeare still had doubts.

*Perhaps, Eliska, you are already the enemy within. Perhaps I am the prize, served on a platter to Spain.*

She reached across and touched his hand. 'This goes back many years.'

'I know your history. Your father worked for the Reformation, and died at the hands of the Inquisition. But is that reason enough to sacrifice your own life? Has Heneage persuaded you to this course?'

'My father was taken in the night, from his own house. He was a great catch for the Spanish. They spirited him away to Madrid, where he was tortured. Torments so foul that my tongue will not speak them. And at the end, after months of ill treatment and starvation and endless demands to recant, he was tried and convicted of heresy, and burnt at the stake in the ritual of *auto de fé*. He died by the very instrument he fought so hard to destroy.'

Shakespeare knew all about the methods employed by the Inquisition. It was the stuff of nightmares.

'I met Thomas Heneage again three years after Father's death,' Eliska continued. 'He was in the Low Countries in '86 with Leicester's army. I travelled there to meet him and I vowed to him then that I would do anything to help defend the Reformation, and to defend England against Spain and the Inquisition. Anything.'

'And so you devised this insane plan?'

'Not at first. But Cecil told me that Fort Crozon had somehow to be taken from the inside. While you were hunting for your son in Oxford, the plan came to me. But I knew straightway that I needed you. There always had to be two of us.'

'Perhaps I could do it alone . . .' Shakespeare said.

She shook her head. 'No. Apart from the practicalities of what we must do, I am expected. They trust me, for I have served them already – in Prague, as well as in England.'

'In England?' Shakespeare bristled with distaste. 'In God's name, what services did you do them in England? Did it involve poison, perchance?'

She smiled with quiet resignation. 'You think I poisoned the earl? Would it matter if I had? He was disloyal and proud and would have wished the crown of England, not just for himself, but for the Pope and Philip of Spain.'

'It all fits. Why else would you have been in Lancashire?'

Eliska hesitated. 'Very well, John, I confess, I lied to you. There was a certain Walter Weld—'

'You told me you spoke of nothing but horses. He fled before I could speak with him.'

'He is a senior intelligencer in the employ of Spain, their most important man in all England. When I discovered this I took the information to Heneage and Cecil. Weld became my intermediary to the Spanish spies in the French embassy. I was in Lancashire because that was where Weld was based, trying his utmost to mould the Earl of Derby to the requirements of his masters in Spain and the Vatican. If you had brought Weld in for hard questioning, as I believed you threatened, then everything would have crumbled to dust. I made him run – I had to save him from you, Mr Shakespeare.'

'So that was why he vanished.'

'It was necessary. *He* was necessary. Yes, he was a traitor and had designs on Dr Dee, but a bigger scheme was afoot, so I had to warn him. With such small sacrifices, great gains are possible. And now you and I must work together, for the Spanish will not trust you without me at your side. There is no other way. I needed someone who had something to offer to Spain – a great deal to offer. You have all the secrets of Walsingham and Cecil. There was never any other man to fit the bill.'

He understood her plan. But would it work? It seemed unfeasible, but perhaps that was its very strength. Perhaps the

Spanish would be thrown off their guard by the sheer audacity of the plot. But whose side was she really on? She confessed she had lied to him once, so was she lying still?

Shakespeare laughed. 'I will be hanged from the battlements or thrown from the cliffs as soon as we arrive – and you will be sent to the Escorial to be tortured or gawped at.'

'You underestimate your value to them, John. They know you have great secrets they want, and they know you were married to a Catholic and have no love for the more extreme Protestants. You are worth a treasure fleet of gold to them.'

Norreys had told him that the stratagem had been many weeks in setting up, that Eliska had passed information to Madrid through the French embassy in London. It was already a well-known route – the route used by the Babington plotters in their conspiracy to raise Mary Queen of Scots to the throne of England.

The story told to Spain was that John Shakespeare could no longer stomach the persecution of Catholics. He wished to defect, bringing the innermost secrets of England's spy network with him. Names of intelligencers, codes, conspiracies. Eliska had vouched for him; so, at her bidding, had Walter Weld.

Now he had to adopt the role of traitor. It was a part that sickened him. If only he had his brother's skill at play-acting . . .

Crozon stretched away in front of them. It was a rocky, sparse outcrop. Trees were bent away from the wind. Hardy cattle and squat stone houses told the nature of those that inhabited this land. Shakespeare laughed. The region was called Finistère – land's end. The end of the world, perhaps. Was ever a place better named?

'We ride on then, my lady.'

\*

By sunset, they stood before the fort's land-facing ramparts. It was a remarkable structure, unlike anything Shakespeare had expected. He had been prepared for an ugly, uncompromising wall, built with but one purpose: to stand against all comers on the landward side, and to attack enemy shipping from the sea-facing walls.

The fort had a magnificent towering gatehouse keep, a dense curtain wall and, on either side, a bastion shaped like the spade suit in a game of cards. Though elegant, it was clearly functional, too. It was there to be impregnable from land, and to menace and control the port of Brest, a mere two miles or so across the water.

Four Spanish guards in morion helmets and steel corslets trained the muzzles of their calivers on the two riders and demanded to know who they were. Shakespeare explained to them in their own language that they came in peace and wished to confer with their commander.

The senior officer ordered them to dismount, then looked them up and down closely and asked their names. He gazed at the monkey, then spat on the ground with derision. But he was clearly satisfied that these people and their pet were no threat, for he nodded and strode away through the main gate without saying another word.

Shakespeare took note of the defensive works. In advance of the curtain wall was a deep ditch preceded by an imposing counterscarp – a thick, sloping hill of earth and stone that would act as bulwark against any bombardment and would be nigh on impossible to scale without coming under heavy fire from the ramparts above. Likewise, the main gatehouse would be protected from cannonfire. The gateway itself consisted of two immensely heavy oak doors, eight feet high with powerful iron straps, designed to foil the use of battering logs. Shakespeare could not see a portcullis. Well, he would discover all in due course.

'The castle of your dreams, my lady,' Shakespeare said.

'I am sure it suits its purpose well.'

He nodded. There could be no doubt about that. More importantly, did it suit *their* purpose?

After a few minutes the chief of guards returned and ordered Shakespeare and Eliska to follow him.

Inside the fort they were confronted by an elaborate trench system, then a row of military houses, each in the Spanish style with flat, pointed façades topped by crosses at the highest point. The one on the right was clearly a guardhouse; the central one was the most elegant and probably housed the commandant and his staff. The one on the left was squat and had a brutally functional air. It had to be the munitions store.

Shakespeare observed that the two bastions, either side of the curtain rampart, had heavy artillery pieces covering the landward approaches. They were a likely match for Norreys's siege train. The bastions were colossal structures.

Through a central alleyway, he saw the main compound, a wide open square for drilling and mustering. Buildings were ranged all around the square: barracks for the men, cookhouse, chapel, stabling.

This was an astonishingly well-constructed fort, impervious to undermining because of the solid rock it stood on. Shakespeare was forced to acknowledge that the military assessment was correct: it had to be taken from the inside.

A soldier was walking towards them. He was a man of fifty or so, with grey hair and a strong, weathered face.

'Mr Shakespeare?' he said in English. 'Lady Eliska? Please allow me to introduce myself. I am Captain Tomas de Paredes. I was expecting you. You are most welcome. I trust your journey here has not been too unpleasant.'

Eliska smiled. 'Indeed not, captain. And I am delighted to

tell you that I bring important information, and a gift of great value.'

Paredes smiled. 'It is as I was told. But first, I am certain, you will both wish refreshments and the chance to wash. These Breton roads are pitted and hard on rider as well as horse. Later we will talk and you can bring me all your secrets regarding the force that is to be sent against me. Then in the morning, you will be given passage with an armed escort to General del Águila, who is presently in the south, at Blavet Harbour. As for your comforts, I have evicted an officer from his chamber for you, my lady. Mr Shakespeare, I fear you will have to share my rooms.'

The commander nodded to the chief of guards, standing stiffly at his side.

'Show the lady Eliska and Mr Shakespeare to their quarters, Captain Ferreira.' He turned back to Shakespeare and Eliska. 'I must apologise,' he said conspiratorially. 'You will find it is not the most palatial of accommodation.'

They spoke over supper in Paredes's apartments. The rooms were comfortable enough, in a masculine, military way. Paredes had a good table of food. Attentive servants brought them some of the best wines of Spain.

'So to business,' Paredes said at last. 'I thank you, Lady Eliska, for your fine gift.'

'The pleasure is all mine, captain. It is the thought of those angry English faces when they discover that it is missing that causes me the greatest joy.'

'So what else do you bring me? Intelligence from Norreys's camp, I trust. Do I have anything to fear?'

Eliska looked at Shakespeare. If she was uneasy, it did not show in her demeanour or beautiful features. Her eyes were as animated and luminous as ever he had seen them.

'That is for you to decide. Let us begin with the complement of his forces, which will soon march from Morlaix. He has five thousand four hundred men, a siege train of six guns, which will be supplemented by navy cannon, and some pieces – and more men – supplied by Aumont. In all, you will face fourteen or fifteen cannon.'

Paredes interrupted. 'You mention Morlaix. Surely, the siege train is needed against the castle there. My messengers have told me the Catholic League is holding the fortress against Baskerville's veterans and some of Aumont's troops. Norreys cannot come while the siege remains; his back would be compromised.'

'The castle fell without a fight, captain. They surrendered as soon as Frobisher appeared off the coast and rolled out his guns.'

Paredes snorted. 'This so-called Catholic League! They should be hanged for cowardice. Which side are the French on?'

'A very good question – and one that troubles the English as much as you, captain. Just ask Norreys.'

'Well, Lady Eliska, the pirate Frobisher's guns will not frighten us so easily. He is already here, you know, and keeps us entertained with his paltry cannon. They may wake you during the night. Pay them no heed, for the balls can scarcely hit the base of the ramparts, let alone clear them. He might as well shoot arrows at the moon.'

Eliska slid a scroll of paper from her sleeve and handed it to Paredes.

'There you will find full details of Norreys's manpower, equipment, gunpowder and munitions, down to the last halberd, trumpet and brick for building ovens.' She touched the paper with her forefinger. 'There, fifty pioneers. Eighteen cannoneers, two hundred thousand pounds of artillery powder and fifty thousand for small arms, two hundred ladders, one hundred mortars.' She stabbed her delicate finger at another section of the paper. 'There you will find the effective companies and the ones you may ignore, the pressed men.'

Paredes read the paper slowly. Every so often he smiled. 'So the Privy Council has sent a thousand spades and fifteen hundred pickaxes for trenchwork and undermining. That should afford us great amusement. We will shoot them one by one as they break their tools and backs on solid rock.'

Every sinew of Shakespeare's being raged against the divulging of these military secrets, and yet he smiled and nodded as Eliska revealed detail after detail. She was giving away the muster numbers, the disposition of General Norreys's army, and probable siege and battle plans. These were the general's most intimate secrets. Under any other circumstance, the passing of such intelligence to an enemy power could lead only to the scaffold and another severed head to decorate the southern gatehouse of London Bridge.

Paredes looked up. 'What of the royalist French troops, Lady Eliska?'

'My knowledge is not so good. I have not shared a bed with Marshal Aumont.'

Paredes laughed.

Shakespeare interrupted. 'Aumont has three thousand men, captain, many of them unreliable and mutinous. They have been drifting away home for the grape harvest. They do not like fighting alongside the English. As for Aumont himself, he tries to rule Norreys, but Sir John won't have it. They quarrel and bicker like old maids. I am not certain they will be able to work together much longer. Aumont will not allow the English into the port of Morlaix, nor into Brest. Norreys is a man of action; Aumont wishes a quiet life and will be reluctant to attack you.'

Paredes signalled a servant to pour more wine for Shakespeare.

'Then we have little to fear.' He tugged at his grey beard and met Shakespeare's eye. 'It was said you were coming here as a friend of Spain, that you were a Roman Catholic at heart. That you had information of a critical nature to impart. That was my intelligence from Don Juan del Águila.'

Shakespeare sat back and looked at his nails with a nonchalant air. 'Indeed, that is so. Do you doubt me?'

Paredes continued to study his face for some sign of dissimulation. 'Well,' he said at last, 'that is for others to rule on when you go to General del Águila on the morrow. But for now, I wish to have your secrets.'

Shakespeare sighed. 'Captain Paredes, I do not wish to cause you offence or insult you in any way, but I worry about your information. Did your messenger not tell you that I was to talk to no one but del Águila in person?'

'No. I was not told that, only that you were both coming to me with vital intelligence.'

'That is so. The military intelligence has now been given to you, by the Lady Eliska. That is all you need. The remainder, which I keep locked away in my head, is political and diplomatic, and will be imparted to Don Juan del Águila alone. He will know the names of every English spy operating in the Spanish empire. He will know the secrets of every code at Cecil's disposal. He will know how many blackened teeth the Queen of England has left in her pox-ravaged face if he so wishes.'

Paredes's eyes were piercing. The moments ticked by. Then suddenly he laughed.

'Of course, you are right not to trust me. I am nothing but a soldier, a common *capitán.*' The smile left his face as quickly as it had appeared. 'But I tell you this, Mr Shakespeare, though I treat you with civility here as an honoured guest, you may not have the same reception at Blavet if you are suspected of false dealing. There are secret chambers there, where masked men with fire and iron can be very persuasive.' He furled the paper Eliska had given him and clutched it tight. Then he smiled. 'More wine, I think. These Breton nights are cold and long.'

Shakespeare did not sleep. He was deeply troubled by the evening, particularly the gift from Eliska to Paredes.

'You mentioned a gift. What did you give him?' he demanded beneath his breath as they were escorted to their chambers.

Eliska lifted her chin and her face glowed in the candlelight. 'Are you jealous, Mr Shakespeare?'

'This is no time for games. Tell me.'

'It is a pistol, a wheel-lock with a handle of solid silver, and the initials J. N. inlaid in red gold. It belonged to Norreys.'

'Does he know you have taken it?'

'I imagine he does now.' She laughed quietly and leant towards Shakespeare to whisper in his ear. 'I would have you warm my bed this night. I had hoped . . . but it seems you are billeted with our host.'

Now, in his single cot bed, he stared by the light of a single candle at a carved wooden figure of the Virgin Mary on the stone wall. For the first time he understood its significance. Mary and Elizabeth . . . Both sides had their own virgin to honour.

Two guards stood outside the room and Paredes snored close by.

Shakespeare turned over and looked away from the wall. He could no longer bear the eyes of Mary, mother of Jesus, upon him. He listened to the wind howl outside as he shifted on the thin mattress, but could find no comfort.

At dawn, he began to drift into sleep, but his peace was shattered by a prolonged discharge of musket shots. Without opening his eyes, he smiled, for he knew what it meant:

Norreys's arquebusiers were here, just as promised. Three hundred of the best shot. The fort was now secured from land and sea. He and Eliska would not be going to Águila at Blavet after all. No one would be moving from this fort. The first stage was in place, thank God. He and Lady Eliska were here for the duration.

# Chapter 43

THE RAIN TEEMED down without respite. Reaphook could not go on. His thigh was turning black where the girl at the farm had stabbed him. He knew he had gangrene, for he could smell its sickly sweetness.

'He's done for, lad,' Pinkney said to Andrew. 'Musket-ball in the heart would be the kindest thing. That's what you'd do for a mastiff when its days were up.'

'Could we not cut the leg away?'

Pinkney shook his head briskly. 'First, we've no surgeon. Second, the wound's too high. The rot's spread to his body. He told me his prick has turned black and it pains him to piss. Even if we could save him, no man wants to live like that. You keep him talking so he don't see it coming. Easier that way.'

The provost marshal turned aside, huddled against the constant rain.

Andrew went and sat by Reaphook. Neither of them had soles to their boots and both had strips of rags wrapped about their feet. They were soaked through. Andrew could not recall the last time his skin had been dry. The stink of Reaphook's rotting body was somehow made worse by the eternal damp, and it almost overpowered him.

Reaphook's breathing was shallow and laboured, but he opened his eyes at the touch of Andrew's hand on his arm.

He was burning up. Andrew handed him a mess-tin of rain-water that he had caught in his cap and Reaphook drank greedily, then clutched at Andrew's dripping cassock with his wasted, claw-like fingers.

'I saw you do that thing with your hand over them Frenchies you killed.'

'The sign of the cross?'

'Aye. What does it do?'

'It's a prayer for their spirit, seeking forgiveness. The extirpation of sins. A blessing.'

'I done a lot of bad things, Private Woode.'

'I know you have, Mr Reaphook.'

'Is it too late for me?'

'God tells us it is never too late. I no longer know if I believe it.'

'But it's got to be worth a try, though.'

'Would you like me to pray for you? Is that what you're saying?'

'Aye.'

'You should repent your sins.'

'What does that mean?'

'Say you're sorry for all you've done wrong, all those you have harmed and robbed and . . . murdered.'

He wanted to say *raped*, too, but could not bring himself to utter the word, for it brought back memories of Ursula Dancer.

'Well, then, I'm sorry.'

'And for what you did to Ursula.'

'For everything. I was born bad. My slut of a mother was bad and I never knew no father.' Reaphook smiled slyly at Andrew. 'You liked her, didn't you? Wouldn't have minded yourself, eh? Ursula pigging Dancer.'

Andrew felt the heat rise to his face. 'You should not have treated her like that. She is a good woman.'

'Like you. High-born. Never fitted in with the likes of us. A haggard, she was – a wild she-hawk that would not be tamed. I used to be copesmates with Staffy, you know. There wasn't always bad blood between us. Used to go sharking, wenching and drinking together when he wasn't so soft. He was sweet on her, but wouldn't touch her. That was the problem – wouldn't let no other man touch her neither. Went against the natural order. Anyone would have thought she was the virgin bloody queen. But once when he was cup-shotten, he told me stuff. I know where she came from. Gentry, her mother was. Squires or lords or somesuch from Grantley Brook. Rich as lions with land and gold. I'd cut all their throats. I'd have cut yours, too, just for being better than us. I wanted Spindle to do it, wanted to watch it and see her face as you died.'

'Is she still alive?'

'Well, she was when bloody Pinkney came back for me. That bastard Spindle had run away in the night, so I was taken in his place. And here I am.'

'Say, "Father forgive me, for I have sinned." That should be enough.'

'Father forgive me, for I have sinned. And you can have my sickle. I bequeath it to you.'

Andrew made the sign of the cross over him and tried not to look past him at the approaching Pinkney, sword in hand.

Reaphook didn't look either. He closed his eyes tight shut in anticipation of impending death. Pinkney pulled back the sword with both arms, then swung it at Reaphook's neck. First strike did it. The head fell away, three-quarters severed, and blood gushed like a fountain.

They buried the body in the muddy earth, along with his sickle; no one wanted it. Then they resumed marching.

Two hours later, just before dark, they reached the English garrison at the port of Paimpol. All they found was the rump of the army; Norreys was long gone westward to Morlaix and, perhaps, to Crozon. Pinkney took on fresh food, munitions and boots, commandeered wagons – and took to the road again. He had no intention of missing *this* fight.

Captain Paredes paced up and down the battlements, looking out across the grey waters of Brest Harbour and beyond to the open sea. He stopped and gazed through a bevelled shooting slit at the English and Dutch ships. They were all stood off, outside Le Goulet – the rock-strewn narrows that led into the harbour – and out of range of the fort's guns, but every so often Frobisher drove one or more of his ships forward. A half-hearted puff of smoke came from a single cannon, followed by the sound of gunpowder exploding and the dull thud of the ball taking a chunk of rock and earth out of the cliff-face below. The Spanish gunners wanted to reply in kind, but Paredes insisted they conserve powder and ball.

'Why does he do this, Mr Shakespeare?' Paredes demanded. 'You must be acquainted with Martin Frobisher – why does he waste gunpowder and cannonballs in this way? He cannot possibly elevate his guns sufficiently to harm us. Nor can he be resupplied easily.'

'It is probably as much to keep his own men occupied as to worry you.'

'It makes no sense. I had thought the English good seafarers and fighting men. But this . . .'

'I cannot argue with you. It makes no sense.'

*But if it is intended to get under your skin, Captain Paredes, it seems mighty effective.*

'How long is it now? How long has Frobisher been here? How long have Norreys and his army been here? How many days has this rain fallen?'

Time was dragging. Days on end of gales and rain, broken

only by the stilllness of dense fogs that seemed to suffocate the rocky headlands. To be enclosed in this impenetrable fort for days and weeks without number was taking its toll. The citadel of El Léon was starting to feel like a cold damp tomb.

In the evenings Shakespeare and Eliska dined with Captain Paredes and his officers, and played cards in a genteel fashion, to the sound of mandolins, as though they were not surrounded by an enemy that wanted their blood. Only the sporadic sound of gunshot and cannon boom intruded on the elegance of the setting.

Shakespeare would have liked time alone with Eliska, but they were closely watched. As a result they always met each other in the company of Paredes or one of his senior officers.

Shakespeare had, however, discovered a great deal more about the fort's structure. Paredes enjoyed his company and took him on his daily rounds. The high, solidly built ramparts and bastions were to be found only on the landward approaches. Its designer, Rojas, must have decided that no army could scale the cliffs to attack, so the seaward defences were less robust. They were lower, too, following the falling-away contours of the clifftop. This was just as Sir Roger Williams had described the fort in his report to the Privy Council. Four culverins faced northwards from these lower ramparts, covering the narrows. Frobisher was in no position to seriously challenge such might; his fleet would merely take a severe battering to which it could not respond. All the English and Dutch ships could do was ensure that no Spanish galleons approached to break the siege.

As far as Shakespeare was concerned, the culverins did not matter. What was crucial was the height of the ramparts on which they were mounted. The walls were visible from the sea to the west of the harbour. Such a view would be impossible to landward.

*

The siege was not going well. The armies of Norreys and Aumont were bogged down, their tents dripping and drenched in mud.

Each day, more soldiers reported sick with the bloody flux. Pioneers had been unable to dig into rock, and so they had built up the thin muddy topsoil into entrenchments above ground, and these were beginning to stink of ordure. The siege train had arrived and had been reinforced by some of Frobisher's ship cannon, hauled ashore at a nearby fishing village and mounted on spars. Keeping powder dry was a major problem, but the fourteen siege guns at last opened up with a brutal onslaught. Ball after ball smashed into the counterscarp. The Spanish merely laughed from the ramparts. Their fort could withstand ten thousand such barrages.

The soldiers passed the time drinking foul ale and apple brandy, staking their non-existent wages on a throw of the dice and trying to keep rust from seizing up the mechanisms of their weapons. They also hurled insults across no-man's-land in broken Spanish and coarse English.

'I fucked your mother last night!'

'I wouldn't fuck yours – I don't fuck dogs!'

There were diversions, some murderous.

The worst of the horrors came on the English side: a company of foot, led by enthusiastic but inexperienced gentlemen volunteers, overran the counterscarp and threw ladders up against the bastions. They were easily hurled back and took casualties. Then a careless gunner sent a spark into a barrel of gunpowder, killing or wounding more than fifty English artillerymen and other soldiers. Gloom descended on the English tents.

The next morning one of Norreys's messengers carried a parley flag aloft and marched to the fort's gates to offer safe passage to all within if they surrendered. Captain Paredes did not hesitate: no surrender, no talks, no quarter asked or given.

And then the weather grew yet worse.

A howling gale roared in and the siege settled into a hopeless stand-off. If Norreys and Frobisher did not launch an all-out attack soon, the siege would be lost to winter.

# Chapter 44

T HE DAY WAS dark. The rain had gone, but a sharp wind chilled their faces. Everyone knew that it had to be this day. There would be no other chance. Águila would soon be snapping at their rear. And sickness was worming its way through the camp at alarming speed.

Provost Marshal Pinkney addressed his company.

'You will be pleased to know,' he said, 'that Captain-General Norreys has affforded us the signal honour of being part of the main attack, with Frobisher's marines. So say your prayers.'

He told them to have valour, to stay alive and to make the Spanish die. Then he ordered brandy to be given to each man, for courage. Every soldier listened with his own thoughts, then, when their captain was done, returned to honing his blade.

Pinkney called Andrew over to him. 'Come, walk with me to the field kitchen. I fight better on a full stomach.'

They walked through the tents and damp, fluttering pennants of the camp. Everywhere, men were forming up, preparing for battle, checking weapons and packs.

'You have shown yourself to be a man of courage, Private Woode,' Pinkney said.

'Thank you, sir.'

It seemed to Andrew now that he had been a soldier all his life. Oxford had receded into a distant dream. Obeying orders, eating porridge and peas, foraging for berries and roots, shitting at the roadside, carrying a halberd and pack as his constant companions, living in a cassock and coat stained with other men's blood, had become his world.

Now, at last, they were in the main camp at Crozon. They had been here two weeks and were rested and better fed. But they had discovered a sense of ill-ease and ominous anticipation in the air. There was a miasma of disease; men had to be kicked from their field-beds to get moving in the mornings. The bodily sickness of some was made worse by the despondency of others. Rumours abounded that the main Spanish army was but ten miles to the rear and would advance to trap and crush Norreys between them and the troops in the fort.

'You know what marines are, do you, lad?'

'I think so, sir.'

'They are seaborne soldiers. Some men say they should stick to seafaring activities like tying knots and hauling anchors, but Norreys seems to think well of them, so we'll have to make the most of it. If you ask me, we'll be like a Forlorn Hope. You know what the Forlorn Hope is, do you?'

'No, Provost Pinkney, sir.'

'They are those that are sent in first to test the enemy fire. When none of them comes back alive, the captain-general knows the fire's hot. Is that well with you, Private Woode?'

'Yes, sir.'

'Good man. And I'll take that bloody useless halberd off you. There'll be no cavalry against us today. This is all about foot soldiers – pike and shot. I'll find you a proper weapon, a petronel. When you're in the mêlée, use your short sword. One chop to the neck, then stab them in the belly. That's all it takes. Then move on to the next. The word is that today is the day. Fine weather for it: grey and dark as hell. Rockets will fly, then the trumpet will sound – and we go in.' They arrived at the field kitchen. 'Ah, mutton broth. Just the thing to stir the loins to action.'

A furlong to the east, the first musket-shot of the day rang out from the fort's ramparts. A cloud of crows flew up from the bushes all around, to join the wheeling seabirds. Pinkney pointed to them.

'Bastards,' he said. 'Gulls to laugh at the dying men, crows to pick out their eyes.'

'Well, Mr Cooper,' Frobisher said, 'do you have the precious tube about your person?'

'Yes, admiral.'

'And is Mr Ivory fit? Can he climb to the mast-top?'

Boltfoot hesitated. They were in Frobisher's cabin at the stern of the royal ship *Vanguard*. Ivory was far from recovered. His left side was palsied. He could not walk, let alone climb up the rigging.

'No, admiral,' Boltfoot said at last. 'Mr Ivory will not be able to climb. He cannot yet walk. I doubt he will ever walk again for the surgeon believes him to have suffered a stroke of God's hand.'

'Then you must know what is to be done. *You* will have to use the perspective glass, Mr Cooper. Your eyesight is sufficient, I trust?'

'Admiral, I . . .'

He looked down at his club-foot. Drake had always excused him topman duties. He had fought alongside the best of the crew, and crafted barrels and spars to a high degree, but he could not bear to climb.

'Yes, Mr Cooper?'

'Is it really necessary to go to the mast-top? Might the instrument not be used here on deck?'

'God's blood, no. You will always have a better view from on high. I say again, is your eyesight sufficient?'

Boltfoot sighed. 'Yes, admiral. My eyesight will suffice.'

Lieutenant Morgan Millwater watched Frobisher being rowed for shore in the cockboat and knew he would have to act soon. There had been feverish activity aboard all the ships. Two thousand marines were already on land, out of range of the fort's guns. Something would happen today, something that would involve the perspective glass. He was certain of it.

Millwater gazed out across the choppy grey water to the cliffs. He was tall and slender with soft, well-bred features, one of the *Vanguard*'s senior officers, just the sort of man that Frobisher liked, for he was a professional and had been at sea with him before, chasing Spanish treasure fleets. What Frobisher did not realise was that Millwater cared nothing for the admiral's opinion of him. His thoughts were all on the perspective glass.

It had all seemed so simple. Have Trayne lure Ivory to a game of chance, then club him and relieve him of the spyglass. And so it had proved – except that the glass in his possession was a fake.

Trayne had not noticed the deception. The device he took *looked* as it should. It was cylindrical, made of stiff hide and had a roundel of glass at either end. Without further ado, he had hidden it deep in a keg of gunpowder. No one would look for it there. No one except Morgan Millwater.

But then came the incident at Paimpol. The plan had been for Trayne to take the glass ashore, ride to the Spanish garrison at Blavet and hand it over to General del Águila. But bloody Cooper had foiled that idea with his inspection of every man's forearm, and his seizing of Trayne. Millwater only discovered all this when he rejoined the *Vanguard* at Morlaix.

With Trayne under guard, he had gone at night to the marked powder keg to remove the perspective glass. That was when he discovered that it was merely a fake, a worthless replica of the perspective glass containing blank roundels where complex lenses should be. In a rage, Millwater tossed it from the ship's stern into the foaming sea. As for Trayne, he was a base hireling, a mere assassin. When he was tossed into the sea, Millwater shed no tears. No one would miss him: food for lobsters and crabs.

But where was the perspective glass?

If Ivory did not have it, someone else must. Who, though? The obvious answer was Boltfoot Cooper, for had he not been assigned to protect both Ivory and the glass? It must be in his possession. Well, today was the day he would find out. And it would be Boltfoot Cooper's last day on earth.

'Do you hear that, John?'

He nodded. Yes, he had heard. Two English cannons shot in quick succession, a count of ten, then three cannon rounds, another count of ten, two more reports, another count of ten, then four more booms. It was the signal. The first three salvoes were the code; the fourth, added to the other three, gave the hour. Eleven. If all went well, the attack would commence at eleven o'clock – forty minutes from now.

Eliska and Shakespeare were on the seaward ramparts. Her voice was a whisper and she smiled as though she was commenting on the weather. They had only one guard now, Gomez, an old veteran who had fought in the Low Countries and in Portugal under Alba. He was white-haired and hunched, but Shakespeare did not underestimate him. He might be slow and ponderous, but if he had survived this long in the bloodiest wars of the century, then he knew how to fight. He would not be an easy man to overpower.

Paredes was striding around the ramparts issuing orders. He had seen ships' boats carrying men and supplies from Frobisher's fleet and he had observed the hugely increased levels of activity among the land forces of Norreys and Aumont. As he approached Shakespeare and Eliska he bowed his head.

'Well, Lady Eliska, Mr Shakespeare,' he said, smiling. 'This is a day the English will rue.'

'I am sure God will look down favourably, captain, for you will be fighting in His name.'

'Indeed, but I must require you to take shelter, for your own safety. Sergeant Gomez will take you to the guardhouse.'

Shakespeare saw that Paredes had a fine pistol in his hand.

Paredes followed his eyes. 'A beautiful pistol, yes? Sir John Norreys must miss it. Today I will discover if it is as good as it looks. It would be appropriate to shoot Norreys dead with his own pistol, I think. Now, if you please, you must make haste.'

The fort was in uproar. Men moved in all directions, hauling kegs of powder on their shoulders; dragging cannonballs up from the arsenal; frantically cleaning muskets and honing swords; hefting spare muskets, crossbows, blades and pikes up to the ramparts; priming, loading and firing cannon; heating cauldrons of oil to tip over any enemy who got close enough to scale the bastion walls. Every man had his task and knew it well. No one was looking at Shakespeare and Eliska. No one but Sergeant Gomez, who plodded behind the captain's guests as they made their way towards the guardhouse, deep beneath the inner wall of the curtain rampart.

'*Sargento*,' Eliska said, smiling, 'if I might be permitted to go first to my chamber. A lady has requirements . . .'

Gomez looked doubtful, but Eliska touched his arm and her voice was as sweet as ripe Mediterranean figs. He nodded briskly and marched them towards the officers' quarters.

She opened the door to her room, then hesitated. Gomez was standing behind her, his sword sheathed, but his hand on the hilt. Shakespeare was at his side.

There was a screech. The monkey bounded across the floor from the other side of the room in welcome. Gomez turned his head towards the animal in surprise.

Just then the English and French siege battery opened up again. Fourteen guns roared with scarce a second's delay between each one. The cannonballs smashed like a hellish hail into the counterscarp, and some overtopped it and hit the curtain wall. The thunderous sound allied to the screeching and jumping of Doda disoriented Gomez. He turned this way and that, a small lapse of concentration, but it was enough for Shakespeare.

He pushed the guard and moved across him in a single, seamless movement.

Gomez stumbled forward. Shakespeare's knee came up sharply into his belly. The Spaniard lurched and toppled headlong. He grunted, then cried out, but his voice was lost in the roar of cannon and the shooting of hundreds of muskets and rampart guns. Shakespeare clutched his hands together and brought his forearms down on to the back of Gomez's neck, pummelling him to the ground.

He lay there, face down, moving feebly. Shakespeare relieved him of his sword, dagger and pistol, then stripped him of his soldier's cassock and mail. He hit his head another crushing blow with the haft of his own dagger. Gomez lay still, his breathing weak. Shakespeare stepped further into the room and took a linen sheet from Eliska's bed. Using Gomez's dagger, he cut it into shreds.

Eliska closed the door behind her. 'What are you doing, Mr Shakespeare?'

'Making twine to bind and gag him.'

'We do not have time for this. Kill him. Put the dagger to his throat.'

Shakespeare ignored her and wound a gag around Gomez's mouth, then tied his arms behind his back. He pulled up the guard's legs and bound his ankles to his wrists. Tight.

Eliska shook her head in dismay. She was undoing the stays on her gold-thread bodice and sleeves. She removed the garment, then took off her undershirt, a bright, corn-yellow chemise. She put the bodice back on, then began attaching the chemise to Gomez's sword.

Shakespeare picked up the guard's dagger and pistol. 'We move as soon as we hear the mine. Is that your understanding?'

'Yes.' She moved closer to him. 'And the attack starts as soon as the rockets go up. If we fail – if *you* fail – the English will all be slaughtered, Mr Shakespeare.'

'Then let us not fail.'

She looked at him with a kind of sadness. 'We are, indeed, a long way from the inn on the moor.'

Shakespeare thrust Gomez's dagger into his belt and began to check that the pistol was properly primed and loaded.

'John . . .'

He glanced at her. There was a light in her eye, glistening. He put down the gun and took her in his arms. He kissed her.

'Surely you must trust me now?' she asked him.

He kissed her again. Her slender body moulded itself to his. He recalled the night they had made love at the inn in Lancashire. Perhaps there would be other times for them, when this was over. He could not entertain such thoughts; their lives hung by the lightest of gossamer threads.

'Why did you weep?' he was about to say, but then stopped himself. He had no right to ask such a thing. 'Yes,' he said. 'Yes, I trust you.'

Trusting *her* was one thing. Trusting the plan was another. Could all the elements of this great, preposterous scheme be in place?

The *Vanguard* was riding at anchor, a little too close to the Fort El Léon battery. Lieutenant Morgan Millwater was in command of the ship. All the marines were ashore with Frobisher at their head.

Millwater stood on the quarterdeck, gazing across to the fort. He listened to the skirmishing. This was the moment. Languidly, he called over to Boltfoot.

'Mr Cooper, I would see you in the captain's cabin.'

Boltfoot was half the length of the ship away, looking up into the rigging. Very little in life frightened him, but this was a task that would test his mettle to the full. In truth he would rather face a dozen Spaniards single-handed than climb this confounded mess of tarred ropes. He turned around at the sound of Lieutenant Millwater's voice.

'Yes, master?' he called.

'I have a matter to discuss with you. Come, Mr Cooper.'

Boltfoot was very clear that he was to go to the main-top now.

'Sir, I am under strict orders from Admiral Frobisher to take this watch. There is to be no delay.'

'God's blood, Mr Cooper. It is the admiral himself who has commanded me to discuss this certain matter with you. There has been a change of plan. Now come with me, sir, or do I have to bring you by force?'

Boltfoot looked up into the shrouds once more and shuddered. The mast-top had to be a hundred feet or more above the deck. He glanced across at William Ivory, slumped against the bulwark.

Ivory shook his head. 'Go up, Cooper. Don't listen to him.'

Ivory's words came out from the side of his mouth like a dribbled stream. 'Go up – or for ever remain the craven dog that you are.'

'Aye. I'll do your work for you yet again. Even without your supposed sharpness of sight, Ivory.'

'Don't be a horse's arse, Cooper. The perspective glass will give any man the eye of a hawk. You don't need my blue eye.'

'Mr Cooper!' Millwater was striding towards them now.

Ivory was frowning. 'Bloody Millwater. Ignore him. I recall him from the *Dainty*. Didn't think much to him then and I don't now. There's only one man to obey here – Frobisher. If you're not up there in short order, you'll miss the signal.'

Boltfoot began to climb. First one step with his good right foot into the lowest of the sagging ratlines. He pulled up his left leg and clumsily placed it into position. He would have to move like this: right foot first, get a firm hold in the swaying ropes, then bring up the left. Same thing, every ungainly step of the way through the stinking ladder of ropes. The sea was choppy and the great ship rocked violently. The air for miles around was filled with the sound of cannonfire and musket-shot. On the headland, smoke billowed above the fort and beyond.

'Mr Cooper!' Millwater bellowed. 'Come here this instant or face the damned consequences.'

William Ivory's body might have been half wrecked by the stroke, but his mind was untouched. He was thinking about Millwater and the bark *Dainty*. Had Millwater known about the perspective glass back then? Captain Thompson certainly knew about it when they took the *Madre de Dios* off the Azores. Had he told Millwater about it after an evening drinking brandy? Or had Millwater merely looked up and guessed what Ivory was about?

The concept of a spyglass was certainly no secret. Mariners in Spain and the Low Countries, even Italy, had talked for years of the possibility that it might one day be created. It was simply a matter of finding the right conformation of glass roundels and the men expert enough to make it.

Saliva dripped from Ivory's mouth. He scrabbled about, trying to move, suddenly horrified, because it was all beginning to make sense. That was why Trayne didn't have the fake glass in his possession, because Millwater had it. Millwater was the confederate.

Boltfoot raised his right foot on to the next tarred rope. He could not bear to look up. Millwater was halfway from the quarterdeck now. He had a pistol in his hand. Boltfoot climbed another rung, then another. Millwater was below him, pointing his pistol.

'Come down now! Else I will bring you down dead.'

A gunshot rent the air, so close that it cut through the thunder of cannon. Boltfoot looked down again. Lieutenant Millwater was clutching his side. Blood was pouring from a wound, washing through his fingers. His face was bemused, as though he didn't realise he had been shot. Boltfoot glanced across at Ivory. A pistol smoked in his right hand. He was grinning, lopsidedly, with the half of his face that still functioned.

'Don't stop, Cooper! Carry on with your bastard climbing or you'll miss the signal.'

## Chapter 45

G OMEZ'S UNIFORM WAS not much of a disguise. Shakespeare's tall figure and pale skin would give him away to any soldier who took a second look. He was relying on them all being too busy, too focused on shooting at the enemy without the walls to note the enemy within.

He nodded to Eliska. She was watching him from the door to her quarters. Behind her back, concealed in her black velvet cloak, she held Gomez's sword, her corn-yellow chemise tied to it like a pennant.

The day was cool, but Shakespeare was dripping with sweat. He had to find a way to create a breach, or the fort would never be conquered. The walls were unbreakable by cannon alone.

Suddenly, a huge explosion shook the ground and the air. He knew instantly what it was. The besieging pioneers had detonated a mine beneath the western bastion wall. For a moment there was silence, then a shouting of orders in Spanish, and men ran towards the scene of the blast. Shakespeare carried on along the course he had set, towards the eastern end of the interior trenchworks.

Shakespeare was relieved. There seemed to be only two Spanish guards at the picket door, inside the arch of the gatehouse. Both of them wore steel breastplates, brigantines and morions.

They carried crossbows, one with bowstring drawn and bolt set in place, the other unloaded. The man with the drawn bow held it loosely in his hand, the other had it perched over his right shoulder. They were both smoking pipes, casually, as if a battle wasn't raging. With the swagger of a senior officer, Shakespeare strode up to them. They looked at him questioningly, as though trying to place him, though they must have seen the *inglés* about the fort. Shakespeare smiled, raised his pistol and shot the guard whose bow was drawn.

The deadly ball hit him in the face, just beneath the lip of his steel helmet. The guard's head snapped back and he fell against the wall, his knees buckling beneath him, dying as he slid to the ground. The second guard dropped his pipe and reached for his sword, but Shakespeare hammered the spent pistol against his head. The man lurched sideways, but did not lose his footing.

Shakespeare had Gomez's curved fighting knife in his left hand. It was a terrible weapon, more like a butcher's blade than a man's dagger. With a backward sweep of the hand, he slashed out with all his strength, catching the man's throat on the left side, cutting deep into his windpipe. Blood leapt from the wound as if it were an underground spring.

Quickly, Shakespeare looked around. No one had seen him. They were either above him on the ramparts, or ferrying munitions. Everyone had a task, hunched over rampart guns or feeding cannon with ball and powder and tamping it home. The only person who could see him was Eliska, huddled inside the lee of the central passageway into the compound. She had seen what he had done and nodded to him. He nodded back and she turned away, walking towards the stable block, the sword-pennant concealed beneath her black velvet cloak. Shakespeare gasped as a guard stopped her. He could see her smiling, then the guard nodded and she walked on. At the stables, she suddenly vanished behind a wall. Shakespeare breathed again.

Their fate was sealed. And the fate of hundreds of English and French soldiers and marines. If they attacked now, at her signal, and there was no breach, then they would be massacred by the defenders on the ramparts above. It would be bloody butchery.

Shakespeare opened the door into the picket house, set into the wall. He pulled the dead guards away from immediate sight. The main gates would resist any battering ram or shot. They were held shut by two heavy bars, slotted into steel fittings driven deep into the thick stone walls at either end. One of the bars was at a height of eight feet, the other at ground level. Opening them was a task for more than one man.

He stepped through the picket door, which was no more than five feet high, its base about a foot from the ground. Inside the little guardroom, there were more weapons, a table, a chair, a ledger. Most importantly, there was another small, heavy door – an iron door to the world outside the fort. It was secured by two bolts. He pulled them back, then cursed. There was a padlock, too. He looked out of the inner door at the bodies of the guards. One of them had a large ring at his belt, with three keys. Shakespeare cut the belt with the man's own dagger, then returned to the padlock and tried a key. It fitted, and turned.

He pulled it open, and prayed that the breach would hold and be enough. He prayed, too, that Eliska had managed to make her way to the unmanned southern ramparts. And that he would see her again.

Boltfoot squinted through the perspective glass. He knew what to expect, but it still astonished him that things in the distance could seem so close. High on the cliffs, above the fortress parapet, through the belching smoke of burning gunpowder, he was almost certain he could see a figure. Was that a woman? She seemed to be dancing in the air, like a tiny sprite, visible one moment, gone into the acrid mist the next. For a few seconds, he just watched, amazed at what he saw, and almost forgot his discomfort at being so high in this swaying mast-top.

He looked harder. His eyesight was good, very good, but not as keen as a falcon-eyed man like Ivory. Boltfoot screwed up his eyes again. He was almost certain. Against the grey-dark sky and smoke, there was a splash of yellow, a summer butterfly, just discernible.

He shouted down to the deck, 'Fire away, Mr Ivory. Fire away.'

Ivory blew on the glowing match in his right hand and touched it to the fuses of the three enormous firework rockets supplied by the Queen's firemaster and, until this day, kept in Admiral Frobisher's own cabin.

'That's the signal, lads. We're moving forward. Do not rush, keep your bucklers raised and your helmets on.'

Pinkney held a pistol in one hand and a short sword in the other. Ranged alongside him were the men he had brought from England along with as many men again, all assigned to him by Norreys.

'If in doubt, follow me. And if I'm dead, follow Admiral Frobisher: he's the devil with the pirates over yonder, at the right flank. Be tigers for Elizabeth and England! Trumpeter Baylie, blow your horn. Advance! Advance!'

As the trumpet sounded and the company moved forward with the marines, a withering fire from muskets and calivers rained down on them. The ramparts were lined with Spanish soldiers throwing everything at them – bullets, stones, bolts, arrows, like lethal hailstones. Andrew gritted his teeth and ran through the mud and storm of lead until he had scaled the counterscarp and jumped into the mud-thick ditch. All around him men were falling. The only thing that separated the quick from the dead was chance, or the will of God.

Three Spanish soldiers were crossing the compound with petronels hard against their mail-clad chests. One let off a shot. Shakespeare ducked, instinctively. The shot smashed into the solid oak behind him and sent splinters flying.

To the north of the fort, brilliant against the glowering sky, the three rockets of fire seemed to hang in the air, raining showers of golden specks. Shakespeare felt a surge of hope. He grabbed one of the crossbows, the loaded one. He was breathing heavily, but his hand was steady. He pulled the trigger and loosed the bolt. He aimed for one of the attackers, high for the body, but the bowstring was not drawn tight enough and the bolt fell short. Damn the guard for his laziness. He scrabbled around for another weapon. He found a bolt in the dead guard's quiver and tried to slot it in place. Another gunshot smacked into the ground, close at his side.

He was cornered here. He could not get through the gate for there was no way of knowing what or who he would meet on the other side. There would be no time to explain to an English soldier that he was one of them, a friend, not an enemy, before the bullet took him or the falchion cleaved his skull. Besides, he had to hold this door as long as possible. He glanced up, wishing he could see the seaward ramparts and Eliska. The powder smoke swirled and eddied.

He wound the bowstring taut and released the bolt. This time it sped true with almost point-blank trajectory, catching the first of the Spaniards in the shoulder, then shearing away. The soldier twisted sideways, his arm savagely cut, even with the protection of chain-mail. But it was too little, too late.

They were almost on him now; he was at their mercy and he knew none would be given.

And then the first of the English soldiers pushed through the open picket door ...

Shakespeare immediately put his hands in the air and shouted, 'English, I am English!'

The first man had a wheel-lock pistol in each hand and two more thrust in his belt. Shakespeare recognised him immediately as Martin Frobisher. He pointed the guns at Shakespeare and his finger seemed about to pull the trigger, then suddenly relaxed.

'So you are. God's teeth, it is you, Mr Shakespeare. Well done!'

A shot cracked and Frobisher spun around. He had been hit. Blood spilt from a wound at his hip. Immediately behind him, three, four, then more marines poured through the gate and shot at the advancing Spaniards, who stopped in their tracks and dived for the shelter of the fort's inner earthworks.

As the English marines burst through the picket door, so more Spaniards raced to the trenches to reinforce their brothers-in-arms and hold the invaders at bay. The English held the gatehouse now and quickly lifted the bars, to throw wide the main gates.

'Get a surgeon, get a stretcher!' Shakespeare shouted. 'Your admiral is wounded.'

'Dog's bollocks, Mr Shakespeare, I am going nowhere until this fort is ours.' Frobisher lifted his head and loosed off two pistol shots in the general direction of the enemy.

Shakespeare, hunched low, bowed his head to Frobisher. 'Forgive me for leaving you like this. Your men will look out for you. If you would give me two of your pistols, there is something I must do.'

Without hesitation, Frobisher thrust two pistols into Shakespeare's sweat-slippery hands. He handed him a horn of powder and a small box of touchpowder, along with a pouch of balls. Shakespeare quickly primed the guns with powder and loaded them, tamping the bullets home hard with cartridge paper.

There was a roar. A cannonball blew past them into the incoming wave of marines, taking one man clean off his feet and carrying him away. Frobisher turned to an adjutant. 'Do for that cannoneer and take control of his machine, sir.'

'Yes, admiral.'

The air was blistered by gunshots, crossbow bolts, the screams of men and the whisper of arrows. Shakespeare broke cover and ran deep into the fort, to the eastern side of the Spanish trenches towards the chapel and the stables. He sensed balls whip past him. Keeping his head low, weaving this way and that, he made it to the stable block where panicked horses were whinnying and stamping, straining to break free from their stalls. A haybarn was ablaze.

Then he saw her. She was standing on a powder keg on the seaward rampart, waving her yellow chemise flag. Surely she must have seen the rocket flares? She must know her work was done. He wanted to shout to her: *Get down, it has worked, make your escape.* He saw Captain Paredes, too. He was striding along the seaward ramparts. His pistol – Norreys's pistol – glinted in the flames of the burning hay. Shakespeare shouted out, but she did not seem to hear. Paredes pulled the trigger, driving a bullet deep into Eliska's back. She had not even seen him coming. She toppled forward, still clutching the hilt of her sword. The flag fluttered down with her.

Shakespeare ran up the steps.

'Murderer! Dog!'

He shot Paredes with the first pistol and the captain went

down. Shakespeare, closer now, pulled the trigger of the second pistol – and Paredes was dead. The first ball had entered his chest and must have ripped into his heart; the second tore into the side of his skull.

Careless for his own safety, Shakespeare went to Eliska and knelt at her side. A squadron of five Spaniards had detached itself from the main fighting force at the landward end of the fort and had followed him. Shakespeare realised in horror that both his pistols were discharged. He tried to powder one, but his hands were shaking now and all he did was spill the black powder on to the stone beneath his feet.

'Eliska . . .'

Her breathing was shallow. He feared she did not have much time; he had to get her to safety. He looked up. The Spaniards were no more than thirty yards away. But instead of coming forward, they stopped and turned to the east for they were now coming under fire themselves, from three English marines with petronels, who had broken through from the gateway contingent and formed a defensive pocket behind a low stable wall.

Their arrival bought him time. He took a deep breath, steadied himself and tried again to load his pistols. This time the shaking had gone. He pushed them into the belt of his breeches, then lifted Eliska in his arms. She was as light as he remembered from their night in the wilds of Lancashire. Her fair hair hung loose, her eyes were open. Was she breathing? He was no longer certain.

From the rampart, steps led down into the side of the cliff where, he knew, there were more storerooms and emplacements. He carried her down. The going was steep and rugged, overgrown and tangled with briars and vines and sharp gorse. Halfway down, he found a room carved into the rock, nothing more than a man-made cave. There was little light in the gloomy room. It was cool in here and the sound of battle was muffled. He placed her gently on the ground, on her side, with her blood-soaked velvet cloak splayed beneath her. He put his ear to her breast and listened for breathing but could hear none; he felt for her pulse in vain. He talked to her, urged her to live. Seconds passed, minutes. Nothing. There was no more any man could do for her. He held her face, kissed her and made supplication to God for her soul.

Suddenly he was riven with anger. Why had she continued to wave the flag after the rockets went up? Why had she still been there, offering herself up as a target when her work was done?

With his thumbs, he closed her eyes.

He turned away and stepped out into the grey daylight. He began to climb back up to the fort, through the thorny undergrowth. At the top he saw that the squadron that had saved him was, itself, in difficulties. The Spanish troops had been heavily reinforced and were raining gunshots and crossbow bolts at them.

Crouching, he loped along close to the parapet. He was getting nearer to the English contingent. He looked up and his heart felt as though it would stop in his chest: Andrew. Andrew was there in helmet and armour, with another he recognised: the pitted face of Provost Marshal Pinkney.

The terror of it was that the powerful Spanish force – a dozen or more men, with pike and shot – was advancing. The English position was about to be overrun.

# Chapter 46

SHAKESPEARE ROSE TO his full height. He had no cover. He raised one of the pistols in his right hand, the wrist supported by his clenched left hand, then pulled the trigger. One of the attackers crumpled. Shakespeare dropped the pistol, fell to one knee, raised the other loaded pistol and fired again. The recoil knocked him back momentarily, as flame and smoke belched from the gun. A Spaniard moaned and doubled up as though he had been punched in the belly. The other Spaniards stopped. Shakespeare leapt down the steps from the rampart and dashed for Andrew and the two others.

'Fair shooting, Mr Shakespeare,' Pinkney said. 'You are full of surprises.' He nodded towards Andrew. 'And see what a pleasant surprise I have for you here.'

Shakespeare threw himself down beside Andrew. This was no time for greetings. Their eyes met, then he set about powdering his weapon.

To their left, a detachment of English pikemen, their eighteen-foot poles raised in the attack position, drove forward into the Spanish trenches. It was a sight to strike terror into the stoutest of hearts, but the defenders merely drew their swords and fought hand to hand, at close quarters. The main gate had now been opened and English marines and soldiers were pouring through. The Spanish were hugely outnumbered, but fought with desperate courage. Even though their captain was dead, no white flags of misericord were raised; no lives were pleaded for.

The fighting raged for five hours. It was slaughter. Blood lay thick, like a coating of red, sticky paint, daubed across the compound and ramparts. Every inch was hard won for the English and the French.

By late afternoon, Norreys and Frobisher had control of the fort. Both the general and the admiral were wounded, but continued to lead their men.

As soon as the way was clear, Shakespeare grasped Andrew by the arm. 'Come with me. You have done enough here.'

Andrew hesitated. He was under military command now. He looked at Pinkney for orders, for approbation.

Pinkney merely nodded. 'Take him, Shakespeare. I had thought to leave him to the wolves when I discovered his connection to you, but I tell you this: I have never met a better soldier.'

Shakespeare looked hard into his eyes. 'What are you, Pinkney? Norreys says you are loyal and strong, but I saw you kill a bound and unarmed man in cold blood. It was simple murder.'

'He was a traitor, an enemy of England. I saved him from a worse fate on the scaffold.'

'He should have had a trial. Every man deserves that.'

'A trial arranged by Mr Topcliffe, perchance? And execution, too . . . the bowelling, the cutting out of the living heart, the quartering of the body. I tell you, I did Mr Lamb a kindness.'

Pinkney's eyes were ruthless and cold: the unremitting eyes of a soldier who had survived battles through hard brutality, who would never surrender, never give quarter. When

Shakespeare looked at Andrew, he saw something of the same. He had to get him away from this before he was lost for ever.

In the distance, from below the cliffs, there were gunshots and shouting.

'I still have Spaniards to kill.' Pinkney shook Andrew by the hand, then led his men forward to the cliffs, where the last of the defenders had fled.


Boltfoot sat at the back of a cockboat as the mariners rowed hard for land. Other ship's boats were all around them, heading for the shore at the bottom of the cliffs.

Dozens of Spaniards were diving and jumping from the rocks into the sea. They bobbed in the surf, struggling to rid themselves of their armour and helmets as they waded away from the English onslaught, fleeing like hares before hounds. Shots peppered the waves around them. Now and then a man cried out, then sank into the boiling red water.

Boltfoot watched grimly. The mariners in the boats leapt out as they reached the exhausted Spaniards in the shallows, then grappled with them, holding their heads under water, drowning them one by one until the sea was awash with sixty or seventy floating bodies. Frobisher arrived on the rocky shore, supported by two men.

'That is enough. No more killing,' he said.

*There are no more to kill*, thought Boltfoot. Never had he seen a crueller day.

# Chapter 47

LANTERNS WERE LIT all through the fleet. Aboard each ship, there was music – viols, lutes, mandolins. Sailors sang and danced. The marines drank themselves into a stupor, each one embellishing tales of his valour or mourning a lost friend.

Shakespeare and Andrew were among a dozen men crowded into Frobisher's cabin. The admiral lay in state, complaining loudly as the surgeon dug a bullet from his hip bone. Shakespeare's arm was around his boy's shoulders. He barely recognised him. Andrew no longer looked like a boy, but a hard-bitten soldier, broad-shouldered, lean and silent.

In the distance, they heard the boom-boom of charges detonating; the pioneers were busy laying mines to blow the fort to rubble. Meanwhile other detachments buried the dead while the wounded sought treatment. The watch stayed alert, for it was feared that Águila could still come at them and try to take their rearguard by surprise.

The toll of dead showed that four hundred Spaniards had died and sixty English. The French had suffered disproportionately, losing hundreds of men in the earlier skirmishes. After Frobisher called his ceasefire, six Spaniards were found cowering among the rocks and were spared.

'I think you need a brandy, Andrew,' Shakespeare said.

He nodded. 'Yes, thank you, sir.'

'You do know I tried to find you? I searched every byway in the shire of Oxford looking for you. I found a girl—'

Andrew suddenly looked up. 'Ursula Dancer?'

'She's in England, safe. You will see her.'

'She saved me, Father. She saved my life.'

Shakespeare clasped Andrew tight to him and held him.

Boltfoot had stayed on deck. He wouldn't drink with the officers in Frobisher's cabin. Shakespeare strolled out to him. A mist was drifting in along the strait. In the distance, the lights of Brest came and went as the fog thickened. There was a chill in the air. Shakespeare handed Boltfoot a pouch of tobacco. He accepted it gratefully and proceeded to fill a pipe. He was thinking of Jane and baby John. He had to get home.

'Where is Mr Ivory, Boltfoot?'

Boltfoot gestured to the far bulwark. 'Playing dice. It seems he can no longer hold cards properly, so he will have to devise a new method of cheating. He is a pimple on the world's buttock, and a dog of a man.'

'Well, at least he saved your life.'

'Not as many times as I saved his.'

Shakespeare smiled. 'Tell me about this man, this Lieutenant Millwater,' he said.

'They've patched him up and locked him away, master. They reckon Frobisher will string him up in the morning.'

'Then I had better see him now. Andrew, stay with Boltfoot. Get drunk.'

Above him there was a chattering noise. Doda was in the rigging, eating titbits given her by the mariners. After the fighting, Shakespeare had brought the little monkey from Eliska's chamber. He would leave her here, aboard the *Vanguard*. She would make a fine ship's pet.

*

Shakespeare knew Morgan Millwater, but he had no idea why. Millwater's eyes were closed and his breathing was strained. He lay on the floor of his makeshift cell, curled up, clutching his wounded side. Shakespeare could tell he was in great pain and wondered whether he would last long enough for his appointment with the hangman.

'Mr Millwater?'

The man opened his eyes and the face half turned. Yes, Shakespeare had seen him before. He knew the profile of that face, with the light hair falling about his shoulders. His features were delicate and handsome. But where had he seen him? The name meant nothing.

Then Shakespeare remembered. He had seen that face just once, and then fleetingly. He had been walking out of the hall of Lathom House. His name was Walter Weld, he had been the household's Gentleman of the Horse and he had left before Shakespeare could question him.

More than that, he now knew, this man was Spain's chief spy in England. Under various names, he had wormed his way most successfully into the body of England. Until now.

'Who are you?'

'My name is John Shakespeare.'

The injured man nodded his head slowly, each breath more laboured as he raised an effort to speak. The words came out slowly.

'Ah, yes . . . I recall. You were to come over to Spain. Eliska turned you . . .' Millwater laughed, then cried out in pain. 'Get me out of here, Mr Shakespeare.'

Shakespeare smiled. 'I fear you are under a misapprehension. Unlike you, I am no traitor. You were duped by a pretty face, Mr Weld.'

Millwater groaned. A dribble of blood fell from his lips. 'For pity's sake . . . have you brought water, ale? I am dying here.'

Shakespeare handed him his own cup of wine.

'Has the surgeon seen you?'

Millwater shook his head.

'Can you sit up and talk?'

'Bring me brandy . . . to dull the pain.'

Shakespeare signalled to the guard who stood by the door. 'Get a flask of brandy.'

The guard was clearly reluctant to leave his post.

'Fear not. This man is dying. He is going nowhere.'

The guard bowed and backed away.

'So, Mr Millwater. You had designs on the perspective glass. How much did the Spanish offer you? A great many ducats, I imagine.'

Millwater said nothing. Shakespeare watched him and waited. At last the guard returned with brandy. Shakespeare knelt at the wounded officer's side and put the neck of the flask to his lips. Millwater drank, then gasped, then drank again, desperate for a taste of oblivion.

'Will you talk now? Aboard this ship, you had a confederate named Janus Trayne.'

'Murdered . . . by that dog . . . Frobisher.'

'And in Lancashire, you had some purpose. Were you hoping to gain the secret of the perspective glass from Dr Dee? Or were you there, perhaps, to murder Lord Strange, the Earl of Derby?'

The words provoked Millwater into movement. Gasping with pain, he struggled up to a sitting position. Shakespeare could see now how gaunt he was, how close to death. And yet his eyes were on fire.

'Murder the Earl of Derby . . . why would we do that? He was our leader . . . our king-in-waiting . . . I would sooner have died a thousand deaths than harm him . . .'

'But he betrayed Richard Hesketh.'

Millwater slumped back. Cold sweat beaded his brow. His clothes were streaked with blood. 'He had no option ... Hesketh was a fool. We tried to stop him . . . He believed himself sent by the Society of Jesus . . . He would not hear us.'

'So you believe Hesketh was sent by others – men hostile to the earl?'

'You know it to be true.'

'Who?'

'Lamb knew. Somehow he found out, but he would not tell me. I think he did not like me, nor trust me. We were made of different stuff. My mission was to help Spain and to bring my lord, the Earl of Derby, to his rightful place on the throne of England. Father Lamb sought only to save souls.'

'There was a letter, a coded letter from Lamb to his masters in Rome. Speak now what it meant, and die with the truth on your lips like a Christian.'

Millwater's eyes closed again. He was sliding down the wall. Shakespeare put an arm around him, trying to prop him up.

'Who are you, really, Mr Millwater? Tell me now. There are many more questions I must ask you. Tell the truth and make your peace with God.'

But it was too late. Millwater was dead.

# Chapter 48

S IR ROBERT CECIL was silent. He sat at his table in his efficient and sparse apartments at Greenwich Palace, staring at Shakespeare. He sighed and shook his head.

'What are we to do with you, John? I was dismayed when I heard that you had abandoned Dr Dee in Oxford to go scouring the countryside for your boy.'

*What would you have done in my place, Sir Robert?* The words remained unspoken. This was a time to listen, not talk. Otherwise he might say something he would come to regret. Shakespeare stood stiffly before his master.

'And then you perform an act of remarkable valour, going into the enemy fort knowing you had little chance of survival. Truly, Her Majesty is delighted. She has demanded that I tell you as much and wishes me to heap favours upon you.'

Shakespeare bowed. Seconds passed and the atmosphere welled unpleasantly between them. He knew what was coming.

'But I cannot square it,' Cecil said as though the words were wrenched from him with a tooth-puller's pelican. 'We have a dichotomy. As hard as I try, I cannot come to terms with your dereliction of duty at Oxford.'

'There was no alternative, Sir Robert. I would to God there had been. I did not have time to take Dr Dee elsewhere. And he was well guarded. I judged him safe.'

'You left him in the care of two of Derby's men and you judged him safe? I sent *you* to be with him, not to abandon him to the questionable care of two untried men. No, sir, he was *not* safe. You put your family before the security of the realm. You have no idea how close we came to abandoning the Crozon venture. Do you realise how much planning went into it? The subterfuge of messages relayed through the French embassy that you and the lady Eliska planned to defect to Spain?'

Shakespeare held his head high. He would not be bowed by this torrent of invective.

'And what of your boy? Is he innocent? I think the college case flimsy and I will try to avoid a hanging, but there are still questions that must be answered.'

'I had thought you a great believer in family, Sir Robert. Should a man's child not come before all else? Is it not the natural order? Your message to me implied understanding of my predicament.'

Cecil's little fist clenched and unclenched. 'Be careful, Mr Shakespeare. I have always shown you the greatest forbearance, but be careful. I will be lectured on morality by no man save my own father.'

Shakespeare bowed again. 'Forgive me, that was not my intent.'

'Besides, you are wrong.' Cecil's voice softened. 'You and the boy are both subjects of Her Majesty, and *her* interests must always take precedence. And, yet, I am told he too showed valour . . .' Cecil's voice tapered away. 'I am sorry it has come to this. We will talk again about the case of your boy and about your future.' His eyes drifted down to the table. The perspective glass lay there. He shook his head again. 'As to the glass, that will stay with me from now on – until we need it again.'

Shakespeare bowed curtly. 'In your letter you said my

indiscretions would be washed away like dust in a summer rain. Well, the season is dry. Fear not, Sir Robert. My resignation will be on your table within the hour.'

He found his old friend Joshua Peace, searcher of the dead, at his lodgings near St Paul's. It was on the third floor of a six-storey tenement in Knightrider Street. Shakespeare judged it one of London's better houses. The other lodgers were all single men of some means, mostly lawyers and scribes.

Peace's rooms were comfortable, full of books, strange surgical implements and well-worn furnishings. Whenever Shakespeare came here, he wondered whether Joshua was lonely, but then dismissed the thought; marriage did not suit all men.

This time, his welcome was more muted than usual. Peace asked him in, but there seemed to be a lack of enthusiasm. Shakespeare frowned.

'Is all well with you, Joshua?'

Peace hesitated, then shook his head. 'In a word, John, no.'

'You do not seem pleased to see me.'

'It is not that . . . Well, yes, it *is* that. I wish to God you had never called me to Lancashire. I confess it, I am rattled and mighty scared. Look at my door. Note the extra bolts I have fitted.'

Peace's eyes were gaunt. Shakespeare saw fear there, and exhaustion: things he had never seen before in his friend. What could possibly have brought a stalwart man like Joshua Peace to such a pass?

'I think you had better tell me everything, Joshua. Might I sit down?'

'Yes, yes, of course. Forgive my ill manners. I will get you some wine.' Peace attempted a smile, but it was strained and his tone was brittle.

'A little wine would be good. Thank you. I fear I have not brought you the Gascon wine I promised, but I shall. All in good time.'

Peace shuffled away to find cups. Shakespeare noticed that he was stooped and slow. He seemed to have aged ten years since last they met.

'Well, Joshua?'

'I scarce know where to start.' Peace was hesitant, finally screwing up his eyes as if deciding this had to be told, however painful. 'Soon after you left, commissioners Egerton and Carey arrived, as did William Stanley, the brother of the dead earl, from the Isle of Man to claim his inheritance as the sixth earl. If the loss of a brother pained him, you would not know it. I am sure he and his bride are settling most comfortably into the dead earl's palace.'

'Bride? Stanley has a bride?'

'Why, yes, where have you been? He has married Sir Robert Cecil's niece.'

'Elizabeth de Vere?' Shakespeare was shocked. He had no idea such a match had even been mooted.

'You have been away from the world, John. Much else has happened besides. Yes, they married at Greenwich with the Queen in attendance. So the Derby line – with all its royal connections – is now secured for the Cecilians. Most convenient, do you not think? As for the bride, all I can say is God help the wretched woman, for the new Derby is a most cold and brusque man.'

Peace told Shakespeare how he had been sent packing from the house, as had the steward, Mr Cole.

Shakespeare listened intently. It must have been humiliating for him to be dismissed so peremptorily.

'But you talked of fear, Joshua. That is a very different matter.'

'There is more, much more. Do you recall the kitchen steward, Michael Dowty? The one you said acted as the earl's taster?'

'Why, yes, of course.'

'It seems he has ambitions. His kitchen days are over. Cecil has sponsored him for Parliament. Soon he will be engaged in discourse with Ralegh and the rest at Westminster. But that is by the by. You cannot hang a man for seizing the main chance.'

*Payment for services rendered?* Was that what Peace was suggesting here? It was a thought Shakespeare disliked intensely, but could not easily cast aside. If the earl was poisoned, who would have more opportunity than his cook and taster?

'Wait,' Peace continued. 'I can see the way your thoughts are going, but listen. There is more. I should have just come home to London straightway, but through some misplaced sense of loyalty to you, I stayed.' The searcher laughed bitterly. 'In future, I shall stick with *dead* bodies; they are a lot less dangerous than the living.'

'What happened?'

Peace went through the whole affair of the meeting with Thomas Hesketh, the implied threat, the demand for the paper found on Father Lamb. And then, the encounter with Mistress Knott and the journey deep into the woods at Knowsley where the old crone had handed him the vial.

Shakespeare sipped the wine and waited. Peace was walking about the room. He looked out of the window, then walked to the door, opened it and looked about, as though he suspected he was overheard. He shut it again and bolted it.

'Tell me of this woman of the woods.'

'She was just a sly old hag, Mistress Knott's ill-favoured mother. I can see why the ignorant local people called her a witch, for she was bent and crooked and unkempt. I am sure she lived there in the woods because she had been shunned and driven out of the village. I am certain, too, that the villagers still went to her secretly. Men and women will always follow the promise of cures and secret knowledge, and she had those a-plenty. Give her money and she would sell them herbs for gout and philtres for love. She had them in twists of paper, boxes and bottles. Probably most of them were no more harmful than the medicines dispensed by those fools from the College of Physicians. But then magical powers are not necessary, are they? Man and nature are quite deadly enough without any assistance from an imaginary world of spirits. Who needs to cast a death spell when you have bullets and knives . . . and poisons?'

Shakespeare nodded gravely. 'What was in the vial that she handed you?'

'Judge for yourself.'

Peace took the little bottle from its hiding place behind a book. Shakespeare removed the stopper and sniffed.

'Death's Cap mushroom,' Peace said. 'The odour of rose petals is faint, but definitely there. Its appearance is certain.'

Shakespeare hurriedly replaced the stopper. 'But surely such a mushroom does not grow in springtime?'

'Indeed not. But what if it had been picked the previous autumn and dried?'

'Would that work?'

'I believe it would retain its potency. If you left it in water, it would become whole again. Then it could be added to any strong-flavoured stew or mess of food.'

Shakespeare was aghast. Every country child in England was taught the dangers of the Death's Cap mushroom. It was a filthy way to die: at first the victim ailed grievously, but then believed himself cured, only for the deadly illness to rage back and bring the sufferer to death. And yes, it fitted, for that was the way things had gone with the earl.

Peace continued his tale. 'The old woman said something to me and laughed. "That's what I sold them," she said. "The monkey woman and the one with the viper's tongue." I wished to hear no more, John. I could not wait to get away from that woman. Outside the hag's cabin, Mistress Knott was waiting for me. I knew by then that she was the old one's daughter. Yet while the mother had no semblance of humanity about her, Mistress Knott had goodness in her soul. I talked to her more and it became clear that she was desperately ashamed of her mother and her dark dealings. When she had learnt of the earl's sickness, she knew immediately that her mother must be involved and went to her to discover the truth. That is why she set up her vigil in the corner of the earl's bedroom. She was trying all in her power to counteract her mother's wicked deed, trying to find an antidote to the mushroom. But as we know, there is no antidote.' He smiled sadly. 'Not even the fabled bezoar stone.'

Shakespeare was listening, but all his thoughts came back to Eliska. *She was the poisoner. Or, at least, the procurer of poison.* He wished he was surprised. Yet the revelation raised more questions than it answered.

'The monkey woman . . . Eliska.'

'And the *viper's tongue*. I have my own theory about that one. Yet I fear there are more involved. Indeed, I believe this conspiracy is like a trail through a labyrinth that continually divides and bewilders. What scares me most is where it might all end. Where is the centre of this maze? Dear God . . .' He laughed savagely. 'I had never thought to hear myself invoking the deity for mercy. You know my thoughts on superstitions of all kinds, be they religious or otherwise. But now I find myself wondering. I go to church not from fear of a fine, but to pray. You see, I know too much, and my life is worth nothing.'

'Joshua, I am here. You are no longer alone.'

'You are no safer than I.'

'Look, Joshua, do you not think your fears and theories might be getting a little wild? Might you be exaggerating the danger? We have witnesses now, Mistress Knott and her mother. This can all be brought to court.'

Peace closed his eyes and said nothing.

'Something has happened?'

At last Peace nodded.

'It was the worst of all. I had arranged to see Mistress Knott one more time, in the village where she lived. In that village there is a large, deep millpond. I arrived just in time to see her and her mother being tried as witches. They were bound, hand and foot, to be thrown into the depths. If they floated, it was said, they must be satanists or anabaptists. If they sank, then they were innocent. They sank . . . and drowned, and all the children and goodwives cheered. Probably at some time each one of them had visited Mistress Knott or her mother for a potion or a cure, yet they stood and applauded their deaths.

'And overseeing it all, smirking, talking to one another and idly smoking their pipes, were the judges at this court of the damned: Thomas Hesketh of the Duchy of Lancaster and one Bartholomew Ickman, whom I believe you know. When he saw me, he winked, and his lips moved, saying, "You next." His tongue seemed to flick like a viper's. I fled Lancashire within the hour and have been expecting death every minute since.'

A little way upstream from Chelsea, at Mortlake, the oarsmen eased their tilt-boat into the landing stage. Shakespeare ordered them to wait, then stepped out. In front of him, less than a hundred yards back from the river, was an imposing house. It was a large property, almost a manor house, with exaggerated lozenge timbering and a new-thatched roof. It was not to his taste, but it was evident that a great deal of money had been spent building it, and it was in a fine position with superb views of the Thames and its adjacent meadows.

There was a bell outside the front door. He clanged it and a servant appeared within seconds. He was a young man in bright new livery of blue, with spotless white nether-stocks and good buckled shoes.

'Is Mr Bartholomew Ickman at home?'

'I shall endeavour to find out, master. Might I be permitted to know your name?'

'John Shakespeare.'

The servant bowed and left him standing in the open doorway. A minute later, the servant reappeared. 'Mr Ickman is in his solar. He will see you, sir. If you would follow me . . .'

Ickman was standing by a leaded window, a small volume in his hand, as though he were reading it. Shakespeare was not fooled for a moment by the studied affectation. Idly, the man looked up from his book.

'Mr Ickman, sir, this is Mr Shakespeare.'

Ickman smiled. 'Why, of course it is. We last met in a field in Lancashire, did we not?' He turned to the servant. 'Bring wine. Our best. With goblets and some cakes.'

The servant bowed preposterously low and backed out as though he was removing himself from the Queen's presence.

'Now then, Mr Shakespeare, how can I help you? I believe you have been spending some little time in western France. Did I not hear a whisper that you were involved in some part in England's great victory over the Spanish at the Crozon peninsula? All London marvels and says you must soon be a minister of the crown. But what a tragedy that Admiral Frobisher should not survive to enjoy the fruits of his labours. For myself, I had rather be hanged by the neck than have a surgeon play his diabolical games with my parts.'

Shakespeare ignored him. 'We had some unfinished business. I called on your lodgings in Ormskirk, but you had disappeared. The landlord wished very much to disembowel you as it seems you had neglected to pay the reckoning.'

Ickman laughed. 'These northern peasants. Are they not droll?'

He was, thought Shakespeare, like a silk-skinned slow-worm, with his golden, beardless face and his exquisitely cut clothes.

'You left in a great hurry. Where did you go?'

'I had matters to attend to.'

'Such as?'

'That is my business. But I will tell you that the main reason I left Lancashire was because I was finding Dr Dee's company exceedingly tiresome. And those brutish men you sent to accompany him, Mr Oxx and Mr Godwit. I could not hold my divining rod steady, so unnerving were they.'

'If you found Dee's company so tedious, why had you gone to him in the first place? Was there something about Lancashire that drew you there?'

'What could there be about Lancashire? It is full of Papists and traitors. No place for a civilised man. The only reason I was there was that Dee and I are old friends. He has always believed I have some talent as a scryer.'

'Ah, yes, you converse with angels.'

'Remarkable, is it not? I can scarce believe it myself. But that was not why the good doctor wished to see me. He was in desperate need of gold, as always, and begged me to help him with my powers of divination. He had a treasure map of great antiquity.'

'What were you hoping to gain?' Pointedly, Shakespeare looked about the room with its sumptuous hangings and expensively carved oak furniture. 'Surely you do not need to go on hopeless hunts for treasure. I do not take you for such a gull. The Ickman family did not get rich by hunting for buried gold or doing work without pay.'

'Believe what you will. It was an act of charity.'

'Nothing to do with hunting for mushrooms, then?'

'Mushrooms? In springtime?'

'Dried mushrooms. Death's Cap mushrooms.'

Ickman's eyes widened and he stepped back with exaggerated horror. 'Dear Mr Shakespeare, what are you suggesting? Do you not realise that such things are exceeding poisonous?'

'I am saying that you poisoned the fifth Earl of Derby. That you did so with Lady Eliska Nováková, Thomas Hesketh, Michael Dowty and others. I am saying you were part of a foul conspiracy, Ickman, and that you will hang for it.'

Ickman laughed with scorn. 'The earl poisoned? Why, that cannot be. The commission of inquiry was quite precise on the matter. They found that he was beguiled with evil spells. Indeed, two foul witches who had copulated with the devil, prick and tail, were apprehended and justice meted out to them.'

'Justice? You drown two women and you call that justice? And by your own twisted logic, does not the fact that they did not float prove their innocence? You are a repulsive man, Mr Ickman. And what of your dealings in the matter of the pitiable Richard Hesketh? You handed him a letter at the White Lion in Islington – a letter that brought him to the scaffold. Was *that* an act of charity? Or did someone pay you to do it? It sounds very close to treason to me.'

The change in Ickman's demeanour was almost imperceptible, but Shakespeare noted it. 'I have heard the tale, but that was not me, Mr Shakespeare. It was all made very clear at the time. As I understand it, the tavern-keeper's boy was given the letter by a stranger to hand to Mr Hesketh. The White Lion is a pleasant inn and one that I sometimes frequent, which is why the boy was confused. He is very young and his mistake was quickly cleared up. That is the advantage of having friends at Her Majesty's court. They can prevent miscarriages of justice.'

The servant reappeared with the wine. Shakespeare ignored the goblet offered him; he would rather sup with the anti-Christ than drink with this man.

'Which friends, Mr Ickman?'

'Great men, powerful men. Rest assured, Mr Shakespeare, I fear no man.' He smiled unctuously. 'Though perhaps *you* should.'

Shakespeare had had enough. His hand lashed out and gripped Ickman's elegant, red and black doublet. 'Do you threaten me, Ickman?'

Ickman brushed him away. He was a great deal stronger than Shakespeare had anticipated. His servant instantly appeared in the doorway with a pair of pistols, both trained on Shakespeare.

From behind the servant another figure emerged and entered the room. Shakespeare shuddered with revulsion. It was Topcliffe. Richard Topcliffe, priest-hunter, torturer and tormentor of souls. His hair was as white as a hoar frost and he leered with pleasure at Shakespeare's discomfiture.

Ickman smiled. 'You think you can assault me, Shakespeare? You think you can step into a man's home and accuse him of felonies? You are treading on hot coals if you believe you can treat an Ickman so. What say you, Mr Topcliffe?'

'I say he will burn for his temerity, Mr Ickman. Burn in hell.'

Shakespeare was appalled and yet not surprised. How could he be surprised to find Ickman close-coupled with Topcliffe? Both men shared a taste for evil.

'Yes,' he said. 'This makes sense. The demon and his acolyte. But which is which?'

Topcliffe bared his teeth. His lips were foam-flecked. 'Derby and all his clan are traitors – as are all the Shakespeares. We'll do for them all, Mr Ickman!'

Shakespeare shrugged his shoulders. There was nothing more to be gained here. He knew Topcliffe well enough to know that he would merely lash out with his silver-tipped blackthorn cane before ever he answered any of his questions. He had already done much harm to Shakespeare and his family. The detestation was mutual. There was nothing more to be discovered about the white dog, but he had learnt something about Ickman this day. He ignored Topcliffe and threw a look of cold scorn at Ickman.

'I have learnt what I wanted. I now know you, Ickman. You and your family are what I had come to believe you were: common felons, hired assassins. Trust me, the eyes of the law are on you now. You will be brought low.'

Yet even as he spoke the words, they sounded hollow. Without Sir Robert Cecil, he had no power against a man such as this.

Ickman and Topcliffe looked at each other and laughed, then Ickman turned to his serving man.

'Remove this object,' he ordered, nodding in Shakespeare's direction. 'He pollutes my air.'

# Chapter 49

JANE SERVED A supper of bream fried in butter, with fresh manchet bread. They sat around the table in the kitchen at Shakespeare's large home in Dowgate: Shakespeare, Boltfoot, Andrew, Jane and the girls, Grace and Mary. Baby John Cooper was close by, asleep in a cot.

It was a fine, large house, built close to the river by the late father of Andrew and Grace Woode, and run as a school for the poor boys of London until the plague and other circumstances forced its closure. Now its future was uncertain.

At the table, the younger children prated merrily and wanted to know all about the great adventures in Brittany. Boltfoot was like a lovesick swain, touching hands with Jane at every opportunity, surreptitiously, as though he somehow thought no one would notice. It should have been a joyous occasion, but Shakespeare felt the darkness of Joshua Peace's fears and his own suspicions clouding all. What in God's name did Topcliffe have to do with all this? Nothing made sense, except for one thing: he knew that the white-haired dog of a man would do anything to harm him or those he loved.

He thought, too, of those brutish men who followed Topcliffe, his band of pursuivants, who wore the Queen's escutcheon, and who had the power to seek out and arrest priests and those who harboured them. They considered such hunts to be sport, the tormenting of men, women and children more satisfying than the chasing of stags or otters. Among their number was one Thomas Fitzherbert, yet another of that difficult clan that included the Papist traitors, and one James Fitzherbert, until recently tutor of St John's, Oxford. He had said he despised his treacherous, exiled Catholic cousins, Thomas and Nicholas. Well, that was possible enough.

But what if he was close to the other Thomas, the one who followed like a slavering pup in the trail of the killing dog Topcliffe? What if Topcliffe and Thomas Fitzherbert, pursuivant, had begged or bribed James Fitzherbert, tutor, to assist in bringing ruin upon Andrew Woode and despair upon the house of Shakespeare? No man had a better chance to daub paint across a painting of the Queen and across the gown and hands of a scholar in his care. And if he was innocent, why was he no longer at the college?

Shakespeare observed Andrew. The boy was taciturn. He had hoped to see Ursula again, but Frank Mills had sent word that she had disappeared from the house at Chevening, stealing a horse into the bargain. They would clearly never see her again. But there was more than that to Andrew's dark mood. Shakespeare could see that he was finding it difficult to adjust to life away from the army, and he was unhappy that the affair at Oxford had not been resolved.

'You will not be hanged, Andrew,' he had told the boy after his meeting with Cecil. Now he repeated the pledge.

'Are you certain? Did Cecil say as much?'

'He does not wish you hanged and I will not allow it. Besides, I have a powerful suspicion who was behind it.'

How, though, would he prove it?

Even though fires were lit, the house was cold and unwelcoming. Chill air whipped off the Thames, through the gaps between the panes and under the doors. The family ate enough, said prayers and were in their beds by nine of the clock. Much remained unresolved, especially Andrew's future. Shakespeare wished him to return to Oxford, but he could tell that the boy had other ideas. Perhaps he was right: the confined world of the scholar might be too suffocating for him now.

In bed, by the light of a single candle, Shakespeare unfolded a letter. It had been handed to him by Cecil before their parting that morning. It was from Eliska.

'She asked me to give this to you if anything happened to her.'

Shakespeare had hesitated before accepting it.

'Take it, John,' Cecil insisted, pushing it towards him.

Now he looked at the letter and thought of the last time he had seen her alive and of the burial at sea they had given her. He wished very much to close his heart to her, to think of her no more. But here was the letter.

His hands hesitated, then opened it. He did not wish to read her confession to murder: that was too much to ask of a man. His reason dissolved like sugar in wine when he tried to make sense of her actions.

As he started to read, the candlelight guttered in the draught and seemed to shift the words, as though they had life.

*'John, if you are reading this letter, it means you have survived and I have died. My sadness is past. We met at a place and time where our joy could only ever be fleeting. I knew you could never be mine, not truly, for your love resided elsewhere and I was set on a course that could not be altered and which, I knew, you would never countenance, not in its entirety.*

*'By the time you receive this, I will have explained to you about my father and his treatment by the Church corrupt. He was the finest man that ever lived and he was my life. You came closer to him than any man I have ever known. Just as I now know you were prepared to sacrifice your career and reputation in your quest*

*for your boy, so I vowed to do all in my feeble power to further the cause my father fought for, for so many years. I think you probably now know what it involved. I will not attempt to justify all I have done, not here. Nor will I ask forgiveness, for I believe I have done no wrong. You will disagree with this, but perhaps one day you will find it in your heart to understand.*

'*And so I bid you farewell. I would ask you to pray for me, and I will give thanks to God that you have lived through our great adventure. Fight for the right, John, with no quarter given. Yours, in love, Eliska.*'

He had not known the depth of her passions. She had concealed them well. Except for once, one night in Lancashire when, unbeknownst to her, he had noted her tears. Now at last he began to understand why she wept.

What was less easy to understand was why she had invited death on the battlements of Fort El Léon. Why had she continued to wave her pathetic yellow flag, long after the need for it had passed? And then he began to realise: it was the same thing that had driven her all this time since her father's killing; it was what made her come to Lathom House and then to Brittany, into the very maw of death. Just one word: *defiance.*

Shakespeare read the letter one last time, then held it to the candleflame and watched as it flared up and fluttered down in black ashes to the floor of his chamber.

He sniffed the air. He had slept only fitfully and was half awake. The room was utterly dark and there was a smell of burning. He did not move from the warmth of his bedclothes. All he wanted was to sleep. The smell must be the ashes of Eliska's letter.

Except that it wasn't. The burning stench was too strong, and there was smoke. He leapt up in his nightshirt. There was a fire. Somewhere in the house, there was fire. He threw open the window shutters and looked out. Flames licked from the window below. Black smoke belched out in the street. The house was ablaze.

'Fire! Fire! Fire!'

He shouted the word again and again. There was no other word in the English language more likely to drag the sleeping into instant wakefulness. Opening the chamber door wide, he shouted again and again, willing his voice to be heard in every room in the house and beyond.

The darkness was absolute. Feeling his way by memory, he stumbled towards the chamber occupied by Grace and Mary. Quickly, he opened their shutters for a little moonlight, then pulled them roughly awake and from their beds. If only he had a lantern, something to light the way out of this building.

Mary began to cry. Grace rubbed her eyes sleepily and fought to return to her bed, but Shakespeare tugged at her arms.

'Grace, we must leave the house. It is on fire.'

He lifted Mary over his shoulder and gripped Grace's hand firmly in his and made for the door from their room.

Andrew called out from the gallery, but Shakespeare could not see him.

'Get Jane and Boltfoot and the baby.'

'They're here. Not Boltfoot, but Jane and little John.'

Andrew coughed and spluttered as he spoke. At Shakespeare's side, Mary began to wail. The smoke was getting to them all. Shakespeare tore scraps from Grace's linen nightgown and gave squares to the children to hold against their faces.

'Don't wait,' Shakespeare ordered into the black darkness. 'Find your way down and try to make your way to the back of the house. If all else fails, break a window and throw yourselves into the river. Where's Boltfoot?'

'He wasn't there when I awoke,' Jane said, fear thickening her voice. 'He must have gone downstairs.'

'Stay close together. Open no doors. The whole of the front is on fire.'

Suddenly there was light. Flames burst through an open door into the hall below, casting hell-like patterns across the walls.

'Run. You can see your way!'

With the fire broken through, they had light but little time. Together, they all made their way down the main staircase, shielding themselves from the leaping flames with their arms. In the hall, Shakespeare handed Mary and Grace over to Andrew.

'Go, take them to safety.'

'Boltfoot,' Jane pleaded.

'I'll find him. Get yourself and the baby out of the house.'

He watched as they ran across the hall, chased by the flames. They made it into the kitchens and Andrew slammed the door shut behind them. Good, thought Shakespeare, anything to give them more time. Now, where was Boltfoot?

He heard a muffled groan. No words, just a deep-throated animal sound, faint and distant. It seemed to be coming from somewhere at the side of the house. Clutching a piece of night-shirt to his face and keeping low, Shakespeare ran towards the sound. The flames were rushing up the walls to the ceiling. This house was wood-framed. The seasoned oak burnt and roared as readily as logs in a hearth. Within a very little time they would be engulfed.

'Boltfoot, where are you? Boltfoot! Boltfoot!'

He heard another sound, from the schoolroom. Shakespeare pushed through the open door. There were flames at the back of the room, curling up around the window. A body lay on the floor: Boltfoot, bound and gagged.

Shakespeare dragged Boltfoot by the arms, crouching low against the choking black smoke that billowed across the room and out into the hall. It was now thick with an acrid cloud. He knew they had to stay below the smoke or, within moments, they would be overcome and die. There was no time to unbind him and he had no blade to cut the cords that held him tight.

He slung his assistant over his shoulder like a sack of beets and thanked God he was a squat, lean man with little in the way of weight to drag them down. Now which way? He was lost, disoriented. He had a sudden horror: they were going to die here, suffocated in their own home.

Scrabbling around, he pulled Boltfoot off his back and dragged him by his shoulders. A face loomed out of the darkness: Andrew. Sweat dripped in soot-black rivulets from his forehead and streaked his cheeks. He was crawling towards them, a damp cloth about his mouth and nostrils. He handed wet rags to Shakespeare, who clamped one about his own face, one on Boltfoot.

'Come, Father,' Andrew said. 'Follow me.'

For hours they fought the blaze, bringing pail after pail of water to douse the flames. Men, women and children from a mile around left their beds to watch the flames light up the night sky or to help. Jane stayed with the children at the house of a neighbour, while Shakespeare, Andrew and Boltfoot joined the local watch and scores of other men ferrying water from the river. It was hot, brutal work that left skin scorched, faces striped with soot and sweat, and hair singed.

At last, soon after dawn, the worst of the fire was out. But what was left was no more than half a house, the remainder just a black carcass of smoking timbers. They had lost important belongings, but they had protected neighbouring properties. For Shakespeare the worst loss was the few jewels and small trinkets of his late wife, Catherine; for Andrew, it was the destruction of a painting of his long-dead mother.

The firefighters quenched their thirst with tankards of ale, while Shakespeare and Boltfoot picked through the half of the house that was saved. Even the part of it that stood was damaged by water and smoke, and would need extensive repairs before it would be habitable again. They found their weapons and some coin, but little else of use.

At last, Shakespeare had a moment to speak with Boltfoot.

'Now tell me. What happened? Who was it?'

'I heard a noise downstairs and went to investigate. I spotted instantly that the front door was open, broken. Then they were on to me from the shadows. Three of them, master. They knew exactly what they were doing, binding and gagging me in moments, without a word spoken. I did not stand a chance. All I could do was watch them as they went from room to room, setting the fire, laying trails of powder and kindling all along the walls, beneath the drapes and hangings.'

'Did you recognise them?'

'No, they were masked in cowls.'

Shakespeare gritted his teeth and swept a hand through his soot-thick hair. He knew exactly who had done this, even if he had not been here in person: Bartholomew Ickman. Joshua Peace had been right to fear him.

And not only Ickman, but Topcliffe, too. His malign presence cast a dank, heavy cloud across this whole affair. London was a great distance from Oxford, but the foul Topcliffe was a monster with a long reach. He should have seen it . . .

*You will burn for your temerity*, he had said.

Shakespeare's hand went to his hip, seeking a steel haft. He was still in his tattered nightgown, but he had fastened his seared sword belt about his waist. His hand gripped the hilt with unreasoning ferocity. He uttered a rare profanity. He wished very much to kill a man this day. Or, better, two men.

Will had two rooms above a cobbler's shop in Shoreditch.

'They are not much, John, but you are welcome here as long as you wish. I shall stay at an inn.'

John Shakespeare looked around the rooms. Papers and books and broken quills were everywhere. Inkstains dotted the floors. The rooms were both of a size, about eighteen feet by twelve. There was enough space for the seven of them; many families lived like this all their lives. But it would be a great imposition on his brother.

'This is where you work.'

Will glanced at his guests: Jane, Boltfoot and the children stood awkwardly at the wall closest to the doorway. All wore clothes borrowed from neighbours. They must have looked a motley group, riding through the streets of London on the horses from their stables. He smiled at them.

'Your need is the greater. Besides, John, you have done much for me.'

Shakespeare shook his head. 'One day and night, Will, that is all we require. On the morrow, we will find other lodgings, more suitable to small children.' He turned to Boltfoot and Andrew. 'Are you armed? Then let us ride.'

Skirting the city along well-used, rain-sodden tracks, the ride to Westminster was no more than four miles, but took them an hour and a half. The dark, baleful stone of Richard Topcliffe's house rose in the shadow of St Margaret's church. It was a house that John Shakespeare knew all too well. A house that stank of sweat and blood. A house where torture was licensed. A house with its own chamber of iron and fire, and a rack that was its owner's pride. A house that stained England.

Shakespeare hammered at the heavy oak door with the haft of his poniard. Boltfoot stood to his left, caliver loaded and ready. Andrew stood to his right, hand gripped on the hilt of his sheathed sword.

The door opened. A young heavy-set man stood there, his straggle-hair slicked with grease. He looked at the three visitors with unconcealed loathing. Shakespeare knew him well: Nicholas Jones, apprentice in cruelty to Topcliffe.

'Where is your master, Jones?'

'You won't find him here.'

He made as if to close the door, but Shakespeare was ahead of him. His hand grasped at the young man's throat, pushing him back into the hallway. Jones stumbled backwards under the onslaught and fell to the floor. Shakespeare, Boltfoot and Andrew looked down at him. The muzzle of Boltfoot's caliver was trained on his face.

'Where is he, Jones?'

Jones spat and Boltfoot pushed the muzzle down harder so that the cold steel flattened his nose. Jones wrenched his head sideways.

'Shall I blast his head away, Mr Shakespeare?'

'All in good time, Boltfoot.'

'Court of Chancery,' Jones spluttered. 'He's at the Court of Chancery!'

Shakespeare brushed Boltfoot's caliver aside and dragged Jones to his feet. He held him against the wall by the lapels of his leather jerkin.

'What is this? What is Topcliffe doing at Chancery? It is a civil court; there are no poor creatures to persecute there.'

'He has brought a suit for non-payment of contract.'

'Tell me more!'

'There is no more.'

'Finish him, Boltfoot.'

'Please, wait.' Jones could see the rage of death in these men's eyes. He had never before believed Shakespeare capable of cold-blooded killing: he did now. 'He is suing Tom Fitzherbert.'

Shakespeare could not disguise his astonishment. How could this square with his theory that Tom Fitzherbert and Topcliffe had conspired with James Fitzherbert falsely to accuse Andrew? Why, if they were co-conspirators, would Topcliffe be suing him in Chancery?

'What is the debt?'

'Five thousand pounds. Fitzherbert promised Mr Topcliffe five thousand pounds.'

'For what?'

Jones hesitated. Shakespeare slammed his head into wall, hard.

Jones cried out in pain, then cringed away. 'Hell's turds, Mr Shakespeare, I'll tell you. It is no secret for it will be heard in court. Tom Fitzherbert pledged to pay Mr Topcliffe five thousand pounds to bring his Papist father to his death so that he might inherit his lands and properties. Old John Fitzherbert has died in the Tower – and yet Tom Fitzherbert will not pay. Mr Topcliffe wants his money. He wants his five thousand. That is what this is about. Go to court yourself and you shall see.'

Shakespeare stared with astonishment into Jones's eyes and saw fear, not dissimulation. Could it be true? Could an Englishman sue a man for non-payment of a contract to kill?

Suddenly, he flung the wretched Jones down the hall, turned on his heel and marched a hundred yards in the direction of Westminster Hall, with Andrew and Boltfoot close behind.

# Chapter 50

SHAKESPEARE STRODE INTO the ancient hall, past the Common Pleas. The Court of Chancery was at the upper end, at the left-hand side. This was where Lord Keeper Sir John Puckering presided, with Master of the Rolls Sir Thomas Egerton at his side. It briefly flickered through Shakespeare's mind to wonder about some link between this court and Egerton's recent role as commissioner inquiring into the death of Lord Derby in Lancashire. At times, he felt, a man could be strangled in the myriad interconnecting twines that linked the great men of England. He shook his head as though to sweep aside the entangled briars; such things might be a matter for another day. This day he wanted but one thing: to find Richard Topcliffe.

A hand touched his sleeve. He turned sharply, as though bitten, and stared into the familiar face of Clarkson, Sir Robert Cecil's most trusted retainer. Shakespeare was about to pull away but Clarkson's grip tightened.

'I must speak with you, Mr Shakespeare.'

'I have no time for talk, Mr Clarkson.'

'Sir Robert Cecil wishes to see you. He is close by, at Whitehall Palace.'

'How did you find me here?'

Clarkson smiled. He was, as always, formally attired in black doublet and hose.

'It was thought probable – and understandable – that you would be seeking Mr Topcliffe this day. I know that Sir Robert wishes to give you certain assurances in that regard.'

Shakespeare laughed without humour. 'Assurances that Topcliffe is to hang? I do not believe it.'

'Please come with me, sir. I am sure it is for the best.'

Cecil welcomed Shakespeare to his offices in Whitehall with a warm smile and gave Clarkson the nod to leave them. The privy councillor personally poured wine into two silver goblets and handed one to his guest. Boltfoot remained outside with Andrew.

'You received my message, John? I am glad you have come, for I know what dread events have taken place. Your house, the threat to your family.'

'And you must know who was responsible, Sir Robert.'

'Indeed, I have grave suspicions.'

'It was Topcliffe and Ickman. They told me as much. They said I would burn.'

Cecil sighed. 'Let me say at once that I consider Bartholomew Ickman no better than a diseased dog that should be disposed of. It was his men that laid the fire. But he will trouble the world no more. Trust me on this.'

'Have you warned him off? He will laugh at you. Or are you trying to tell me something else? What *are* you saying?'

'Nothing. I am saying nothing. Read nothing into my words. But worry about him no more.'

'You ask a great deal, Sir Robert. My inclination is to kill him for what he has done to my home and my family. And what of Topcliffe? Now he sues his confederate Thomas Fitzherbert for not paying the agreed price for murder. Has England come to this?'

'John, Her Majesty is beside herself with fury at Topcliffe.

She can barely speak for anger. I have not seen such rage in her, no, not even when Ralegh was wed against her wishes.'

Cecil sat down. He looked for all the world like a mannequin put into place by a puppet-master, his feet barely touching the floor. He patted a cushion at his side. Shakespeare hesitated, then sat at the other end of the settle, so that they could see each other but were not touching.

'I pledge you this, John: Topcliffe's days of power are done. This court case . . . I tell you that if he is not brought to ruin within a six-month, then you may call me a liar. Her Royal Majesty has already ordered Puckering to hear it in closed session. I cannot overemphasise her displeasure. Never again will Topcliffe have access to her presence.'

'Why are Topcliffe and Fitzherbert not simply brought to trial for conspiracy to do murder?'

Cecil clenched his eyes closed as though the question pained him, then opened them. 'Because old John Fitzherbert was lawfully detained in the Tower for his seditious ways. And though he was tormented, he died of natural causes. That, it seems, is why his son refuses to pay the money Topcliffe believes is owed him. So there is no murder.'

'And yet there was a contract to do murder. Is that not offence enough?' Shakespeare hammered his fist into his hand. 'But this is not my concern. What I care for is my own family. Was Topcliffe involved with James Fitzherbert the tutor? Did they conspire against Andrew?'

Cecil was silent a moment. When he spoke his voice was quiet and his words were precise.

'I have no proof, John, but I can speculate on what happened. I surmise that Tom Fitzherbert was under a great deal of pressure from Topcliffe for the five thousand pounds that is now in dispute. To try to prevent Topcliffe's suit proceeding, he offered him a trade-off. Knowing of Topcliffe's loathing for your family, he would bribe or beg his cousin James Fitzherbert to bring false accusations against your boy at Oxford. Topcliffe went along with the idea. But your son's redemption put an end to the deal, and now they are in court.'

Shakespeare could sit no longer. He rose from the settle and paced the room.

Cecil's eyes followed him.

'I know you are sceptical. I know you believe that I am some sort of Machiavel creature and that I had something to do with the events at Oxford and in Lancashire. I think you even believe me responsible for the death of the Earl of Derby. But ask yourself this: if I was organising a conspiracy and murder in Lancashire, why would I have sent you there in the first place? I know you well enough to realise that you would be bound to inquire into such an event. God's blood, John, I wanted you at Lathom House to protect the secret of the perspective glass. With good cause, as it happens, for the man Walter Weld, or Millwater, or whatever his true name was, did indeed have designs on the instrument. And I needed you to meet Eliska Nováková.'

'But you *know* that the earl was murdered. We both know that.'

Cecil shook his head. 'I know nothing of the sort. I know that there were some curious goings-on at Lathom House. I know, too, that many people might have wished him dead. I confess that it suits my own purposes that he is succeeded by his brother William, whose loyalties are more certain. But that does not mean I killed him. Nor do I have any reason to believe that he died of anything but natural causes. A rupture of the gut, perhaps, a canker within, some bad shellfish . . . These things happen every day. Did he take his own life, deliberately, with some poison? He was always of a melancholy humour. We will never know what killed him. It is a tragic waste of a young life, but nothing out of the ordinary. If he was murdered, it was not by me, nor by my command and not with my knowledge.'

Shakespeare downed his goblet of wine. It was good wine, but it felt raw against his throat. His very nerve endings felt raw.

Cecil reached out and gripped Shakespeare's hand, briefly.

'A man in my position must do many bad things, John, but I promise you this: I have never stooped to murder, nor ever would. I have called you here today because it is important to me that you know that and believe it.'

'And Eliska? What of Eliska? I know she obtained poison in Lancashire.'

'Then you know more than I do.' Cecil nodded slowly. 'Dear Lady Eliska. That is where my deceit lies. I realise now that I should have told you more about her before you went to Lathom House. I wanted you to observe her without prejudice. She seemed desperate to do some harm to Catholicism and the Inquisition, but I couldn't be sure whose side she was really on. There were times when I confess I doubted her. I knew she had to go to the French embassy, but who could know what really passed within those walls? In the end, we know that she spoke truth, that she was on our side; she had a rare passion and we made use of it, which you may think shames England. But it was what she yearned for. With this in mind, Sir Thomas Heneage had great plans for her – plans that needed your assistance. First, though, I wanted your reaction, for I trust your judgment.'

'As you say, you should have told me before sending me to her. It might have saved much grief.'

Cecil threw wide his hands. '*Mea culpa*, as the Romans say.' He stood up from the settle and walked across the room. '*Mea maxima culpa*, John.' He took a paper from a shelf. 'Do you believe me? May I tear this up?'

Shakespeare saw that it was his letter of resignation.

'No,' he said. 'Not yet.'

He looked hard at Cecil. Did he really not know of the poisonous mushroom and Eliska's role in acquiring it?

'John, I need you. England needs you. You will be recompensed in full for all Ickman has done to you, I promise you. But I need you in my service. Your actions in Brittany . . . I can think of no other man who could have done such a thing.' Cecil's fingers hovered over the paper, ready to rip it to pieces.

'Arrange an audience for me with Sir Thomas Heneage. When I have spoken with him, I will give you my answer. First, I have business elsewhere.'

Shakespeare bowed curtly and walked to the door. Cecil watched him go, deep foreboding in his careful eyes.

Sending Boltfoot and Andrew back to the family, Shakespeare went alone to Mortlake. Cold rage had supplanted the unreasoning fury he felt before. He still had violence in his heart but now he considered the consequences beyond the act. He could not implicate Boltfoot and Andrew in this.

At first the door to Bartholomew Ickman's opulent dwelling was not opened. Finally, at the third beating of his poniard and fist against the oak, he heard a shuffling of feet from inside and the door was opened. A serving woman stood there in apron and smock.

'Mr Ickman is not here, master.'

'Where is he?'

'Gone. He left soon after noon.'

'Where is his manservant?'

The woman looked from side to side, as though fearing she might be overheard.

'Speak, woman.'

'He left soon after, sir. I think . . .' She hesitated.

'Yes?'

'I think he has fled, master. In truth I do not know what is going on this day. Others have run away, too. There is a great fear, sir.'

For a moment, Shakespeare wondered whether the woman was going to break down in tears. He pushed past her into the house and strode from room to room. He went to the solar where he had met Ickman and Topcliffe. The hall echoed with silence. The whole place seemed deserted. What in God's name was going on here?

The serving woman was still cowering by the door when he returned.

'I will be back,' he said. 'Tell your master that there is no hiding place on earth from me.'

Two men were standing by the river. Shakespeare recognised them instantly. Provost Pinkney and his giant of a sergeant, Cordwright. They were watching him and he noticed that they both smiled.

He walked over to them and they made no attempt to avoid him.

'Mr Shakespeare, we meet again,' Pinkney said. 'How fares private soldier Woode? Itching for blood and steel?'

'He fares well enough.'

Shakespeare turned to Cordwright. The last time he had seen him, he was wasting away in a Weymouth gaol cell. Now he seemed almost back to his immense strength.

'And how did you slip the hangman's noose, Mr Cordwright?'

Pinkney laughed. 'Takes more than a gaol cell to hold my sergeant.'

'So it appears. Well, Mr Pinkney, it seems a mighty

coincidence to find you here. Are you friends of Mr Ickman? Perhaps you lay fires for him.'

'Indeed not, Mr Shakespeare. We are here because our word is our bond, as always. Small tasks for great gentlemen. No, indeed not, we are no friends of Mr Ickman, though it would be fair to say we have made his acquaintance.'

'And where is he now?'

'Why, I believe he is in the woods. Did he not venture into those woods yonder for his morning perambulation, Mr Cordwright, along that path?'

Pinkney nodded towards the thick woodland that stretched away from Ickman's property.

'Yes, sir, Provost Pinkney, I believe he did.'

'But enough of common chatter, Mr Shakespeare,' Pinkney said. 'Our work here is done and we must be away. Be so good as to convey my greetings to private soldier Woode.'

Shakespeare had already noted two horses tethered to a tree close by. Pinkney and his sergeant walked towards them, mounted and rode away slowly in the direction of London, without turning back. Shakespeare watched them depart, then followed the path into the woods.

The body of Bartholomew Ickman hung from the branch of a tree, swaying gently in the breeze. Shakespeare gazed upon his grotesque face without emotion. The dead man was wearing the buttercup silk doublet he had worn in the fields of Lancashire, divining for treasure with Dee. His arms were unbound and a stool was on its side close to his dangling feet as though he had stood on it and kicked it away to take his own life. But Shakespeare knew better. He had a very good idea how Ickman had died.

## Chapter 51

D R JOHN DEE was waiting when Shakespeare arrived back at his brother's rooms in Shoreditch. Shakespeare glared at him with angry disdain.

The old alchemist was dressed in his flowing gown once again. He stood rigidly, with his back to the window, and looked nervous. Shakespeare wondered why he was here. He did not wish to see this man; he had enough problems of his own to contend with.

'I was told I might find you here,' Dee said tentatively. 'Your Dowgate neighbours.'

'Why are you here, Dr Dee?'

'I heard about your home. The blaze . . . a terrible mishap.'

'It was no mishap. The fire was deliberately set. It was arson, attempted murder of three adults and four children. It was a monstrous act.'

'I know. That is why I am here. I can keep silent no longer.'

Will was out at the playhouse. Andrew and the children were in the other room with Jane. Boltfoot was here, though, eyeing Dee with wary curiosity. Shakespeare turned to him.

'Boltfoot, please bring Dr Dee some wine. I think I wish to hear what he has to say. Sit down, Dr Dee.'

'Thank you.'

'But I must warn you to be straight with me. I have little patience today.'

Dee sat on the hard wooden settle. His beard was growing again and he looked much like his old self. He folded his hands in his lap, his voluminous sleeves draped across his thighs. He closed his eyes, as if summoning up some divine energy to enable him to say what had to be said. Shakespeare watched him closely, and waited.

'Here.' Boltfoot handed Dee a beaker of sweetened wine.

Dee opened his eyes, took the beaker, sipped it, then put it on the settle at his side.

'What I am about to say does not come easy, Mr Shakespeare. But at the hazard of my immortal soul, I must tell you certain things.'

Shakespeare watched and listened, but said nothing.

Dr Dee produced a paper from his sleeve. 'This is the letter you found about the person of Father Lamb. When I was at Chevening, Mr Mills showed it to me, for it meant nothing to him. He thought to try whether my intellect would fare better.'

'And did it?'

Dee nodded his head gravely. 'I told Mr Mills that I could not understand it, that it was all about birds and seemed meaningless. But that was a lie. In truth, I saw instantly what it meant. It was an acrostic of sorts, and the words leapt from the page at me. Look now, examine the initial letters of the verse you uncovered.'

'Hand me the letter.'

Dee leant across and placed the paper in Shakespeare's hands. He gazed at the hidden words that had been revealed by heat.

'*The killing birds wait in line. The hawks edge nearer, even as golden eagles under soaring eyries dive. Malevolent dove, evil nightjar, baleful ibis and twisted hoodcrow toss overhead, preying on insects, shrews or newts. Let dogs fester, orphans rot, ere rooks lay down and die.'*

Shakespeare took a quill from his brother's table and dipped it in an inkhorn. He scratched the initial letters of the message on a piece of blank paper, then examined what he had written:

TKBWILTHENEAGEUSEDMDENB
IATHTOPOISONLDFORERLDAD.

The letters seemed to have neither sense nor reason, except for one word that stood out like the back-end of a boar among sows.

'I see the word poison in there, nothing more. Explain to me, Dr Dee.'

Dee shifted close and placed his long forefinger on the paper, smudging the wet ink.

'At the beginning and end there are nulls, blanks – letters that mean nothing. That is why Mills could not see it. Reading from the H, the first two words become clear – *Heneage used.* You then have four sets of initials for names: MD, EN, BI and TH. After that, it clearly says *to poison LD.*'

'LD – Lord Derby.'

'Indeed.'

'And the four sets of initials?'

'You know them as well as I do, Mr Shakespeare.'

'Say the names to me. I wish to hear you say the names.'

'Very well. MD, Michael Dowty; EN, Eliska Nováková; BI, Bartholomew Ickman; and TH, Thomas Hesketh.'

*EN. Eliska Nováková. Evil nightjar.*

'Then it was as I thought. They were all in it, working together.'

'On the orders of Sir Thomas Heneage, Chancellor of the Duchy of Lancaster.'

'Political murder.'

If this letter had succeeded in reaching Lamb's Jesuit masters in Rome, the enemies of England would have spread it abroad with glee and rejoicing. No more could England claim moral authority over King Philip of Spain and his despised political assassinations.

'My question, Dr Dee, is how you were able to see this so clearly from a rag-tag scrawl of letters?'

'Because I already knew of the conspiracy, Mr Shakespeare. And Father Lamb heard it from my lips.'

'You told Lamb? In God's name, why?'

'Because I wanted to stop it. I wanted to save the earl. I had already done far too much harm, and I was overcome with guilt and remorse. I still am, Mr Shakespeare. That is why I am here today. I seek to expunge my sin. I am an old man. I do not have long to find redemption.'

'So you were part of the conspiracy, but had second thoughts: is that what you are saying?'

'No. No, I never meant murder against any man.'

'What, then, was your sin?'

Dee sighed deeply and his tight jawline throbbed. For a moment it occurred to Shakespeare that he might weep.

'My sin, Mr Shakespeare, was my involvement in the original plot to ensnare the earl, the plot that ended with poor Richard Hesketh's cruel death on the scaffold. Richard was my good friend of many years' standing, and I used him most foully.'

Shakespeare threw a questioning glance.

'You wish to know why I betrayed my friend. It was not intentional. It all began when Heneage invited me to dine with him in the early summer of last year. The talk turned to my time in Prague and he asked me who I knew there. I mentioned several names, including Richard. Heneage seized on the name and questioned me about him.

'I thought no more about it, but Heneage called me to his home at the Savoy again a few days later and told me about the Privy Council's fears that Lord Strange – Lord Derby as he would become – was a crypto-Catholic, and that he was manoeuvring secretly against the Queen. Heneage told me the Council wished to compromise him, bring his plans out into the open and thus dash his hopes of ever succeeding to the throne. To this end, they had conceived a scheme. A letter would be brought to him from Catholics in Prague, begging the earl to be their figurehead. If he did not reveal the letter to Queen and Council, he would be proved a double-dealer, just like Mary of Scots before him. It was suggested that Richard Hesketh should bring the letter to the earl, as if it had come from exiles. Heneage needed my assistance, though, for Richard would trust me above all men. If he did this thing, all former charges against him would be dropped, I was told, and he would be allowed to live unmolested with his family once more. As for me, in return for my small help, I would be offered a living, perhaps Winchester or the collegiate church of Manchester.'

'Did you have no misgivings at this stage?'

'Of course I did. But Thomas Heneage is a charming and most persuasive man. He told me that I would be helping England and my sovereign. I persuaded myself, too, that I would be doing Richard Hesketh a great favour.'

'What happened next?'

'On Heneage's instructions, I sent a letter to Richard, explaining that I had been assured he would be forgiven past misdemeanours and would be allowed safe passage back to his wife and children in Lancashire. All he had to do was pick up a certain package at the White Lion in Islington and take it to his master at Lathom House. The letter was sent and I hoped for the best. Three months later, I heard that Richard had been arrested and was to be executed for treason. My blood ran cold, Mr Shakespeare, for I was responsible. Then, to compound my guilt, I discovered that the incriminating package had been handed over to Richard by Bartholomew Ickman, my former scryer, and I realised I had involved myself in something evil. Ickman would have known of my friendship with Richard Hesketh. I began to believe that he was behind the whole plot and gave Heneage the idea of using me . . .'

Dee hung his head.

'Please continue, Dr Dee. Allow me to guess. You were so overcome with remorse that you vowed to look after Isabel Hesketh and her family with donations of money. You even went to her husband in his cell at St Albans, begged forgiveness and vowed that you would do this for them. You were the noble gentleman of whom she spoke to me.'

'Did she tell you that?' He nodded. 'Yes, that was me.'

'And you will be pleased to know that when I saw her, she was big with her husband's child. It must be born now, so her need of money will be yet greater.'

Dee sighed heavily and shook his head with something approaching despair.

'I still have no money for her. Heneage has not given me the living I was promised. That was why I was reduced to digging in a field in quest of Roman gold. That was why I was in Lancashire. My meeting there with Ickman was entirely coincidental. He was there on a mission to poison. Knowing the depth of my involvement, he happily boasted as much to me. "If we can't get the traitor one way, we'll do it another," were the words he used. He told me more. He was full of it, how clever the plot was, how pleased Heneage and the Privy

Council would be, what riches would be bestowed upon the Ickmans. I could bear to listen to it no more. That was when I went to Father Lamb and begged him to save Lord Derby. But it was too late by then, as you know. The earl had already been poisoned.'

'What part did Eliska play in all this?'

'We were friends in Prague. The next I knew of her was when she appeared at Lathom House. It was Ickman who told me how she had helped soften up Richard Hesketh to bring the earl his fateful letter. She had come to Lancashire, he said, to finish her work. She knew all my sins. On the night of your brother's play, she was berating me. She suspected I had communicated something to Father Lamb.'

Shakespeare eyed the old doctor coldly. For a man of intellect, he was dangerously foolish. Not a man to trust with your friendship if he could be so easily swayed by designing men – and women. Poor Richard Hesketh must have been easy meat to the likes of Ickman and Eliska, and his own ambitious brother Thomas Hesketh.

And what of Michael Dowty, soon to be a Cecilian member of Parliament? His role was obvious: he fed his master the dish with the deadly mushroom, having pretended to taste it himself. Was this the England that Shakespeare had fought for all these years? He felt befouled by the whole dirty conspiracy.

'You have great reason to feel shame, Dr Dee.'

'It is true. I have nothing to say in my defence. No penitence or contrition will ever expiate my sin.'

Shakespeare was thinking hard. What was to be done about any of this? He stood up and began pacing, then stopped and nodded slowly.

'You have done the right thing in coming to me this day. Will you speak all this in a court of law?'

The light drained from Dee's eyes. He shook his head violently. 'I cannot, Mr Shakespeare. No man could.'

'Your immortal soul—'

'No, not even for that. There is worse. Look again at the secret code in the verse.'

Shakespeare picked up the paper. 'What, pray, am I looking for?'

'It says, "Heneage used MD, EN, BI and TH to poison LD . . ." and then there are nine more letters, though only the first five of those need concern you: FORER.'

Shakespeare saw it straightway: *for ER*. For Elizabeth Regina. Her Majesty the Queen. If the letter was true, then the conspiracy could not go higher.

No, this could not be brought to a court of law. It had to be settled by other means.

# Chapter 52

SIR THOMAS HENEAGE, son of a Lincolnshire landowner, was a man of immense charm. Some said he was the only courtier who managed to be friends with everyone from the Queen downwards. He even got on with Ralegh and could bridge the divide between the most bitter of rivals so that he was as much at ease in the camp of the Cecils as he was with Essex and the Bacons.

But above all, he was known as the truest friend of the Queen. Fiercely Protestant, he had caught Elizabeth's eye in the earliest days of her reign and had remained close to her ever since.

He stood in the hall of Lancaster mansion at the Savoy to welcome John Shakespeare. His smile was warm and genuine and his words of praise for Shakespeare's efforts on behalf of Queen and country were undoubtedly heartfelt.

Shakespeare had come here to this bend in the Thames by Westminster with deep antagonism in his soul. He had been ready to do violence to Heneage. Instead, he smiled back and thanked Sir Thomas for receiving him so quickly.

'Sir Robert said you wished to see me. He has told me everything. Your fears and your suspicions. Let me tell you, John – if I may call you that, in friendship – that I am delighted to meet you again so that I may explain my side of the tale to you. You may not like me for it, but I believe you will respect me.'

'Sir—'

'Please, John, hear me out. I wish to say at first that I know the affection in which you were held by Eliska. If she loved you, as I believe, then I too must hold you dear.'

Shakespeare tried to interject again. 'Sir Thomas, I have questions—'

'And I have answers. What I tell you here in this room will explain everything to you, but you will never repeat it to any man or woman, and neither will I. Even Sir Robert Cecil does not know what I will tell you, for it would be unfair to compromise his integrity with such knowledge. You and I will maintain silence to death, for our sovereign, her realm and her Church. I will not ask you to make a promise to that effect, for I know it is unnecessary.'

'Do you?'

'I know you are a man of courage and honour. As I recall, we spoke before of the Bond of Association. Surely you signed it.'

Shakespeare shook his head. It had been placed in front of him by Walsingham but he had refused to sign it, for it was the rule of the mob. All those who signed the bond – and there were thousands, including the whole Privy Council – had made an oath to take instant vengeance on anyone conspiring to harm the Queen. No trial, just instant death. Summary justice. The bond had been drawn up by Walsingham and Burghley in 1584 in the aftermath of the Throckmorton plot and a year later was encoded into the law of the land. Walsingham had not been pleased by Shakespeare's stance, insisting that it was his patriotic duty to sign, haranguing him in that cold, relentless way that broke so many men's will. Shakespeare would have none of it.

'Well, I did, John,' Heneage said. 'As did many others, some with no more than a cross of ink to signify their mark. But in 1586, when Mary Queen of Scots plotted against her cousin's life, the Bond proved worthless. The Scots devil's gaoler, Amyas Paulet, refused to kill her for her sins, though he himself had signed the Bond in seeming good faith and though Walsingham wrote begging him in such wise to do his duty as a man. It would have been the easy way out for all concerned. A drop of poison in her food or wine, an unfortunate accident out riding. It would have been the decent, manly thing to do. But Paulet was squeamish and cowardly. "God forbid that I should make so foul a shipwreck of conscience," he wrote back. So, instead, the whole burden was laid on Her Majesty. She had to sign the warrant of death and suffer the onslaught of venom from the world outside England. I believe the beheading of her cousin did age Her Majesty ten years.'

Shakespeare was not convinced. Being monarch came with responsibility as well as privilege.

Heneage sensed his doubts. 'She may be our sovereign, yet she is a woman, too, and a virgin. She has no husband to protect her, so we must. On bended knee, I vowed to her then that she would never be placed in such a position again.'

'So you had the Earl of Derby killed, believing him a traitor?'

'Yes.'

'Then you are a murderer.'

'Executioner.'

'Why are you telling me this? Do you not fear what I might do with such information?'

Heneage smiled. 'I am telling you because there is no reason not to. We are both on the same side, Mr Shakespeare, a fact that Mr Ickman forgot, to his great misfortune. Besides, I am sure you would not flatter yourself that you pose any threat to me.'

'And does Her Majesty know of your part in Lord Derby's death?'

'No. She must never know. It was done *for* her and for England, but I could not place such mortal sin on her slender shoulders. I am a loyal subject and a man. Derby *was* a traitor. As I was Chancellor of the Duchy of Lancaster, it fell to me to deal with him. He came under my jurisdiction. It was my duty to judge him and see sentence carried out. My responsibility.'

'Do you have proof of his supposed treason?'

'He was plotting with the Jesuits to be king. You yourself saw the hiding place he kept for the priest Lamb. Harbouring a Jesuit? That is enough to have any common husbandman or goodwife, yeoman or burgess, taken to the scaffold. His followers and retinue were almost all Catholic; the whole palatinate of Lancashire is a very pestilence of recusancy. My Duchy attorney Thomas Hesketh, who also signed the Bond, swims against a great floodtide of rebellion. Even his own brother was a betrayer.'

'You should have had Derby brought before a court and tried.'

'Then we would have had to ask the Queen to sign the death warrant for yet another cousin. What sort of man would require that of his sovereign lady? We are at war, Mr Shakespeare. Did Throckmorton or Babington or Parma or Philip of Spain demand a trial for Elizabeth before doing their utmost to assassinate her? If I am morally wrong, then God will punish me and I will accept His judgment, as we all must. But even faced with the eternal fire, I will not repent, for I know I did the correct thing. I did my duty.'

'Then there is nothing more to say. Everything in the Lamb letter was true. Here.' Shakespeare took the letter from his doublet and handed it to Sir Thomas. 'You should have this. Do with it what you will.'

Heneage took the letter and laid it aside. A fire was burning in the hearth, but he did not place the letter in the flames.

'Thank you, John. It is better in my hands than the Pope's, that is certain.'

Heneage put out his hand. Shakespeare looked at it, but did not take it.

'It is the hand of friendship, John. I never meant you harm. I accept that I erred in using the services of Ickman. What he put you and your family through was beyond enduring. But he will trouble us no more. He has paid the price.'

What was it the sergeant, Cordwright, had said while he awaited death in Weymouth gaol? *When we are not a-soldiering, Provost Pinkney and me do little tasks for a certain great personage, a man whose word is his bond.* Perhaps they, too, had signed the wretched Bond of Association.

Heneage's eyes met Shakespeare's. His hand waited, but Shakespeare did not take it.

Instead he turned away and walked towards the door. He liked Heneage. He found much to respect in his unquestioning love and loyalty for his monarch. Yet he could not admire the man, and he would never shake his blood-stained hand.

Shakespeare and Andrew reined in beside a field in Cambridgeshire. The day was cold. Flurries of snow were in the air, though none of it was settling on the ground.

They looked across a bleak field of beet that had failed and fallen to weed and rot.

'Over there,' Andrew said.

A thin trail of smoke rose from a small fire at the other side of the field, near a spinney. A horse was tethered to a tree and a piece of tarpaulin had been stretched across a lattice of branches to make a small shelter.

They kicked on across the field. A figure rose from beside the fire and edged towards the horse as though about to mount up, ride away and escape. But then the figure stopped.

They could see her clearly now. Her fair hair and pinched face, her slender arms and waist. And she could see them, for she started walking towards them. Andrew slid from the saddle and walked towards her. Shakespeare held back and watched from twenty yards' distance.

Ursula had a blanket wrapped around her shoulders. She hunched into it.

'Andrew pigging Woode,' she said. 'Fancy you being alive.'

'Thanks to you, Ursula pigging Dancer.'

She laughed. 'Soldier, now, are you?'

He nodded and glanced across to Shakespeare, who shrugged his shoulders. He had other ideas.

'So what are you doing here?'

'Looking for you. Reaphook told me where you came from. I thought you'd come looking for your family.'

She laughed again, but without smiling this time. 'Shouldn't have bothered, should I? Knocked at the door of their great manor house and this old servant told me to go away. I said I was family, long-lost kin. He looked at me as if I was a dog turd and went away. Then he came back with this evil old woman with a walking stick. Well, she stared at me and it was as if she'd seen a pigging ghost or something. Staffy always said I looked like my mother, so I suppose she thought I was her. I think the woman was my grandmother, but all she did was start hitting me with her stick. Beat me around the head with it, and she could hit hard for an old one.'

'What did you do?'

'I ran. What else should I do? I know when I'm not pigging wanted. Shouldn't have gone there. Why would I want anything to do with people like that?'

'Come home with us. We're your family now.'

She huddled deeper into the blanket and looked away.

'There's nothing for you here, Ursula. You just said so yourself.'

She was shaking her head. 'I won't fit in. Didn't fit in at that house in the shire of Kent, did I? They treated me like a skivvy and kept making dirty remarks about me. And they knew I heard them. Called me slut and drab and thief.'

'Well, you *are* a thief! You stole their horse to prove it.'

'I didn't steal the nag, I borrowed it. Anyway, that's by the by. I'm not a slut nor a drab.'

'No, you're not. So come with us. What have you got to lose?'

'I don't know.'

Shakespeare had dismounted now. He walked to her and put an arm around her shoulder. 'You'll work for us, but you won't be a skivvy. You'll help Jane with the children and the running of the house, and we'll give you an education. Teach you to read and write.'

'What do I want with reading and writing? How will that help me go a-sharking?'

'There'll be no more of that. And you'll understand why you should learn to read and write, once you try it.'

'Why you doing this for me?'

'Because we esteem you highly. And we need an extra pair of hands. We're moving into a new house and there will be a great deal to do. More than anything, you'll cheer the place up. The children have had a tough time these past months. I know they'll take to you. Say you'll come. We like you.'

Her face creased up. For a moment, Andrew thought he saw a tear forming in her eye, then rejected the very notion as ridiculous. Ursula Dancer didn't cry.

'Well?' he said.

'Oh, of course I'll pigging come.'

# Acknowledgments

As always, I am indebted to many people for their support and help. I would particularly like to mention Michael Riordan, archivist of St John's and the Queen's Colleges, Oxford, for giving me his valuable time, and Bill Clements, chairman of the Fortress Study Group, www.fsgfort.com. My thanks, too, to my wife Naomi, editor Kate Parkin and agent Teresa Chris.

Books that have been especially helpful include: *Hamlet's Divinity* by Christopher Devlin; *The Queen's Conjuror* by Benjamin Woolley; *Sir John Norreys and the Elizabethan Military World* by John S. Nolan; *The Fraternitye of Vacabondes* by John Awdeley; *A Caveat or Warning for Commen Cursetors vulgarely Called Vagabones* by Thomas Harman; *The Art of War and Renaissance England* by John R. Hale; *Shakespeare's England*, edited and introduced by R. E. Pritchard; *Elizabethan Military Science* by Henry J. Webb; *Elizabeth's Wars* by Paul E. J. Hammer; *Elizabeth's Army* by C. G. Cruickshank; *The Elizabethan Militia* by Lindsay Boynton; *The English Yeoman* by Mildred Campbell; *The Works of Sir Roger Williams*, edited by John X. Evans; *Martin Frobisher* by James McDermott; *The Telescope* by Richard Dunn; *Surveillance, Militarism and Drama in the Elizabethan Era* by Curtis C. Breight; *Shakespeare's Military Language* by Charles Edelman; *Manavilins* by Rex

Clements; *The University of Oxford: A New History* by G. R. Evans; *The Colleges of Oxford: Their History and Traditions*, edited by Andrew Clark; *The Earls of Derby 1485–1985* by J. J. Bagley.

# *Historical Notes*

## The Hesketh Affair: Timeline
### *1581*

Dr John Dee, astrologer to the Queen, scientist and alchemist, is noted by spies as being friendly with Lancashire cloth merchant Richard Hesketh. Hesketh was in Antwerp as agent, a diplomatic post representing England's commercial interests in the city. He shared an interest in alchemy with Dee, who was then in England, and the two men corresponded. Dee cast Hesketh's horoscope.

### *1589*

Richard Hesketh, now returned to Over Darwen, Lancashire, is implicated in the murder of a local landowner, Thomas Hoghton, in a dispute over cattle. Hesketh flees to Prague (then in Bohemia), where he joins the circle of Edward Kelley, a former counterfeiter from Lancashire, and also a former 'scryer' – medium – to Dr Dee.

### *1591*

*Christmas*: Lord Strange's Men – the players' company that presented the first plays of William Shakespeare – triumph at court, staging six plays before the Queen at the seasonal court festivities.

Ferdinando, Lord Strange, who is descended from Henry VII through his mother's line, is a prime claimant to the throne of England and the toast of high society.

## 1592

*13 June:* A spy in Brussels named Robinson reports to his masters in England, 'There is certainly intelligence between Strange and the Cardinal [William Allen].' Strange is now suspected of being a crypto-Catholic. His younger brother William, a friend of Dr Dee, is more favoured by the Cecil faction at court.

## 1593

*9 September:* Richard Hesketh lands at Sandwich in Kent, having sailed from Hamburg. Apparently, he has been exonerated by someone on the Privy Council of any blame in the murder that caused his exile. He walks to Canterbury where, at the Bell Inn, he meets a young soldier named Trumpeter Richard Baylie, whom he takes on as a servant. Together, they travel to Rochester, then to Gravesend, London and Hampstead.

*16 September:* They stay at the White Lion, Islington. As they are leaving, a boy named John Waterworth hands Hesketh a letter 'from one Mr Ickman (or Hickman) to take to the Earl of Derby'.

*20 September:* Bartholomew Ickman (like Kelley, a former 'scryer' to Dee) visits Dr Dee at his home in Mortlake.

*22 September:* Hesketh and Baylie arrive at Over Darwen. They stay there with Hesketh's wife, Isabel, for two days before travelling south again to Lathom House in Lancashire, home of the Derby dynasty.

*25 September:* Hesketh arrives at Lathom House in Lancashire, the palatial home of Lord Strange, and hands him a letter urging him to snatch the crown of England for Catholicism – as well as supposedly threatening him with a wretched death if he reveals their plan. Though Hesketh says he picked up the letter in Islington, the letter is later claimed by prosecutors to be from the exiled Cardinal William Allen, head of the Catholic resistance to Queen Elizabeth's Protestant regime. Hesketh had intended returning to his wife, but Lord Strange – who succeeds this very day to the title Earl of Derby on the death of his father – urges Hesketh to stay over Michaelmas. Hesketh seems flattered by the attention and agrees to accompany the earl to court.

*2 October:* On the way to court, Hesketh stops at Brereton in Cheshire. From there, he writes to his wife, Isabel, and to his brother, Thomas, a fiercely anti-Catholic lawyer. The letters are carried by Trumpeter Baylie.

*9 October:* Lord Strange, the new Earl of Derby, reports directly to the Queen at Windsor and shows her the treasonable letter brought by Hesketh, who is immediately arrested.

*15 October:* William Wade, clerk to the Privy Council, begins Hesketh's interrogation.

*4 November:* Hesketh, weeping and wailing, confesses to treason, though he maintains he was an innocent dupe in the matter and did not know the contents of the letter. Lord Strange, the fifth Earl of Derby, is excluded from the proceedings by the Cecils and their allies. No witnesses are called at the trial.

*29 November:* Hesketh is drawn on a hurdle to the scaffold at St Albans, where he is hanged, quartered and beheaded.

*Christmas:* It is a very different festive season to the one enjoyed by the earl two years earlier. Now he stays away from court, alarmed by malicious rumours circulating about him. Hesketh's brother, the Protestant lawyer Thomas Hesketh, is known to be among those slandering him, trying to further the cause of the Duchy of Lancaster and under-mine the power of the earl in the North.

*27 December:* Lord Burghley refuses to give the Chamberlainship of Chester to the Earl of Derby, a position that should have been the earl's by right. Instead it is given to Sir Thomas Egerton. On top of that, the earl's old friend, the Earl of Essex, has turned against him and is luring away his retainers. These snubs confirm what the earl and his wife, Alice, most fear: that they are 'crossed in court and crossed in his country'.

## 1594

*23 March:* At Mortlake, Dr Dee gives a horse to Bartholomew Ickman, his former 'scryer' and near-neighbour. Ickman heads north.

*5 April:* The Earl of Derby – Ferdinando, Lord Strange as was – becomes violently ill after a day's hunting. The next day he begins to vomit blood.

### The Strange Tale of Alice and Thomas

There is a curious postscript to the mysterious illness of the fifth Earl of Derby. Six years after the events described in this book (much of it true, though, of course, fictionalised), the humbly born man who investigated the affair went on to marry the earl's aristocratic widow.

That investigator was Sir Thomas Egerton, bastard son of a Cheshire landowner. The widow was Alice, dowager Countess of Derby, née Alice Spencer of Althorp.

At one time, early in his career, Egerton had been a mere aide to the family of Lord Derby, dependent upon their lar-gesse. But by 1594 he had risen to become one of the greatest lawyers in the land, a former attorney-general and newly appointed Master of the Rolls.

So when he arrived at Lathom House in Lancashire to investigate the devastating illness that had laid low the Earl of Derby, his relationship with the family was very different.

By now, Egerton, a convert from Catholicism, had a reputation as a fervent Protestant, an implacable prosecutor of Catholic priests and those who harboured them. He had taken a leading – and uncompromising – role in bringing Edmund Campion, Mary Queen of Scots and the Babington plotters to their deaths on the scaffold.

He was responsible for ordering prisoners to be tortured and was close to the Queen's despised priest-hunter, the cruel and relentless Richard Topcliffe.

And so his eventual marriage at the age of sixty to the cultured, beautiful Alice (a patron of the arts and the widow of a man who sponsored the early theatrical endeavours of William Shakespeare, among others) seems something of a mismatch – which is just as it turned out.

Yet it was Egerton who suffered the most. If he had hoped his marriage would bring him the aristocratic lustre he so desired, he was to discover only misery, for the haughty Alice – twenty years his junior – despised him and treated him with disdain.

She became one of the great hostesses of the court, a favourite of Elizabeth, performing in masques, and supporting playwrights and poets including Edmund Spenser and the young John Milton. Yet she had a cutting way with words and proved avaricious and careless with money, spending their great wealth with impunity, which displeased the frugal Egerton.

In the latter years of his life, Egerton (by now Lord Chancellor) confided in his son John that the marriage had brought him nothing but despair and he spewed out his venomous feelings towards his wife, accusing her of having 'a bitter tongue'. He wrote to his son: 'I thank God I never desired a long life, nor ever had cause to desire it since this, my last marriage, for before I was never acquainted with such tempests and storms.'

## Fort El Léon: The Aftermath

The cruelty of war is aptly demonstrated by the aftermath of the battle for Fort El Léon near Brest in Brittany on 7 November 1594.

After five hours of bloodshed, only half a dozen of the four hundred Spanish defenders were found alive, hiding in the rocks of the cliff beneath the fort. The English commander, Sir John Norreys, spared them and sent them back to the main Spanish army of General Juan del Águila.

Instead of being welcomed, however, they were hanged for cowardice.

Another casualty was Martin Frobisher, the commander of the English fleet and hero of the English assault. He had personally led his marines into the fort's breach and had been shot in the hip. The wound in itself was not life-threatening, but the surgeon who removed the bullet left wadding in the wound and the subsequent infection led to gangrene, which killed Frobisher on his return to England.

# Vagabonds in the Sixteenth Century

The word 'vagabond' conjures up an image of romance and freedom on the open road, but the life of such people in the sixteenth century was anything but romantic.

They were the dispossessed of the age. They had no land, no welfare and were driven on from town to town. When apprehended, they could face the whip, mutilation or death by hanging.

If the Elizabethan historian William Harrison is to be believed, then the vagabonds of England were subjected to virtual genocide during the reign of Elizabeth's father, Henry VIII.

In his *Description of Britain*, Harrison wrote in 1577 that Henry 'did hang up three score and twelve thousand of them in his time'. So, out of a population of probably no more than 3 million, he executed 72,000 vagabonds (the equivalent for today's population would be about 1.5 million).

Harrison said that Henry's brutality seemed to terrify the vagabonds into submission, but that since the king's death their numbers had greatly increased and there were now over 10,000 roaming the land and they had become so well organised that they had their own social structure and cant (some of which has survived in common usage, as you will see from the short lexicon below).

Yet Harrison clearly had no time for able-bodied vagabonds. He said: 'They are all thieves and caterpillars in the commonwealth and, by the word of God, not permitted to eat since they do but lick the sweat from the true labourers' brows.'

Facing such hostility, the vagabonds sought protection in numbers, forming themselves into large bands. This, of course, only served to make them seem more menacing and they came to be seen as a great social nuisance by the burgesses of towns and by the government. In London, they would be rounded up and thrown into Bridewell for whipping and forced labour.

Respectable townsfolk were both afraid of them – and fascinated by their lifestyle, much in the way we now find old-time pirates glamorous.

In 1565, the printer and writer John Awdeley brought out a small volume entitled *The Fraternitye of Vacabondes*, which was so popular that it was immediately reprinted – and then brought out again ten years later. His book was followed by Thomas Harman's equally famous *Caveat*, published in 1567.

Both men claimed to have talked extensively with vagabonds to obtain their information, and there are great similarities between their accounts.

## A Vagabond Who's Who
This is the hierarchy of the vagabond bands, as outlined by Awdeley (and modernised and shortened by this author):

**Upright Man:** One that goes with a staff. He has so much authority that meeting with any of his profession he may call them to account and command a share of all that they have gained. And if he do them wrong, they have no remedy against him, even though he beats them. He may also command any of their women, which they call doxies, to serve his turn.

**Curtall:** Much like an upright man, but his authority is not so great.

**Kitchen co:** an idle, renegade boy.

**Kitchen mort:** A girl. She is brought at her full age to the Upright Man to be broken, and so she is called a doxy, until she comes to the honour of an Altham [the wife of a Curtall].

**Abraham Man:** He walks bare-armed and bare-legged, and feigns himself mad and calls himself Poor Tom.

**Ruffler:** Carries a weapon and seeks work, saying he has served as a soldier in the wars. But his main trade is robbing poor wayfarers and market women.

**Prigman:** Steals clothes and poultry and carries them to the alehouse, which they call the boozing inn, and there sits playing at cards and dice until he spends all he has stolen.

**Lackman:** One that can read and write and sometimes speak Latin. He makes counterfeit licences [i.e., to prove he has permission to beg alms], which they call 'gybes'.

**Whipjack:** He uses counterfeit licences to beg as though he were a mariner, but his chief trade is to rob booths at a fair, which they call 'heaving of the booth'.

**Frater:** He goes with a licence to beg alms for a hospital and preys upon poor women.

**Quire bird:** One that came lately out of prison and goes to seek work in service. He is commonly a stealer of horses, which they term a Prigger of Palfreys.

**Washman:** Also called a palliard [one who wears a patched cloak]. He lies in the path, begging with lame or sore legs or arms, bitten with spickwort and sometimes with ratsbane.

**Patriarch co:** He makes marriages, until death do part the married couple, which happens like this: when they come to a dead horse or any dead cattle, then they shake hands and so depart.

# A Lexicon of Vagabond Slang

**Abram:** naked
**Betty:** picklock
**Bleating cheat:** sheep
**Bubble-buff:** bailiff
**Bube:** pox
**Chive:** knife
**Clapperdudgeon:** someone born a beggar
**Collar the cole:** lay hold of the money
**Cull:** a fool
**Dads:** old man
**Dell:** a young wench not yet broken by the Upright Man
**Elf:** little
**Fambles:** Hands
**Fencer:** receiver of stolen goods
**Fog:** smoke
**Gage:** excise man
**Grub:** food
**Hog:** shilling
**Horsebread:** poor-quality bread made of beans or bran, designed for horses
**Hum:** strong
**Jem:** ring
**Jet:** lawyer

**Kick:** sixpence
**Kin:** thief
**Leake:** Welshman
**Mauks:** whore
**Mish:** smock
**Mort:** a female
**Mort of Rome:** the Queen of England
**Nan:** maid of a house
**Nap:** an arrest
**Nimming:** stealing
**Nip a bung:** cut a purse
**Otter:** sailor
**Plant the whids:** mind what you say
**Popps:** pistols
**Ruffmans:** woods
**Rumbo ken:** pawnbroker
**Rum mort:** fine woman
**Shark:** to swindle; prey upon
**Smeer:** painter
**Snaffler:** highwayman
**Tip:** give
**Tit:** horse
**Tom Pat:** parson
**Tout:** take heed
**Tripe:** belly
**Wobble:** to boil
**Yam:** to eat
**Yelp:** town crier
**Zad:** crooked

The fifth historical thriller featuring John Shakespeare,
available soon in hardback

# *The Heretics*

## RORY CLEMENTS

England survived the Armada threat of 1588, but when
Spanish galleys land troops in Cornwall seven years later, is it
a dry-run for a new invasion? Or is there a more sinister
motive? The Queen is speechless with rage. Intelligencer John
Shakespeare tries to get a grip on events, but one by one his
network of spies is murdered. What has this to do with
Thomasyn Jade, driven to the edge of madness by the rituals
of exorcism? And what is the link to a group of priests held
prisoner in Wisbech Castle?

From the torture rooms of the Inquisition in Seville to
the marshy wastes of fenland, and from the condemned
cell at Newgate to the stench of brimstone, *The Heretics*
builds to a terrifying climax.

Now read on . . .

www.roryclements.com

# Chapter 1

THE KNOCK AT the door came as John Shakespeare unhooked his sword belt from a nail in the wall. 'Come in,' he said.

His assistant Boltfoot Cooper limped into the comfortable library of his master's house in Dowgate, close by the river in the city of London, and bowed. 'You have a visitor, master.'

'Not now. I am expected elsewhere.' He began buckling his belt. 'Pass me my cloak, Boltfoot.'

Boltfoot picked up the old black bear fur from the coffer where it had been flung and held it up for Shakespeare to pull about his shoulders.

'It is a man named Garrick Loake, sir. He begs you to spare him two minutes. He says he has most urgent business, of great import to the safety of the realm.'

'Who is he?'

Boltfoot's coarse seafarer's brow twisted in a frown. 'I know not, but from the varied colours of his attire, I might guess him to be a player or a poet. He did mention that your brother William recommended him to come to you.'

Shakespeare sighed. 'Send him in. Tell him he has two minutes, no more.'

*

Loake did indeed wear colourful clothes. They were in the Italian style, including a hat with an enormous feather. Boltfoot was right: he could not be anything but a player.

'Mr Loake? Is it true that my brother sent you?'

Loake bowed with a dramatic flourish. 'He did, Mr Shakespeare. And I am most honoured to make your acquaintance for I have heard a great deal of your bold exploits.'

'*Why* did Will send you here?'

'I took the liberty of confiding in him that I had concerns about a certain matter and he said straightway that you were the man to talk with.'

'Mr Loake, I have little time to spare you. Perhaps you would return tomorrow when I am less pressed.'

'I beg you to listen for a brief moment. I know what a busy man you are.'

Shakespeare remained standing. The library fire was blazing away and soon he would overheat in this fur. But he kept the cloak on. He did not wish to give this man the impression that he would stay and talk with him.

'I know your distinguished brother from the Theatre, Mr Burbage's fine playhouse in Shoreditch,' Loake continued. 'If you are as straight dealing as he is, then I am certain I can trust you.'

Shakespeare, a tall man with long hair, waited, merely smiling. His presence alone was often enough to lure men into revealing their secrets.

'I sometimes play there myself,' Loake went on. 'I am not a member of the company, but there is usually work for me as a hired man in one capacity or another. Yesterday, I was working with the costumes.' He twirled to display his brilliant outfit. 'I borrowed this, Mr Shakespeare. It is Capulet's apparel. Do you not think it becoming? Am I not a noble Veronese gentleman?'

'The certain matter, Mr Loake—'

'Forgive me, I shall come to that straightway. I have a secret to impart, you see. A secret involving papist intrigue. I believe young Cecil will pay very well for such intelligence.'

'You mean Sir Robert Cecil.' Shakespeare was not about to let his chief man be referred to as 'Young Cecil' by a stranger.

'Indeed, not old Burghley. It is the young Caesar who runs the Privy Council these days, is it not? His father holds the purse-strings, but the boy spends the gold. Your brother mentioned that you might have a pathway to that purse.'

Shakespeare was losing patience. He could not imagine that Will had said anything of the sort. 'Tell me the matter, Mr Loake. And do not refer to Sir Robert Cecil as *the boy*.'

'My information is worth twenty sovereigns, I am certain of it. Twenty gold sovereigns.'

'I fear you are ill informed.' The figure was laughable. There were too many snouts in the trough already. 'Very little is worth even twenty shillings. Twenty sovereigns is out of the question.'

'Well, that is my price. I have great need of gold, and I need it in haste, which is why I have come to you. I cannot go a penny below my asking price.'

Shakespeare stepped away from the oppressive heat of the fire and moved towards the door. 'Tell me what you know. And be quick about it.'

'What I know,' Loake said, 'is that there is a most foul conspiracy unfolding. It wafts from the papist fastness of eastern England, gathers force in the seminaries of Spain, but it will blow into a tempest here.' He lowered his voice for dramatic effect. 'A conspiracy the like of which England has never seen.'

'How do you know this?'

'It is my business to listen well, for I sometimes hold the book and prompt the players.'

'Names,' said Shakespeare wearily. 'Give me names. What manner of plot is this? Tell me the circumstance.'

'I will, Mr Shakespeare, when you give me twenty sovereigns. For the present, I must hold my peace, for if I say more, then you will know as much as I do, and I will have no power to bargain.'

Shakespeare suddenly caught a whiff of sweat. This man was scared and desperate. 'You are wasting my time. Say what you know.'

Loake put up his right hand, which had a ring on each finger. It shook. 'I will tell you one thing, one thing only. The seminary involved is the College of St Gregory in Seville.'

'The English college of Jesuits?'

'The very same. So you will tell young Cecil to give me a purse of twenty gold sovereigns, as agreed?'

Shakespeare laughed. 'Mr Loake, I have agreed nothing. Now I must go. If you have something to tell me, then return in the morning.' He waved a hand in dismissal.

Many men came to Shakespeare's door, scratching like curs for coins in return for information; at times of want it was a daily occurrence. Most of the intelligence was worthless, scraps of tittle-tattle overheard in taverns and gaols. But it all had to be listened to and some of it, no more than a tiny portion, had to be investigated. There was something in the demeanour of this man that interested Shakespeare. He would like to see him again, to delve more deeply. But not now.

'Twenty, I must have twenty. Sovereigns.'

Despite himself, Shakespeare stayed. It was plain to him that Loake had no concept of how to conduct a negotiation; no idea that you must demand a high price so you can meet somewhere in the middle.

'Even if we could agree a figure, I would need to seek authorisation for the payment, and that would be impossible without first knowing the details of your intelligence. Trust is required on both sides in such a transaction. I promise you this: if you tell me a secret as valuable as you claim, then I shall obtain up to five pounds on your behalf. Is that not fair dealing, Mr Loake?'

'I cannot go so low.'

Shakespeare rested his hand on the hilt of his sword as if to underline who held the power here.

'You must bear in mind, Mr Loake, that you have now informed me that you have knowledge of some treachery directed at this realm. If you do not tell me all you know, then you will be laying yourself open to a charge that you are an accessory to that treason.'

Loake drew himself up to his full height, which was not great, and wiped a sleeve of gold and blue across his sweat-glistening brow and prominent nose. 'Did your brother then lie when he said you were to be trusted?'

Shakespeare shook his head. 'I will not listen to insults, Mr Loake.'

Should he have Boltfoot take the man to Bridewell or the Fleet prison for the night? He rejected the notion; it would be a betrayal of his brother.

'Come back when you have collected your wits. I may have an offer for you if you tell me enough of interest. Be here half an hour after first light and I will see you.'

## Chapter 2

I T WAS DUSK by the time Shakespeare got to Newgate
prison. He came in secret, wearing his hat low over his forehead, his body swathed in black fur, concealing his identity
from the long lines of curious onlookers already gathering for
the next day's entertainment. The gloom was lit by a dozen
bonfires and blazing cressets. Makeshift stalls had been put
up to sell food and ale to those who would camp out here in
this long, cold night to ensure the best view in the morning.
Some among the waiting crowds stared at Shakespeare, but he
ignored their insolent gaze and walked on with purpose.

He stopped at the main entrance beside the gate in the city
wall. The road beneath his feet was cobbled and slippery; the
gaol, towering above him, rose five storeys high into the darkening London sky. The last of the day's carts and drays clattered
through the archway into the city. A flock of geese, driven by a
man in a smock, waddled in to meet their fate. Shakespeare
hammered with the pommel of his dagger on the gaol's heavy
oak door. The head keeper, who had been waiting, opened it to
him, welcoming his visitor with a bow and a sweep of the arm.
The ring of keys that hung from his broad oxhide belt jangled
as he ushered Shakespeare inside.

'How is he faring, Mr Keeper?'

'He does well, master. Never have I met so rare a man.'

Shakespeare turned and pushed back his hat to look into the keeper's eyes, gratified by what he saw there: honesty and genuine affection. He was not surprised; the condemned prisoner had that effect on many people. Shakespeare held the keeper's gaze. 'Where is he? In Limbo?'

The keeper nodded, a pained expression curling his lips. Limbo was a dark pit in the lower reaches of the ancient gaol, lacking light and air, where the condemned prepared themselves for the hangman. Its meagre bedding of straw was clogged with the ordure of frightened men.

'But at least he is alone there, master. No other felons await death.'

'Bring him to an upper cell. Let him breathe before he dies.'

'Mr Topcliffe commanded me, master—'

'Damn, Mr Topcliffe. I am here under orders from Sir Robert Cecil. Bring the prisoner up.'

The keeper hesitated, but then uttered some sort of grunt and shuffled off into the rank depths of the gaol. Shakespeare pulled his hat back over his brow and waited.

Within a minute, the keeper returned. 'I have ordered him brought to a cell on the second floor. I will take you there now. You will not be disturbed.'

The single window was barred by a grating of iron rods, embedded into the stone walls. It was a small aperture, scarcely big enough to admit the last of the day's light. The cell was clean and the cold air as fresh as could be hoped for in such a dungeon.

Shakespeare had not seen Father Robert Southwell in eight years and the passage of time had not treated him well. The years of solitary confinement in the Tower and episodes of torture at the hands of Richard Topcliffe had broken his body. His once serene face was now gaunt and his slender back bent, yet his eyes shone in the grey light. It seemed to Shakespeare that he had the exquisite fragility of church glass.

Southwell, his palms together in prayer, sank to his knees at the sight of his visitor, but Shakespeare raised him to his feet and clasped his hands. He turned to the gaoler, still hovering by the iron-strapped door. 'Bring us a flagon of good wine, Mr Keeper.' He dug fingers in his purse and pulled out a coin. 'That will pay for it.'

The keeper bowed and departed, leaving the door open.

'I could overpower you, Mr Shakespeare, and make my escape.'

Shakespeare smiled at the sad jest. Southwell would be hard pressed to do battle with a kitten.

'Shall we sit down, Father?'

There was a table and three stools, but the condemned Jesuit shook his head and continued to stand. His breathing was fast. Thin trails of vapour shot from his mouth and nose and vanished in the cold air. 'There is time enough for these bones to rest.'

'Are you being treated well?'

'I count the keeper as my friend. Many good people have sent in offerings of food and he has brought it to me, along with their messages of support. I never ate so well in the Tower as I do here.'

'Well, that is something at least.'

'Their generosity of spirit gladdens my heart, Mr Shakespeare. And on the matter of kindness, will you not tell me of your beloved wife, Catherine? You have a child, I believe.'

Shakespeare stiffened. Long before he had met Catherine in the year of eighty-seven, she had been a friend of Southwell and had received the sacraments from him. But now Catherine lay in her grave.

Southwell saw his pain. 'I am sorry. I see I intrude on some grief. Is she with God?'

'I must pray that she is.'

'Forgive me, I had not heard of your great loss, Mr Shakespeare. In the Tower, I heard nothing of the world beyond my four walls. I loved Catherine as a daughter or sister. I will pray for you both . . . and the child.'

'The child is well. She is called Mary. Catherine did not suffer . . .'

Shakespeare's voice broke and he shuddered, for the word resonated icily in this room. *Suffer*. He knew what agonies Southwell would have to suffer on the morrow. Convicted of treason at the court of King's Bench this day, he would be collected from his cell at dawn and dragged on a hurdle along the jarring road to Tyburn. There he would be hanged in front of a crowd of thousands, then cut down while he lived so that the butchers could tear his belly open and rip out his entrails to burn before his eyes. And at last, he would be quartered and beheaded.

Southwell noticed his visitor's unease. 'I think you are right, Mr Shakespeare. I will sit down. Come, sit with me. There are things I must tell you, though I am sure you are a busy man. Does Mr Cecil know you are here?'

'Yes, Sir Robert knows.'

'Ah – so he has been knighted. You see, I hear nothing. Well, I am sure it is deserved. He is my cousin, you know.'

'Yes, I know that. And I know that he admires your courage, if not your religion. And I can tell you, in confidence, that the Queen also knows I am here. She wishes to be told the contents of your heart. She wishes to know why one so holy and poetical should strive to bring about the destruction of her estate.'

Southwell frowned, as if he did not comprehend the question. 'I fear she has been fed falsehoods. I never meant the destruction of Her Majesty, nor any harm to England. I sought nothing but the eternal good of souls, including hers. Even now I call on the Lord God to enlighten her, and her Council, and not to hold them guilty for my death.'

'But your Church excommunicated her. The Jesuits support invasion by Spain—'

'Many errors have been made on all sides, Mr Shakespeare. You may tell Her Royal Majesty that I honour her as my sovereign lady. I have prayed for her daily.'

'I will tell her. Is that why you asked me to come here, Father?'

The keeper arrived with the wine and two goblets. Setting a tallow rushlight on the table between Shakespeare and the condemned man, he bowed and backed away to the door, without a word. Again, he left the door open. Shakespeare poured the wine.

'He watches and listens, Mr Shakespeare,' Southwell said quietly. 'He fears I will take my own life. He has been ordered to keep me alive so that my death is witnessed as a warning to others.' Southwell reached out and grasped Shakespeare's arm in his thin fingers. 'Did you ever hear of a Catholic priest that hurt himself so? Why should we add the destruction of our souls to the demise of our bodies?'

Shakespeare understood. He sipped his wine and waited.

'And so to your question. I asked for you, Mr Shakespeare, because there is something I must beg of you. One favour. If you will do this one thing for me, then I may go to my death in peace in the hope that I will be saved by the Passion of our Lord, Jesus Christ.'

'Then you had better tell me what it is, Father.'

The priest sighed, closed his eyes for a moment, then spoke, little more than a whisper. 'There is a girl, Mr Shakespeare. A girl named Thomasyn Jade. I want you to find her.'

Shakespeare got up and walked to the door. A figure shrank

back into the passageway beyond. Shakespeare shut the door, then returned to sit at the table.

'This harks back nine years to the dangerous days of summer in eighty-six,' Southwell said, his voice still low. 'It can be no secret to you that I was newly arrived in England, for I know that you were then working for Mr Secretary Walsingham, and his spies had told him of my coming.'

Shakespeare nodded. He recalled all too well those feverish, fearful days and weeks. It was the time of the Babington plot that had led to the downfall of Mary, Queen of Scots, and brought so many foolish young Catholic men to the scaffold, condemned for plotting to assassinate Elizabeth and put Mary on her throne.

'Within a month of my arrival the so-called plotters and others had been rounded up. Some were racked, many were executed. Among those held was Father William Weston of the Society of Jesus.'

'I know all this.'

London had been a cacophonous circle of the inferno. The bells of the city churches pealed all day long and into the night; the streets were ablaze with fires celebrating that the plot had been uncovered and foiled. And on the river, an endless procession of captured conspirators and priests was carried upstream, bound hand and foot, from the baleful Tower to the courts at Westminster, and then drawn to the place of execution. It had seemed as though the slaughter would never abate.

'Indeed, Mr Shakespeare. And I am sure, too, that you will know of the other dark events that occurred in those months, when certain Catholic priests carried out exorcisms on unfortunate souls possessed by demons.'

Shakespeare's mouth turned down in distaste. It had been a disgusting affair. Young women and men had been held for days and weeks on end, being subjected to the most repulsive treatment by a group of priests and their acolytes, all in the name of ridding them of supposed demons. Many who had been sympathetic to the popish cause had been turned against it by the whole foul story.

'Yes, I remember it, Father Robert, for I spoke with Weston himself, but I believe the practice stopped at about the time of your arrival in England.'

The priest's eyes were downcast. His fine features brought to mind the name he had been given by the townsfolk of Douai in Flanders when he had attended the English College there as a young man: *the beautiful English youth*. That youth was now long gone, worn away by pain and deprivation, yet Shakespeare could still see the strange, troubling beauty in his soul.

'Yes, the exorcisms were halted. But much damage had already been done, and not just to the Catholic cause. The real victims, I fear, were some of those whom the priests were trying to help.'

'Was Thomasyn Jade one of them?'

'She was. It is no secret now that I met my Jesuit brother William Weston soon after my arrival and not long before his arrest. I did not know it at first, but it seems he was the prime mover of these exorcism rites. We travelled together to a house in Buckinghamshire – I will not tell you more than that – to confer and rest. We stayed there a week. During that time, a girl of seventeen or eighteen – Thomasyn – was brought to us by certain priests to be rid of devils. She had already undergone many more such ordeals at Denham House, near by, which, as you must know, was the centre of these goings-on.

'I watched in horror as the ritual was played out. She was stuck with pins to catch the devils beneath her skin and she was made to drink concoctions of herbs. The holy thumb of the martyr Campion was thrust in her mouth. Brimstone was burnt beneath her nose so that I believed she would choke to death. I was affronted, Mr Shakespeare, for I saw that those who did these things were in mortal error. Those who witnessed the events were struck with such fear that they quaked and trembled and wept most bitterly. Within a short while, I brought the ceremony to a halt and, though Father Weston was my superior, I advised him that he would do well never to partake in such things again.'

Shakespeare was surprised to hear Southwell voice such open criticism of a fellow of the same order.

The priest waved his hand. 'Do not misunderstand me. I have nothing but admiration for the work and ministry of Father Weston. He is a saintly man. Perhaps too saintly sometimes, too unworldly. He did what he did out of fine motives, trying to save souls. But he was misguided in subscribing to the rite of exorcism, nor am I alone among the Catholic fraternity in thinking this way. I have sometimes wondered since whether the simple fact of his failing eyesight might have made him easily deluded by others less honest. I do not believe he saw evil spirits under the girl's skin, nor do I believe he truly saw them coming from her mouth and . . .' He hesitated, scarce able to say the shameful words. 'And from her privy parts. But *he* believed he did.'

'Why do you want me to find the girl?'

'Because she was ill used by us. When she came to the house, she was shaking with fear; she was halfway mad with frenzy and weeping. I should never have allowed the exorcism to proceed as far as it did.'

'And what became of her at the end of the day's torments?'

'She was given cordials and food, and I spoke soothing words to her. I tried to discover more about her, but she could not speak. I tried to pray with her, but she became yet more distressed. I was at a loss. I did not know what to do for her. With five sisters of my own, I understand women's ways, but I am aware that the years among men at the Society colleges have made me less easy in their company. Thomasyn could not stay at that house and I could not take her with me. Instead she was taken away by the priests who had brought her, back to the house near by whence she had come.'

'Denham House?'

'Indeed.'

Shakespeare gave a wry smile. He had heard much about Denham House, a putrid place, a dark hole of corruption and wickedness.

'I fear I did not do well by her, Mr Shakespeare. Three weeks later the priests who housed her were themselves arrested, as was Father Weston. Thomasyn Jade was taken away by the pursuivants, but her story reached certain courtiers and she was soon freed into the care of a great Protestant lady, the Countess of Kent. It was hoped that she would undo the priests' efforts to reconcile the wretched girl to the Church of Rome, and take her back to Protestantism. But within a few days I heard that she had disappeared. I prayed for her every day and worried for her, for she was an afflicted young woman and in need of proper care and spiritual nourishment. I sought her as best I could, but in the year of ninety-two, as you know, I was myself arrested. I have heard nothing of her since. Her memory haunts me, and I cannot go easily to my death.'

'And if I find her?'

'My family and friends have set aside money on her behalf. They will be as godparents to her and she will be well cared for. There is nothing sinister, no more exorcisms. Nor will they seek to influence her choice of faith. I ask only that you find her . . . if she is alive.'

'Why should I do this for you, Father Southwell? You came to England as a traitor. Since then you have longed for martyrdom. You must see that you are my enemy.'

Robert Southwell crossed himself. 'You know that is not so, Mr Shakespeare.'

It was true. They were not enemies. And while Shakespeare could never comprehend Southwell's quest for death, nor like the way he held to the superstitions of Rome, he admired his courage, his piety and his poetry. If it was true, as the English state insisted, that some Jesuits contrived the death of princes, then Southwell was not one of them. Either way, though, he was about to have his martyrdom.

Shakespeare nodded slowly. This man had once risked life and liberty to help him; he could not refuse him now. 'I will do what I can, Father. You had better tell me every detail you know.'

Just over a mile north-east of Newgate, near Bishopsgate, Garrick Loake sat alone in an alehouse booth. He had downed four pints of strong beer and was beginning to feel hazy. Yet he was not drunk, not enough to ignore the uncomfortable feeling that his meeting with John Shakespeare had gone badly. Would it go any better on the morrow? A fresh tankard was slopped down in front of him. He paid the maid a penny, then picked up the vessel and drank deeply.

The problem was there was no going back now. He had told Shakespeare too much to shirk their next meeting, and so he would be at his house in the morning. What about tonight, though? He couldn't go home; it wasn't safe there. Not now. He looked around at the other drinkers in the taproom. Every man seemed a threat.

He fished out his purse and saw that his hand was shaking. Counting the meagre contents, he gauged that if he drank no more, there might just be enough for a room for the night at one of the cheaper inns. And he would say a prayer that Mr Shakespeare would save his skin.